PHARMACEUTICAL ORGANIC CHEMISTRY

[As Per Revised Syllabus for S.Y.B. Pharm. Sem. III & IV]

Useful For

B. Pharmacy, B.Sc., M.Sc., Chemistry Students of All Indian University Students

Prof. S. C. Shetty
M.Sc. Pharma. Chem., M. Phil .[Ph.D.]
Asst. Prof. in Department of Pharmaceutical Chemistry,
Rajgad Dnyanpeeth's College of Pharmacy,
Bhor. Dist. Pune 412 206

Dr. R. V. Shete
M. Pharm., Ph.D.
Principal, R.D.'s College of Pharmacy,
Bhor. Dist. Pune 412 206

Dr. R. D. Kankariya
M.Sc. M.Phil. Ph.D.
Principal, Pratibha College of Commerce & Computer
Sciences Pimpri, Pune

Prof. K. J. Kore
M.Sc., M. Phil.
Asst. Prof. R.D.'s College of Pharmacy,
Bhor. Dist. Pune 412 206

NIRALI PRAKASHAN
ADVANCEMENT OF KNOWLEDGE

N1638

PHARMACEUTICAL ORGANIC CHEMISTRY   **ISBN 978-93-51647-95-9**

Second Edition   :   May 2016
©   :   Authors

Published By :
NIRALI PRAKASHAN
Abhyudaya Pragati, 1312, Shivaji Nagar
Off J.M. Road, PUNE – 411005
Tel - (020) 25512336/37/39, Fax - (020) 25511379
Email : niralipune@pragationline.com

➤ DISTRIBUTION CENTRES

PUNE

Nirali Prakashan : 119, Budhwar Peth, Jogeshwari Mandir Lane, Pune 411002, Maharashtra
Tel : (020) 2445 2044, 66022708, Fax : (020) 2445 1538
Email : bookorder@pragationline.com, niralilocal@pragationline.com

Nirali Prakashan : S. No. 28/27, Dhyari, Near Pari Company, Pune 411041
Tel : (020) 24690204 Fax : (020) 24690316
Email : dhyari@pragationline.com, bookorder@pragationline.com

MUMBAI

Nirali Prakashan : 385, S.V.P. Road, Rasdhara Co-op. Hsg. Society Ltd.,
Girgaum, Mumbai 400004, Maharashtra
Tel : (022) 2385 6339 / 2386 9976, Fax : (022) 2386 9976
Email : niralimumbai@pragationline.com

➤ DISTRIBUTION BRANCHES

JALGAON

Nirali Prakashan : 34, V. V. Golani Market, Navi Peth, Jalgaon 425001,
Maharashtra, Tel : (0257) 222 0395, Mob : 94234 91860

KOLHAPUR

Nirali Prakashan : New Mahadvar Road, Kedar Plaza, 1st Floor Opp. IDBI Bank
Kolhapur 416 012, Maharashtra. Mob : 9850046155

NAGPUR

Pratibha Book Distributors : Above Maratha Mandir, Shop No. 3, First Floor,
Rani Jhanshi Square, Sitabuldi, Nagpur 440012, Maharashtra
Tel : (0712) 254 7129

DELHI

Nirali Prakashan : 4593/21, Basement, Aggarwal Lane 15, Ansari Road, Daryaganj
Near Times of India Building, New Delhi 110002
Mob : 08505972553

BENGALURU

Pragati Book House : House No. 1, Sanjeevappa Lane, Avenue Road Cross,
Opp. Rice Church, Bengaluru – 560002.
Tel : (080) 64513344, 64513355,Mob : 9880582331, 9845021552
Email:bharatsavla@yahoo.com

CHENNAI

Pragati Books : 9/1, Montieth Road, Behind Taas Mahal, Egmore,
Chennai 600008 Tamil Nadu, Tel : (044) 6518 3535,
Mob : 94440 01782 / 98450 21552 / 98805 82331,
Email : bharatsavla@yahoo.com

niralipune@pragationline.com | www.pragationline.com

Also find us on ⨍ www.facebook.com/niralibooks

Dedicated
To
Late: Dr. Abdul Kalam Azad

PREFACE

We take an immense pleasure to present this book entitled **"Pharmaceutical Organic Chemistry"** specially for Pharmacy Students of Savitribai Phule Pune University. Since from the inception of Pharmacy Course the Pharmacy Students of Pune University are referring many books for their study. Students are not getting all the contents in one book, they are searching many books. Yet the concepts are not understanding. So we tried to solve this problem, so that the students will easily understand the concept in this single book without any confusion.

We express our deepest gratitude and sincere thanks to our Rajgad Dnyanpeeth's, President, Respected Anantraoji Thopte Saheb, Sau. Nirmalatai, Shree Sangramdada and Sau. Bhagyashreetai Patil and all the Trustee and members of Rajgad Dnyanpeeth, Bhor for their valuable support and encouragement.

We take this opportunity to express our sincere thanks to Sau. G.J. Kshirsagar, Shri. Y. K. Phanse Sir, Prof. Hangarge Sir, Prof. Nikam Sir, Prof. V.C. Bhagat Sir, Prof. A. R. Dastetwar, Prof. Sonawane, Prof. Gokul Madam, Prof. S.D. Sawant, Prof. S.S. Kadam Sir, Prof. K. R. Mahadik Sir, Prof. Pattan Sir, Prof. Gandhi Sir, Prof. Bhandhari Sir, Prof. Rajurkar Sir, Prof. Satish Ingale Sir, Prof. Bhosale Sir, Prof. Pawar S. S., Prof. Chavan, R., Prof. Godse Madam and all the teachers of Pharmaceutical Chemistry Department of Pune University for their valuable suggestions and co-operation during this book publication.

We record deepest appreciation to our family members for their valuable understanding and co-operation during the preparation of the book.

We also take this opportunity to express our sincere thanks to Shri. Dineshbhai Furia, a pioneer in publication field. We are also grateful to Shri. Jignesh Furia for his encouragement. We are also thankful to Shri. M. P. Munde, Shri. Kiran Velankar, Shri. Akbar Shaikh, Miss Chaitali Takle, Shri. Ravindra Walodare and all the staff of Nirali Prakashan for their valuable co-operation and timely publication of this book.

Although every care has been taken to avoid mistake and misprint, yet it is very difficult to claim perfection. Any undetected, unintentional errors, omission, suggestions etc. from students and readers. For improvement brought to our notice in good spirit are most welcome.

Authors

SYLLABUS

●●●

CONTENTS

•••

Chapter **1** ...

STEREOCHEMISTRY

Syllabus ......

Significance of Stereochemistry in Biological Activity.

Stereoisomerism, Geometrical Isomerism, E & Z Nomenclature, Optical Isomerism, Chirality, Fischer Representation, R & S Nomenclatures, Diastereomerism, Resolution of Racemic Modification, Newman and Sawhorse Representation, Conformational Isomerism, Conformational Isomerism in Ethane and n-butane, Conformations of Cyclohexane, Monoalkyl and Dialkyl Cyclohexanes, Conformation in Decalin.

1.1 SIGNIFICANCE OF STEREOCHEMISTRY IN BIOLOGICAL ACTIVITY

The stereochemical nature of an organic molecule decides the biological activity in most of the circumstances. Thus stereochemistry plays significant role in the biological activity of organic molecule or drugs.

The presence of different stereochemical form of a drug molecule is responsible for a particular biological activity or adverse side effect or toxicity. Hence the exact stereochemical form is required for a particular biological activity.

The Significance of Stereochemistry in Biological Activity can be observed in the following examples:

1. In case of Thalidomide, a drug which was used to suppress morning sickness was a racemic mixture of R and S form. Among these R-form is active against morning sickness, whereas its isomer S-form is found to be toxic and teratogenic which adversely affect the pregnant woman and is responsible for defects in baby, and the babies born without limbs.

R-(+)-Thalidomide   S-(−)-Thalidomide

The defected baby limbs due to Thalidomide toxicity.

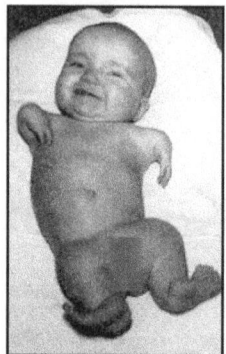

2. The Levorphenol exhibits a potent analgesic activity. In contrast its conformational isomer Dextromethorphan exclusively shows an antitussive activity.

| Morphine | Levorphenol | Dextromethorphan |

3. The diastereomers like Pseudoephedrine is biologically inactive whereas its isomer Ephedrine exhibits CNS stimulatory actions like antiallergic and antiasthamatic activity.

(1R, 2S)-(−)-Ephedrine
(−)-erythro-Ephedrine

(1S, 2R)-(+)-Ephedrine
(+)-erythro-Ephedrine

(+)-threo-Ephedrine
(1S, 2S)-(+)-Pseudoephedrine

(−)-threo-Ephedrine
(1R, 2R)-(−)-Pseudoephedrine

4. The positional isomers, Pentobarbital and Amobarbital having same empirical formula exhibit variation in their biological activity. The Pentobarbital acts as short acting barbiturate whereas its isomer Amobarbital acts as an intermediate acting barbiturate.

Chemical Properties:

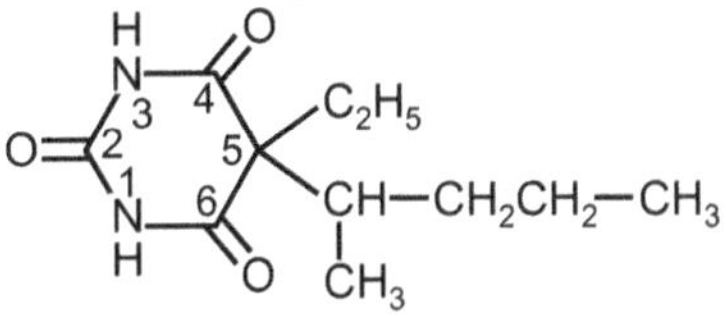

Pentobarbital (I) 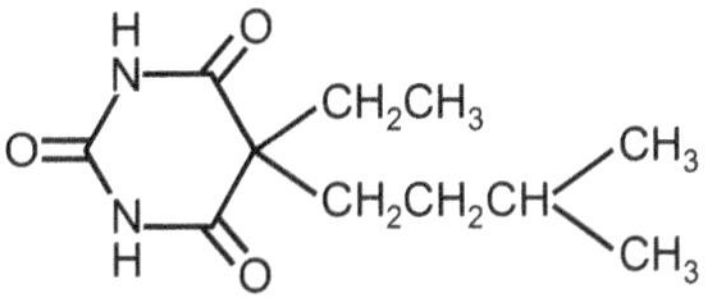   Amobarbital (II)

5. The different conformational isomers also affect the biological activity of molecule. In reality Dopamine(I) may exist in an infinite number of conformations about the single side chain C-C bond. However, two such conformations namely Dopamine(II) [θ = 60° gauche] and Dopamine (III) [θ = 180° gauche] show the maximum biological activity than its other conformations.

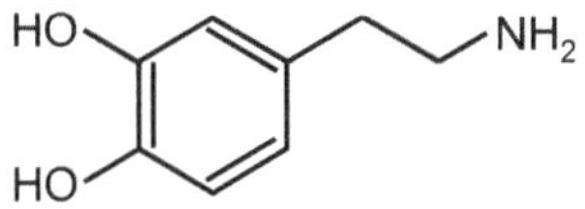

Dopamine

6. The enantiomer (S)-(+) Naproxen sodium acts as an analgesic, antipyretic and anti-inflammatory drug whereas its isomer (R)-(-) Naproxen sodium is inactive and may be poisonous.

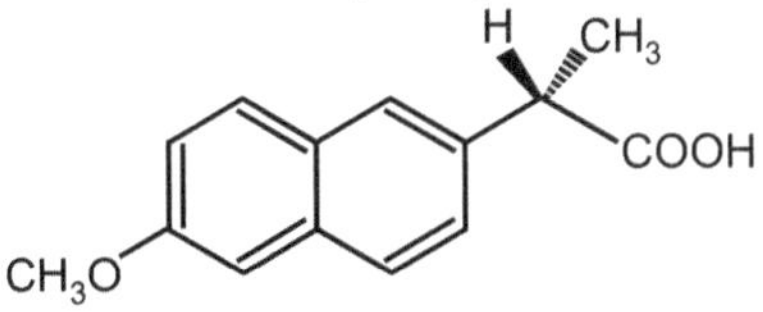

(S)-Naproxen
anti-inflammatory agent   (R)-Naproxen
liver toxin

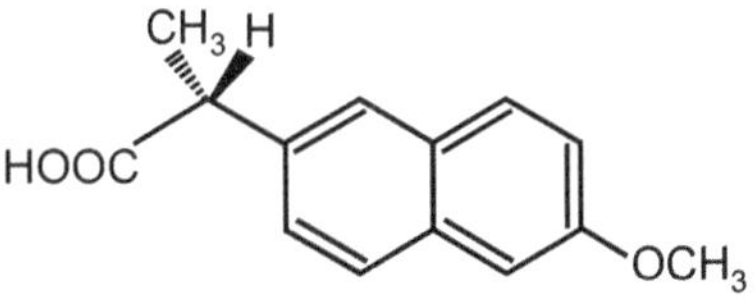

7. In case of Ibuprofen, S-Ibuprofen is having analgesic activity whereas its isomer R-Ibuprofen is found to be inactive towards analgesic activity.

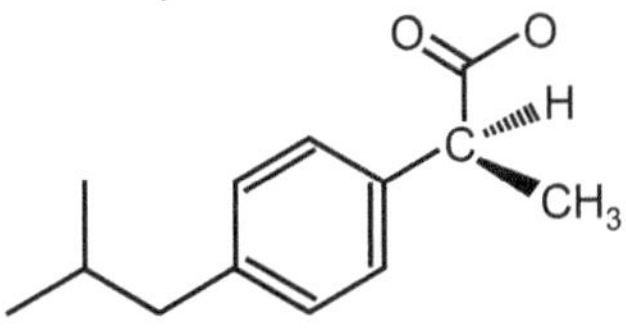

S-Ibuprofen 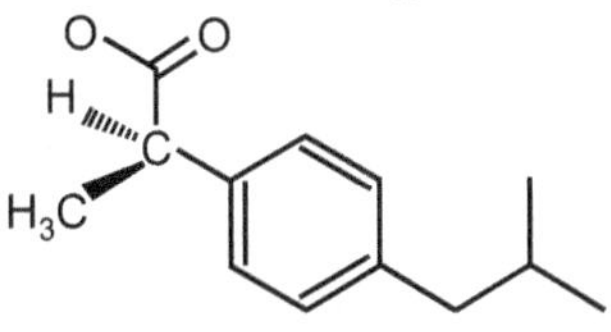   R-Ibuprofen

8. One of the enantiomer of Limonene smells like Lemon and its other isomer smells like orange.

(R)-(+)-Limonene   (S)-(−)-Limonene

9. Our body can make digest starch found in potato and bread, but not cellulose found in wood and plant fibre, even though both are just polymers of glucose because of different stereochemistry of starch and cellulose.

Thus the above example shows the significance of stereochemistry in biological activity.

1.2 STEREOCHEMISTRY

The detailed study of three-dimensional structure of organic compounds is termed as *stereochemistry*. The most stable covalent bonds are formed with a preferred three-dimensional structure and its orientation can be understood by the study of stereochemistry.

1.3 ISOMERISM

Definition: "The compounds having same molecular formula but differ from each other in physical and chemical properties are called isomers". This phenomenon is called as Isomerism.

Example: Ethyl alcohol and Dimethyl eher have the same molecular formula, i.e. C_2H_6O but both possess different physical and chemical properties.

CH_3-CH_2-OH CH_3-O-CH_3

[Ethyl alcohol]   [Dimethyl ether]

Classification: Isomers are mainly classified into two types viz.

I. Structural isomers

II. Stereoisomers

Further these are subclassified as shown in the following chart.

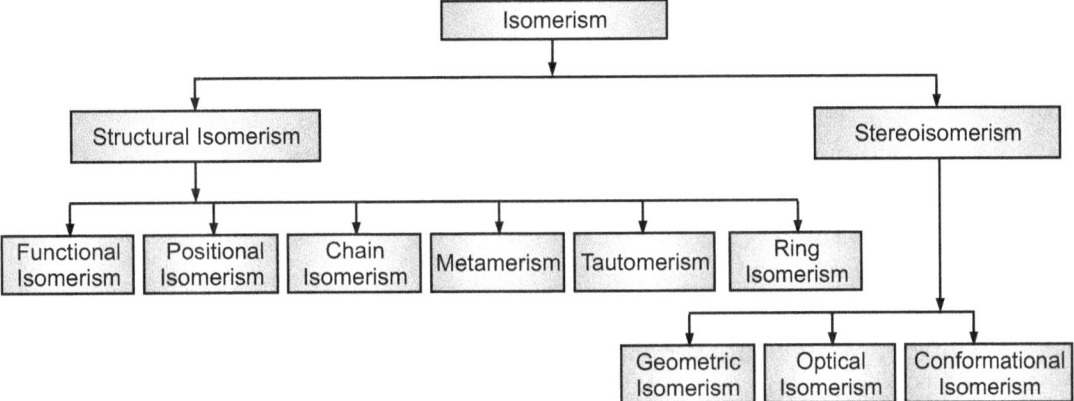

1.3.1 Structural Isomers

The isomers having the same molecular formula but different structural formula are called structural isomers and the phenomenon is called as structural isomerism.

Structural isomerism is classified into following types:

(i) **Chain Isomerism:** The structural isomers having the same molecular formula but differ in pattern/arrangement of carbon atoms bonded to each other are called as chain isomers and this phenomenon is called as chain isomerism.

Examples:

$$CH_3 - CH_2 - CH_2 - CH_3$$

n-butane

$$CH_3 - \underset{\underset{CH_3}{|}}{CH} - CH_3$$
Isobutane

Molecular formula for both is [C_4H_{10}]

$$CH_3 - \underset{\underset{CH_3}{|}}{CH} - CH_2 - CH_3;$$

2-Methyl butane

$$CH_3 - \underset{\underset{CH_3}{|}}{\overset{\overset{CH_3}{|}}{C}} - CH_3 \longrightarrow C_5H_{12}$$

2, 2-Dimethyl propane

Molecular formula for both is same i.e. [C_5H_{12}]

(ii) **Positional Isomers:** The structural isomers having the same molecular formula but differ in the position of functional group on the carbon chain, are called as positional isomers and the phenomenon is termed as positional isomerism.

Examples:

$$Br$$
$$|$$

$CH_3 - CH_2 - CH_2 - CH_2Br$ $CH_3 - CH - CH_2 - CH_3$

     1-Bromobutane   2-Bromobutane

Molecular formula for both is same i.e. $[C_4H_9Br]$

$$OH$$
$$|$$

$CH_3 - CH_2 - CH_2 - OH$ $CH_3 - CH - CH_3$

     n-propyl alcohol   Isopropyl alcohol

Molecular formula for both is same i.e. $[C_3H_8O]$

$CH_3CH_2CH = CH_2$ $CH_3 - CH = CH - CH_3$

     1-Butene   2-Butene

Molecular formula for both is same i.e. $[C_4H_8]$

(iii) Functional Isomers: The structural isomers having the same molecular formula but possess different functional groups, are called functional isomers and the phenomenon is termed as functional isomerism.

Examples:

(a) $CH_3 - CH_2 - OH$ $CH_3 - O - CH_3$

      Ethyl alcohol   Dimethyl ether

      Molecular formula for both is same i.e. $[C_2H_6O]$

$$O \qquad\qquad\qquad\qquad O$$
$$|| \qquad\qquad\qquad\qquad ||$$

(b) $CH_3 - C - CH_3$ $CH_3 - CH_2 - C - H$

      Acetone   Propionaldehyde

      Molecular formula for both is same i.e. $[C_3H_6O]$

(iv) Metamerism: The structural isomers having the same molecular formula as well as functional group but differ in the distribution of carbon atoms on either side of the functional group are termed as metamers and the phenomenon is known as metamerism.

Examples:

(a) $CH_3 - CH_2 - O - CH_2 - CH_3$ $CH_3 - O - CH_2CH_2CH_3$

      Diethyl ether   Methyl propyl ether

      Molecular formula for both is same i.e. $[C_4H_{10}O]$

$$H \qquad\qquad\qquad\qquad\qquad H$$
$$| \qquad\qquad\qquad\qquad\qquad |$$

(b) $CH_3 - CH_2 - N - CH_2\ CH_3$ $CH_3CH_2CH_2 - N - CH_3$

      N, N-Diethylamine   N-Methyl-N-Propylamine

      Molecular formula for both is same i.e. $[C_4H_{11}N]$

(v) Tautomerism: These are special type of functional isomers in which the isomers are in dynamic equilibrium with each other and interconvertible into each other in the presence of catalyst is termed as tautomers and this phenomenon is called as tautomerism.

Example: Ethyl aceto acetate is an equilibrium mixture of keto form and enol form. At room temperature the mixture contains 93% keto form and 7% of enol form.

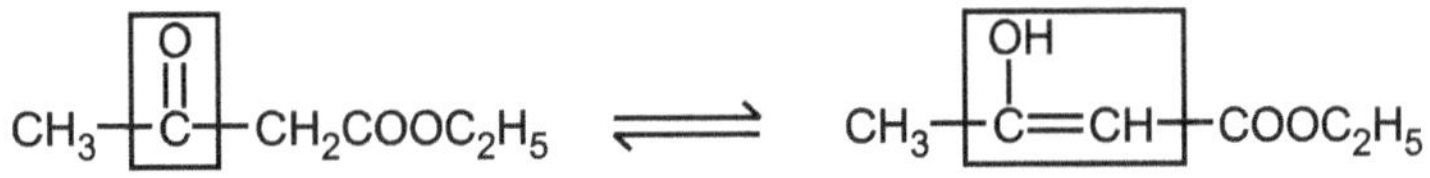

$$CH_3-\underset{\underset{\text{Keto form}}{}}{\overset{\overset{O}{\|}}{C}}-CH_2COOC_2H_5 \rightleftharpoons CH_3-\underset{\underset{\text{Enol form}}{}}{\overset{\overset{OH}{|}}{C}}=CH-COOC_2H_5$$

(vi) Ring Isomerism: The structural isomers having the same molecular formula but exist in chain and ring forms are called ring isomers and the phenomenon is called as ring isomerism.

Example:

1. $CH_3-CH=CH_2$; Prop-1-ene.   2. 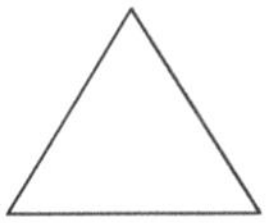 △ = Cyclopropane
    Molecular formula for both is same i.e. $[C_3H_6]$.

1.3.2 Stereoisomers

The isomers having same molecular formula as well as structural formula but differ in spatial arrangement i.e. 3-dimensional arrangement of atoms in space are called as stereoisomers and the phenomenon is called as stereoisomerism.

Stereoisomers are further classified into three types viz.

1. Geometrical / Cis-Trans Isomer
2. Optical Isomer
3. Conformational Isomer.

1.4 GEOMETRICAL ISOMERISM

"The stereoisomers that result from a restriction in rotation about double bonds or about single bonds in cyclic compounds are called as geometrical isomers and the phenomenon is termed as geometrical isomerism. It is also called as cis-trans isomerism.

This was first time recognized in 1875 by Vant Hoff and Le Bel.

Examples:

H – C – COOH   H – C – COOH
     || ||
H – C – COOH   HOOC – C – H

Maleic acid (cis)   Fumaric acid (trans)

M.P. = 130°   M.P. = 286°

Explanation:

The geometrical isomerism in double bonded carbon atom exhibits due to the restriction in rotation about double bonds along C = C bond.

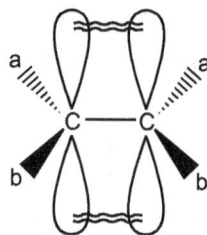

The carbon atoms of the C = C double bond are sp^2 hybridized. The C = C double bond consists of a σ-bond and a π-bond. The σ-bond is formed by the overlap of sp^2 hybrid orbitals. The π-bond is formed by the overlap of p-orbitals. The presence of π-bond locks the molecule in one position. The 2 carbon atoms of C = C bond and 4 atoms that are attached to them lie in one plane and their position in space are fixed. Rotation around the C=C bond is not possible because rotation would break the π-bond.

The Ball and Stick models of geometrical isomers of an organic compound are given below. Here the two black balls (represent carbon atoms) are joined by two spring rods/sticks (representing the double bonds between two carbon atoms) and further each black ball is having two white balls A and B (representing two different atoms or groups). Now since the two balls are joined by means of two spring rods, free rotation of the black ball around the spring is not possible and thus the positions of both A and B are fixed with the result the white balls A and B can be arranged in the following two different ways about the doubly bonded black balls.

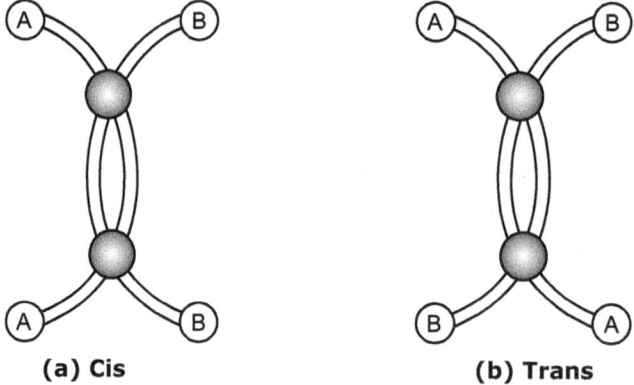

(a) Cis   **(b) Trans**

Geometrical isomerism can further be illustrated beautifully by the following board and nail models; when the two boards are joined by a single nail, the free rotation of either of the two boards is possible and hence the black ends of the boards cannot be arranged relative to each other i.e. this type of model cannot exhibit geometrical isomerism.

On the other hand, when the two boards are joined by two nails in different holes, free rotation is not possible and hence the relative position of the black and white ends can be fixed in two definite ways corresponding to cis and trans isomerism.

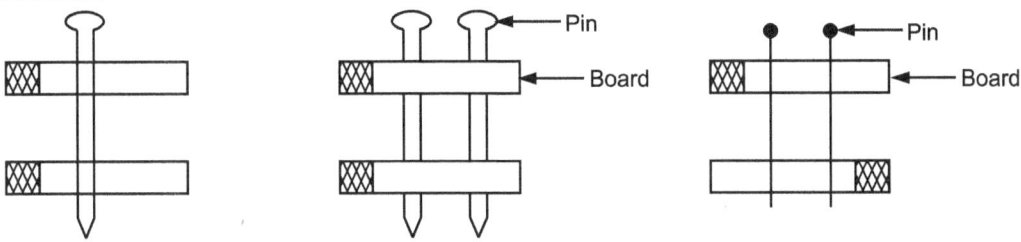

Cis isomer   **Trans isomer**

Example: 2-Butene exists in two spatial arrangements.

$$CH_3 - CH = CH - CH_3$$

Cis-2-butene   **Trans-2-butene**
(B.P. = + 1°C)   **(B.P. = + 1°C)**

Types of Geometrical Isomers: Geometrical isomers can be classified into two types viz.

    1. Cis Isomer

    2. Trans Isomer

1. Cis Isomer: The geometrical isomers in which the similar groups lie on the same side of double bond are called as Cis isomers.

2. Trans Isomer: The geometrical isomers in which the similar groups lie on the opposite side of double bond are called as Trans isomers.

Examples:

Maleic acid (cis-isomer)   Fumaric acid (trans-isomer)

General Properties of Geometrical Isomers:

    1. The interconversion of cis-isomer into trans-isomer or vice versa is possible only if either of the isomer is heated to high temperature. The heat supplies the energy to break the π-bond so that rotation about σ-bond becomes possible. Upon cooling the reformation of π-bond can take place in two ways giving mixture of two isomers.

    2. The trans isomers are more stable than the corresponding cis isomers. This is because, in the cis isomer the bulky groups are on the same side of double bond, the steric repulsion of groups makes this cis isomer less stable than trans isomer in which the bulky groups are far apart i.e. they are on the opposite side of the double bond.

3. All alkenes do not show geometrical isomerism. Geometrical isomerism is possible only when each double bonded carbon atom should be attached to two different atoms or groups.

Example: Prop-1-ene does not exhibit geometrical isomerism.

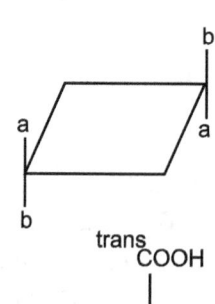

⟶ No isomer

4. In addition to alkenes the geometrical isomerism is also exhibited by the following types of compounds.

(a) Compounds containing C=C bond:

e.g.

Maleic acid (cis-isomer)   Fumaric acid (trans-isomer)

(b) Compounds containing C=N bond:

e.g.

syn/cis   anti/trans

(c) Compounds containing N = N bond:

e.g.

←Lobes

cis   trans

(d) Cyclic compounds:

e.g.

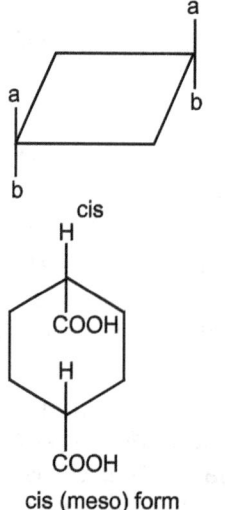

cis   trans

cis (meso) form   trans form

(Cyclohexane-1, 4-dicarboxylic acid)

NOMENCLATURE

The different nomenclature system of geometrical isomers are as below:

1. **Cis and Trans Nomenclature:** In this type, the isomers in which the similar groups lie on the same side of the double bond, are assigned as *cis* whereas the isomers in which the similar groups lie on the opposite side of the double bond are assigned as *trans* form.

   Example:

Maleic acid (cis)   Fumaric acid (trans)

2. **Cis-Trans Nomenclature:** The simple cis and trans nomenclature is not possible when the ethylenic carbon atom possesses four different atoms / groups. In such cases, the prefixes cis and trans should indicate the disposition of the first two group names.

   Example:

   cis-1-bromo-2-iodo-1-chloroethylene   cis-1-chloro-2-iodo-1- bromoethylene
   trans-1-chloro-2-iodo-1-bromoethylene   trans-1-bromo-2-iodo-1-chloroethylene

3. **E and Z Nomenclature:** When three or more functional groups are there as in above case can lead to confusion in naming such isomers. So IUPAC has adopted E – Z system of nomenclature for such compound.

   {In German: Z = Zusammen = together = cis, Cis = Z, C = Z

   E = Entgegen = against = trans, Trans = E, E = T}.

   The E – Z system of nomenclature is based upon the Cahn – Ingold – Prelog [CIP] sequence rules for naming optical isomers as in R – S system.

The following procedure is followed in specifying the E and Z configuration of such compounds.

1. Assign the priority order to the two atoms/ groups attached to each of the doubly bonded carbon in accordance with the CIP sequence rules.

CIP Sequence rules for determining the priority order to atoms or groups attached to doubly bonded carbon atom:

(a) Higher priority is assigned to atoms (directly attached to double bonded carbon atom) of higher atomic number.

   Example:

(b) If isotopes of the same element are attached then the isotope with higher mass number will have higher priority.

   Examples:

   1. Among H and D, 'D' gets 1st priority.
   2. Among C^{13} and C^{12}, C^{13} gets higher priority.

(c) If the priority cannot be decided by the above rule then it is determined by comparing the next atom in the group and so on.

Example:

Br, C=C, CH₂CH₃ / H, CH₂CH₂—CH₃ (Higher priority)

(d) A double or triple bonded atom is considered as equivalent to two or three such atoms. Thus, carbonyl group is considered as if carbon had two single bonds to oxygen.

Example:

$$\text{C=O} \Rightarrow \text{C—O}$$

(e) In case of geometrical stereoisomeric groups, the cis group precedes trans group. Similarly, in case of optical isomers (enantiomers), the (R-) group precedes the (S-) group. In case of pseudoasymmetric centre, the symbols (R) and (S) are replaced by (r) and (s).

2. Select the atom/group with higher priority on each doubly bonded carbon. If the atoms/groups of higher priority on each carbon are on the same side of the double bond, the isomer is assigned as the configuration 'Z' i.e. Z = C.

On the other hand if the atoms/groups of higher priority on each carbon are on the opposite side of the double bond, the isomer is assigned as the 'E' configuration. 'E' = trans i.e. E = T.

Methods of determining configuration of Geometrical Isomers:

By configuration it implies the arrangement of atoms or groups in space around a chiral carbon atom.

Physical methods:

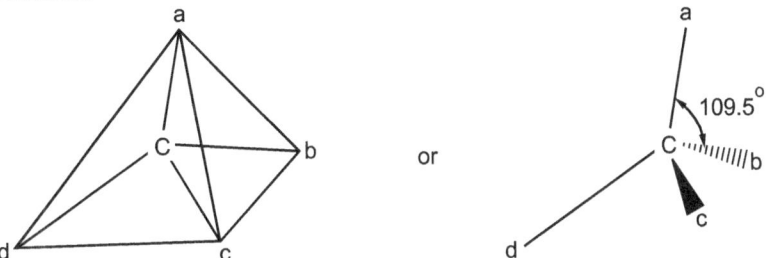

1. Dipole moment:

Cis isomers have greater dipole moment 'μ' than its corresponding trans isomer.

Examples:

$$\text{H} \diagdown \text{C} = \text{C} \diagup \text{Cl}$$
$$\text{Cl} \diagup \qquad \diagdown \text{H}$$

μ = 0.00 D
trans-1, 2-dichloroethylene

$$\text{H} \diagdown \text{C} = \text{C} \diagup \text{H}$$
$$\text{Cl} \diagup \qquad \diagdown \text{Cl}$$

μ = 1.89 D
cis-1, 2-dichloroethylene

Note: In the cis isomer the individual bond moments are additive while in trans isomer the vector sum is zero.

$$\text{H} \diagdown \text{C} = \text{C} \diagup \text{H}$$
$$\text{COOC}_2\text{H}_5 \diagup \qquad \diagdown \text{COOC}_2\text{H}_5$$

μ = 2.54 D
cis-diethyl maleate

$$\text{H} \diagdown \text{C} = \text{C} \diagup \boxed{\text{COOC}_2\text{H}_5}$$
$$\boxed{\text{COOC}_2\text{H}_5} \diagup \qquad \diagdown \text{H}$$

μ = 2.38 D
trans-diethyl maleate

2. Physical Constants and Solubility:

The trans isomers have higher melting point and lower solubility than corresponding cis form.

Example:

Isomer	M.P.	Solubility
Cis Maleic acid	130°C	78.8 gm/100 ml
Trans Fumaric acid	300°C	0.78 gm/100 ml

A.E. Van Arkel gave a dipole rule, which states that the isomer of higher dipole moment has also the higher boiling point, density and refractive index (R.I.).

3. Acid Strength:

Cis isomers are more acidic than their corresponding trans isomers.

Examples:

$$\text{H} \diagdown \text{C} = \text{C} \diagup \text{H}$$
$$\text{COOC}_2\text{H}_5 \diagup \qquad \diagdown \text{COOC}_2\text{H}_5$$

μ = 2.54 D
cis-diethyl maleate

$$\text{H} \diagdown \text{C} = \text{C} \diagup \boxed{\text{COOC}_2\text{H}_5}$$
$$\boxed{\text{COOC}_2\text{H}_5} \diagup \qquad \diagdown \text{H}$$

μ = 2.38 D
trans-diethyl maleate

4. X-ray and Electron diffraction:

X-ray crystallographic analysis although tedious, but it is the best method of determining the configuration of geometrical isomers, wherever it is applicable.

Example: Complete X-ray crystallographic analysis of the **sorbic acid** gave it the trans-trans structure.

trans-trans-sorbic acid

5. Spectroscopy Method:

UV spectroscopy: The configuration of geometric isomers can be assigned by UV spectra on the basis that, trans isomers generally have higher λ_{max} than the corresponding cis isomers (since steric factor, which hinders the resonance in the cis isomer and thus cis isomer has lower λ_{max} than trans).

Examples:

λ_{max} = 278 nm
cis-stilbene

λ_{max} = 294 nm
trans-stilbene

Chemical Methods:

1. Method of cyclization:

This method can be applied only for those geometrical isomers in which either of the form is easily capable of forming a ring. The method is based on the principle that intramolecular reactions occur easily when the reacting groups are close together. The cis-dicarboxylic acid, on heating loses a molecule of water and an anhydride is formed, whereas trans form remains unchanged.

Example: Among the two acids, maleic acid and fumaric acid, only the former gives anhydride on gentle heaving. So in maleic acid the two reactive groups (–COOH) are close together and hence it is the cis isomer and fumaric acid is trans.

Sometimes trans form is also converted into cyclic compound under vigorous conditions only.

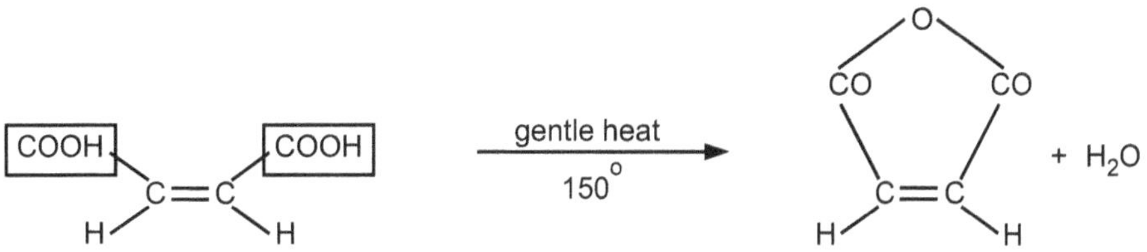

Maleic acid ($C_4H_4O_4$) cis   gentle heat 150°   Maleic anhydride ($C_4H_2O_3$) + H_2O

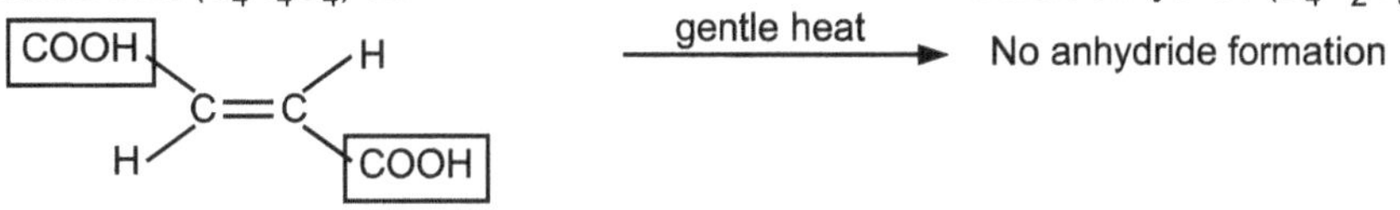

Fumaric acid (trans)   gentle heat   No anhydride formation

Similarly,

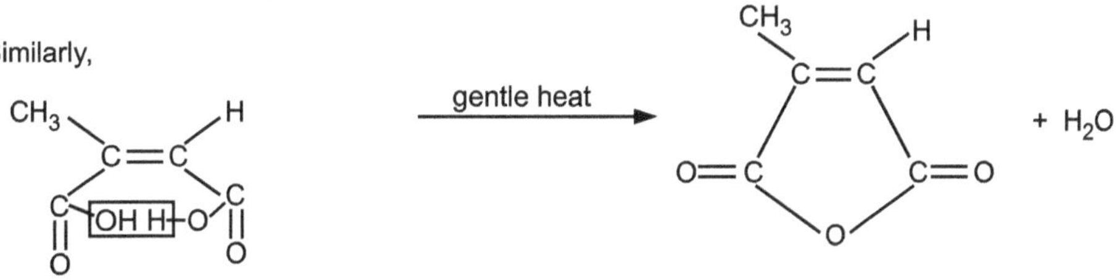

Citraconic acid ($C_5H_6O_4$) cis   gentle heat   Citraconic anhydride ($C_5H_4O_3$) + H_2O

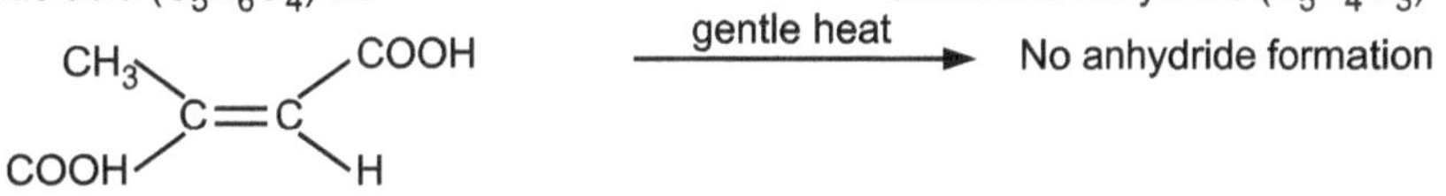

Mesaconic acid ($C_5H_6O_4$) trans   gentle heat   No anhydride formation

2. By converting into compounds of known configuration:

In some cases, a geometrical isomer of the pair can be converted into a compound of known configuration by certain chemical reactions. Now if we assume that, there is no isomerisation during the reaction the configuration of the product will also be the configuration of the starting compound.

Example: One of the trichlorocrotonic acid is converted into fumaric acid on hydrolysis, crotonic acid on reduction. So this trichlorocrotonic acid must be the trans isomer. The other isomer of trichlorocrotonic acid does not give fumaric acid on hydrolysis and form isocrotonic acid on reduction. Hence isocrotonic acid and the corresponding trichlorocrotonic acids are cis isomers.

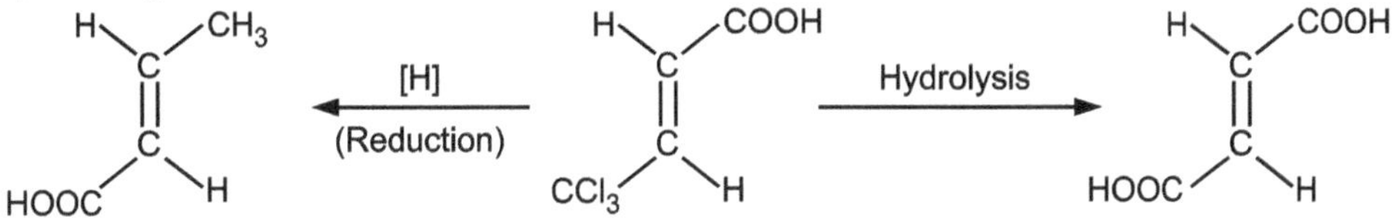

Crotonic acid (trans)   [H] (Reduction)   Trans-Trichloro crotonic acid   Hydrolysis   Fumaric acid (trans)

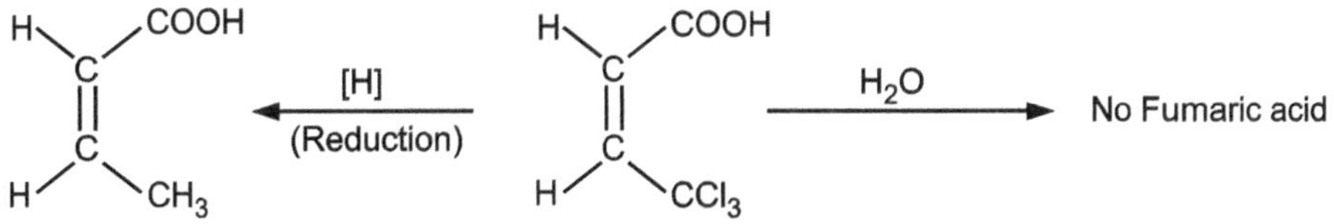

Isocrotonic acid (cis)   [H] (Reduction)   Cis-Trichlorocrotonic acid H_2O No Fumaric acid

3. Method of optical activity:

In certain cases, among the two members of geometrical isomers, only one form is optically active, whereas the other is optically inactive, due to the presence of an element of symmetry. Hence, the optically active form can be resolved and may be used to establish its configuration and it is trans form, because it is resolvable. For example, hexahydropthalic acid, the trans form of which has been resolved.

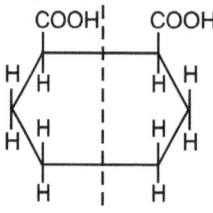

Optically inactive due to
plane of symmetry (cis)

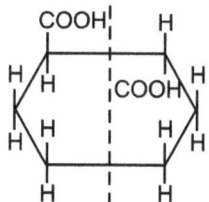

Optically active and
hence resolvable (trans)

4. By Stereoselective and Stereospecific Addition and Elimination Reactions:

Stereoselective reactions: The reactions in which the yield is predominantly one stereoisomer of several possible stereoisomers are called stereoselective reactions.

Example: Addition reactions of alkynes, alkenes and cycloalkenes.

Stereospecific reactions: Stereospecific reactions are those reactions in which stereochemically different reactants give stereochemically different products. All stereospecific reactions are necessarily stereoselective but all stereoselective reactions are not stereospecific. In these reactions, the formation of product is specific with respect to stereoisomer i.e. different stereoisomeric starting materials give rise to different stereoisomeric products.

Example: Hydroxylation of maleic and fumaric acid.

Addition Reactions:

Stereoselective reaction:

$$R-C\equiv C-R$$

$\xrightarrow{\text{Na-NH}_3 \text{ (liq.)}}$

Trans (98%)   +   Cis (2%)

$\xrightarrow{\text{H}_2 - \text{Pd}}$

Cis (98%)   +   Trans (2%)

Stereospecific reaction:

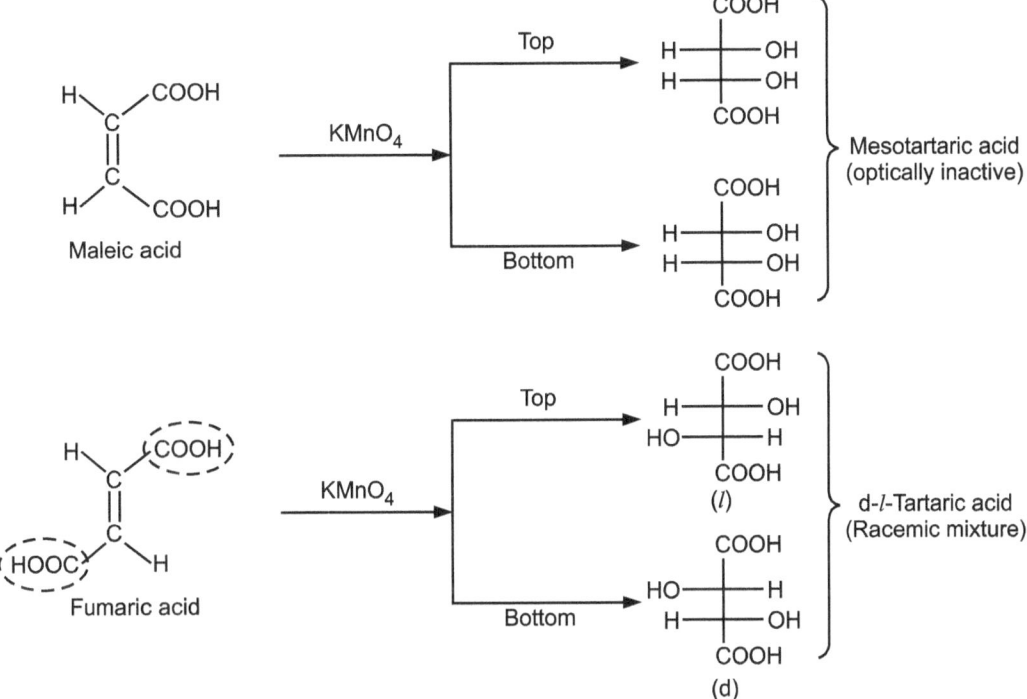

Thus if we know the stereochemical course of the addition/elimination (i.e. whether the given reaction takes place in the cis or trans manner) then by knowing the nature of the product, we can ascertain the configuration of the starting compound.

⇒ Cis addition → meso compound (optically inactive)

    Trans → Racemic mixture

Reduction:

Catalytic hydrogenation of an olefin or acetylene normally gives the cis addition product and hence the reaction will form meso product with cis isomer and (±) product with trans isomer.

Hydroxylation: Like the catalytic hydrogenation, hydroxylation of olefins by means of OsO_4, $KMnO_4$ or H_2O_4 proceeds in the cis fashion.

Example: Maleic (cis) and fumaric (trans) acids on oxidation with either of the above reagents give meso and (±) tartaric acid respectively.

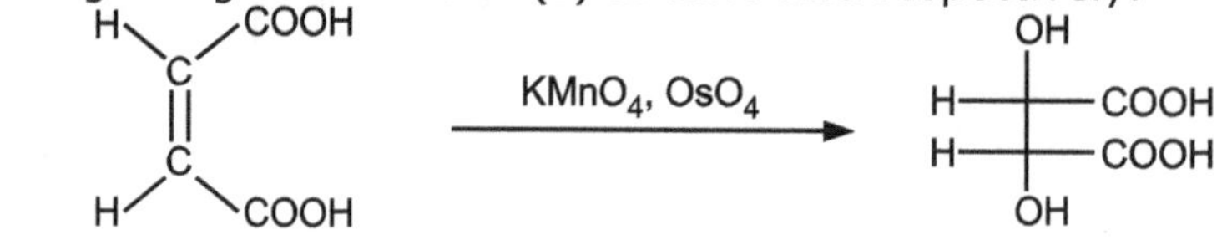

(Cis)   KMnO₄, OsO₄   Mesotartaric acid

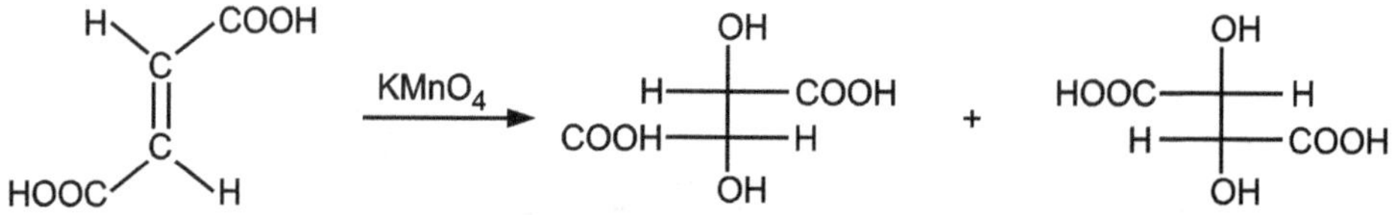

(Trans)   KMnO₄   (±) Tartaric acid

Polar addition of halogens and halogen acids:

Many electrophilic reagents add on olefin to form trans product. Bromide (Br^+) adds on maleic and fumaric acids to give (±) and meso-α, α'-dibromo succinic acids respectively.

Robert and Kimball proposed the following mechanism to account for the trans addition.

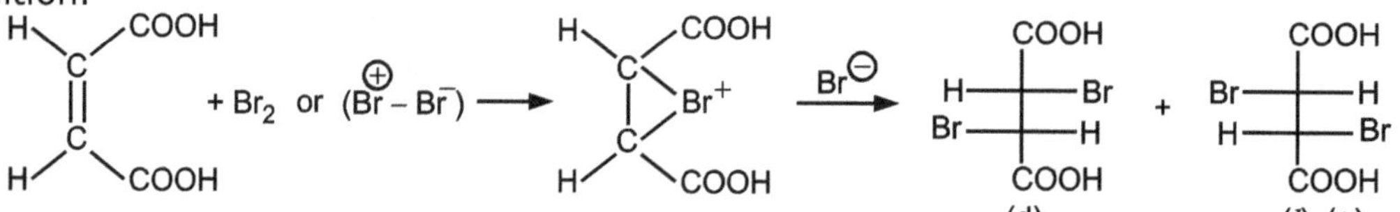

Maleic acid (Cis)   + Br₂ or (Br – Br)   Bridged bromonium ion   (d)   (l) (±)

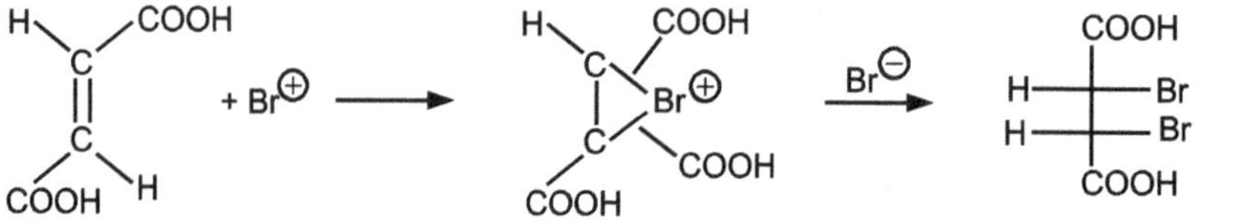

Fumaric acid (Trans)   + Br⊕   Meso

Free Radical Addition:

Free radical addition to double bonds usually proceeds in trans manner.

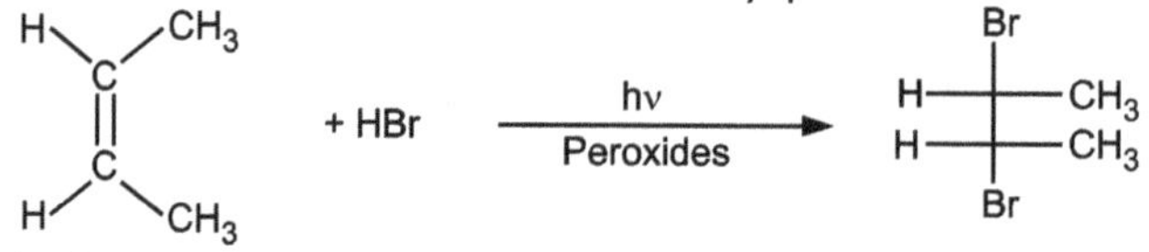

Cis-2-butene   + HBr   hv / Peroxides   Meso

Cis   HBr/hv   (+)   (–)

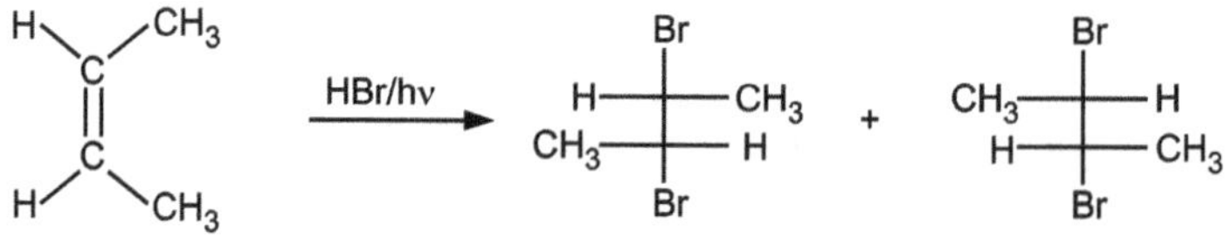

Diels-Alder Reaction:

Since the configuration of a cyclic adduct can easily be determined, the Diels-Alder reaction provides a means of ascertaining the configuration of the **dienophile**.

Example: The configuration of two cinnamic acids can be established by determination of configuration of their stereoisomeric adducts with butadiene.

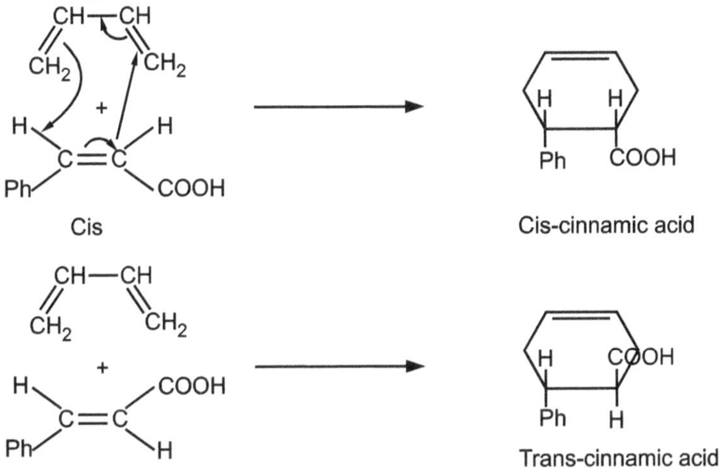

Cis

Cis-cinnamic acid

Trans-cinnamic acid

Addition of Carbenes:

Carbenes add on the olefinic double bonds in the cis fashion.

Example: Carbene adds on cis and trans but-2-ene to form cis and trans 1,2-dimethyl cyclopropane respectively.

Example:

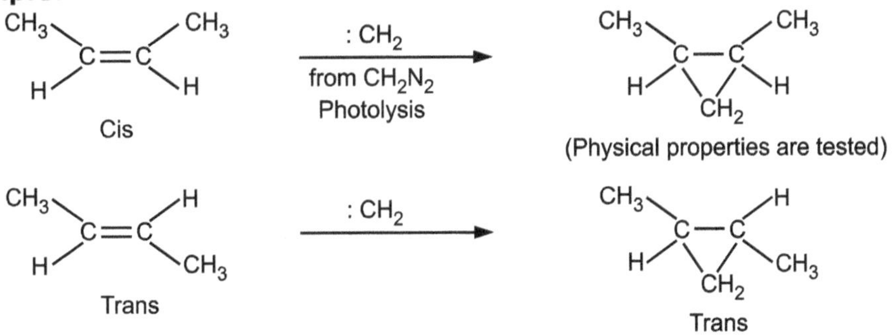

Cis

(Physical properties are tested)

Trans

Trans

Elimination Reactions:

Formation of acetylenes: It has been observed that when the atoms or groups to be eliminated are in the trans position with respect to each other, then the reaction proceeds rapidly as compared to that when the two groups are cis to each other.

Example:

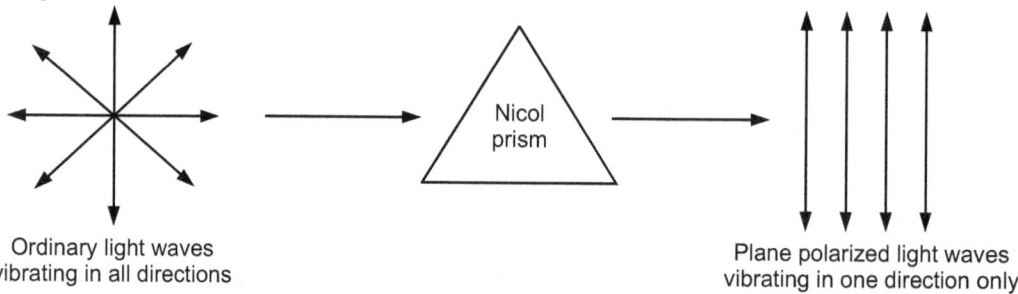

Trans-2-bromo-but-2-ene   But-2-yne   Cis

1.5 OPTICAL ISOMERISM

Definition: "The compounds which have same molecular and structural formula but differ only in their action towards the plane polarized light or optical activity are known as optical isomers and the phenomenon is known as optical isomerism".

Explanation:

Ordinary light waves
vibrating in all directions

Nicol
prism

Plane polarized light waves
vibrating in one direction only

When a plane polarized light is passed through certain substances or their solution, its plane of polarization is rotated either towards right (clockwise) or towards left (anti-clockwise) by a certain angle. Such substances which rotate the plane polarized light are known as **optically active** substances / compounds and the phenomenon is referred as **optical activity**. The substances which rotate the plane polarized light towards right are called **dextro-rotatory** compounds and indicated by 'd' or (+) and those which rotate the plane polarized light towards left are called **laevo rotatory** compounds and designated as 'l' or (−).

The extent of angle of rotation of plane polarized light or the optical activity of a substance is measured by an instrument known as polarimeter.

The magnitude of rotation depends on the following factors:

(a) Nature of the compound

(b) Concentration of the solution

(c) Length of tube containing the solution

(d) Nature of the solvent. Solvent if used is generally indicated in bracket with specific rotational value.

(e) Temperature of solution.

(f) Wavelength of light used, usually sodium 'D' lamp (λ = 589 nm).

Optical activity: When a beam of plane polarized light passes through enantiomer, the plane of polarization rotates. The property to rotate the plane of polarized light is called as optical activity.

The optical activity of a substance is expressed in terms of **specific rotation**. The determination of specific rotation is done using wavelength of sodium at room temperature at 20°. The specific rotation is denoted by $[\alpha]_D^{20}$ or if done at any other t°C then $[\alpha]_D^{t°}$.

Specific rotation: It is defined as the angle of rotation in degrees which the plane of polarized light undergoes on passing through 1 decimeter (10 cm) column of solution of concentration in grams per millilitre (g/ml) as given below:

$$\left[[\alpha]_D^{t°} = \frac{\alpha}{l \times C} \right]$$

where, α = observed angle of rotation in degrees

               l = the length of solution of column in decimeters

               C = the concentration of test substance in g/ml.

1.5.1 Conditions for Optical Activity

The necessary and sufficient condition for a molecule to show optical activity is that, the **geometrical structure** of the molecule should not superimpose on its mirror image (allowing for internal rotation about single bond) i.e. it must exist in enantiomorphic form.

Example:

Plane of symmetry

Centre of symmetry
in ethane molecule

Further, it should be devoid of following elements of symmetry i.e.

1. A plane of symmetry
2. A centre of symmetry
3. An alternating axis of symmetry

Superimposable mirror images; when the mirror image on right superimposes on the right, is rotated by 180°.

1. Plane of symmetry:

A molecule is said to have plane of symmetry, if it can be divided into two equal parts in any plane and the atoms or groups on one side of the plane form mirror image of those on other side.

Example:

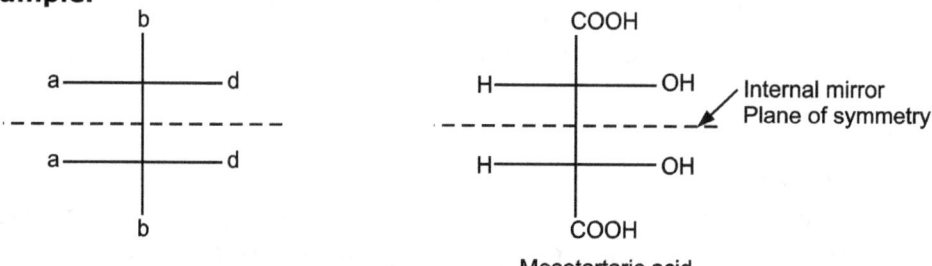

Mesotartaric acid

2. Centre (Point) of symmetry:

A molecule is said to have centre of symmetry, if an imaginary point in the centre of a molecule from which lines are drawn, on any group on both sides to an equal distance it divides the molecule into two equal halves which are the mirror images of each other.

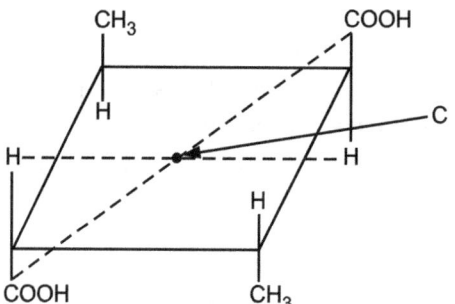

Example:

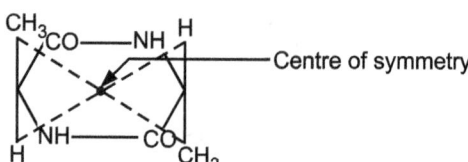

Cis-dimethyl ketopiperazine	Trans-dimethyl ketopiperazine
No centre of symmetry	(Has centre of symmetry)
(Optically active)	(Optically inactive)

3. Alternating axis of symmetry:

A molecule is said to possess an n-fold alternating axis of symmetry if, when it is rotated through an angle of $360°/n$ about this axis and then reflected across a plane perpendicular to the axis, an identical structure is obtained.

OR

A molecule rotated around an axis by $360°/n$, an image is taken through a mirror placed perpendicular to the axis, the mirror image looks identical with the original.

Until 1955, no compound was known which exhibit the optical inactivity due to the presence of only an alternating axis of symmetry, but in 1955, McCasland and Proskow (1956) prepared the first compound 3, 4, 3', 4'-tetramethyl-spiro-(1, 1')-dipyrrolidinium p-toluene (I). The molecule possesses neither a plane nor a centre of symmetry. But on the other hand, when it is rotated through 90° about the axis and then reflected across the plane through N-atom, we get an identical and the mirror image II of the I. So the optical inactivity of the molecule is due to the presence of only a **four-fold alternating axis of symmetry**.

(I)   (II)

Similarly, 3, 4-dichloro-3, 5-dimethylhexane is found to be optically inactive due to the presence of two-fold alternating axis of symmetry.

A   B   C

1.5.2 Relation between Chiral Centre and Chirality

Chiral centre/Asymmetric carbon: A carbon atom having four different monovalent atoms or groups is known as chiral/asymmetric carbon or chiral carbon or chiral centre. The necessary condition for a molecule to exhibit optical isomerism is dissymmetry or chirality.

Most of the optically active organic compounds contain atleast one chiral carbon atom. The term chiral is derived from the Greek word cheir means hands.

Similarly, the term chirality means handedness in reference to our two hands each of which is the non-superimposable mirror image of the other.

Thus, we can say that the terms chiral and chirality are used in reference to compounds, whose mirror image is non-superimposable over itself.

The term Chiral:

The mirror image of the right hand is the left hand. Conversely, the mirror image of the left hand is the right hand.

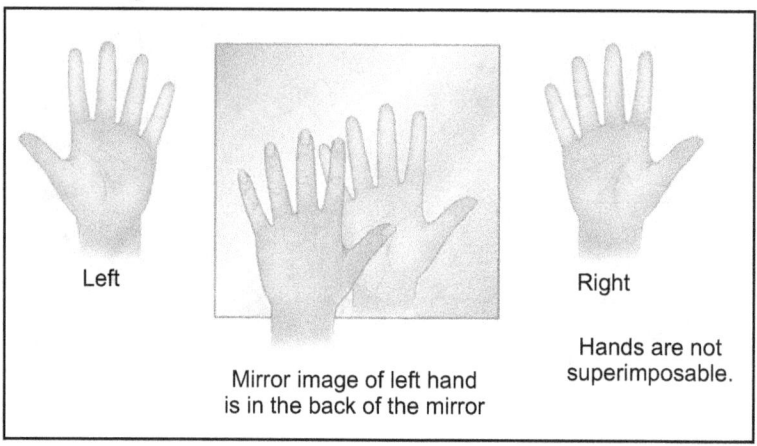

Left

Right

Mirror image of left hand
is in the back of the mirror

Hands are not
superimposable.

The mirror image of left hand is a right hand   **Left and right hands are not superimposable**

The word chiral (Greek word Cheir, meaning hand) is used for those objects which have right-handed and left-handed forms, i.e. molecules which have handedness and the general property of handedness is termed as chirality.

It is observed that,

- Many (but not all) molecules that contain a chiral centre are chiral.
- Some molecules although contain chiral centres yet are achiral. e.g. Mesotartaric acid.
- Some chiral molecules do not have any chiral centre.

  e.g. 2, 3-pentadiene $CH_3 - CH = C = CH - CH_3$.

  Thus, the presence / absence of a chiral centre is no criterion of chirality but possibility of chirality.
- In case a molecule has only one chiral centre, it will always be chiral.

  e.g. Lactic acid
$$\begin{array}{c} CH_3 \\ | \\ H - C - OH \\ | \\ COOH \end{array}$$

- A molecule having more than one chiral centre may be achiral or chiral.

e.g. Mesotartaric acid (Achiral)   Tartaric acid (Chiral)

- Chiral centre is represented by an asterisk*.

Compounds containing one Chiral Carbon Atom:

A compound containing one asymmetric carbon atom is always optically active and exist in 3 forms viz. (+), (–) and (±) (dextro, laevo and d//racemic).

Example: In lactic acid $\left(CH_3 - \overset{*}{CH} - COOH \atop \qquad\;\; | \atop \qquad\;\; OH \right)$, one carbon atom is linked to four different atoms or groups. It gives rise to two isomeric forms or antimeters.

$$
\begin{array}{c}
CH_3 \\
| \\
H - C - OH \\
| \\
COOH
\end{array}
\qquad\qquad
\begin{array}{c}
CH_3 \\
| \\
HO - C - H \\
| \\
COOH
\end{array}
$$

Mirror

Lactic acid in actual practice is known to exist in three forms.

1. One form of lactic acid known as sarcolactic acid extracted from muscles, rotates the plane polarized light to the right side. It is called as optically active d-lactic acid or (+) lactic acid. Its specific rotation $[\alpha]_D^{20} = +2.24$.

2. Second form is obtained by fermentation of lactose (milk sugar), and it rotates the plane polarized light to the left side. It is called as optically active l-lactic acid or (–) lactic acid. Its specific rotation $[\alpha]_D^{20} = -2.24$.

3. The third form obtained in laboratory synthesis of lactic acid is optically inactive as it contains equivalent amount of d and l isomers is known as dl-mixture or Racemic mixture or (±) lactic acid. Specific rotation $[\alpha]_D^{20} = 0.00$.

1.5.3 Compounds Containing Two or More Dissimilar Chiral Carbon Atoms

The number of optical isomers in a molecule containing n number of dissimilar chiral carbon atoms can be predicted by the relation 2^n. Furthermore, there will be 2^{n-1} pairs of enantiomers and the same number of racemic modifications.

Example: Cinnamic acid dibromide.

$$
\begin{array}{cc}
Br & Br \\
| & | \\
C_6H_5 - CH & - CH - COOH \\
* & *
\end{array}
\quad \therefore\; 2^n = 2^2 = 4.
$$

i.e. Four optical isomers, two enantiomers and two racemic mixture.

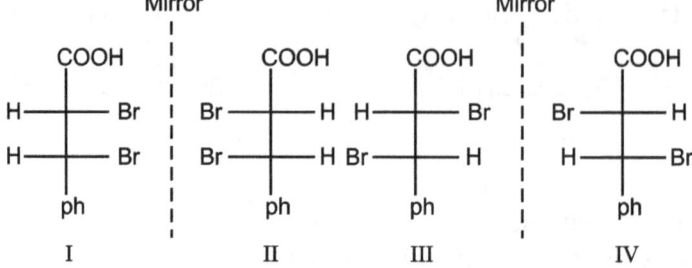

Enantiomers: I and II, III and IV.

1.5.4 Compounds Containing Two or More Similar Chiral Carbon Atoms

In general the number of stereoisomers in a compound containing 'n' number of similar chiral carbon atoms is always less than 2^n.

Example: Tartaric acid: COOH – CH – CH – COOH with OH, OH on the CH carbons (marked *)

Mesotartaric acid
(optically inactive)

1.5.5 Types of Optical Isomers

1. Enantiomers / Enantiomorphs (Gk. enantio – opposite, morph – form)
2. Diastereomers.

1. Enantiomers:

The optical isomers which possess non-superimposable mirror image of each other are called enantiomers.

Example: Left and right hand.

Characteristic properties:

1. Enantiomers have identical physical properties like M.P., B.P., densities, R.I. etc. but they differ only in their action towards the plane polarized light i.e. one will be '*l*' and other will be d.

2. Enantiomers have identical chemical properties except their action towards optically active compound.

   Example: Both the d/*l* enantiomers of lactic acid will react in the same way with same rate. However, the two enantiomers react with different rates when treated with an optically active reagent.

   Example: The rate of esterification of (+) lactic acid or (−) lactic acid with the same (+)− sec. butyl alcohol would be different. Here only one lactic acid reacts and other does not react at all.

   Such situations are quite common in biological system where enzymes and other optically active compounds react with only one of the enantiomers.

   Example: d-glucose is easily metabolized in animal and is fermented by yeast. While (−) glucose is neither metabolized by animals nor undergoes fermentation.

3. When the two enantiomers are mixed in equimolecular quantities, it results in the formation of an optically inactive compound called racemic mixture or d*l* or (±) form.

   The racemic modification has some physical properties different from those of the two enantiomers.

2. Diastereomers:

Stereoisomers which are optically active isomers but not mirror images are called diastereoisomers or diastereomers.

Example:

Characteristics of Diastereomers:

1. Diastereomers have different physical properties such as M.P., B.P., densities, solubilities, R.I., dielectric constant and specific rotations.

2. Diastereomers other than geometric isomers may or may not be optically active.

3. Diastereomers show similar but not identical chemical properties. The rates of reactions of two diastereomers with a given reagent are generally different.

4. On account of differences in their physical properties, techniques such as:

(a) fractional distillation due to their differences in boiling points;

(b) fractional crystallization due to their differences in solubility;

(c) chromatography due to their different molecular shapes and polarity.

Diastereomers can be separated from one another.

1.6 REPRESENTATION OF CHIRAL COMPOUNDS IN FISCHER, FLYING WEDGE DOTTED LINE, SAWHORSE AND NEWMANN AND THEIR INTER-CONVERSION

Flying Wedge Notation:

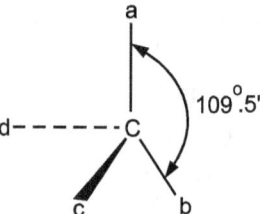

This notation is very often used to depict molecules with a single chiral centre with the implication that the uniform lines lie on the plane of the paper, the thick wedge is infront of the plane (projecting towards the observer) and the dotted line is behind the plane (projecting away from the observer).

Fischer Projection Formula:

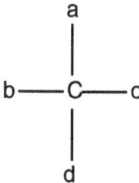

This is used in literature for their simplicity and it is desirable to know their characteristics and limitations which are as follows:

(i)   By convention, the horizontal substituents are in front (up) of and the vertical substituents are behind (down) the plane of Fischer projection formula.

(ii) The structures are not to be lifted out of the plane; they can however, be rotated in the plane through $180°$ and $360°$ which keep the horizontal substituents horizontal and vertical substituents vertical without mixing them up.

(iii) Rotations of $90°$ and $270°$ are not permitted since such operations exchange horizontal substituents (up) with the vertical ones (down) contravening the convention (i).

(iv) Conversion of one Fischer projection formula into an equivalent one with the substituents differently ordered may be done in two ways, by exchanging two pairs of substituents as shown below:

$$
\begin{array}{ccc}
b & & a \\
| & & | \\
d - C - a & \xleftarrow{\ A\ } & c - C - b \\
| & & | \\
c & & d
\end{array}
$$

Or by rotating the substituents in a group of three, keeping the fourth one fixed (i.e. 'a') as shown below.

$$
\begin{array}{ccc}
a & & a \\
| & & | \\
b-C-c & \xrightarrow{\ A\ } & c-C-d \\
| & & | \\
d & & b
\end{array}
$$

(v) Exchange of a pair of substituents leads to the enantiomeric structure (both in Fischer projection and in any 3-dimensional structure).

(vi) The carbon chain of the compound is arranged vertically with the most oxidized carbon at the top.

(vii) Represent the asymmetric carbon(s) as the intersection of crossed lines to show the asymmetric carbon.

$$
\begin{array}{c}
COOH \\
| \\
H \!-\!\!\!-\!\!\!-\!\!\!-\!\!\!-\!\! OH \\
| \\
CH_3
\end{array}
$$

Newmann projection formula:

In the Newmann projection formula, the front carbon and the groups attached to it are represented by equally spaced radii and the rear carbon atoms/groups attached to it are represented by a circle and equally spaced radial extensions.

e.g.

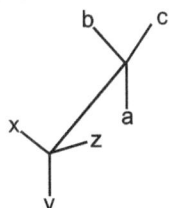

Sawhorse projection:

It is a perspective formula indicating the spatial arrangement of bonds on two adjacent carbon atoms. The bond between two atoms is represented by a diagonal line, the left hand bottom end of which locates the atom nearer the observer and right hand top end of the atom that is further away.

Interconversion of Fischer projection, Sawhorse and Newmann projection formula:

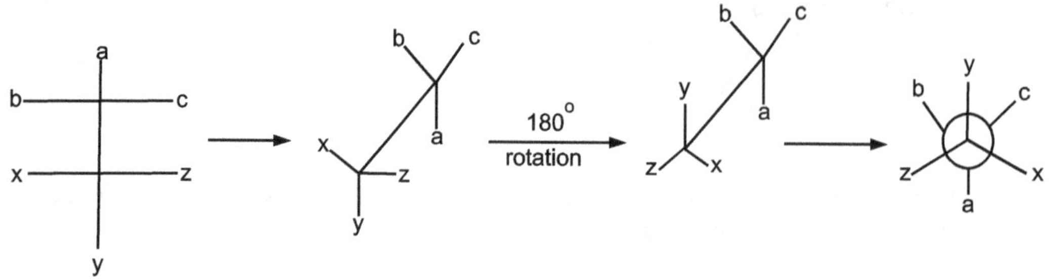

In order to convert Fischer into Sawhorse formula, the bottom chiral centre is written at the front and the top one at the rear, while the substituents are placed in front (up) and behind (below) as implied in Fischer. The front carbon is again rotated through 180° in each case to give conventional staggered sawhorse formula.

1.7 CONFIGURATION

The arrangement of atoms or groups around the asymmetric centre. Types of configuration:
1. Relative configuration
2. Absolute configuration

1. Relative configuration:

In this type, the configuration is compared with standard configuration.

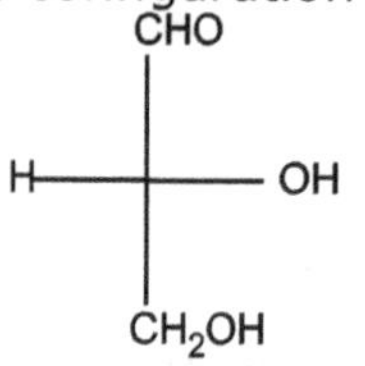

'D' (having -OH to the right side) 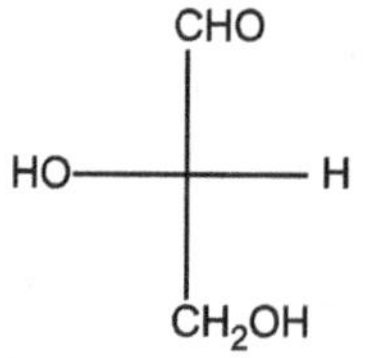   'L' (having -OH to the left side)

After comparison with the standard configuration if OH is to the right side then configuration is assigned as 'D' and if OH is to the left side then the configuration is assigned as L-configuration.

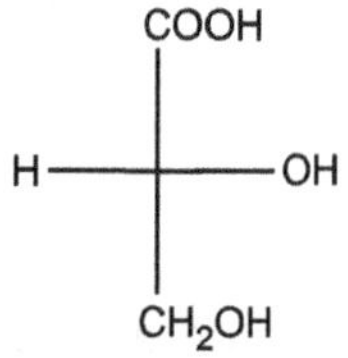

D (−) - Glyceric acid 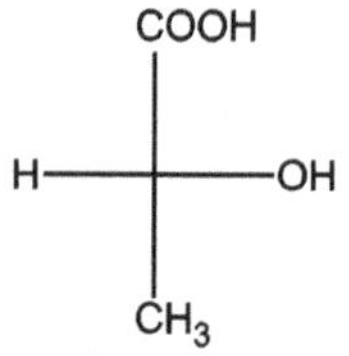   D (−) Lactic acid

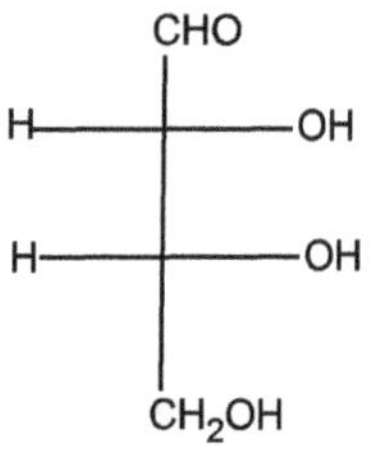

D (−) Erythrose 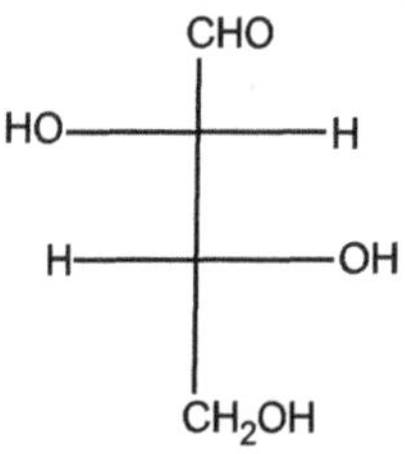   D (−) Threose 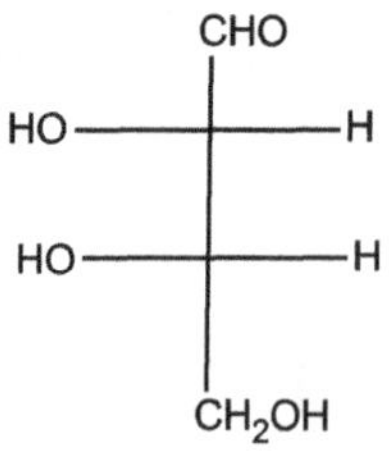   L (+) Erythrose 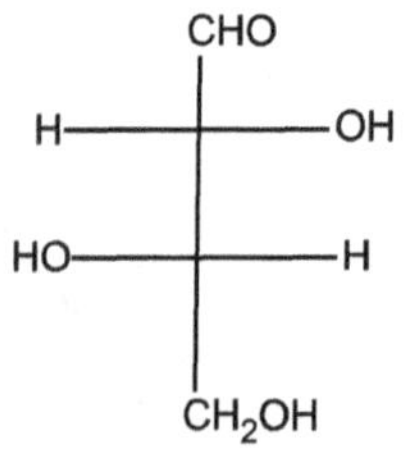   L (+) Threose

Sometimes if two or more carbon containing OH groups are present then lowest carbon is considered.

Similarly for amino acids, standard taken is L(−) serine and D(+) serine.

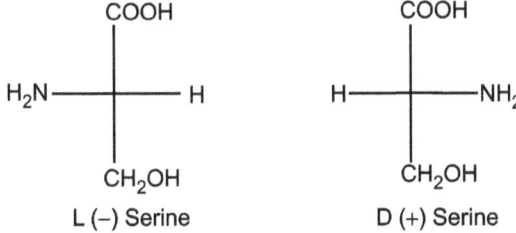

If the compound contains both $-NH_2$ and − OH groups, then the configuration is assigned with respect to either standard serine or glyceraldehyde.

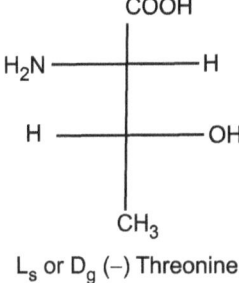

L_s or D_g (−) Threonine

2. Absolute configuration (Latin R = rectus-right and S-sinister-left configuration)

This was proposed by Cahn, Ingold and Prelog and based on the actual 3-dimensional formula and following rules:

1. The four different groups attached to the asymmetric carbon atom(s) are arranged in a priority sequence in accordance with a set of rules known as sequence rules (as described in EZ nomenclature).

2. It must be remembered that while using a Fischer projection formula, it is necessary to carry out an even number of exchanges of pairs of group, so that the group of lowest priority is situated at the top or bottom.

3. After assigning the priorities of the four groups or atoms attached to the chiral carbon, the molecule is imagined to be placed in a position where the atom or group of the lowest priority is directed away from us. Now the arrangement of the remaining groups is viewed in decreasing order of their priorities. In looking so, if the eye travels in a clockwise direction, the configuration is specified as "R". While in case eye travels in the anticlockwise direction, the configuration is specified as "S".

4. When the molecule contains more than one asymmetric centre, the same procedure is applied to each chiral centre.

Compound X_{abcd} where a > b > c > d.

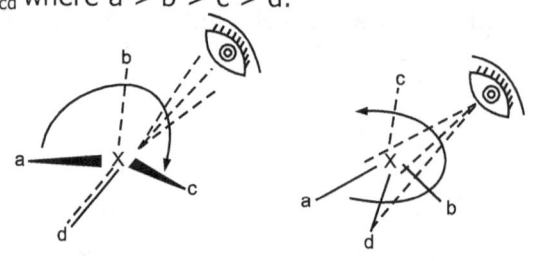

R - configuration   S - configuration

Examples:

1.

CHO — H—OH — CH₂OH

D - glyceraldehyde   'R' - configuration

'R' - configuration

2.

L-Serine   S-Serine   L-Amino propionic acid   'S' - configuration

3.

(2S, 3R) Tartaric acid   (2S, 3R) Threonine

4.

COOH

H————Br

OCH$_3$

Bromo methoxy acetic acid

$\equiv$

CH$_3$O—①Br—COOH③②

H

'R' - configuration

COOH

H————OH

Ph

Mandelic acid

$\equiv$

① OH

Ph—③②COOH

H

'R' - configuration

1. Draw and specify the R and S enantiomers of 2-chloropentane.

Cyclohexane diol-1 (R), 2(S)

$\equiv$

CH$_2$
③C①OH
H
:2:
:3:
CH$_2$—②C—OH
H :1:

2. Draw the structure for S-3-chloro-1-pentene and (R) (Z)-2-chloro-3-heptene.

Cl

CH$_2$=C————CH$_2$CH$_3$

H

Cl
CH$_3$—C—C=C—CH$_2$ CH$_2$ CH$_3$
H   H   H

1.8 R AND S NOMENCLATURE IN BIPHENYLS

In biphenyl isomerism, we encounter optically active molecules without asymmetric atoms. In this if one look at a biphenyl in the conformation in which the two rings are perpendicular along the axis of the bond joining the rings and then projects the four ortho substituents on a plane at right angles to this bond, one obtains a representation of the biphenyl which is very similar to Fischer projection formula. For the sake of uniformity, one can place the front benzene ring horizontally and the rear ring vertically, but this is of no consequence. The molecule is then named in the form in which it is projected as in figure. as if this projection represented an asymmetric carbon. There is however a complication, because of the different nature of biphenyl isomerism as compared with isomerism due to an asymmetric atom, two or even more of the atoms or groups projected may be the same. Therefore, here the sequence rule is insufficient to determine precedence in biphenyls. Therefore, a new rule had to be established, namely "NEAR GROUPS PRECEDE FAR GROUPS'. This rule takes precedence over the sequence rule.

Thus in the following molecules, the horizontal (near) groups automatically take precedence over the vertical (far) groups.

(1)

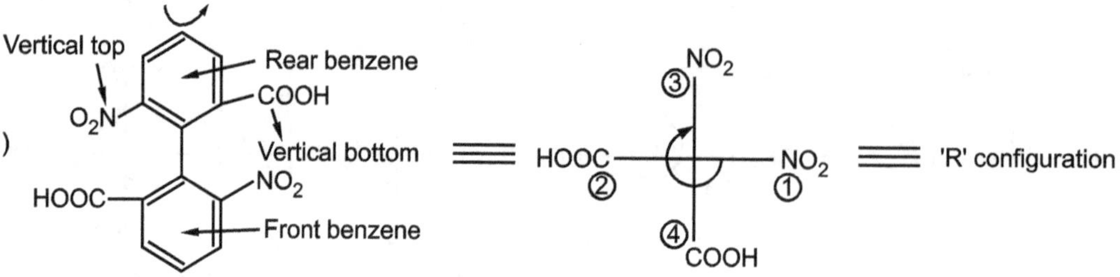

'R' configuration

(2)

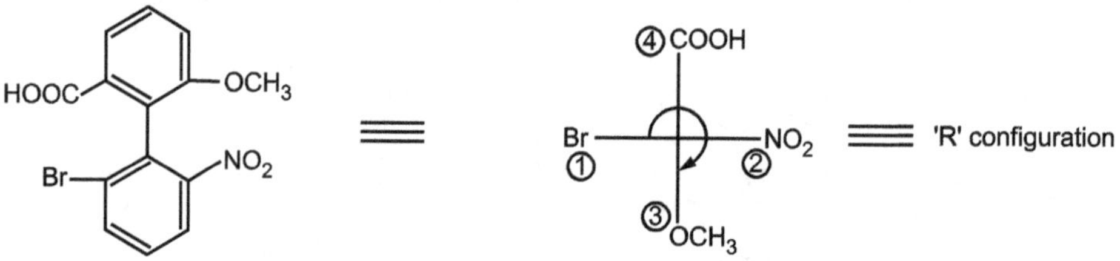

'R' configuration

(3)

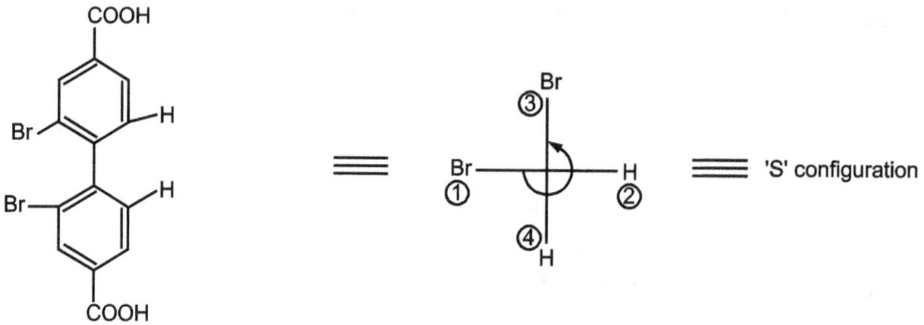

'S' configuration

(4)

'R' configuration

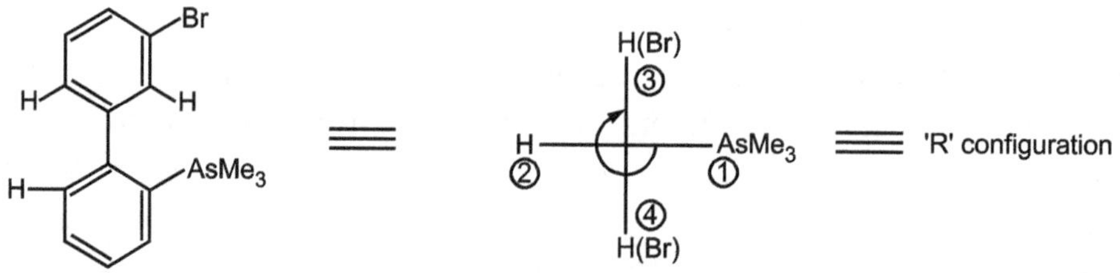

In some cases, the nature and position of the substituents is immaterial from which end the molecule is viewed. The rule, "Near Group precede Far Groups", in this case is interpreted to mean that the ring that has substituents off the main axis of the molecule nearest to an external observer is to be placed in front. Thus, whenever there are 3 substituents, the ring in which it occurs is placed infront is the 3, 5-substituents rather than the 2, 6 substituents determine the sequence.

Examples:

(1) 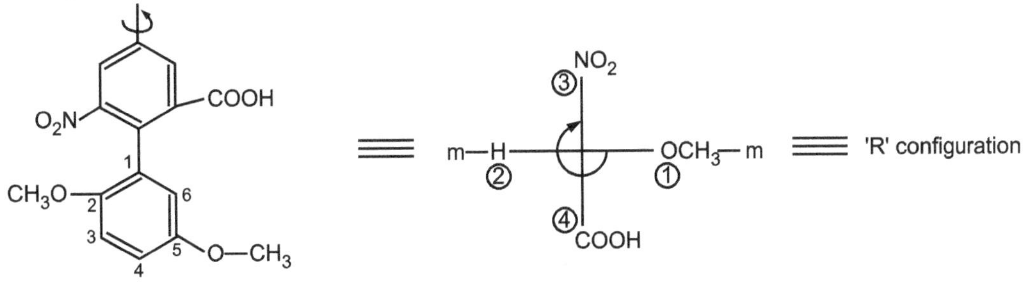 $\equiv$ m—H ... OCH$_3$—m $\equiv$ 'R' configuration

(2) 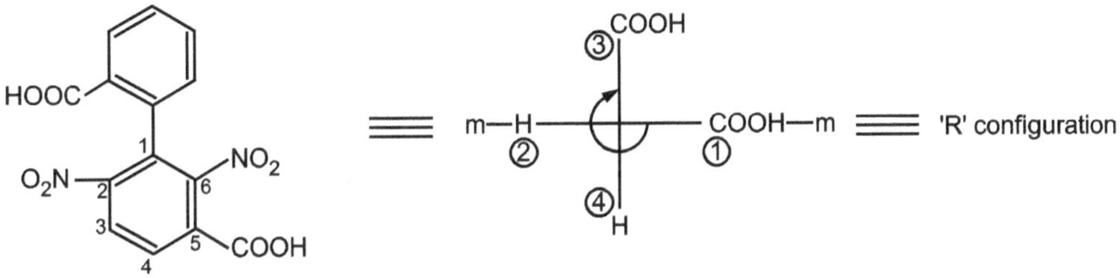 $\equiv$ m—H ... COOH—m $\equiv$ 'R' configuration

1.9 R AND S NOMENCLATURE FOR ALLENES

Rules:

1. The molecule can be viewed from either end of the stereo axis to give the same descriptor. The near groups are given priority over far groups.

2. For better visualization it is always better to put the groups nearest the view direction on a thick line (horizontal or vertical).

Example:

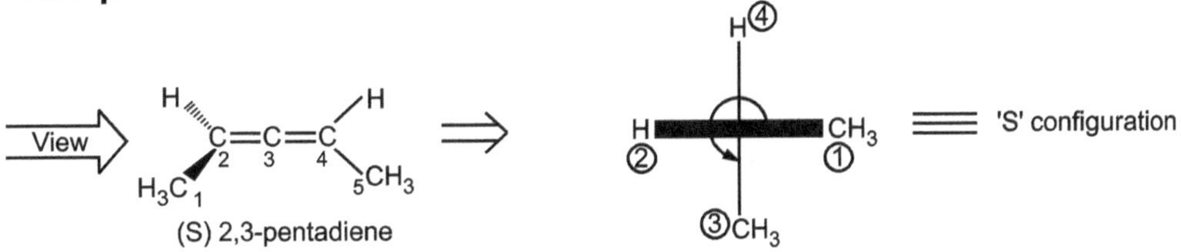

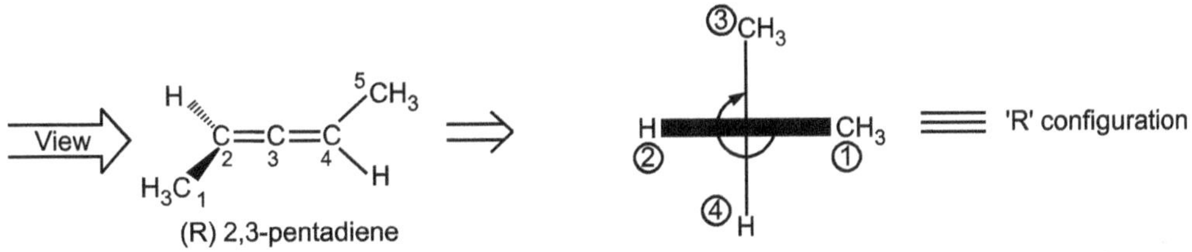

(S) 2,3-pentadiene $\equiv$ 'S' configuration

(R) 2,3-pentadiene $\equiv$ 'R' configuration

3. It makes no difference which end of the structure is viewed, the stereo-descriptor will remain unchanged. Consider (S)-2, 3-pentadiene. Now view from other direction as compared to that in above example. Now the far groups become the near groups and consequently get priority. These are placed on the thick vertical line and the configuration again comes out to be (S).

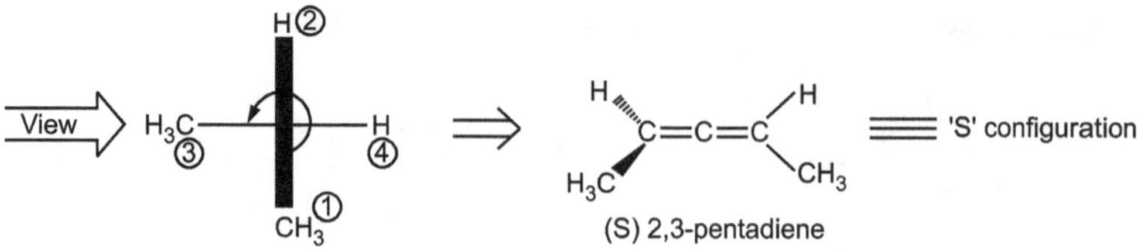

(S) 2,3-pentadiene

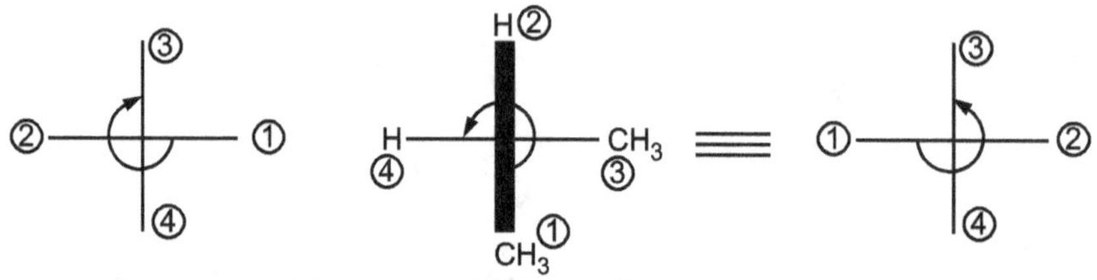

4. Interchange of two geminal groups at one end in these molecules gives the enantiomers.

For example, (R)-2, 3-pentadiene is obtained from the (S)-enantiomer.

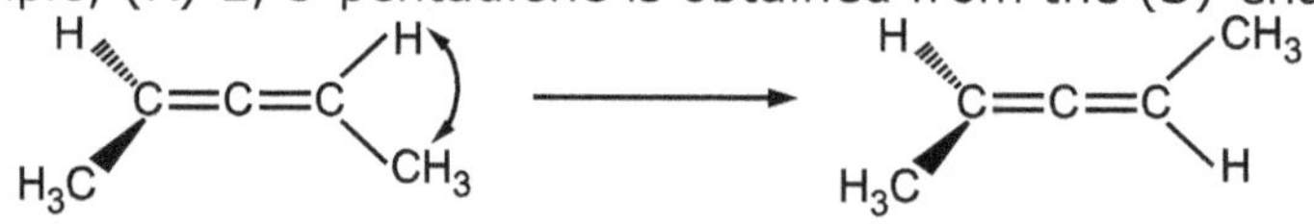

(S) - 2,3-pentadiene   (R) - 2,3-pentadiene

1.10 R, S NOMENCLATURE IN SPIRANES AND ALKYLIDENE – CYCLOALKANES

These compounds possessing axial chirality are assigned configurational descriptors in the same way as discussed for allenes. As in allenes, the interchange of the two geminal groups in these molecules also leads to enantiomers.

(i)

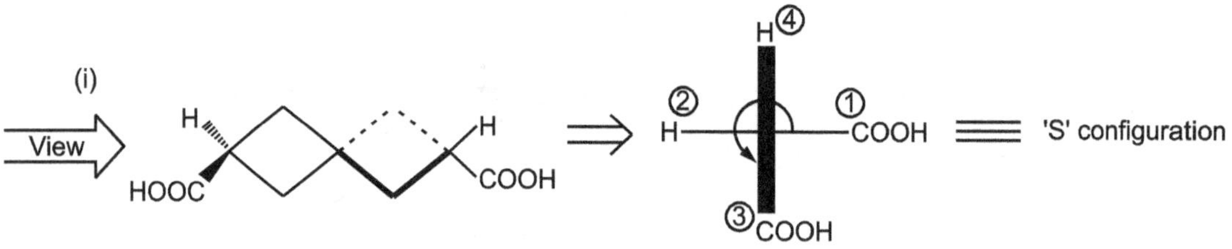

'S' configuration

(ii)

'R' configuration

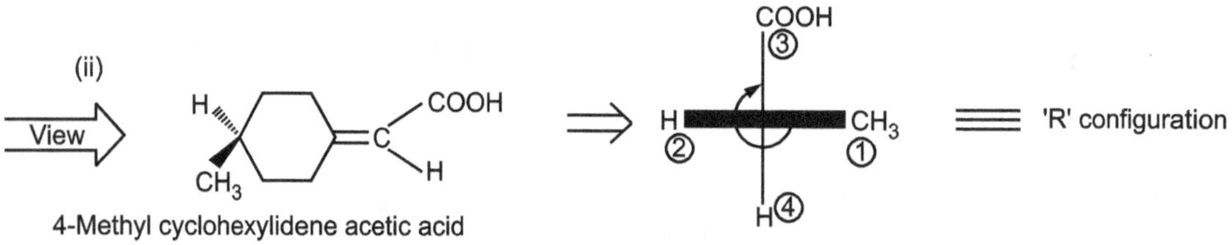

4-Methyl cyclohexylidene acetic acid

1.11 R, S NOMENCLATURE OF COMPOUNDS WITH PLANAR CHIRALITY

To assign configuration to compounds with chiral planes, the sequence rule is extended by choosing a pilot atom. This is a priority atom directly linked to the plane but it is not itself in the plane, thus it is first out of the plane atom. The pilot atom is chosen from that side of the plane which is most preferred (CIP rules). In case of scheme 1, the preferred side of the plane is the one which has the orthobromine and therefore the methylene group on the left hand side is the pilot atom. When both the sides are equivalent, the pilot atom can be chosen from any side of the plane. Then one classifies the adjacent 3 atoms of the plane as these are encounted along the bonds and given numerals 1, 2 and 3. Now view from the pilot atom. If the order 1 → 2 → 3 describe a clockwise array in the chiral plane, the configuration is 'R'. If the array is counter-clockwise the configuration is S.

Examples:

1.

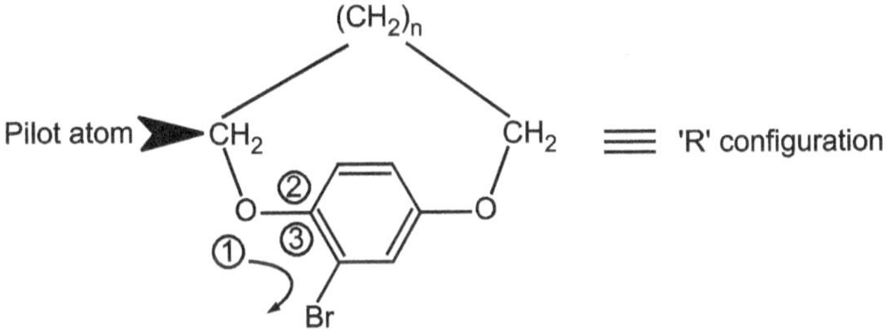

Paracyclophanes

2.

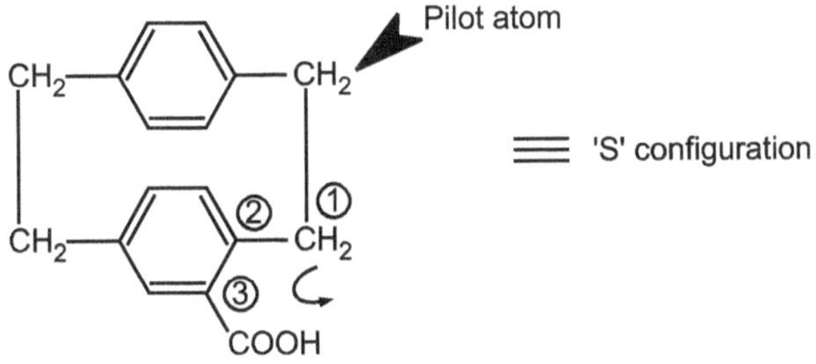

3.

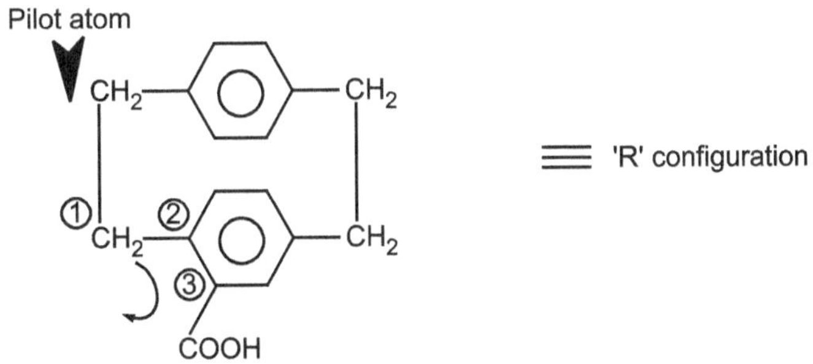

1.12 RESOLUTION OF RACEMIC MIXTURES

"The process of separation of a racemic modification into its two pure enantiomers is known as Resolution".

Following methods are used for resolution of racemic mixtures.

1. **Mechanical Separation or Spontaneous Resolution:**

   It was the first method used by Pasteur (1884) for the resolution of sodium ammonium tartarate which crystallizes out in the form of racemic mixture below 27°C. In this method, crystals of the two forms have different shapes, being mirror image of each other. They can be separated with the help of magnifying lens and small forceps. This method is laborious and is applicable to only those isomers having different crystal shape.

2. **Preferential crystallisation by inoculation (Gernez-1866):**

   This method involves the seeding of a saturated solution of the racemic mixture with a pure crystal of one of the two enantiomers. The solution now becomes supersaturated with respect to the added enantiomer and after sometimes cooling it begins to crystallise out.

   Example: Harda (1865) obtained total optical resolution of free α-amino acids with the aid of 'l' or d-isomers of the corresponding amino acid.

   Sometimes seeds with a crystal of optically active form of another molecule are also possible.

   Example: Crystal of (–) asparagine crystallises out (+) sodium ammonium tartarate from solution of racemic modification.

3. **Biochemical separation:**

   This method is based on the fact that when certain micro-organisms (e.g. bacteria, yeast, mould, fungi) are grown in dilute solution of a racemic modification they assimilate on one enantiomer rapidly than the other.

   Example: The mould penicilium glaucum preferentially destroys the (+) isomer of racemic ammonium tartarate and thus leaves the (–) ammonium tartarate in solution.

   This method has certain disadvantages viz.

   (a) One isomer is always destroyed and sometimes some of the other isomer is also destroyed.

   (b) Sometimes it is impracticable to find a microorganism (enzyme) applicable to a given racemic form.

   (c) Sometimes the racemic modification may be toxic for the micro-organism and may destroy the enzyme or may not be attacked by either of them.

   (d) Since dilute solutions are generally used, the yields are very poor.

4. By diastereomerism (Pasteur – 1858):

It is the best method for resolution of racemic modification. It consists in converting the enantiomers of a racemic modification to diastereomers with the aid of a pure enantiomer of other compound. Since diastereomers are non-identical, they have different physical properties (especially different solubility) and hence can easily be separated into its two compounds by fractional crystallization. After the complete separation of the two diastereomers, they are converted back into original chemical constituents by an appropriate reaction.

Hence success depends upon:

(a) Diastereomers – easily formed in crystalline form.

(b) Easy to convert back into parent compound.

(c) Resolving agent should be cheaper or readily prepared and recoverable.

The selection of optically active enantiomer of another compound, the conversion of d*l*-mixture into diastereomeric mixture depends upon the chemical nature of the compound to be resolved and the physical properties of resulting diastereomers.

Examples:

Acids:

Resolution of racemic modification of acids is carried out with the help of optically active bases like alkaloids (brucine, quinine, morphine etc.).

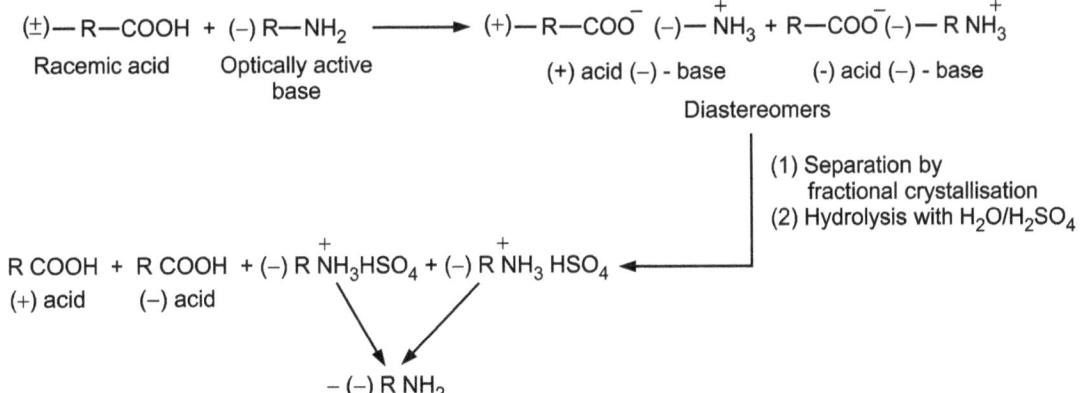

Similarly, for base pure optically active acids are used such as camphor, β-sulphonic acid, tartaric acid etc.

Amino acids are resolved after blocking the amino group via acetylation or formylation and then treating with an optically active base.

Alcohols:

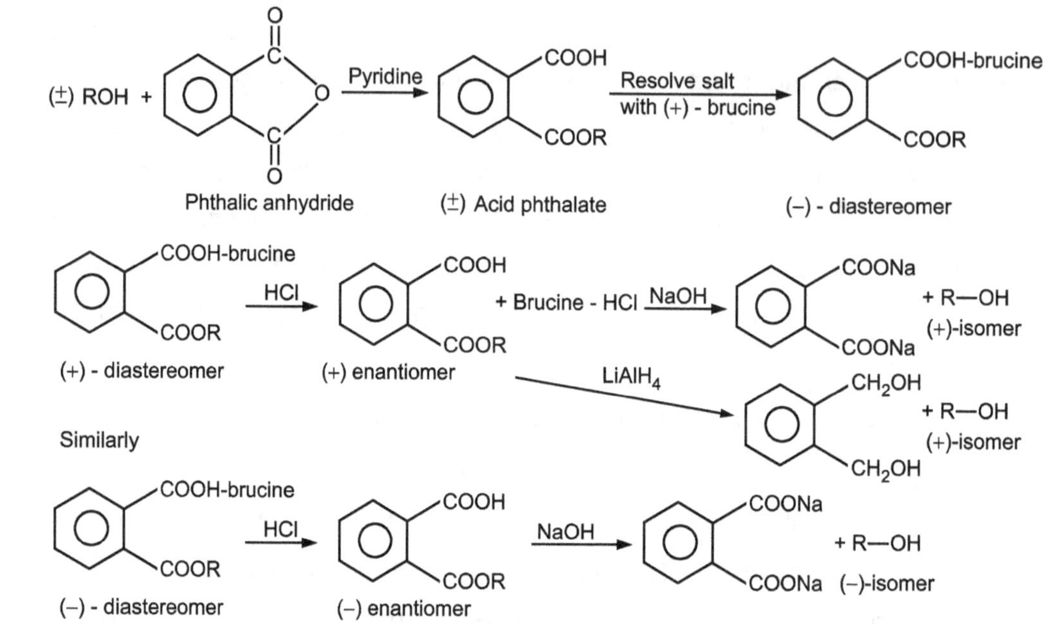

Phthalic anhydride   (±) Acid phthalate   (−) - diastereomer

(+) - diastereomer   (+) enantiomer

Similarly

(−) - diastereomer   (−) enantiomer

Aldehydes and Ketones:

Shilington et. al. (1958) reported another method which is devoid of racemisation for resolving carbonyl compounds. The method involves the conversion of carbonyl compounds into their 4-carboxy phenyl semicarbazone by means of 4-carboxy phenyl semicarbazide. The semicarbazones are acidic in nature and hence can be resolved with optically active base (e.g. brucine) and then hydrolysed to give back the optically active carbonyl compounds.

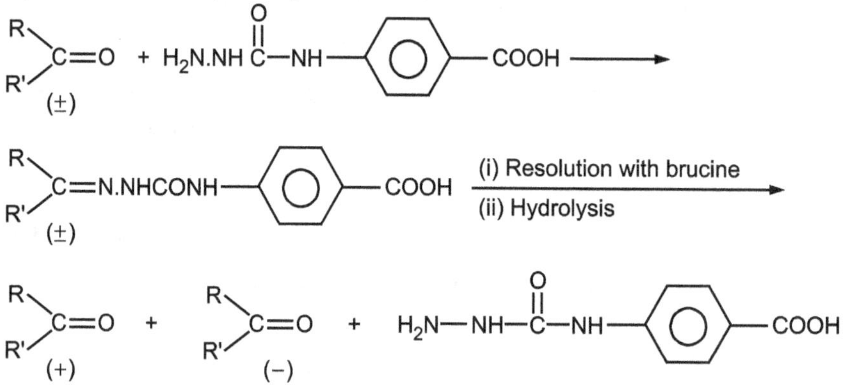

5. Complex formation:

Sometimes a racemic modification forms crystalline diastereomeric complexes with a disymmetric reagent. If the two diastereomeric complexes possess different solubilities, one will precipitate out in preference to the other. After this the two original enantiomers can be obtained from the two complexes by decomposition, by heat, dissolution, chromatography or chemical treatment on the basis of this method.

Windaur et. al. (1955) resolved 1-naphthyl-sec-butyl ether (I) by means of α (2,4,5,7) – tetranitrofluorenyldienimino-propionic acid-II.

6. Chromatography:

Chromatography method of resolution is of limited use. The process involves the addition of a solution of the racemic modification over an optically active adsorbent and collecting the two enantiomers from the adsorbates. Since the adsorbates formed by the combination of enantiomers and adsorbents are diastereomers, they are not equally stable and hence one of them will pass through the column faster than the other. The two enantiomers are then obtained from the two diastereomers by means of careful elution. By the application of this method, (±) p-phenylene bis imino camphor has been resolved on lactose column by Henderson and Rule 1939.

7. Kinetic method:

This method is based on the fact that one of the enantiomers of same racemic modification reacts faster than the other with an optically active compound.

Example: (–) menthol reacts faster with (+) mandelic acid than with (–) enantiomer. Now if reaction is stopped before completion or insufficient (–) menthol is used, the resulting product will contain predominantly (–) menthyl (+) mandate and hence the unchanged acid will predominantly be of (–) form.

8. Asymmetric Transformation:

The phenomenon of asymmetric transformation is exhibited by the optically unstable compound i.e. when the enantiomers are readily interconvertible (+) ⇌ (–).

Asymmetric transformation may be:
(i) First order and
(ii) Second order.

Example: Suppose an equimolecular amount of an optically stable (+) base and an optically unstable (±) acids are dissolved in a solvent. Just at the time of mixing the solution will contain equal amounts of the two possible diastereomers, but since the acid is optically unstable at the time of equilibrium, the two diastereomers will be present in unequal amounts. This establishment of equilibrium in solution between the diastereomers having a real existence is known as **first order asymmetric transformation**. On the other hand whenever either of the diastereomers crystallizes out from solution i.e. they need not have a real existence in solution the phenomenon is termed as **second order asymmetric transformation.**

So by means of asymmetric transformation, especially second order, whole of the optically unstable compound may be converted into the crystallisable form which may be (+) or (–) depending upon the nature of base and solvent.

Example: Miller and Elliot (1928) resolved both forms of N-benzene sulphonyl-8-nitro-1-naphthylglycine with brucine as a base and methanol or acetone as a solvent.

1.13 CONFORMATIONAL ISOMERS

Definition: Conformation may be defined as the term used to denote any one of the infinite number of spatial arrangement of atoms of a molecule that can arise from rotation about a single bond and such conformations are called **conformational isomers**.

Newmann projection formulae are generally considered to be the best representation for conformation analysis.

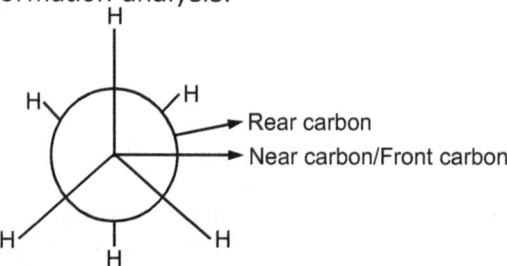

In Newmann projection formula, the carbon atoms nearer to the eye and groups attached to it are represented by an equally spaced radii and the distant carbon atom and the groups attached to it are represented by a circle with three equally spaced radial extensions.

1.13.1 Conformational Analysis of Ethane

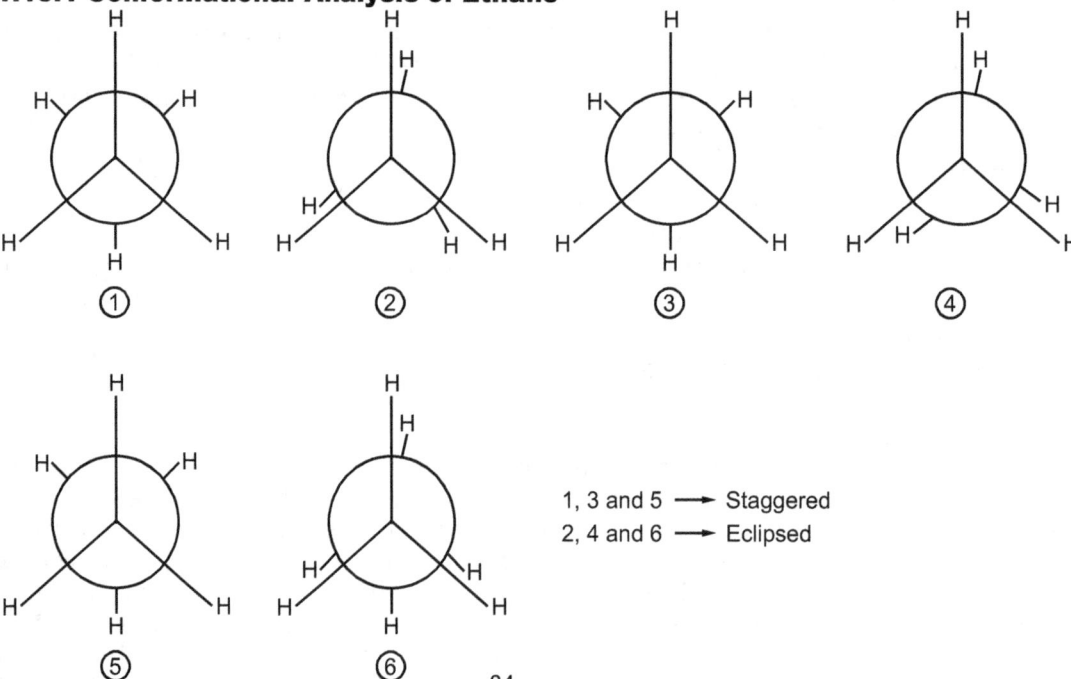

1, 3 and 5 ⟶ Staggered
2, 4 and 6 ⟶ Eclipsed

84

If one of the methyl group is allowed to rotate along the C-C axis keeping the rest of molecule undisturbed, 6 possible conformations are obtained, out of which **3 are staggered** form in which the two hydrogen atoms on the different carbon atoms are as far apart as possible (1, 3 and 5) and there are **3 eclipsed** form in which the two hydrogen atoms on the different carbon atoms are as close together as possible (2, 4 and 6).

Since the potential energies of 1, 3 and 5 are same, they are equally stable. Similarly, the conformations 2, 4 and 6 are equally stable as they also possess the equal energy. But the potential energy of 1, 3 and 5 is less than that of 2, 4 and 6 because in the later case, the hydrogen atoms on the two carbon atoms are very close to each other and hence exert a repulsive force against each other (steric repulsion due to non-bonded interaction of H-atom). Therefore, staggered conformations (1, 3 and 5) are more stable than eclipsed conformations (2, 4 and 6).

Potential Energies (P.E.)

PE of various conformations can be made more clear by plotting a graph between P.E. versus angle of rotation of methyl group w.r.t. the other.

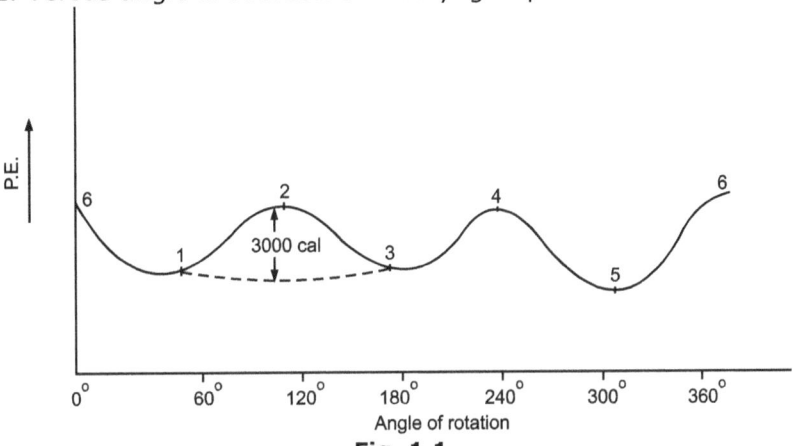

Fig. 1.1

1.13.2 Conformational Analysis of Substituted Ethane

Example: 1, 2-Dichloroethane.

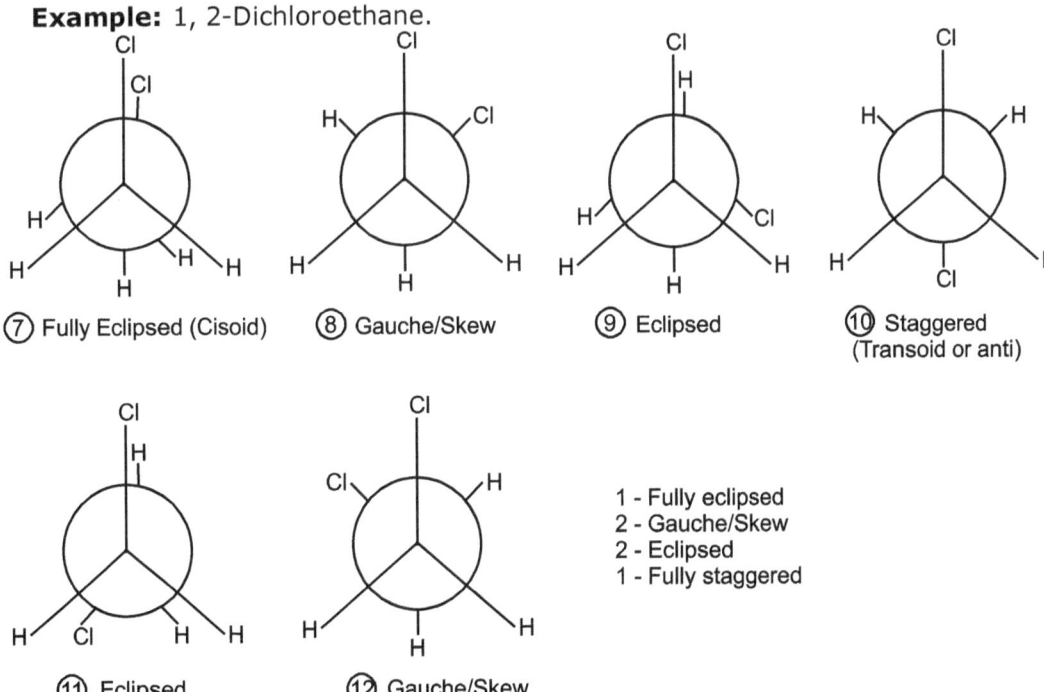

⑦ Fully Eclipsed (Cisoid)   ⑧ Gauche/Skew   ⑨ Eclipsed   ⑩ Staggered (Transoid or anti)

⑪ Eclipsed   ⑫ Gauche/Skew

1 - Fully eclipsed
2 - Gauche/Skew
2 - Eclipsed
1 - Fully staggered

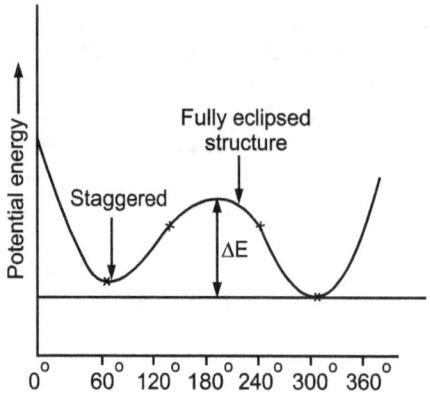

Fig. 1.2: Conformational energy diagram for 1, 2-Dichloroethane, staggered and eclipsed structure

Fig. 1.3: Conformational energy diagram for 1, 2-Dichloroethane 7, 8, 9, 10, 11 and 12 structures

In ethane all the staggered or eclipsed conformations are of equal energy but 1,2-dichloroethane have different amount of energies because of interaction of H–H, H-Cl and Cl-Cl.

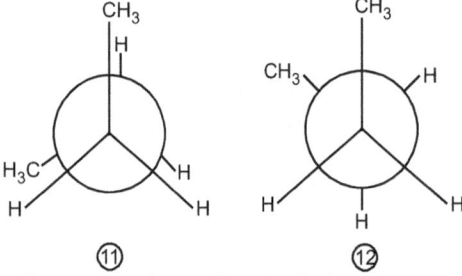

Conformational Analysis of Butane:

Similar to as that of 1, 2-dichloroethane.

1.13.3 Conformations of Cyclohexane

Since the 'C' atom in cyclohexane is tetrahedral so the molecule is not planar. Mohr in 1918 proposed two strainless or puckered conformations in which all the angles are tetrahedral. These two puckered conformations are the chair or Z and boat, flexible or C form.

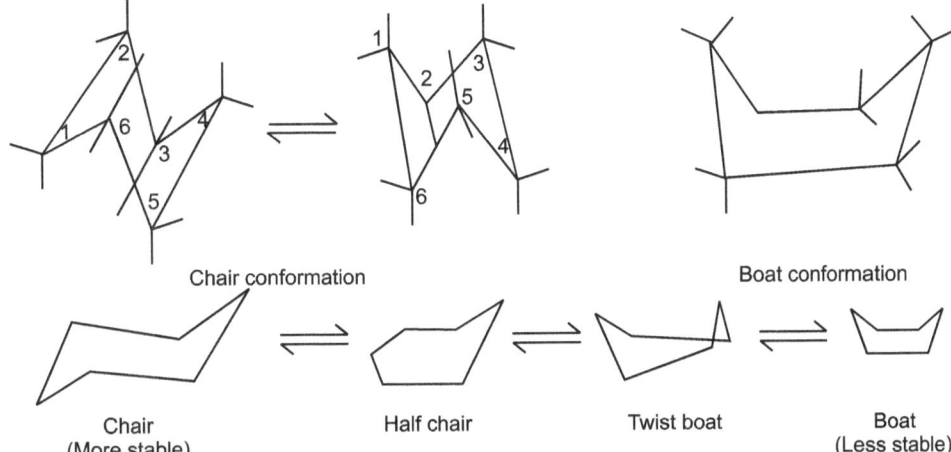

The chair form of cyclohexane exists in two forms each being convertible into the other via the flexible form. During this transformation the axial bonds of one become the equatorial bonds of other and vice-versa.

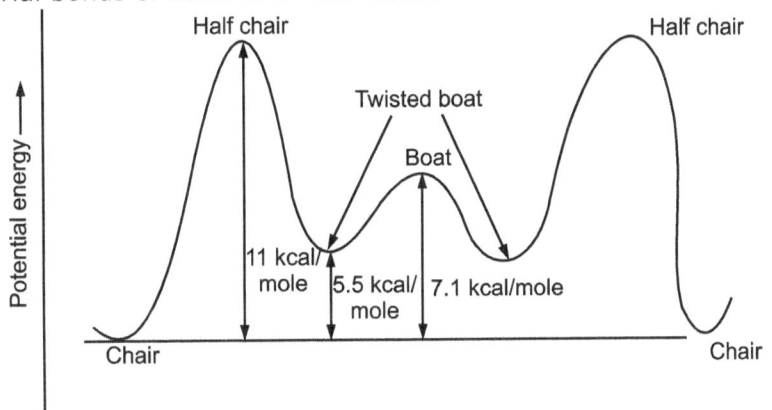

Fig. 1.4: Relative energies of the conformations of cyclohexane molecules

Equatorial and Axial Hydrogens:

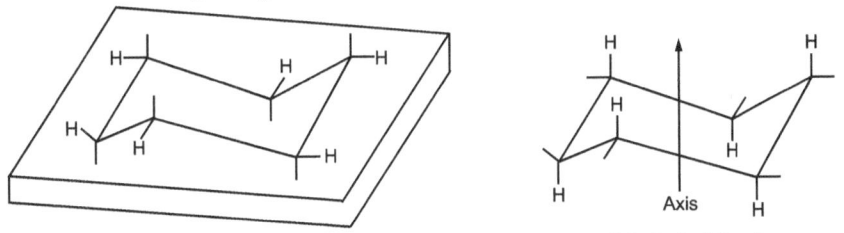

(a) Equatorial hydrogens   **(b) Axial hydrogens**

Fig. 1.5: The equatorial and axial hydrogens of cyclohexanes

(a) Equitorial hydrogens lie in the plane of ring carbons;
(b) Axial hydrogens lie up or down parallel to the perpendicular axis.

Conformation of Monosubstituted Cyclohexanes (Methyl Cyclohexane):

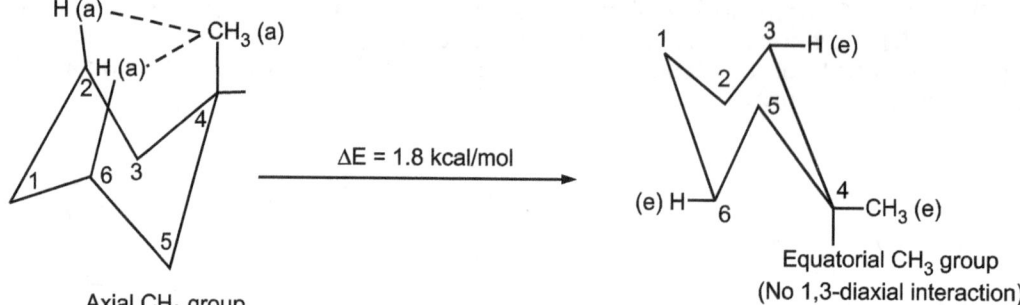

Axial CH₃ group
(presence of two 1,3-diaxial interaction)

Equatorial CH₃ group
(No 1,3-diaxial interaction)

In the axial conformation of methyl cyclohexane, the axial CH_3 group on C_4 is close to the two axial hydrogens on C_2 and C_6, which develop repulsive forces or steric strain in the molecule. Note that, the repulsive force (steric strain) is between axial CH_3 group and axial H atom present on 2, 6 position to each other, such non-bonded interaction is therefore called as 1,3-diaxial interaction. Each such 1, 3-diaxial interaction increases the energy of the molecule by 0.9 kcal/mol. Since there are two such 1, 3-diaxial interactions in the present case, the axial conformer has 1.8 kcal/mol more energy than the corresponding equatorial conformer in which equatorial $-CH_3$ group and the equatorial hydrogen atoms on the adjacent carbon atoms are far away from each other. Thus, the equatorial conformation should be more stable than the axial by 1.8 kcal/mol.

1.13.4 Conformations of Disubstituted Cyclohexane

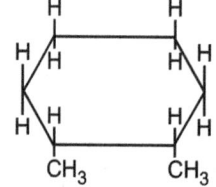

Cis - 1,2-dimethyl cyclohexane

Trans - 1,2 - dimethyl cyclohexane

1.13.5 Conformation of Cis and Trans-1, 2-dimethyl cyclohexane and Conformation of Cis-1,2-dimethyl cyclohexane

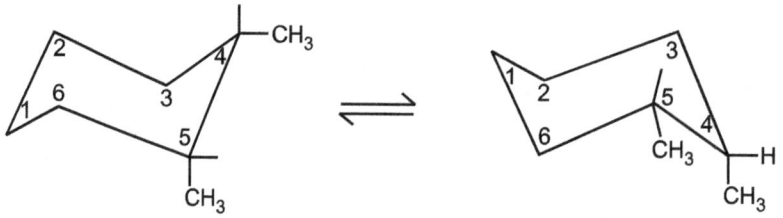

ea (equatorial - axial conformation)

ae (axial - equatorial conformation)

In cis-1,2-dimethyl cyclohexane, one CH_3 group must be axial and other equatorial, such conformations are generally referred to as ea or ae conformation.

Regarding their relative stabilities, we can say that since both of them possess one methyl group in axial position and one in equatorial position (i.e. equal 1, 3-diaxial interaction and equal energy), they are equally stable and thus half of the molecule exists in the conformation (ae) and other half in the conformation (ea).

∴   ea is equally stable as ae conformations.

∴ $\boxed{ae \ = \ ea}$

Conformations of Trans-1, 2-dimethyl cyclohexane:

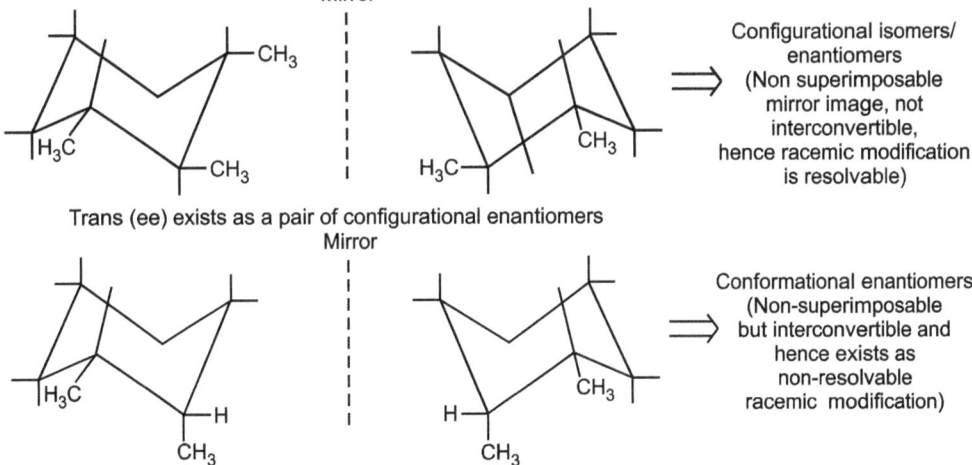

aa (Less stable)   ee (More stable)

In trans-1, 2-dimethyl cyclohexane both the methyl groups are either present in equatorial or axial positions and hence these are generally referred to as ee or aa conformations respectively.

Now since the methyl groups in ee (diequatorial) conformation have less 1, 3-axial interaction than in aa (diaxial) conformation. Hence ee conformation is more stable than aa conformation.

∴ $\boxed{ee \ > \ aa}$

$\boxed{Trans \ ee \ > \ cis \ ae/ea \ > \ Trans \ aa}$

Optical Isomerism in 1, 2-dimethyl cyclohexane:

Trans (ee) exists as a pair of configurational enantiomers

Configurational isomers/ enantiomers (Non superimposable mirror image, not interconvertible, hence racemic modification is resolvable)

Cis (ea) exists as a pair of conformational enantiomers

Conformational enantiomers (Non-superimposable but interconvertible and hence exists as non-resolvable racemic modification)

Conformation of 1, 3-dimethyl cyclohexane:

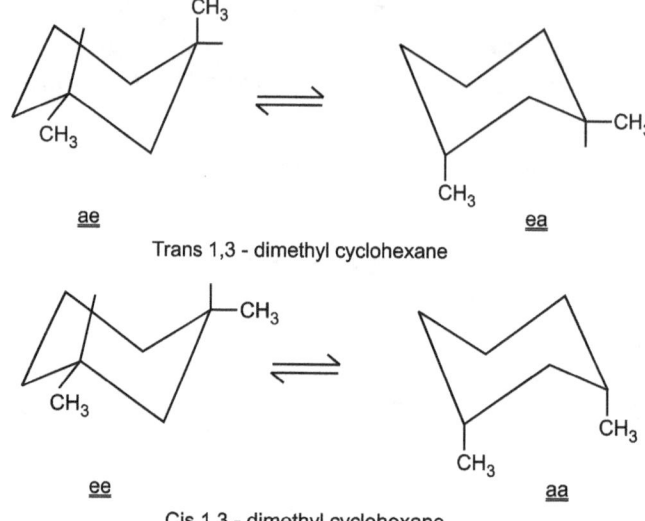

Trans 1,3 - dimethyl cyclohexane

Cis 1,3 - dimethyl cyclohexane

In case of 1,3-dimethyl cyclohexane, the cis-isomer is more stable than the trans isomer.

∴   cis ee > trans ae/ea > cis aa

Conformations of 1, 4-dimethyl cyclohexane:

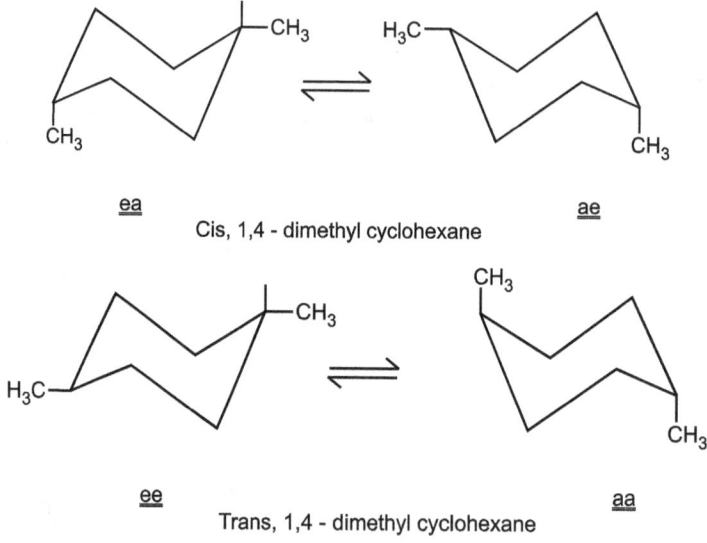

Cis, 1,4 - dimethyl cyclohexane

Trans, 1,4 - dimethyl cyclohexane

∴   Trans ee > cis ea/ae > Trans aa

1.13.6 Newmann Projection Conformations of Cyclohexane

Cyclohexane:

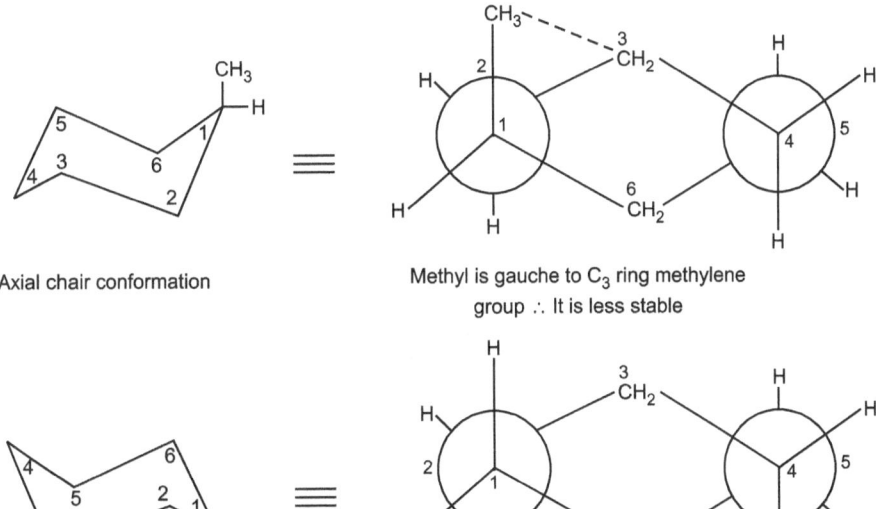

Planar structure   Chair conformation

Newmann projection conformation for cyclohexane

Methyl cyclohexane:

Axial chair conformation

Methyl is gauche to C_3 ring methylene group ∴ It is less stable

Equatorial chair conformation

Methyl group is anti to C_3 ring methylene group ∴ It is more stable

1.14 ATROPISOMERISM (Optical Isomerism due to Restricted Rotation)

Definition: "The stereoisomers (optical isomers) occurring due to restriction in rotation about single bonds (where the isomers can actually be isolated) are called atropisomers and the phenomenon is called as atropisomerism".

Example: Non-planar ortho substituted biphenyls (Biphenyl isomers).

(6, 6' - dinitrophenic acid)

The more crowded the ortho substituents are in the planar form, the higher the energy maximum and more difficult the enantiomers are to racemize. As the ortho substituents are made smaller, the energy barrier between the enantiomers becomes lower and the substance becomes more and more easily racemized.

Most of the available evidence of biphenyl isomerism is in agreement with the simple picture summarized in figure. Tetra ortho substituted biphenyl of the type

can usually be resolved.

In the transition state for racemization, two pairs of bulky groups (a-c and b-d) must slip past each other which is usually difficult so that, the enantiomers, once obtained are usually stable. However, it is clear that, the energy barrier for racemization must depend on the bulk of the ortho substituent. If these are very small, racemization becomes so fast that resolution fails. When one pair of small becomes o fast that resolution fails. When one pair of small ortho substituent and one pair of medium sized ortho groups are just opposed, resolution becomes possible but the enantiomers are racemized on warming. When atleast two of the four ortho substituents are large or if all four are atleast medium sized, optically stable enantiomers can be obtained.

When the conformations of the biphenyl in which the two rings are at right angles to each other has itself a plane of symmetry, these molecules are not resolvable because of symmetry. But the addition of a substituent in the meta position destroying the symmetry (B) will lead to resolvability if the ortho substituents are bulky enough.

A (Non-resolvable)   B (Resolvable)

The characteristic of atropisomerism is that they cannot be represented by any type of formula, as in the case of allenes, spiranes, and centrally chiral compounds, since the stereochemistry depends on the bulk of the ortho substituents which restrict the rotation about the single bond. Thus, even a 2, 2'-6 6'- tetra substituted biphenyl may be non-resolvable, an example is difluoro-dimethoxy derivative (3). On the other hand, biphenyl-2,2-disulphonic acid with only two ortho-substituents is resolvable because of much higher bulk of –SO₃H.

In addition to physical proof and chemical evidence for the non-planar configuration of the optically active biphenyl is provided by the examples (5), (6) and (7). The compounds (5) as well as (6) derived from it are resolvable. But the compound (7) in which the ortho positions are joined by planar rings is non-resolvable, since the non-bonded interaction has been converted into a bonded one.

Pivotal bone

①   ②

③   ④

⑤   ⑥   ⑦

It may be noted that the two diastereomeric planar conformations (1) and (2) represent the energy maxima, the one with similar groups on the same side (cisoid) having higher energy than the other with similar groups on opposite side (transoid). Racemization therefore takes place with greater ease through the transoid configuration. The bulkier the ortho substituents are, the higher is the energy barrier separating the enantiomers and when it exceeds 80-100 kJ mol^{-1}, the stereoisomers may be separable at room temperature. This type of isomerism which owes its existence to restricted rotation around a single bond is known as **atropisomerism** and isomers are called **atropisomers**. They are actually torsional isomers about single bonds.

1.15 CONFORMATION IN DECALIN / BICYCLO [4, 4, 0] DECANE

Cis-decalin   C$_2$ Cis

Trans-decalin   C$_2$h   Trans

Decalin exists in two diastereomeric forms, a cis form in which the two rings are cis fused and a trans form, in which the two rings are trans fused.

The cyclohexane units in both cis and trans decalins exist in chair conformation. Torsional angles around all C-C bonds including the common bond of the rings are approximately 55-56°, the same as in cyclohexane.

The trans decalin in which the two rings are fused through ee bonds has a rigid structure and cannot undergo **ring inversion** which would lead to a highly strained a, a ring fusion.

On the other hand, cis decalin in which the rings are fused through a, e bonds can invert by interchanging a, e bonds in the ring junction as below:

I$_a$ I$_b$

The two interconvertible structures I_a and I_b are mirror images of each other and cis-decalin thus exists as ($\pm$) pair similar to cis-1, 2-dimethyl cyclohexane.

Torsion angle of junction is the torsion angle (ϕ) in each ring which has the common bond as its central bond as shown in Newmann projection formula. Those in the two enantiomeric forms of cis-decalin, usually their values are $55°$ so that $\phi + \phi' = 110°$. For the trans isomer their signs are opposite and fixed while for the cis isomer, their signs are identical and they can be changed simultaneously. Thus, in the trans structure, if the molecule is rotated around the 10-9 bond in an anticlockwise direction, the torsion angle of junction in ring A closes up but that in ring B opens up - a process not energetically favourable (ring 'B' becomes more puckered). On the other hand, in cis form, a decrease of torsion angle of junction in ring A follows a similar decrease of its counterpart in ring 'B' and if the process is continued, cis form is finally converted into its other form and vice-versa. Such a concerted change in torsion angles of junction is energetically quite feasible which explains the ring inversion in cis but not in trans decalin.

QUESTIONS

Answer the following questions:

1. Define the following terms:
   (a) Stereochemistry
   (b) Isomerism
   (c) Geometrical isomerism
   (d) Optical isomerism
   (e) Conformational isomerism
2. Give the classification of isomerism.
3. What is the necessary condition for an alkene to exhibit geometrical isomer ?
4. Differentiate between cis and trans isomers.
5. Give the general properties of geometrical isomers.
6. Explain why trans isomer is more stable than its corresponding cis isomer ?
7. State and explain the CIP sequence rules.
8. Explain the EZ system of nomenclature for geometrical isomers.
9. Classify the following compounds into E and Z configuration.

(a)

(b)

(c)

(d)

(e)

(f)

10. Explain with suitable example the various physical and chemical methods of determining configuration of geometrical isomers.

11. What is plane polarized light and optically active compound ?

12. Define the following terms:
   (a) Specific rotation
   (b) Enantiomers
   (c) Diastereomers
   (d) Chiral centre.

13. Explain the various types of elements of symmetry with a suitable example.

14. Explain the relation between chiral centre and chirality.

15. Give the characteristic properties of enantiomers and diastereomers.

16. Write a note on the following:
   (a) Flying wedge notation
   (b) Fischer projection formula
   (c) Newmann projection formula
   (d) Sawhorse projection

17. Write a note on D and L configuration.

18. Explain in detail how the R and S configuration can be determined for a compound containing single chiral centre.

19. Assign the R and S configuration to the following compounds:

$$CHO$$
$$HO——H$$
$$CH_2OH$$
(a)

$$COOH$$
$$H——NH_2$$
$$CH_2OH$$
(b)

$$Cl$$
$$CH_2{=}C——CH_2CH_3$$
$$H$$
(c)

$$COOH$$
$$Br——H$$
$$OCH_3$$
(d)

$$Ph$$
$$H——OH$$
$$COOH$$
(e)

$$COOH$$
$$H——NH_2$$
$$H——OH$$
$$CH_3$$
(f)

$$OH$$
$$OH$$
$$NH_2$$
(g)

$$CHO$$
$$H——OH$$
$$HO——H$$
$$CH_2OH$$
(h)

$$CHO$$
$$H——OH$$
$$HO——H$$
$$H——OH$$
$$CH_2OH$$
(i)

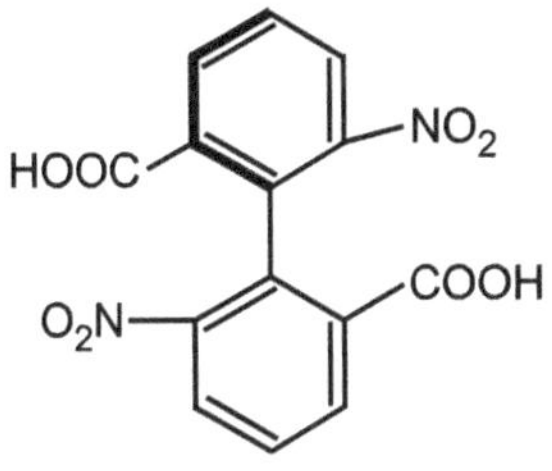

(j)

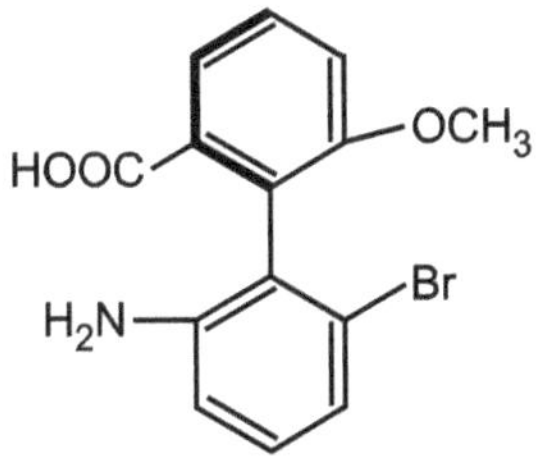

(k)

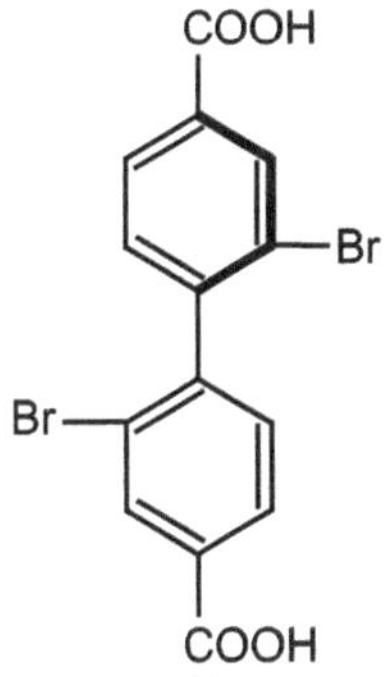

(l)

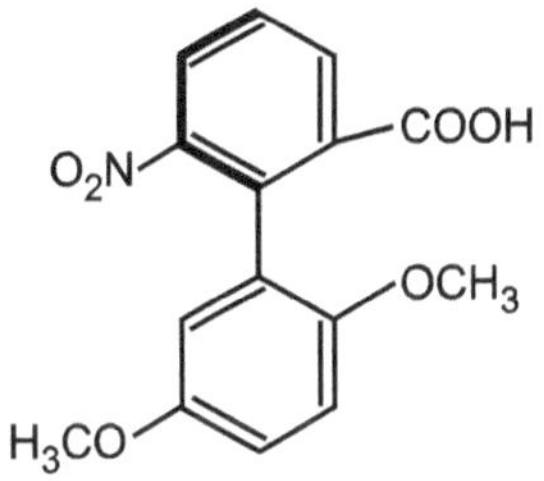

(m)

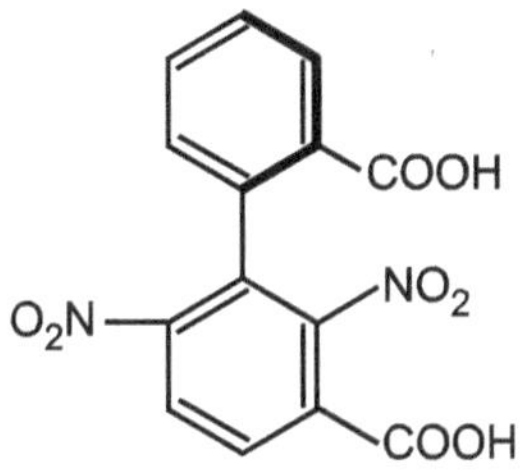

(n)

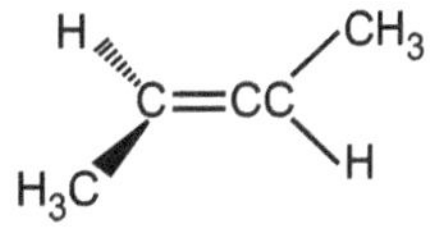

(o)

(p)

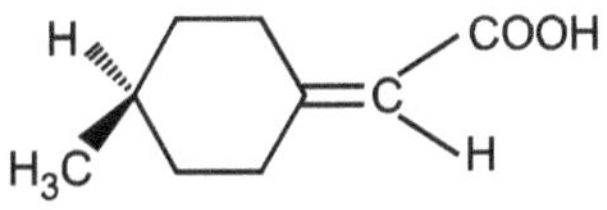

(q)

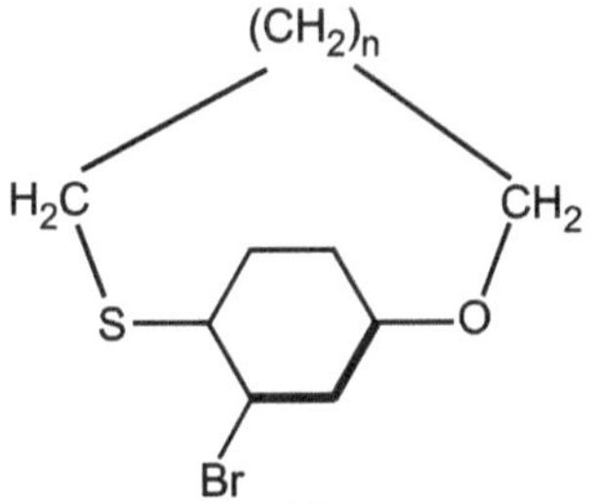

(r)

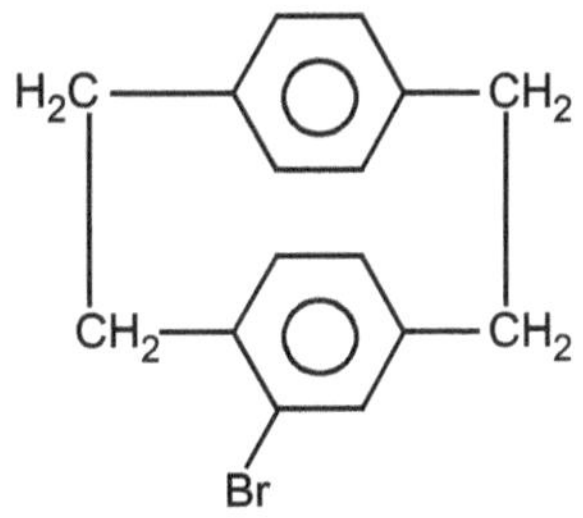

(s)

20. What is racemic mixture ?

21. Explain various methods for resolution of racemic mixture.

22. What are conformational isomers ?

23. Explain the Newmann conformational analysis of:

    (a) Ethane

    (b) 1, 2-Dichloroethane

    (c) Butane

    (d) Methyl cyclohexane

24. Explain the chair conformational analysis of

    (a) Methyl cyclohexane

    (b) Cis and trans 1, 2-dimethyl cyclohexane

    (c) Cis and trans 1, 3-dimethyl cyclohexane

    (d) Cis and trans 1, 4-dimethyl cyclohexane

25. Explain in detail the conformational analysis of Decalin.

26. Define the term Atropisomerism and mention the necessary conditions for a compound to exhibit Atropisomerism.

27. Write a short note on significance of stereochemistry in biological activity.

28. Explain briefly a relation between elements of symmetry and optical activity.

29. Write the Fischer projection for (R)-2-iodobutane and convert it into its wedge and dotted line representation.

30. Which of the following molecules are chiral ?

    (a)   (b)   (c)

31. Assign the absolute configuration to the following compounds and draw their Fischer projections.

    (a)   (b)   (c)   (d)

32. Given the priorities, designate the structures below as R or S.

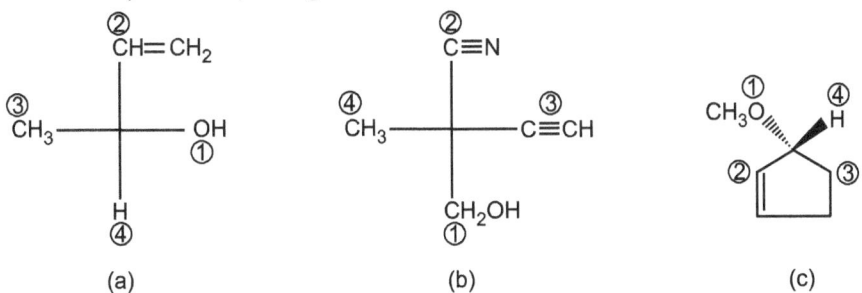

(a)   (b)   (c)

33. Draw the structure of (R)-3-ethylcyclohexene.

34. Draw the Fischer projections of all the possible stereoisomers for 2, 3-butanediol.

35. Comment on the chirality of the naturally occurring antibiotic mycomycin.

36. Write the structure of mesotartaric acid in Newmann projection and translate it into Fischer projection.

37. Draw all the possible stereoisomers of 3-pentene-2-ol.

38. $HC \equiv C - C - C \equiv C - CH = C = CH - CH = CH - CH = CH - CH_2COOH$

Fill in the blanks:

1. Molecules which are not superimposable on their mirror images are called _____.

2. Generally a molecule is chiral if it has no plane of symmetry or _____ of symmetry.

3. A molecule is achiral when it has any _____ of symmetry.

4. Enantiomers are related as object and mirror image, the stereoisomers which are not so related are called _____.

5. A stereocentre can be tetrahedral or _____ planar.

6. A chiral molecule can have no centre or plane of symmetry but can have a simple _____ of symmetry.

7. Meso compounds are _____ and are _____ on their mirror images.

8. The allenes of the type $abC = C = Cab$ are _____ due to non-planar arrangement of four groups called as chiral _____.

9. The stereoisomers due to restricted rotation about single bonds with high rotational barriers which permit their isolation are called _____.

10. Trans isomers are _____ stable than their cis isomers.

11. The equimolar mixture of d and *l* isomers is called _____ mixture.

12. Compounds containing a single chiral centre are always _____.

13. The number of optical isomers in a molecule containing 'n' number of dissimilar chiral carbon atoms can be predicted by the relation _____.

14. 1-propene does not exhibit _____ isomer.

(Answers: (1) chiral, (2) centre, (3) elements, (4) diastereomers, (5) trigonal, (6) axis, (7) achiral, superimposible, (8) chiral, axis (9) atropisomers, (10) more, (11) racemic, (12) chiral, (13) 2^n, (14) geometrical**).**

■■■

Chapter 2

MOLECULAR REARRANGEMENT REACTIONS

Syllabus ......

Rearrangement of electron deficient systems, migration to oxygen, nitrogen, and carbon, Mechanism and stereochemistry of Baeyer-Villiger oxidation and Dakin oxidations, Wagner Meerwein rearrangements, Pinacol-Pinacolone rearrangement, Beckmann, Curtius, Lossen, Hofmann and Schmidt rearrangements. Rearrangements of electron rich system inclusive of Stevens, Sommlet, Favorskii, Neber and Benzilic acid rearrangement. Rearrangement to aromatic nucleus including mechanism of Fries and Claisen rearrangement.

Pericyclic Reactions: Electrocyclic, Cycloaddition and Sigmatropic reactions (Cope rearrangement).

2.1 DEFINITION

It is the reaction which involves reshuffling of the sequence of the atoms to form a new structure.

Molecular rearrangement refers to the migration of a group from one atom to another within the same molecule.

$$\text{Example:} \quad \overset{\displaystyle R}{\underset{\displaystyle |}{A}} - B \longrightarrow A - \overset{\displaystyle R}{\underset{\displaystyle |}{B}}$$

2.2 TYPES OF MOLECULAR REARRANGEMENT

1. Intramolecular rearrangement: If rearrangement occurs within the same molecule, they are said to be intramolecular. In these rearrangements, the migrating group does not get detached completely from the system in which rearrangement is taking place.

Example: Butane + Aluminium trichloride $\xrightarrow{\Delta}$ Isobutane

$$CH_3 - CH_2 - CH_2 - CH_3 + AlCl_3 \longrightarrow CH_3 - \overset{\overset{\displaystyle CH_3}{|}}{CH} - CH_3$$

2. Intermolecular rearrangement: If rearrangement involves the migration of the group between two molecules, they are said to be intermolecular. In these rearrangements the migrating group is first detached and reattached at another site. For example, on treating with dil. HCl, N-chloro acetanilide gets converted into a mixture of o- and p-chloroacetanilide.

         N-Chloro acetanilide   o-Chloro acetanilide   p-Chloro acetanilide

2.3 TYPES OF INTRAMOLECULAR REARRANGEMENTS

1. **Nucleophilic Rearrangement / Rearrangements or Migration to electron deficient atoms:** Here migrating group is nucleophilic and thus migrates to electron deficient centre.

   Example:

2. **Electrophilic Rearrangement / Rearrangements or Migration to electron rich atom:** Here migrating group is electrophilic and thus migrates to electron rich atom.

   Example:

   where B = carbanion (negative ion)

3. **Free Radical Rearrangement:** Here migrating group moves to a free radical centre.

   Example:

2.4 TYPES OF REARRANGEMENTS

[A] Nucleophilic Rearrangements:

(I)   Rearrangement / Migration to electron deficient carbon

    (a) Change in carbon skeleton:

        1. Pinacolone rearrangement

        2. Wagner-Meerwein rearrangement

        3. Benzilic acid rearrangement

        4. Wolff rearrangement

    (b) No change in carbon skeleton:

        1. Sommelet Hauser rearrangement.

(II) Migration to electron deficient nitrogen

    1. Hoffmann rearrangement

    2. Curtius rearrangement

    3. Lossen rearrangement

    4. Schmidt rearrangement

    5. Neber rearrangement

    6. Beckmann rearrangement

(III) Migration to electron deficient oxygen

    1. Baeyer-Villiger oxidation

    2. Dakin reaction

[B] Electrophilic Rearrangements

    1. Stevens rearrangement

    2. Wittig rearrangement

    3. Favorskii rearrangement

[C] Aromatic Rearrangements:

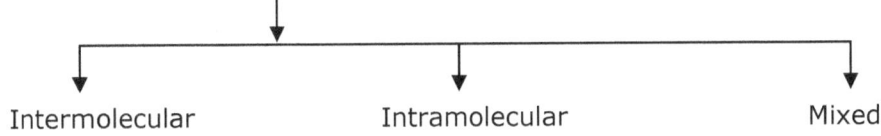

Intermolecular	Intramolecular	Mixed
1. Willgerdot reaction	2. Claisen rearrangement	3. Fries rearrangement
		4. N-Halormide rearrangement

[D] Migration involving double and triple bonds:

    1. Cope rearrangement

2.5 NUCLEOPHILIC REARRANGEMENTS

Here the migrating group (X) which is nucleophilic in nature moves from a carbon atom to an adjacent electron deficient atom (C, N or O). The electron deficiency arises by loss of some electronegative group (: $\bar{Y}$) with its bonded electrons during the reaction. These rearrangements are referred as Whitmore's 1, 2-shift and the migrating nucleophilic species (X) may be carbon, hydrogen, heteroatom: (O^{2-} | N^{3-} | S^{2-} | Cl^- | Br^- | I^-). The migrating group remains partially bonded to the molecule during the migration and forms a cyclic intermediate i.e. bridged or non-classical carbonium ion which in presence of base or solvent, forms the rearranged product.

Nucleophilic rearrangements are further divided into three types. On the basis of the nature of the atom where the migrating group moves.

1. Nucleophilic rearrangement to electron deficient carbon (C).
2. Nucleophilic rearrangement to electron deficient nitrogen (N).
3. Nucleophilic rearrangement to electron deficient oxygen (O).

(I) Nucleophilic rearrangement to electron deficient carbon (Carbonium ion rearrangement):

This rearrangement takes place far more readily than those involving either a free radical or carbanion. In the carbonium ion transition state, there is a new molecular orbital which is formed as a result of combination of an atomic orbital of the migrating group with the atomic orbitals of the other two carbon atoms. This molecular orbital can accommodate only two electrons. On the other hand, free radical and carbanion rearrangements have to pass through cyclic transition states in which 3 or 4 electrons respectively are to be accommodated in molecular orbital embracing three carbon atoms and therefore these should be less stable than the carbonium ion transition states.

Carbonium ion rearrangements are most likely to occur when normal reaction produces an unstable carbonium ion which can be converted to a more stable one ($3° > 2° > 1°$) by 1, 2 shift.

These arrangements can further be divided into two types viz.:

(a) Carbonium ion rearrangement with change in carbon skeleton.

(b) Carbonium ion rearrangement without change in carbon skeleton.

(a) Carbonium ion rearrangement with change in carbon skeleton

1. **Pinacol-Pinacolone rearrangement (Pinacol rearrangement):** "The conversion of pinacols (1, 2-diols/glycols) to their corresponding ketones or aldehydes in the presence of dilute mineral acids is known as pinacol rearrangement".

Example:

1.

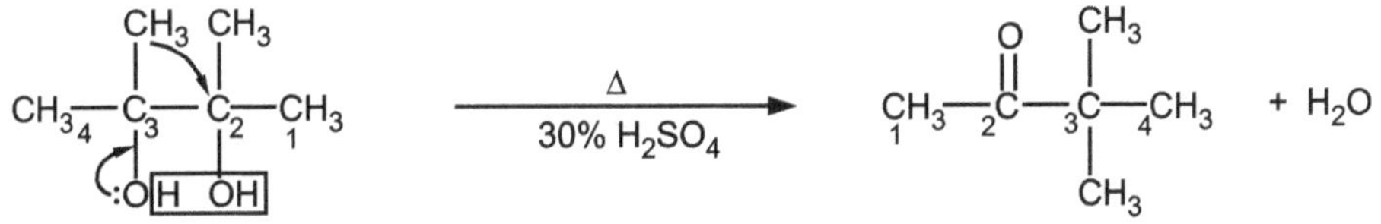

2,3-Dimethyl-2-3-butane diol
(Pinacol)

3,3-Dimethyl-2-butanone
(Methyl-t-butyl ketone)
Pinacolone

2.

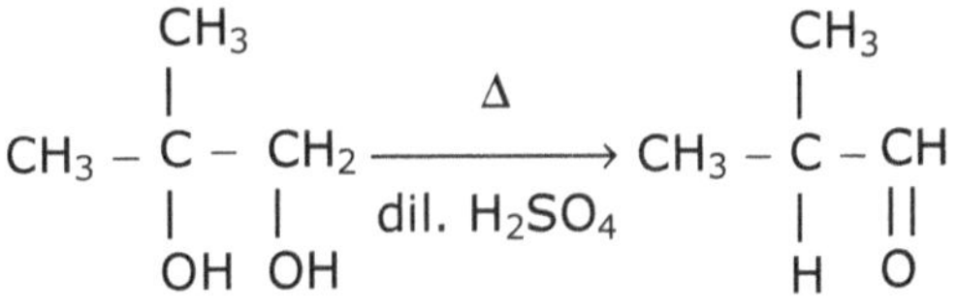

2-methyl propan-1-2-diol   isobutylaldehyde

Mechanism: It involves following four steps:

1. Protonation of an –OH group to form an oxonium ion.

2. Loss of H_2O to form a carbocation.

3. 1, 2-shift of H, R or Ar to form more stable cation/rearranged cation.

4. Loss of $H^\oplus$ to form product.

It is interesting to note that vicinal diols other than 1, 2-diols even pinacols undergo normal dehydration in the presence of Al_2O_3 / aq. HBr to form normal products i.e. olefins.

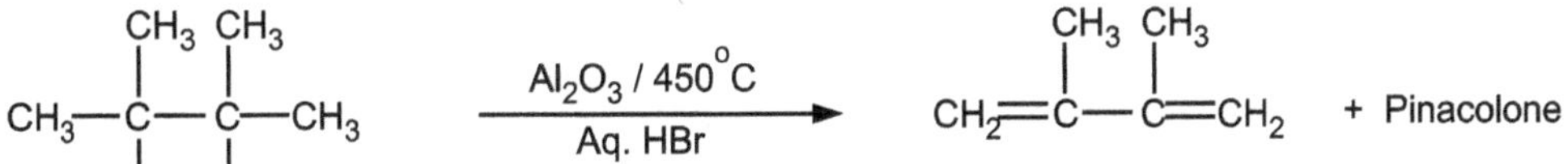

2,3-Dimethyl-1-3-
butadiene (< 75%)

(< 25%)

Mechanism:

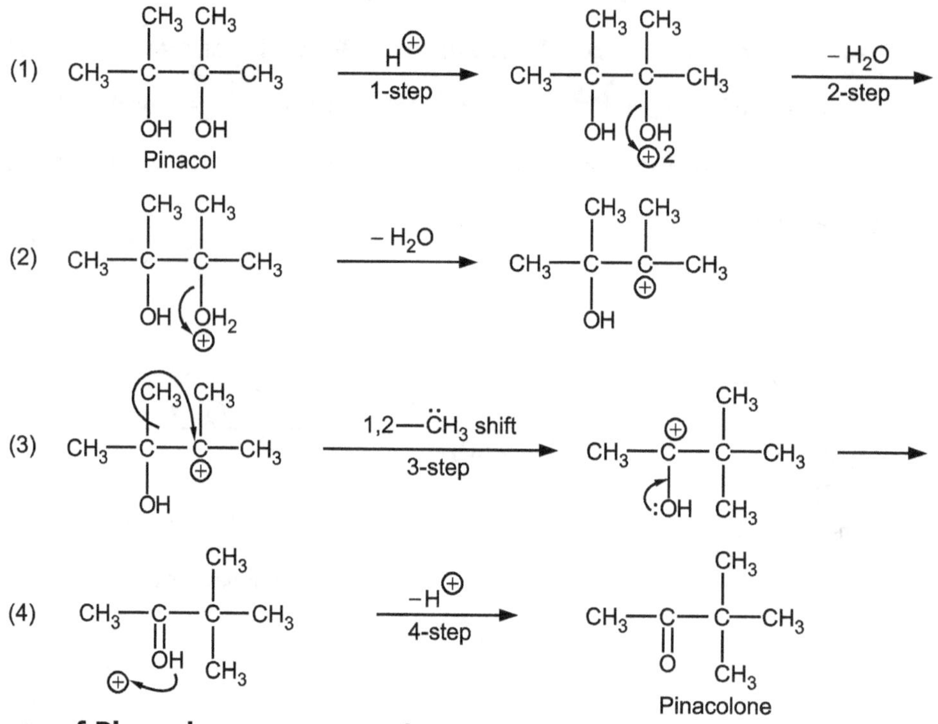

Features of Pinacol rearrangement:

1. Stability of the carbonium ion: When there is a choice as which OH group will be preferentially removed i.e. when two –OH groups are different then that OH group will be removed which produces more stable carbonium ($C^{\oplus}$).

Example:

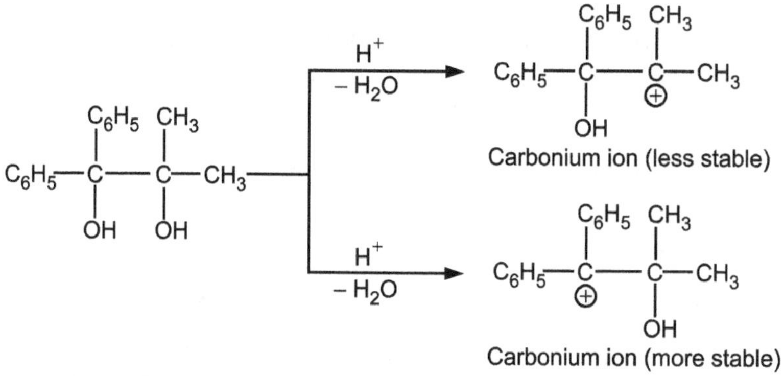

2. Migratory aptitude of group: The migrating group in the pinacols may be alkyl, aryl or H. Hydrogen may migrate in preference to R or Ar. However, H does not always preferentially migrate. Sometimes it is observed that with a given pinacol either H or R can migrate, depending upon experimental conditions. In case when there is a competition between R and Ar groups, generally order of migratory aptitude is Ar > R. But however the actual migrating group depends upon the individual glycol.

Lastly, when the migratory competition is between two aryl groups then the one which is better nucleophile migrates preferentially.

Thus, p-anisyl > p-tolyl > phenyl > p-chlorophenyl > o-anisyl.

Steric effect: The migration of the group is also effected by steric factor viz. o-meo C_6H_4 group migrates thousand times less than p-meo C_6H_4 group.

Example:

Transmigration: The migrating group migrates to the trans (opposite) side of the leaving group.

Example:

Extension and Application: In addition to 1, 2-diols, β-amino alcohols on treatment with nitrous acid form pinacolone. This extension of pinacol rearrangement has a synthetic application.

Example: Synthesis of **cycloheptanone** from amino methyl cyclohexanol which in turn is obtained from **cyclohexanone**.

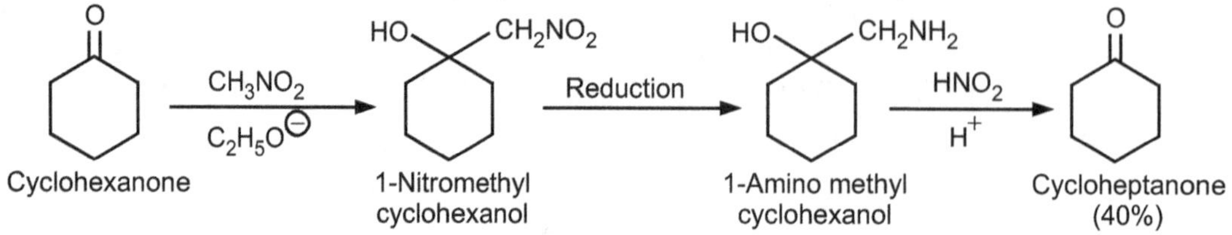

Cyclohexanone →(CH_3NO_2 / $C_2H_5O^{\ominus}$)→ 1-Nitromethyl cyclohexanol →(Reduction)→ 1-Amino methyl cyclohexanol →(HNO_2 / H^+)→ Cycloheptanone (40%)

The yield of cycloheptanone is considerably better than other normal reaction.

3. Wagner-Meerwein Rearrangement (W.M.R.):

"The rearrangement which involves the transformation of lesser stable carbonium ion into a more stable carbonium ion (by 1, 2-shift) is collectively known as Wagner-Meerwein rearrangement".

Example:

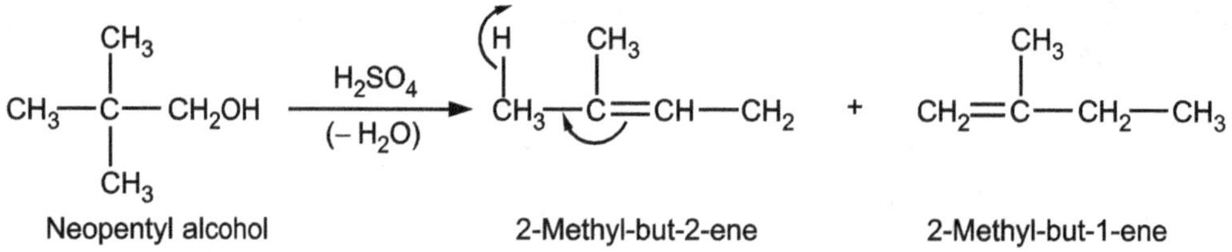

Neopentyl alcohol →(H_2SO_4 / $(-H_2O)$)→ 2-Methyl-but-2-ene + 2-Methyl-but-1-ene

Mechanism:

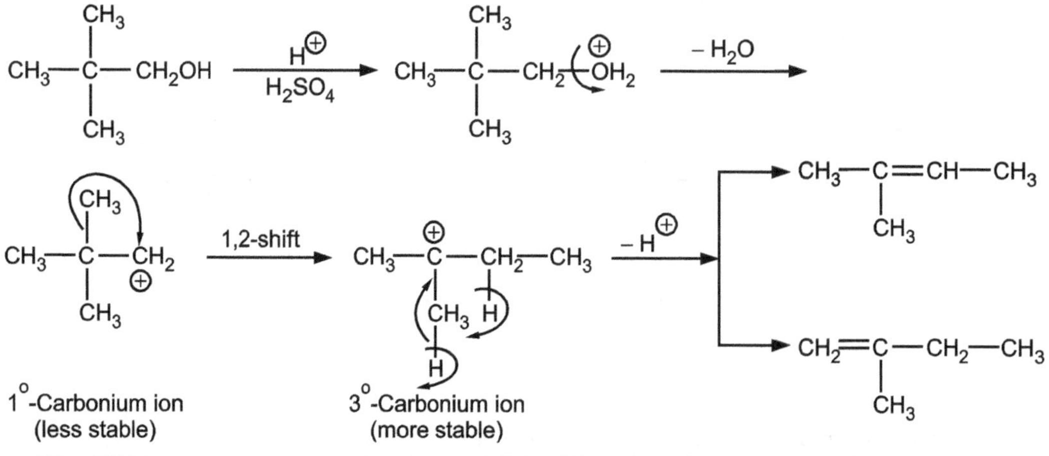

1°-Carbonium ion (less stable) →(1,2-shift)→ 3°-Carbonium ion (more stable) →($-H^{\oplus}$)→

The W.M. rearrangement is also exhibited by alicyclic compounds.

Example: (a) Pinene hydrochloride to Bornyl chloride.

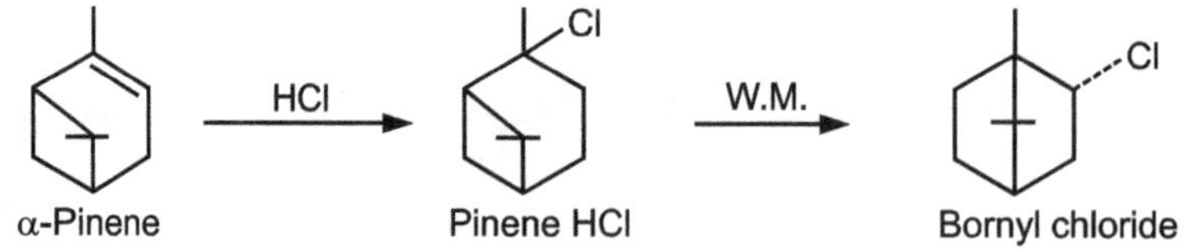

α-Pinene →(HCl)→ Pinene HCl →(W.M.)→ Bornyl chloride

Mechanism:

(a)

| Camphene HCl | Isobornyl chloride | | Camphene |

(b)   (c)

Principle features of W.M. Rearrangement:

1. The carbonium ion in general may be generated in a variety of ways:

   (a) From a halide:
   $$Me_3C - CH_2 - Cl \xrightarrow{Ag^+} Me_3C - \overset{\oplus}{C}H_2 + AgCl$$

   (b) From an alcohol:
   $$Me_3C - CH_2 - OH \underset{}{\overset{H^+}{\rightleftharpoons}} Me_3C - \overset{\oplus}{C}H_2 + H_2O$$

   (c) From an amine:
   $$Me_3C - CH_2 - NH_2 \xrightarrow[(- H_2O)]{HNO_2} Me_3C - CH_2 - N^+ \equiv N \xrightarrow{- N_2} Me_3C - \overset{\oplus}{C}H_2$$

   (d) From an olefin:
   $$Me_3C - CH = CH_2 \xrightarrow{\overset{\oplus}{H}} Me_3C - \overset{\oplus}{C}H - CH_3$$

2. Migrating aptitude: Migrating group may be H, R or Ar. Aryl groups have far greater migratory aptitude than alkyl group.

   Ar > R.

3. The rearrangement is stereospecific in the fact that the migrating group attaches to electron deficient carbon atom and thus inversion of configuration occurs at electron deficient carbon.

4. In some cases, two or more rearrangements may occur successively.

   e.g. The initial carbocation obtained by treating diethyl cyclobutylcarbinol with acid rearrangement by ring expansion to a secondary carbocation which in turn undergoes a further rearrangement to yield a 3° carbocation. The latter then undergoes deprotonation and forms the olefin.

| | Secondary carbocation | Tertiary carbocation | 1,2-Diethyl cyclopentene |

2.6 BENZILIC ACID REARRANGEMENT

"The transformation of α-diketones to α-hydroxy acids by means of hydroxide ions (NaOH/KOH: Pfeif in 1956 observed Barium and Thallium hydroxides are more effective than KOH (NaOH)) is known as benzilic acid rearrangement".

Example: Conversion of benzil into benzilic anion (benzilic acid).

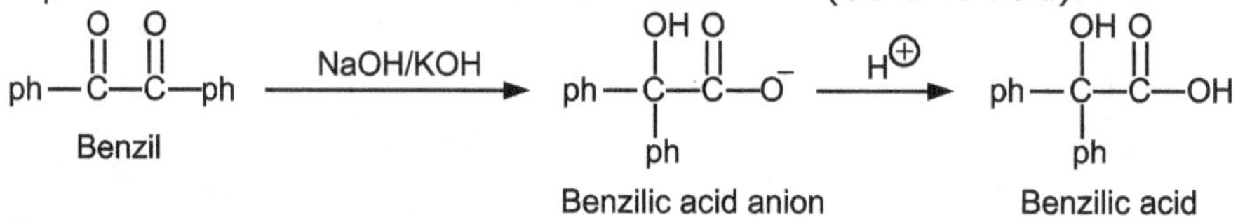

Benzil → Benzilic acid anion → Benzilic acid

Mechanism:

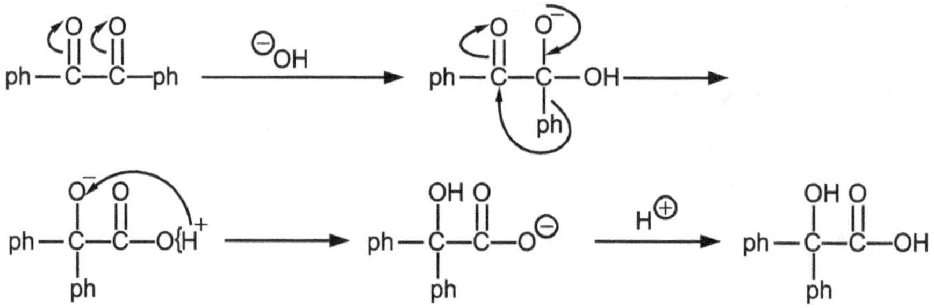

In the benzilic acid rearrangement, when there is competition between the two possible aryl groups, the less electron releasing group will preferentially migrate because the more electron releasing group will tend to neutralize the +ve charge on the carbonyl carbon atom to which it is attached by supplying the electrons and thus the hydroxide ion will attack carbon atom of the other carbonyl group. Since the phenol group is involved, it is possible that during this 1, 2-shift of a phenoxium ion is formed as an intermediate.

Extension and Applications of Benzilic Acid Rearrangement:

Extension:

Doering et. al. (1956) extended the reaction to the formation of corresponding ester by replacing the normal **alkali** by **alkoxides**.

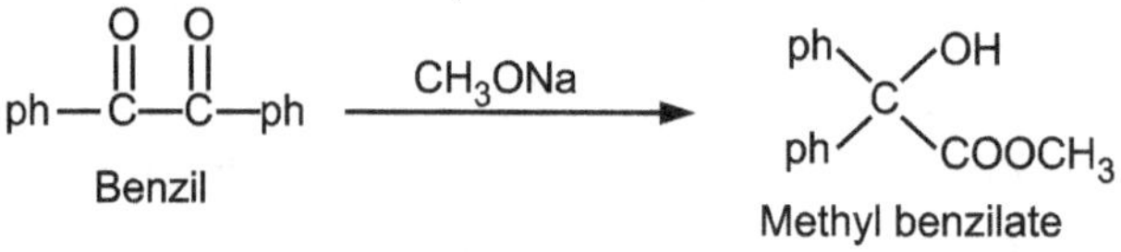

Benzil → Methyl benzilate

Applications:

(a) The reaction may be used for the preparation of α-hydroxy acids from the easily accessible starting material.

Example:

1. Benzil ⟶ Benzilic acid

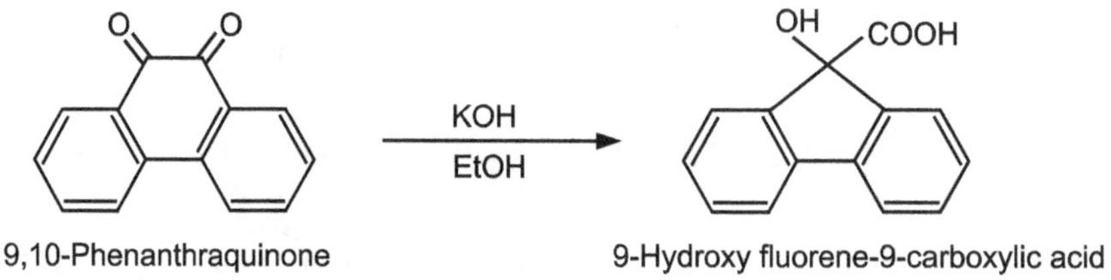

9,10-Phenanthraquinone → 9-Hydroxy fluorene-9-carboxylic acid

(b) Although the reaction is mainly applicable to aromatic ketone, but aliphatic ketone (ketopinic acid) undergoes the rearrangement to form citric acid.

$$\underset{\text{Ketopinic acid}}{HOOC - CH_2 - \overset{\overset{O}{||}}{C} - \overset{\overset{O}{||}}{C} - CH_2\,COOH} \xrightarrow[\text{(ii) } H^+]{\text{(i) KOH}} \underset{\text{Citric acid}}{HOOC \cdot CH_2 - \overset{\overset{OH}{|}}{\underset{\underset{COOH}{|}}{C}} - CH_2COOH}$$

2.7 WOLFF REARRANGEMENT

1. When an acid chloride is allowed to react with a diazo compound to form corresponding "diazoketone which by 1, 2 shift to form corresponding ketene". This reaction is called as Wolff rearrangement.

Note: The ketene obtained is of higher carbon number present in the product.

$$\underset{\text{Acid chloride}}{R - \overset{\overset{O}{||}}{C} - Cl} \xrightarrow[\text{Diazomethane}]{CH_2 - N_2} R - \overset{\overset{O}{||}}{C} - CH\,N_2 \xrightarrow{h\nu/\Delta} \underset{\text{Ketene}}{R - CH = C = O}$$

Mechanism:

Stereochemistry:

Much experimentation indicates that only one of the two possible stereoisomers of the diazoketone can give ketene directly. The two stereoisomers of diazoketones are syn and anti i.e.

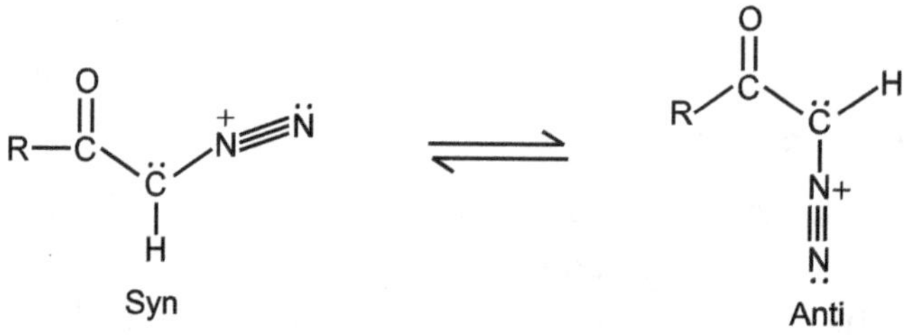

Syn   Anti

Among these two isomers of diazoketone, only the syn isomer can rearrange easily to a ketene. The syn isomer is set up for migration of R with displacement from the rear in what is really an intramolecular SN^2 reaction. By contrast, the anti-isomer would have to do a front side SN^2 for R to migrate as the nitrogen leaves.

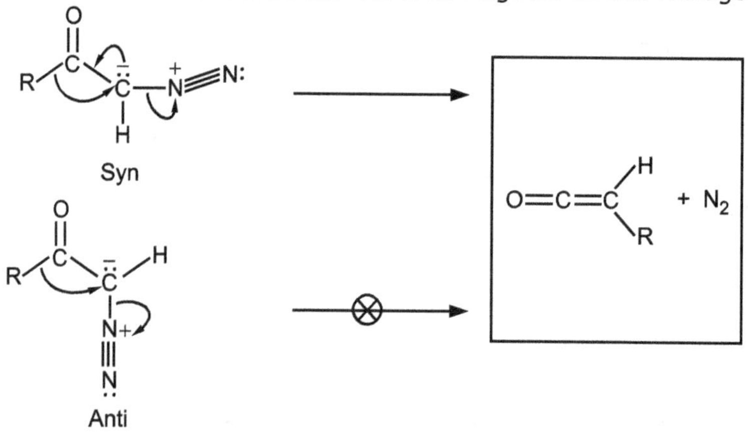

Syn

Anti

$$O=C=C \Big\langle {}^{H}_{R} \ + \ N_2$$

2. **Wolff rearrangement:** When acyl halide is converted to diazo ketone on reacting with diazo compound, when this diazo ketone is treated with water and silver oxide or silver benzoate and trimethylamine, it gives rise to **carboxylic acid** with increased number of carbon chain by one. Such rearrangement is called as Wolff rearrangement.

Example:

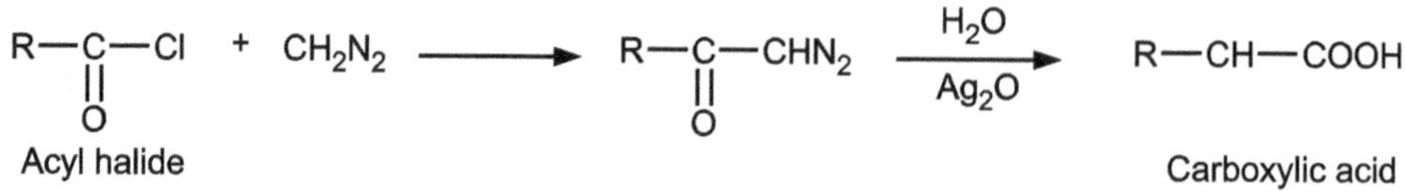

Acyl halide   Carboxylic acid

3. The rearrangement of acyl carbenes to ketenes is also called as Wolff rearrangement.

    Example:

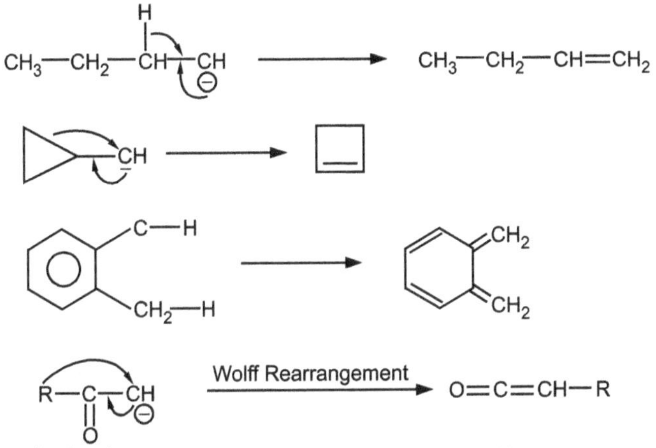

$$CH_3-CH_2-\overset{\overset{H}{|}}{CH}-\overset{\ominus}{CH} \longrightarrow CH_3-CH_2-CH=CH_2$$

$$R-\overset{\overset{\parallel}{O}}{C}-\overset{\ominus}{CH} \xrightarrow{\text{Wolff Rearrangement}} O=C=CH-R$$

Acyl carbene   Ketene

(B) Carbonium ion rearrangement without change in carbon skeleton
Sommelet – Hauser Rearrangement:

Benzylic quaternary $\xrightarrow[\text{NaNH}_2/\text{Low temp.}]{\text{S – H Rearr}}$ Benzylic tertiary amine
ammonium salt

This involves the reaction of benzyl quaternary ammonium salts with alkali-metal amides to form a substituted benzyl 3° - amine.

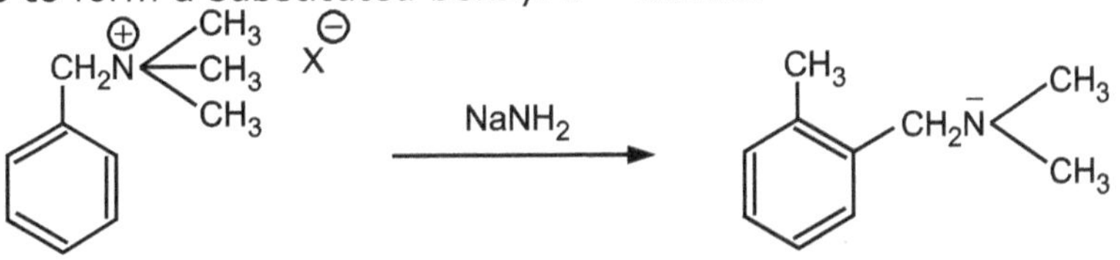

Mechanism: $Na_2NH_2 \rightarrow \overset{+}{Na} + \overset{\ominus}{NH_2}$

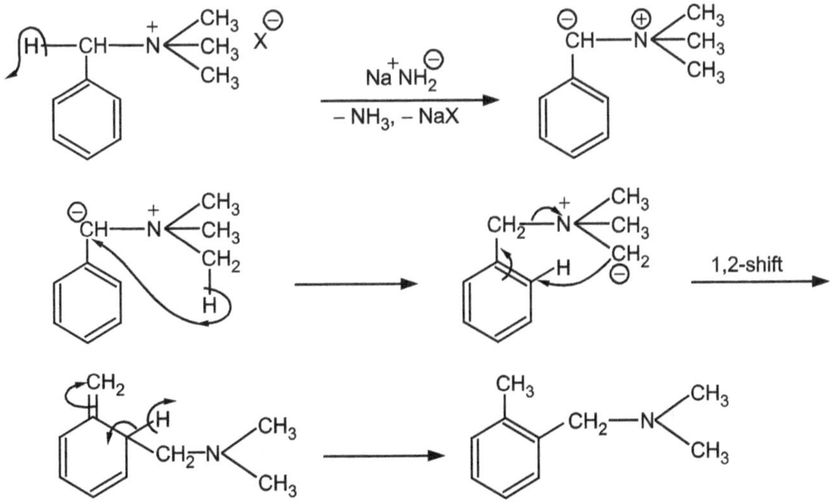

In this protons are first removed from the more acidic benzyl position and subsequently from a methyl group.

The rearrangement occurs only when none of the alkyl groups of the quaternary ammonium salt has β-hydrogen. Remember that quaternary ammonium ions having β-hydrogen atoms undergo E_2 reaction (Hoffman's elimination) with base. Moreover, if none of the alkyl groups has a β-hydrogen but one has a β-carbonyl group the compound undergoes Stevens rearrangement.

Nucleophilic Rearrangement at Electron deficient N-atom

Hoffmann rearrangement or Hoffmann degradation of Amides:

The conversion of an amide to an amine with one carbon atom less by the action of alkaline hypohalite or bromide in alkali is known as the Hoffmann reaction".

$$R - \overset{\overset{O}{\|}}{C} - NH_2 + Br_2 + 4\ KOH \longrightarrow R - NH_2 + 2\ KBr + K_2CO_3 + 2H_2O$$

Mechanism:

$$Br_2 \longrightarrow Br^{\oplus} + Br^{\ominus}\ ,\ KOH \longrightarrow K^+ + OH^{\ominus}$$

$$R - \overset{\overset{O}{\|}}{C} - NH_2 \xrightarrow[- HBr]{Br_2} R - \overset{\overset{O}{\|}}{C} - \overset{..}{N}HBr \xrightarrow[- H_2O]{OH^{\ominus}} R - \overset{\overset{O}{\|}}{C} - \overset{..}{\underset{..}{N}} - Br \xrightarrow{- Br^{\ominus}}$$

N-bromamide   Anion of N-bromamide

$$R - \overset{\overset{O}{\|}}{C} - \overset{..}{\underset{\oplus}{N}}: \longrightarrow R - N = C = O \xrightarrow[H^+/OH^-]{H_2O} R - NH - \overset{\overset{O}{\|}}{C} - OH \xrightarrow[- CO_2]{\Delta} R - NH_2$$

Isocyanate   Carbamic acid

Features:

It has been observed and established that Hoffmann reactions are accelerated if the migratory group 'R' has an increased electron releasing capacity. A strongly electron donating migrating group not only eases the departure of Br from the bromamide anion but also enables to satisfy the electron deficiency of the residual nitrogen atom more effectively. Thus, the rate of amine formation from p-hydroxy benzamide is more rapid than that for benzamide itself due to the activating effect of the phenolic –OH group.

CONH$_2$ $\xrightarrow{Br_2/KOH}$ NH$_2$ / Br / OH

In general, the p-substituted benzamides show the following order of reactivity.

  $- OCH_3 > - CH_3 > - H > - Cl > - NO_2$

It undergoes with complete retension of configuration about the chiral centre of migrating group and no cross products are formed.

Applications:

1. Preparation of primary aliphatic and aromatic amines:

$$R - CONH_2 \xrightarrow{\text{Br}_2/\text{KOH}} RNH_2$$

$$CH_3CONH_2 \xrightarrow{\text{Br}_2/\text{KOH}} CH_3NH_2$$

2. Preparation of β-aminopyridine:

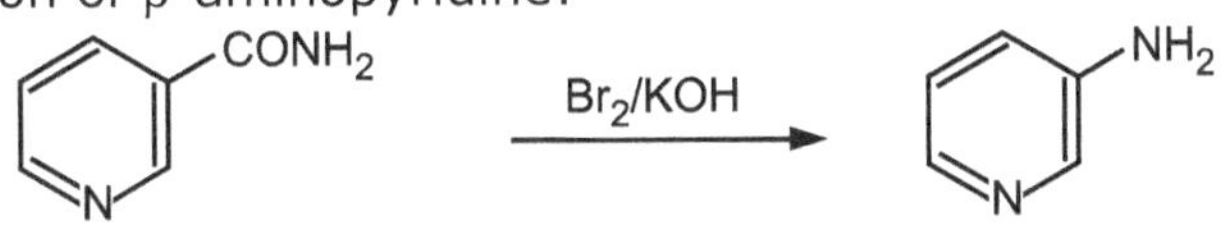

(65-79%)

3. Preparation of amino acids:

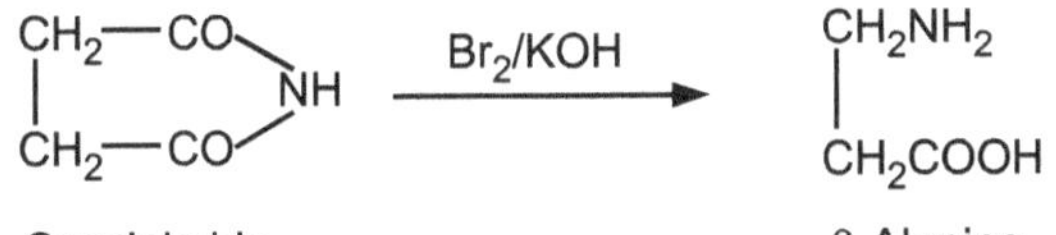

Succinimide   β-Alanine

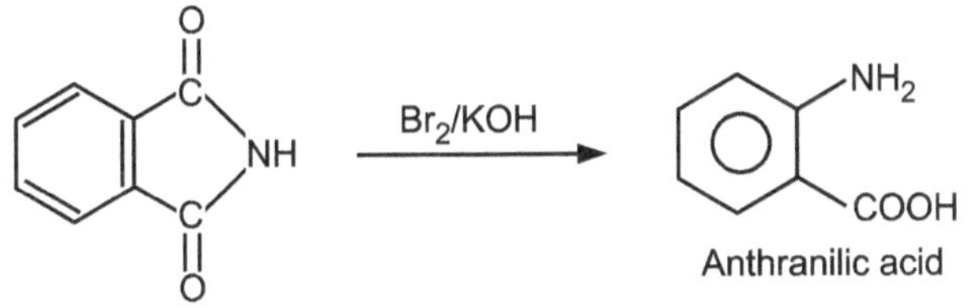

Anthranilic acid

4. Preparation of aldehyde:

$$R - CH = CH - CONH_2 \xrightarrow{\text{Cl}_2/\text{NaOH}} R - CH = CH \, NH \, COCH_3 \xrightarrow{\text{HCl}} RCHO$$

In short, the sequence leading to the production of primary amine from carboxylic acid would be:

carboxylic   acyl   acyl azide   isocyanate
acid   chloride

$$\xrightarrow{\text{H}_2\text{O}/\text{H}^+} R - NH_2$$

1° amine

(C) Curtius Rearrangement:

"The thermal/photochemical conversion of acyl azides to corresponding isocyanate on heating or irradiating is called Curtius Rearrangement".

Acyl chloride   Acidic or   Isocyanate
                Alkaline medium
                or heating   Acyl azide

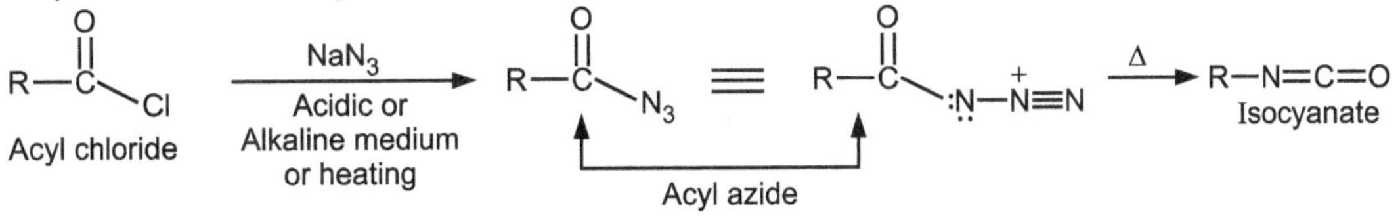

Mechanism:

It is quite similar to Hoffmann's reaction.

$$R-C(=O)-N^+-N\equiv N: \xrightarrow[\text{Photochemical decomposition}]{\text{Thermal or}} R-N=C=O + N_2$$

Applications:

1. This reaction is useful in the preparation of primary amines which are prepared in mild condition but it is required in the preparation of azides.
2. Preparation of α-amino acids. e.g. Glycine.
3. Preparation of urethane: R – NH – COOR.
4. Preparation of aldehydes. e.g. phenylacetaldehyde ($C_6H_5CH_2CHO$)

2.8 LOSSEN REARRANGEMENT

"The conversion of hydroxamic acids or its esters in the presence of base into primary amines is known as Lossen reaction".

$$R-C(=O)-N(H)-OH \xrightarrow{OH^{\ominus}} R-NH_2 + CO_2$$

Mechanism:

$$R-C(=O)-N-OH \xrightarrow[-H^{\oplus}, OH^- = H_2O]{OH^{\ominus}} R-C(=O)-N-OH \xrightarrow[\oplus H_2O/H^+]{-OH^{\ominus}} R-N=C=O \quad \text{Isocyanate}$$

OR

$$\text{or } R-C(=O)-N-O-C(=O)-OR' \xrightarrow[-H^{\oplus}]{OH^{\ominus}} R-C(=O)-N-O-C(=O)-OR' \xrightarrow[+OH^-]{-COOR^{\ominus}} RN=C=O \quad \text{Isocyanate}$$

$$R-N=C=O \xrightarrow{H^+/OH^{\ominus}} R-N(H)-C(=O)-OH \xrightarrow[\Delta]{-CO_2} R-NH_2 + CO_2$$

Carbamic acid

The mechanism of Lossen rearrangement is closely related to that of Hoffmann rearrangement, except that in the former the leaving group is a **carboxylate anion** while in the latter it is the **bromide anion**.

Since the esters give higher yields than the hydroxamic acid itself, generally o-acetyl or o-benzyl hydroxamic acid are used as the starting materials. In case hydroxamic acid itself is used, the leaving group is hydroxide ion which will be removed as H_2O in the presence of a strong inorganic acid.

Application: Since the hydroxamic acid is difficult to obtain, the reaction is of limited importance.

2.9 SCHMIDT REACTION

"Carboxylic acids react with hydrazoic acid in the presence of conc. H_2SO_4 to give amines directly. This is known as Schmidt reaction.

1. $$R - \overset{\overset{\displaystyle O}{\|}}{C} - \boxed{OH + H}N_3 \xrightarrow{\text{conc. } H_2SO_4} R - NH_2 + CO_2 + N_2 \uparrow$$

"The reaction also takes place between aldehydes or ketones and hydrazoic acid to form mixture of cyanides and formyl derivatives of primary amines and amides respectively.

2. $$R - \overset{\overset{\displaystyle O}{\|}}{C} - H + HN_3 \xrightarrow[\text{Hydrazoic acid}]{\text{conc. } H_2SO_4} R - CN + R - NH - CHO$$

3. $$R - \overset{\overset{\displaystyle O}{\|}}{C} - R + HN_3 \xrightarrow{\text{conc. } H_2SO_4} R - \overset{\overset{\displaystyle O}{\|}}{C}NHR + N_2 \uparrow$$
   $$\text{amide}$$

Mechanism:

The reaction mechanism with acids is similar to that of Hoffmann and Curtius reactions. While with aldehydes and ketones, it resembles the Beckmann rearrangement.

Reaction with acid:

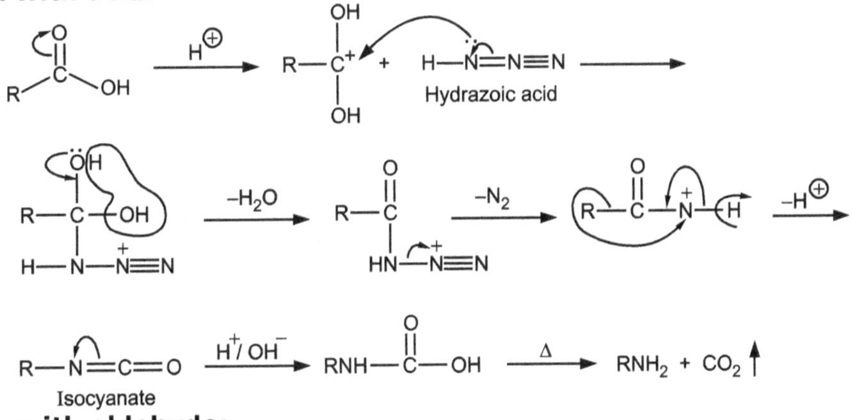

Reaction with aldehyde:

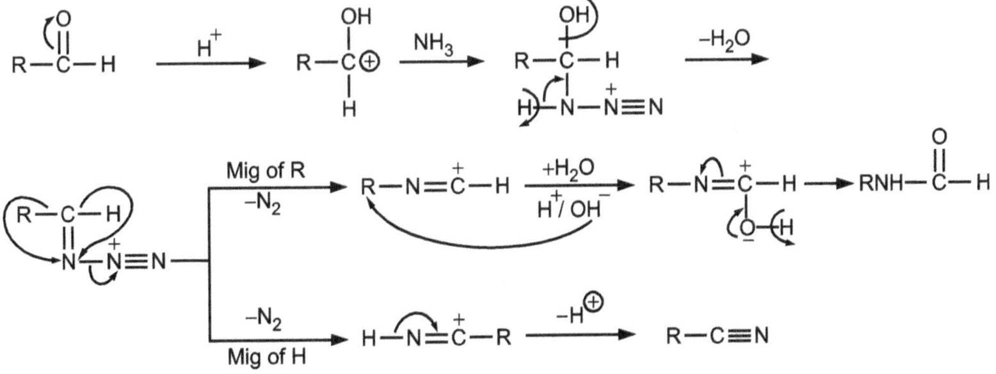

Reaction with aldehyde:

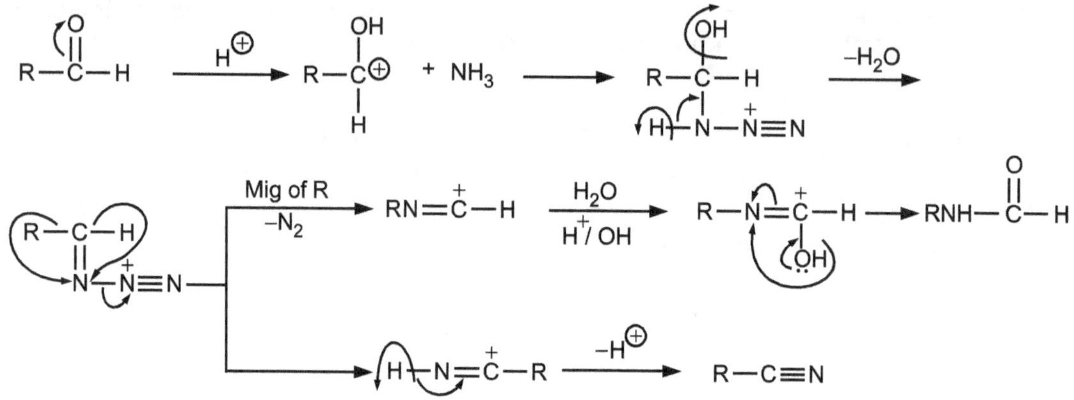

Reaction with ketone:

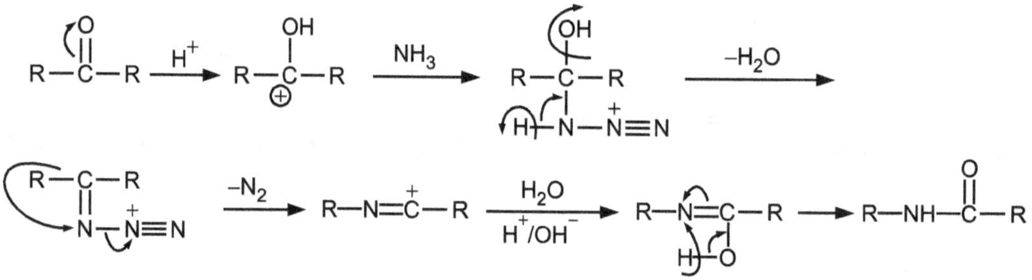

Applications:

1. Preparation of primary amines: It is direct method for preparation of 1°-amine from carboxylic acid and give better yield than Hoffmann Curtius reaction but it is somewhat dangerous because H_3N somewhat explosive so applied with caution. It is important to note that this reaction is applicable only when the carboxylic acid used does not contain any group sensitive to conc. H_2SO_4.
2. Preparation of α-amino acids from acetoacetic ester.

2.10 NEBER REARRANGEMENT

"Treatment of ketoxime tosylates with a base such as ethoxide ion, pyridine etc. to form α-amino ketones is known as Neber Rearrangement".

p-Toluene sulphonates = Tosylates

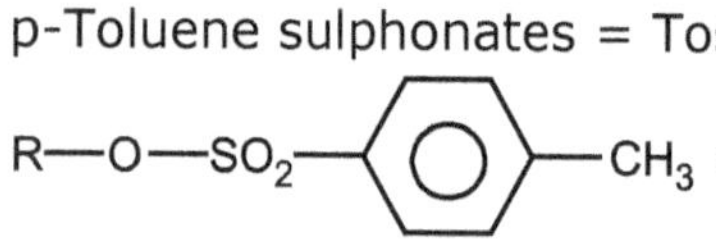 = structure of Tosylate = OTs

where, R = alkyl or hydrogen

R' = alkyl or aryl group

1.

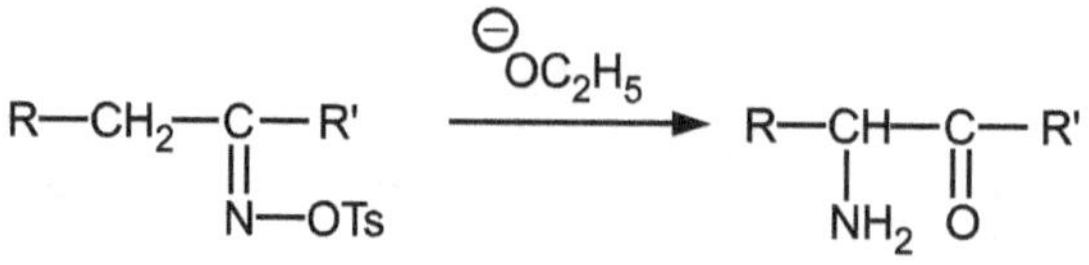

Mechanism:

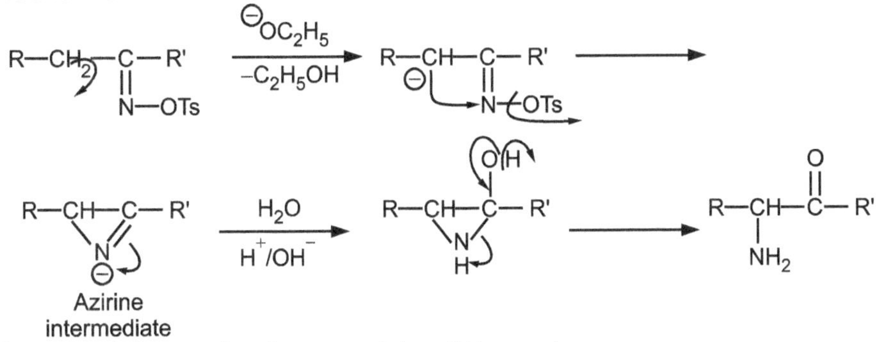

Azirine
intermediate

The complete mechanism consists of three steps:

(i)   The loss of proton to form carbanion.

(ii) The rearrangement of carbanion to form azirine intermediate.

(iii) Hydrolysis of azirine to form α-amino ketone as the final product.

Neber rearrangement can also be applied to N, N-dichloroamines:

2. 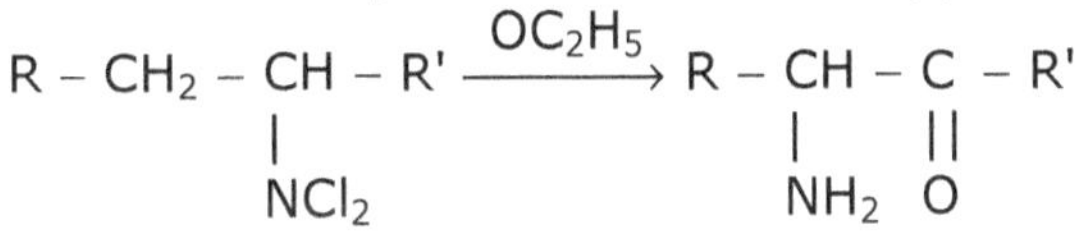 $R - CH_2 - CH - R' \xrightarrow{OC_2H_5} R - CH - C - R'$
               | | ||
               NCl_2 NH_2 O

2.11 BECKMANN REARRANGEMENT

The Beckmann rearrangement consists of the conversion of ketoximes to N-substituted amides by heating with acidic reagents viz. conc. H_2SO_4, H_3PO_4, HCOOH, BF_3, P_2O_5, PCl_5, SO_2, $SOCl_2$, $C_6H_5SO_2Cl$, silica gel etc.

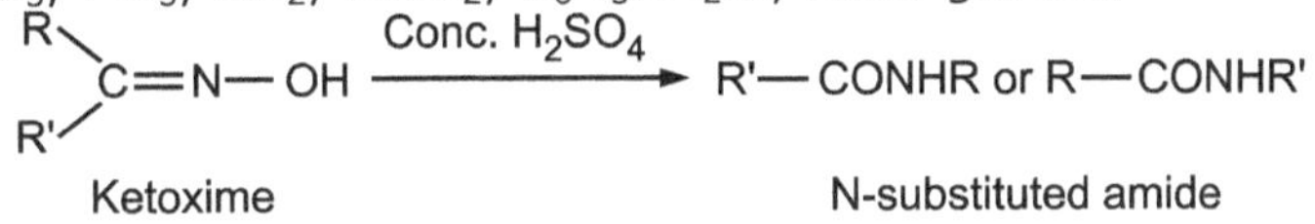

Ketoxime   N-substituted amide

Mechanism:

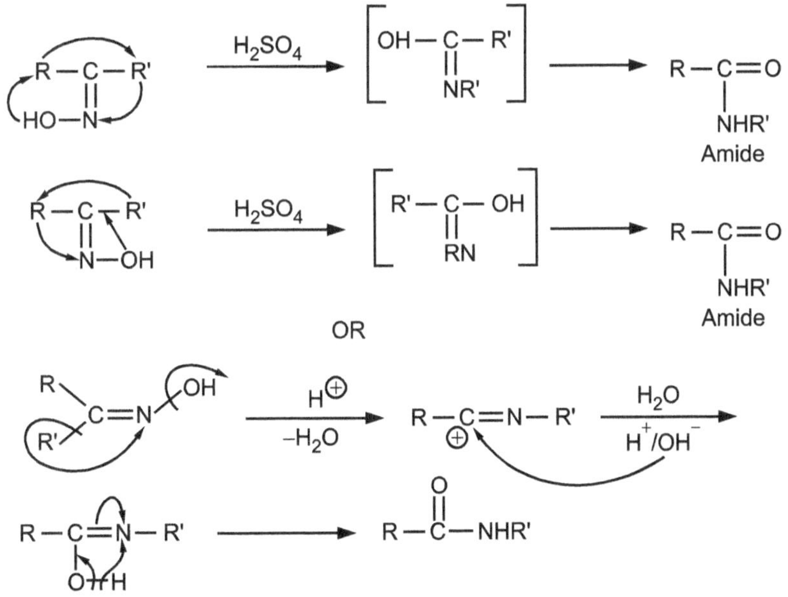

Applications:

(i) Determination of configuration of ketoximes: It is based on the fact that the two isomeric ketoximes viz. syn and anti give different amides via Beckmann rearrangement. The amide in turn can be identified by their hydrolysis product.

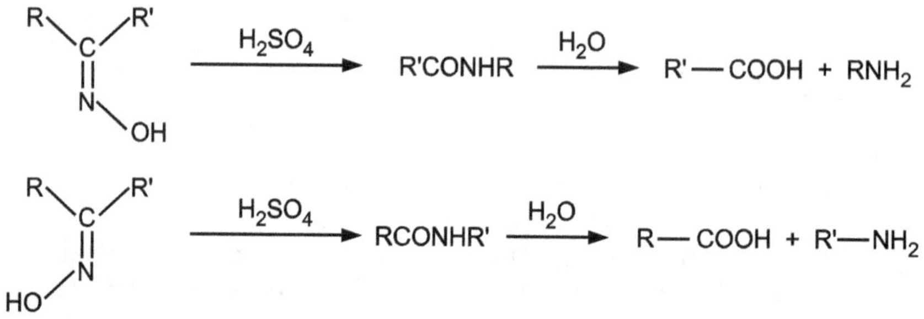

$$R'CONHR \xrightarrow{H_2O} R'—COOH + RNH_2$$

$$RCONHR' \xrightarrow{H_2O} R—COOH + R'—NH_2$$

(ii) Synthesis of isoquinoline:

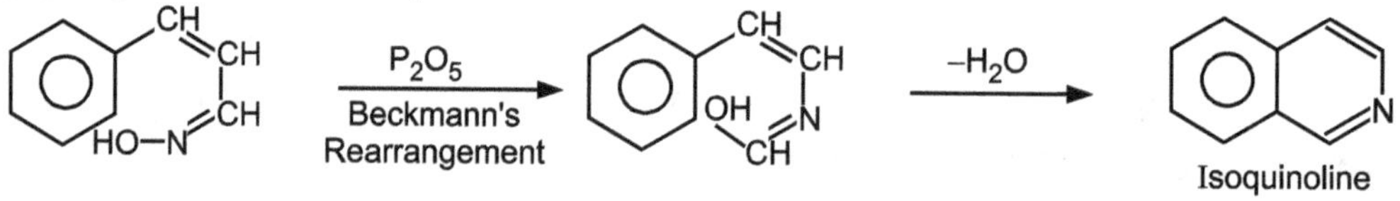

Isoquinoline

(iii) Synthesis of ∈-caprolactum:

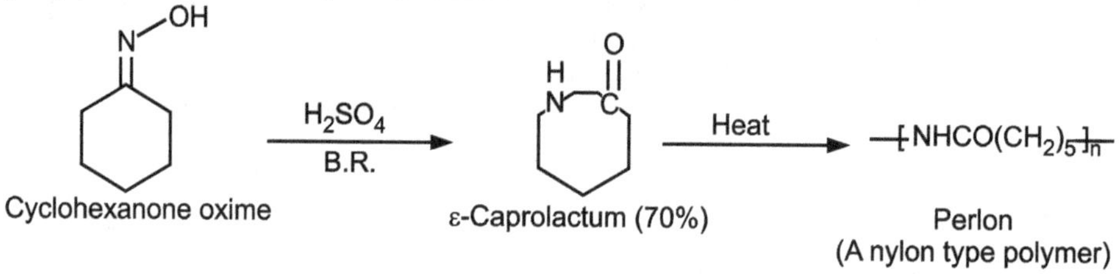

Cyclohexanone oxime   ε-Caprolactum (70%)   Perlon (A nylon type polymer)

Nucleophilic Migration to Electron deficient oxygen:

1. Baeyer - Villiger Oxidation:

"The reaction in which oxidation of ketones into an ester by means of peracids is called Baeyer - Villiger oxidation. Cyclic ketones give lactones.

Ketone + Alkyl per acid ⟶ Ester   +   Carboxylic acid

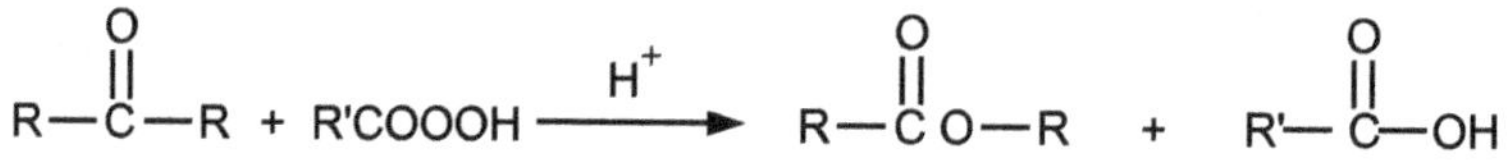

$$R—\overset{O}{\overset{\|}{C}}—R + R'COOOH \xrightarrow{H^+} R—\overset{O}{\overset{\|}{C}}O—R + R'—\overset{O}{\overset{\|}{C}}—OH$$

Cyclic ketone + Alkyl per acid ⟶ Lactone

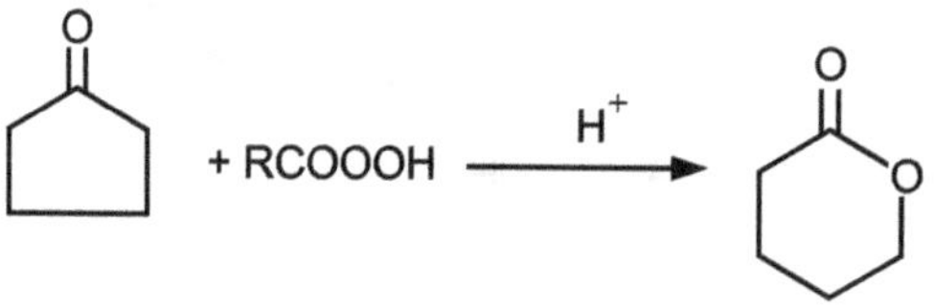

Mechanism:

A number of peracids viz. trifluoroperacetic, peracetic, perbenzoic, etc. have been successfully used in the reaction. But trifluoroperacetic acid is the most reactive among all the above mentioned peracids.

The general mechanism is supported by the fact that the reaction is catalysed by acid and is accelerated by electron releasing groups in the ketone and by electron withdrawing groups in the peracid. Further that the oxygen atom of the carbonyl group of the ketone is the same one as in the carbonyl group of ester.

During the mechanism we see that an alkyl group migrates from carbon to oxygen. The order of this migratory aptitude in the alkyl series is $3° > 2° > 1°$.

Example:

$$Me_3C - \overset{\overset{\displaystyle O}{\|}}{C} - CH_3 \xrightarrow{\text{R-CO}_3\text{H}} CH_3 - \overset{\overset{\displaystyle O}{\|}}{C} - O - CMe_3$$

  pinacolone   t-butyl acetone

Among the aryl series the order is p-anisyl > p-tolyl > phenyl > p-chlorophenyl > p-nitrophenyl > p-aminophenyl etc. When aryl and alkyl both groups are present the migratory aptitude of various groups is

$3°$ alkyl > $2°$ alkyl, aryl, benzyl > $1°$ alkyl > methyl

$$\therefore \quad C_6H_5 - \overset{\overset{\displaystyle O}{\|}}{C} - CH_3 \xrightarrow[\text{(Peracids)}]{\text{RCOOOH}} CH_3 - \overset{\overset{\displaystyle O}{\|}}{C} - O - C_6H_5$$

   Acetophenone   Phenyl acetate

It must be remembered in mind that the reaction is intramolecular and thus the migrating group retains its configuration.

Applications:

1. The reaction is frequently used for the synthesis of the following types of compounds.

    (a) Esters and acids:

$$R - \overset{\overset{\displaystyle O}{||}}{C} - R' \xrightarrow{\text{RCOOOH}} R - O - COR' \xrightarrow{\text{HOH}} R'COOH + ROH$$

    (b) Anhydride:

$$CH_3 - \overset{\overset{\displaystyle O}{||}}{C} - \overset{\overset{\displaystyle O}{||}}{C} - CH_3 \xrightarrow{\text{RCO}_3\text{H}} CH_3 - \overset{\overset{\displaystyle O}{||}}{C} - O - \overset{\overset{\displaystyle O}{||}}{C} - CH_3$$

    (c) Lactones:

Cyclohexanone   ε-Caprolactone

2. This reaction is also useful in the degradation of organic molecules for proof of structure.

2.12 DAKIN REACTION

"This reaction involves replacement of the aldehyde (or ketonic) group of the o-hydroxy, p-hydroxy or o-amino benzaldehyde (or ketone) by a hydroxyl group of the action of alkaline H_2O_2".

Example:

o-Hydroxy benzaldehyde   Catechol

Mechanism: $NaOH \rightarrow Na^+ + OH^{\ominus}$

                $H_2O_2 \rightarrow H^+ + {}^{\ominus}OOH$

Applications:

1. The Dakin's reaction is especially useful in the preparation of polyhydric phenols from naturally occurring hydroxy aldehydes.

Example:

o-Vanillin   Pyrogallol-1-monomethyl ether

2. Dakin's reaction is used industrially to convert

$$Toluene \xrightarrow[H_2O_2]{Alkaline} Phenol$$

$$Aromatic\ Aldehyde \xrightarrow[H_2O_2]{Alkaline} Phenol$$

$$Aromatic\ Ketone \xrightarrow[H_2O_2]{Alkaline} Phenol$$

But there must be an OH^- or NH_2 group in ortho or para position. This is called as **Dakin's Reaction**.

2.13 ELECTROPHILIC REARRANGEMENTS: STEVEN REARRANGEMENT

Steven rearrangement involves the rearrangement of keto-quaternary ammonium or sulphonium salts to amino ketones under the influence of a strong base such as NaOR or $NaNH_2$.

α-Dimethylamino-α-Benzyl acetophenone

Benzyl methyl phenyl sulphonium ion   α-Methyl mercapto-α-Benzyl acetophenone

Mechanism:

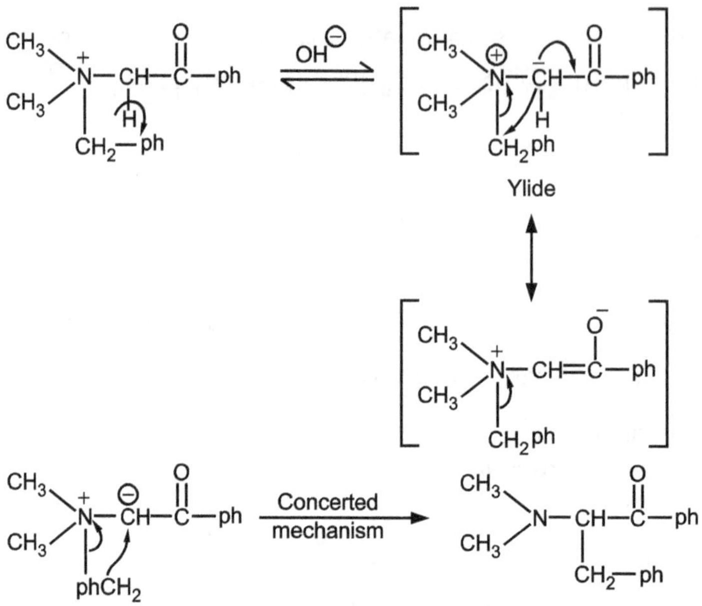

The concerted mechanism rearranges ylide to amino ketone by radical-pair mechanism or ion-pair mechanism in a solvent cage.

2.14 WITTIG REARRANGEMENT

"Wittig reaction involves the preparation of alkenes or olefin by the interaction of aldehydes/ketones (aliphatic/aromatic) with triphenyl phosphine alkylidenes".

Example:

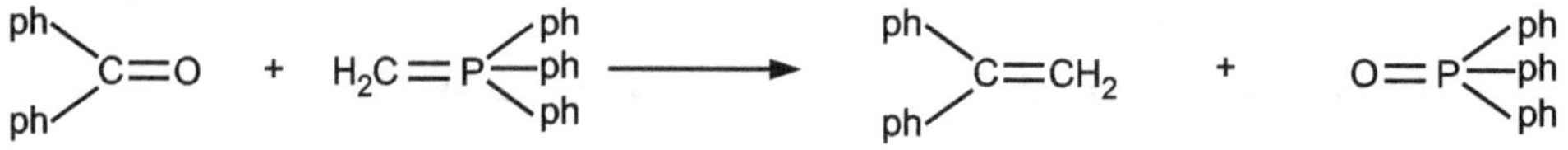

| Benzophenone | Methylene triphenyl phosphorous (phosphines) (Ylide) | 1,1-Diphenyl ethylene | Triphenyl phosphine oxide |

Mechanism:

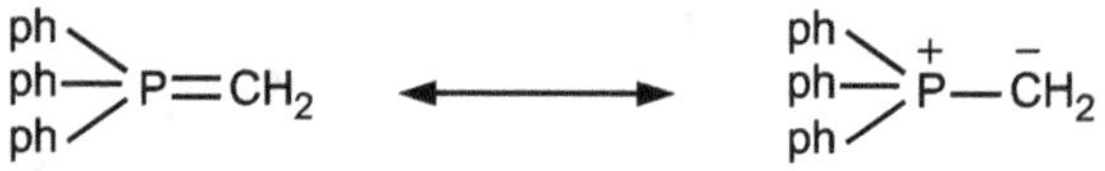

Methylene form

Ylide form

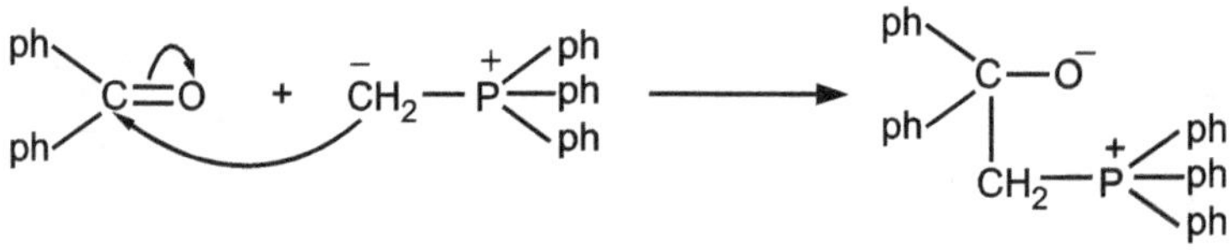

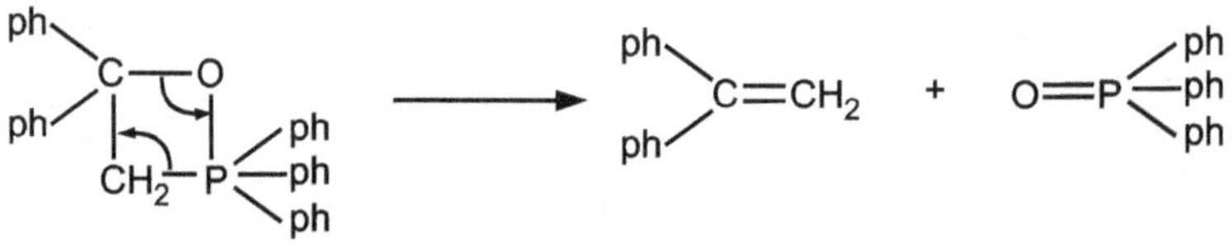

Betaine

Triphenyl phosphine

The triphenyl phosphine alkylidene, which is a resonance hybrid of methylene and an ylide structure attacks on the carbonyl compound and forms a new C-C bond between electronegative atom of the phosphorane and the electronegative carbon atom of the carbonyl group. The dipolar transition state (betaine) then collapses by intramolecular attack of the negatively charged oxygen on the positively charged phosphorous atom via a four centre transition state to form corresponding olefins.

Applications of Wittig Reaction:

1. **Preparation of Olefins:**

(a)

$$\underset{\text{Acetophenone}}{\underset{CH_3}{\overset{ph}{>}}C=O} \quad \xrightarrow{CH_2=P(ph)_3} \quad \underset{\alpha\text{-Methyl styrene}}{\underset{CH_3}{\overset{ph}{>}}C=CH_2}$$

(b)

$$\underset{\text{Benzaldehyde}}{\underset{H}{\overset{ph}{>}}C=O} \quad \xrightarrow{CH_2=P(ph)_3} \quad \underset{\text{Styrene}}{ph-CH=CH_3}$$

(c)

$$\underset{\text{Cyclohexanone}}{\bigcirc=O} \quad \xrightarrow{CH_2=P.(ph)_3} \quad \underset{\text{Methylene cyclohexane}}{\bigcirc=CH_2}$$

(d)

$$\underset{\text{Benzaldehyde}}{\underset{H}{\overset{ph}{>}}C=O} \quad \xrightarrow{COOC_2H_5-CH=P(ph)_3} \quad \underset{\text{Ethyl cinnamate}}{ph-CH=CH\cdot COOC_2H_5}$$

(e)

$$\underset{H}{\overset{ph}{\underset{|}{CH=CH-C=O}}} \quad \xrightarrow{(ph)_3P=CH_2} \quad \underset{\text{1-Phenyl butadiene}}{ph\,CH=CH-CH=CH_2}$$

(f) PhCHO

$$\xrightarrow[\text{Vinyl methylene ylide}]{(ph)_3P=CH-CH=CH_2} \quad \underset{\text{1-Phenyl butadiene}}{ph-CH=CH-CH=CH_2}$$

2. **Preparation of carbodi-imides:** Carbodi-imide is the important reagent used during the synthesis of polypeptides and nucleic acids can be prepared from isocyanate.

$$RN = C = O + RN = PR_3 \longrightarrow \underset{\text{carbodi-imide}}{RN = C = NR} + R_3P = O$$

3. Stepping up of aldehyde:

$$R \cdot CHOH \cdot CHO + (Ph)_3P = CH \cdot COOC_2H_5 \longrightarrow RCHOH \cdot CH = CH \cdot COOC_2H_5 \xrightarrow[HClO_4]{OsO_4}$$

$$R \cdot CHOH \cdot CHOH \cdot CHOH \cdot COOH \longrightarrow R - \overset{\boxed{\quad O \quad}}{CH \cdot (CHOH)_2 - CO} \xrightarrow[\text{or NaBH}_4]{Na \cdot Hg}$$

$$R \cdot CHOH(CHOH)_2 \cdot CHO$$

4. Synthesis of natural products: Bisabolene, squaline, β-carotene, lycopene, crocetin, binin esters, vitamin A, vit. D₃ corticoids etc.

2.15 FAVORSKII REARRANGEMENT

The reaction of α-haloketones with alkoxide ion to give rearranged esters is called the Favorskii rearrangement. The cyclic **α-haloketones** lead to **ring contraction**.

In general, α-haloketones + Alkoxide ions ⟶ Ester

In case, hydroxide ion or an amine is used as base in place of alkoxide ion, the final product is free acid and amide respectively.

Mechanism:

The first step of the reaction involves the formation of carbanion which undergoes rearrangement to form a cyclopropane intermediate I (1,3-elimination). The cyclopropane intermediate undergoes subsequent addition of OH, followed by ring opening to yield the more stable of the two possible carbanions (benzyl > primary), followed by proton exchange to give the rearranged ester as the final product.

Note that the first step of the above mechanism involves the removal of α-hydrogen atom from the other side of the carbonyl group Ketones that do not have such hydrogen atom also undergo rearrangement to give the same product. This is usually called as quasi-Favorskii rearrangement.

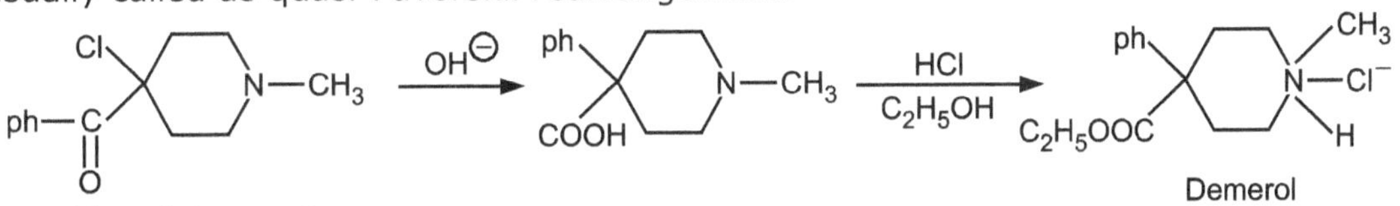

No α-Hydrogen atom

Demerol

Example:

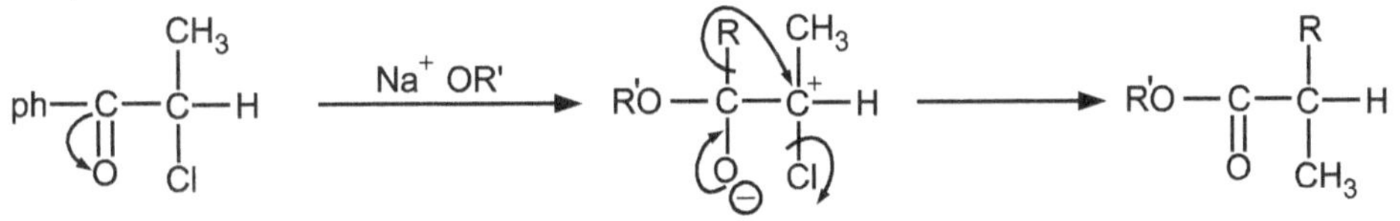

The mechanism of quasi-Favorskii rearrangement does not involve the formation of cyclopropane intermediate. The mechanism is called semi benzilic mechanism involving inversion at the migration terminus.

The semibenzilic mechanism is also found to operate in the ring contraction of α-halocyclobutanones.

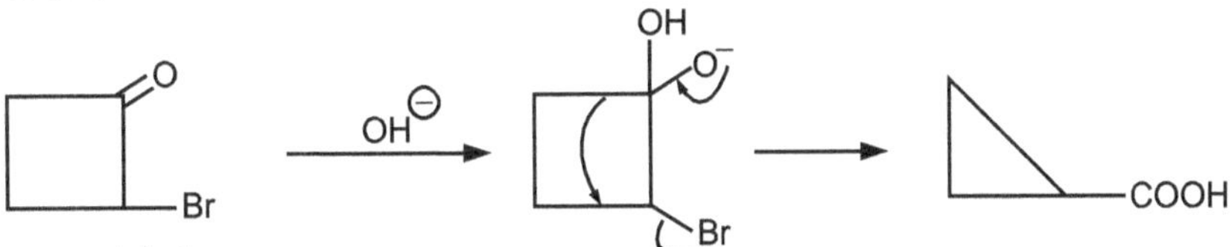

α-Bromo cyclobutanone

Aromatic Rerrangements:

Aromatic compounds of the type I undergo rearrangement in the manner mentioned below.

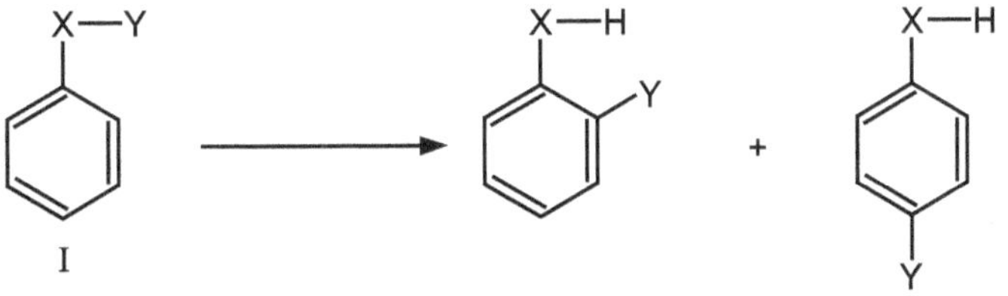

The element X from which group Y migrates may be "N" or [O]. Furthermore, rearrangement may be intermolecular, intramolecular, mixed or of indefinite type.

1. Intermolecular rearrangement : Orton rearrangement / N-chloroacetanilide
2. Intramolecular : Claisen reaction
3. Mixed type : Fries rearrangement

2.16 ORTON REARRANGEMENT

(REARRANGEMENT OF N-CHLOROACETANILIDE)

"The conversion of N-chloroacetanilide into a mixture of o and p chloroacetanilides by means of HCl is known as Orton rearrangement.

N-Chloroacetanilide   o-Chloroacetanilide   p-Chloroacetanilide

The reaction is specific for HCl.

Mechanism: (i) $HCl \rightarrow H^+ + Cl^{\ominus}$ (ii) $Cl_2 \rightarrow Cl^+ + Cl^-$

Here the migrating group, the chlorine atom, becomes completely detached from the rest of the molecule for a significant period of time during the reaction and then combines with the $Cl^{\ominus}$ from HCl to form Cl_2 molecule. The succeeding reaction is a normal electrophilic aromatic chlorination to form a mixture of o and p-chloroacetanilide.

2.17 CLAISEN REARRANGEMENT

Claisen rearrangement involves the conversion of phenyl allyl ethers to ortho (or para if o-positions are preoccupied) allyl phenols by means of heat at about 200°C

200°C. (Phenyl allyl ether $\longrightarrow$ Ortho allyl phenol).

Mechanism:

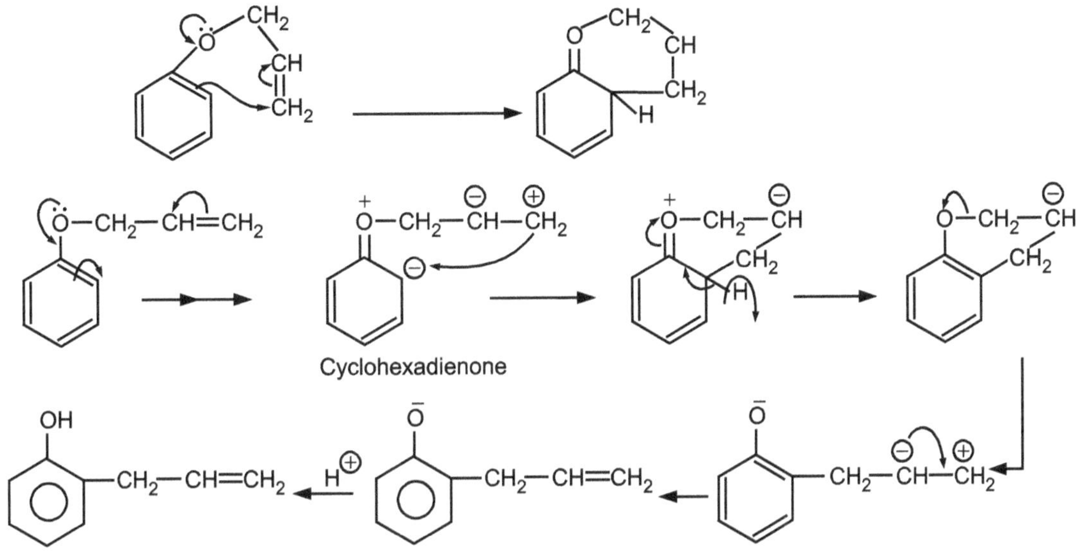

Cyclohexadienone

Ortho allyl phenol

Salient features of Claisen rearrangement:

1. The reaction does not require a catalyst and follow first order kinetics showing thereby that each individual act of rearrangement involves only one molecule.
2. If a mixture of two different ethers is heated together, no cross product is formed.

For example, a mixture of α-naphthyl allyl ether and phenyl cinnamyl ether gives only 2-allyl-α-naphthol and o-α-phenyl allyl phenol formed by the separate rearrangement of each.

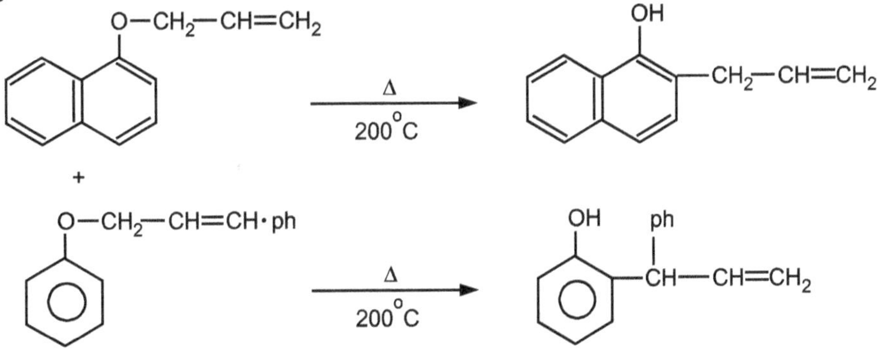

Extension and Applications:

(a) The rearrangement is also applicable to allyl ethers of enols.

e.g.

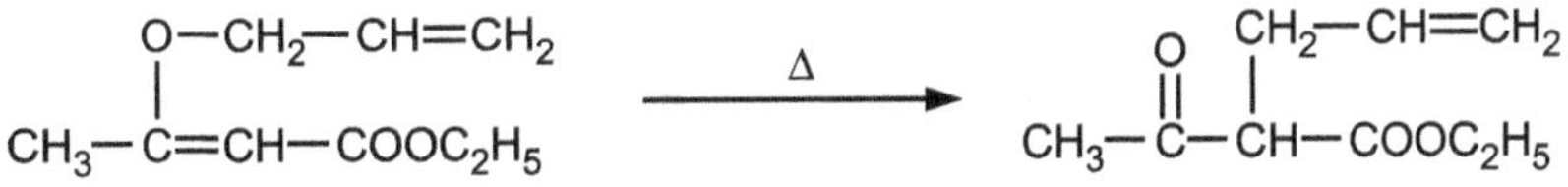

o-allyl acetoacetic ester

(b) Rearrangement of allyl esters

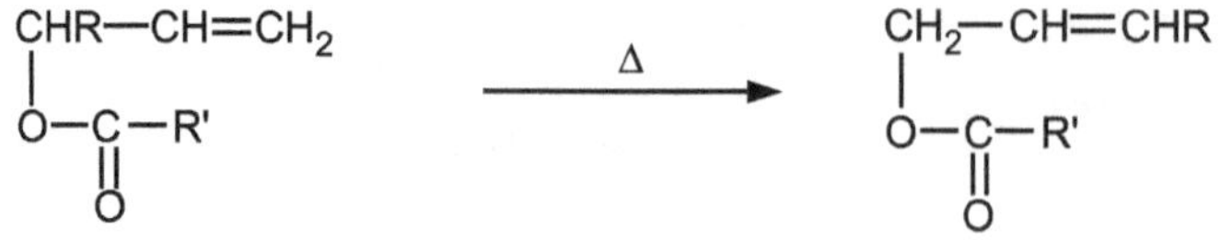

(c) Rearrangement of allyl vinyl ethers

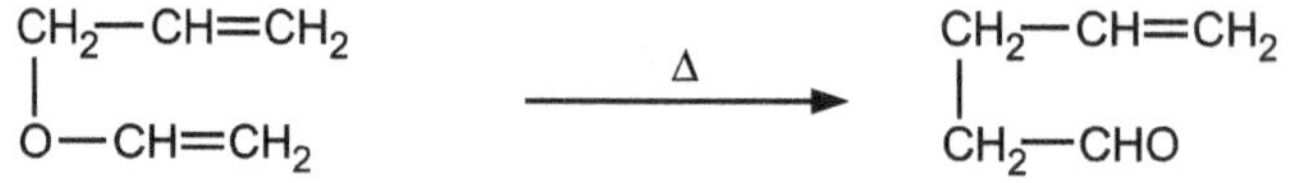

(d) Rearrangement of allyl amine oxides

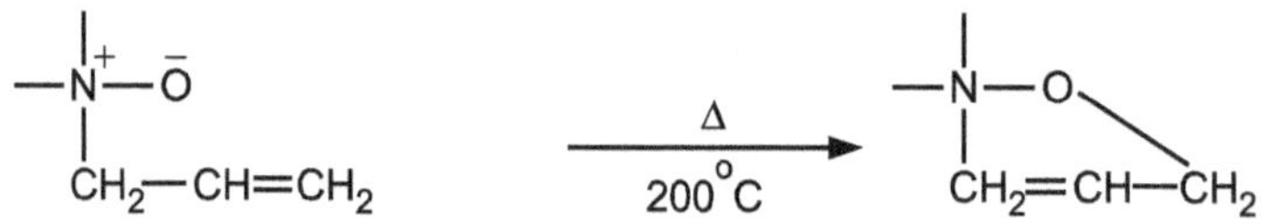

(e) Rearrangement of 1, 5-hexadienes (cope rearrangement)

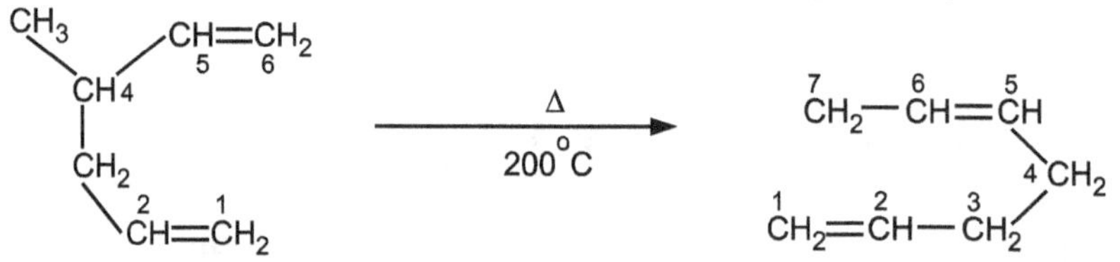

4-Methyl 1,5-hexadiene   1,5-heptadiene

2.18 FRIES REARRANGEMENT

Phenolic esters or aryl esters can be rearranged by heating with Friedel-Crafts catalysts (Lewis acid) – $AlCl_3$ gives rise to o- and p-acyl phenols can be produced is called as **Fries rearrangement**. It is possible to select conditions so that either ortho or para product dominates. The ortho/para ratio depends on the temperature, solvent and amount of catalyst used. Low temperature favours para products and high temperature favours ortho products. The R-group may be aliphatic or aromatic.

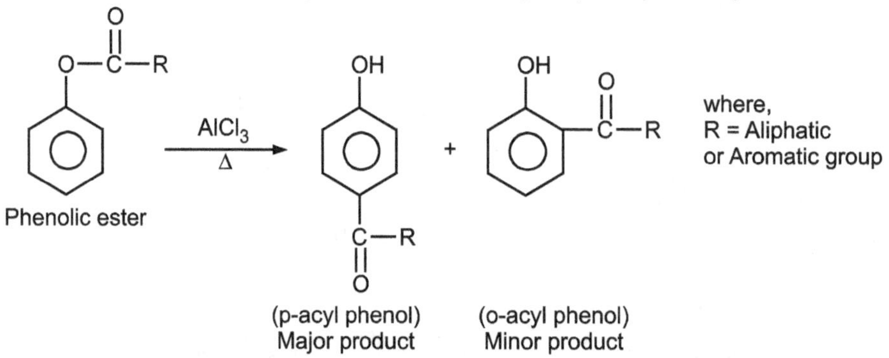

where,
R = Aliphatic
or Aromatic group

Phenolic ester

(p-acyl phenol)
Major product

(o-acyl phenol)
Minor product

where R = aliphatic or aromatic group.

Example:

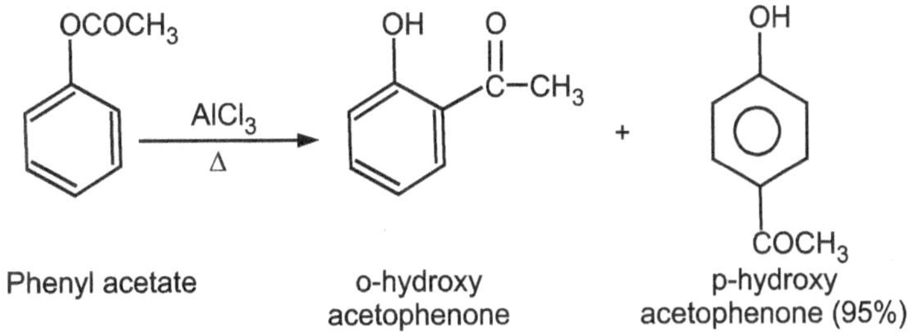

Phenyl acetate   o-hydroxy acetophenone   p-hydroxy acetophenone (95%)

Mechanism:

There is evidence for the intermolecular (Baltzly et. al. 1948) as well as intramolecular (Crawford 1954) mechanism and hence the rearrangement is best regarded as a combination of two mechanisms occurring simultaneously.

Intermolecular mechanism (2-step process)

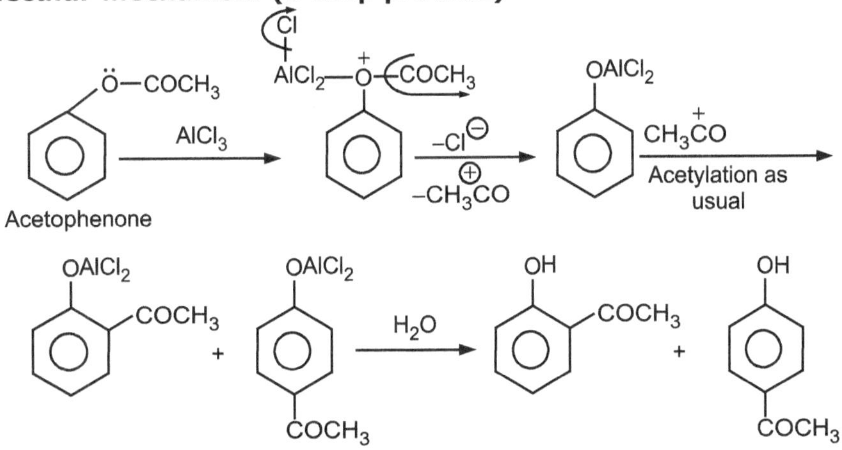

Intramolecular mechanism (1 step process)

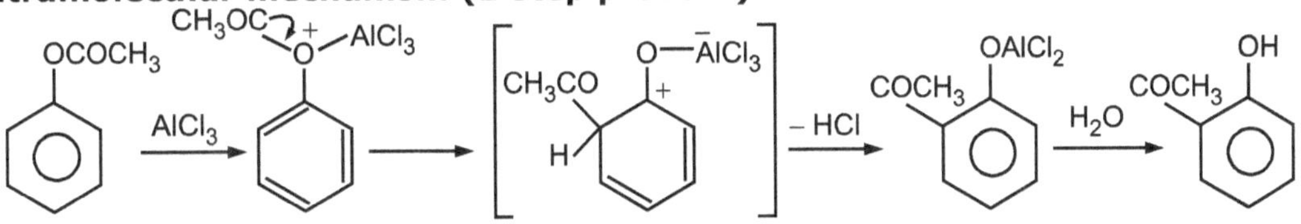

Therefore whatever might be the mechanism of the rearrangement, it generally forms a mixture of p- and o-isomers. The relative amount of each isomer depends upon several factors viz. temperature, solvent, amount of catalyst and structure of ester.

     (i)   **Effect of temperature:** Generally, low temperature (60° or less) favours the formation of p-isomer while high temperature (above 60°C) favours the o-isomer.

     (ii)   **Effect of solvent:** Although Fries rearrangement generally does not require any solvent, sometimes the use of some solvent reduces the temperature at which reaction proceeds at a useful rate.

Example:

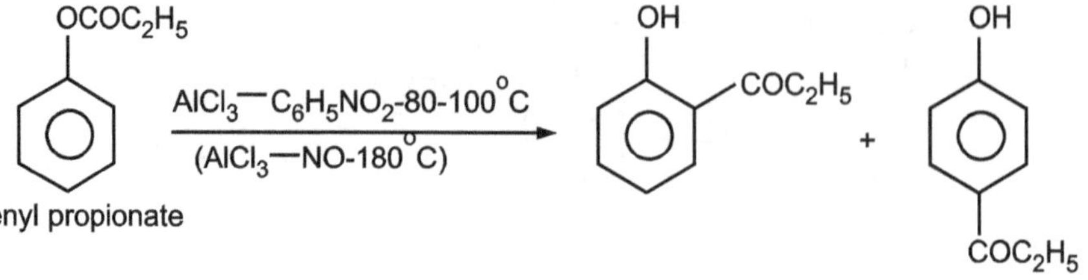

Phenyl propionate

35%   50%

(iii) Ratio of the starting materials:

Ratio of AlCl$_3$ to ester	Ratio of o- to p-hydroxy compounds
0.5	2.93
1.0	2.41
2.0	10.1

(iv) Structure of esters: Generally presence of m-directing group retards the reaction. The effect of the position of the group in the aromatic nucleus to the product can be judged from the following examples in which methyl group is present in all three different positions.

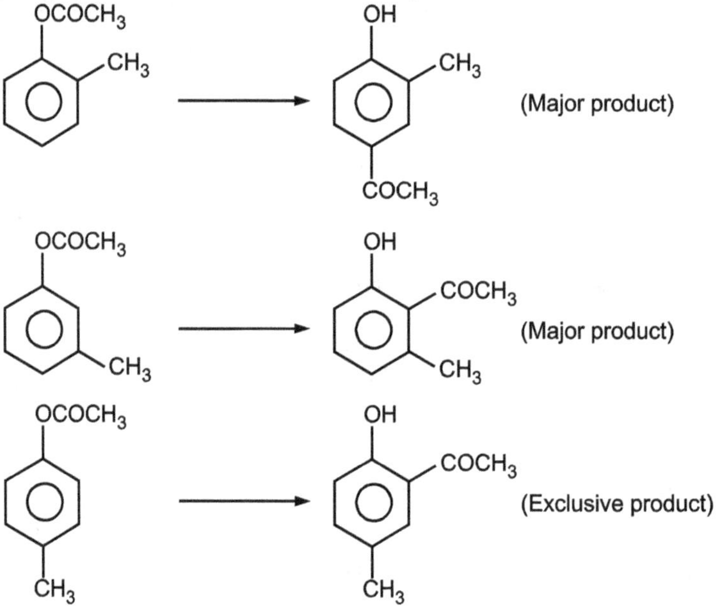

Applications:

1. Since the direct synthesis of **aromatic hydroxy ketones** from phenols is not possible owing to the formation of insoluble aluminium phenoxide, Fries rearrangement provides important route for the preparation of hydroxy ketones.

2. Fries rearrangement may also be extended to the esters of enols to give 1, 3-diketones.
   Example:

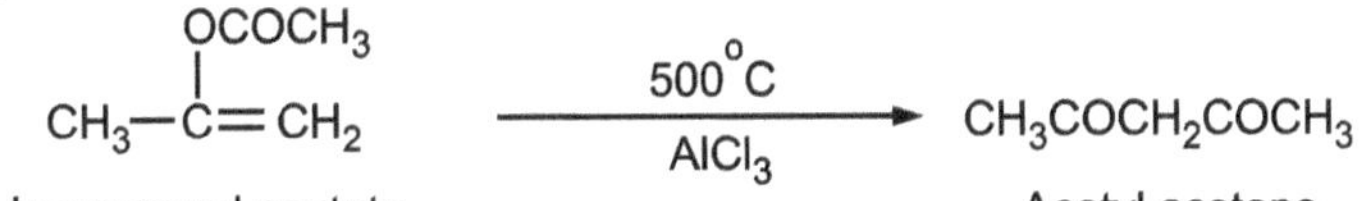
OCOCH3
CH3—C=CH2
500°C
AlCl3
CH3COCH2COCH3

Isopropenyl acetate Acetyl acetone

3. Synthesis of adrenaline, the heart stimulant.

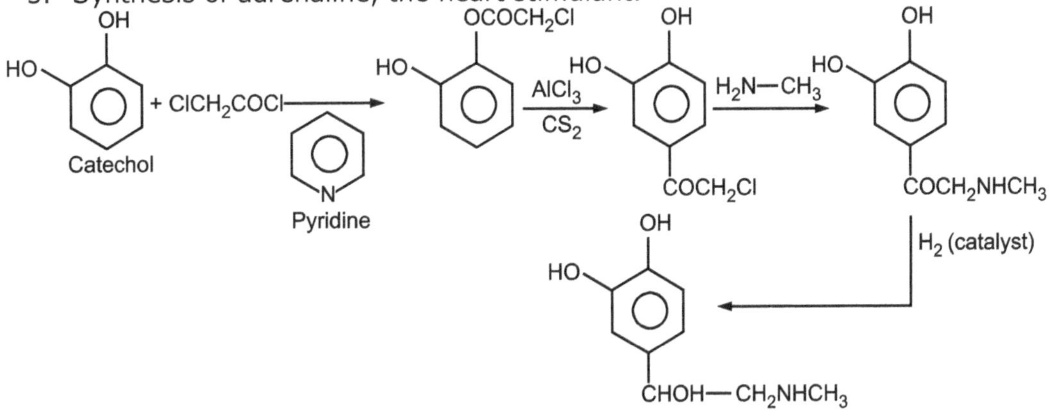
OH
HO
+ ClCH2COCl
Catechol
N
Pyridine
OCOCH2Cl
HO
AlCl3
CS2
OH
HO
COCH2Cl
H2N—CH3
OH
HO
COCH2NHCH3
H2 (catalyst)
OH
HO
CHOH—CH2NHCH3

(±) Adrenaline

2.19 PHOTO FRIES REACTION

Fries reaction can also be carried out in the presence of UV light.

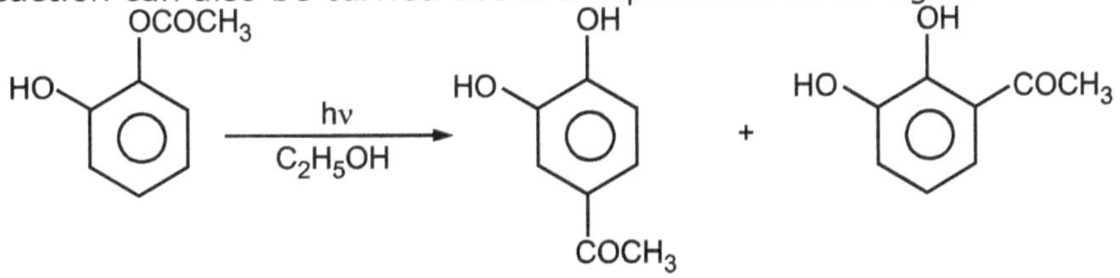
OCOCH3
HO
hν
C2H5OH
OH
HO
COCH3
+
OH
HO
COCH3

o-hydroxy phenyl acetate 2-hydroxy acetophenone

Mechanism:

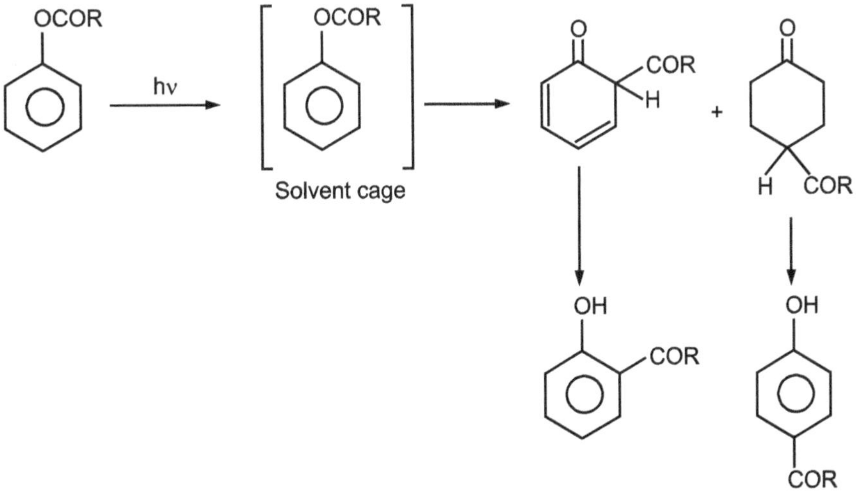
OCOR
hν
OCOR
Solvent cage
O
COR
H
+
O
H
COR
OH
COR
OH
COR

2.20 WILLGERDOT REACTION

"The conversion of a ketone into an amide having the same number of carbon atoms by means of yellow ammonium polysulphide is known as Willgerdot reaction".

$$ph-\overset{\overset{O}{\|}}{C}-CH_3 \xrightarrow{(NH_4)_2S_n} ph-CH_2-CONH_2 \; + \; ph-CH_2COONH_4 \; + \; phCH_2CH_3$$

Acetophenone   Phenyl acetamide   Ammonium   Ethyl
                    (50 %)   phenyl acetate   benzene
                                  (13.5%)

Mechanism:

Not known with certainty.

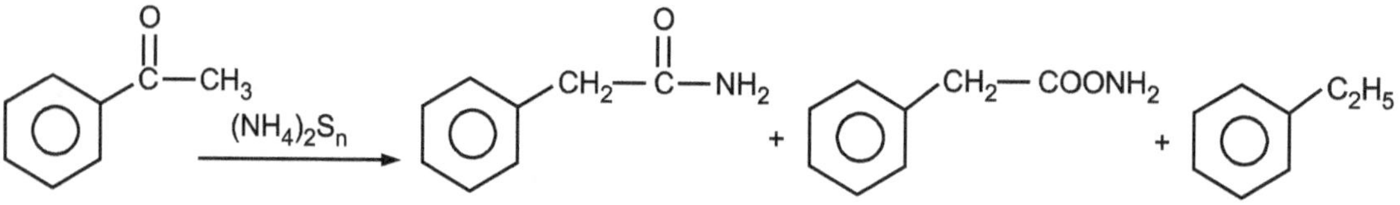

Application:

Preparation of aryl substituted aliphatic acids.

2.21 COPE REARRANGEMENT

When 1, 5-dienes are heated they isomerize in a [3, 3] sigmatropic rearrangement to give more stable product.

Example:

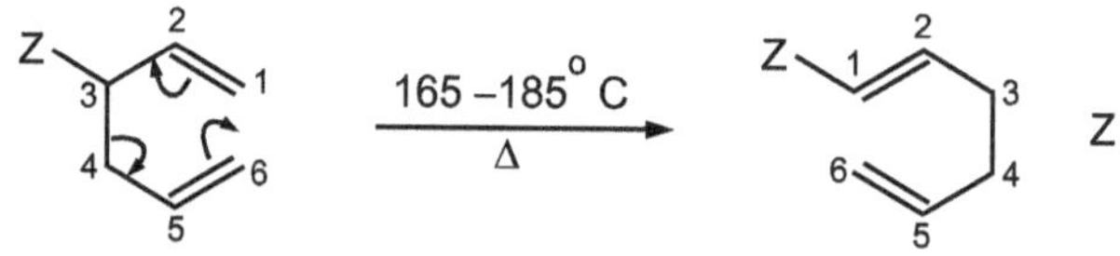

1,5-hexadiene,   1,5-dienes,
3-functional group   1-functional group

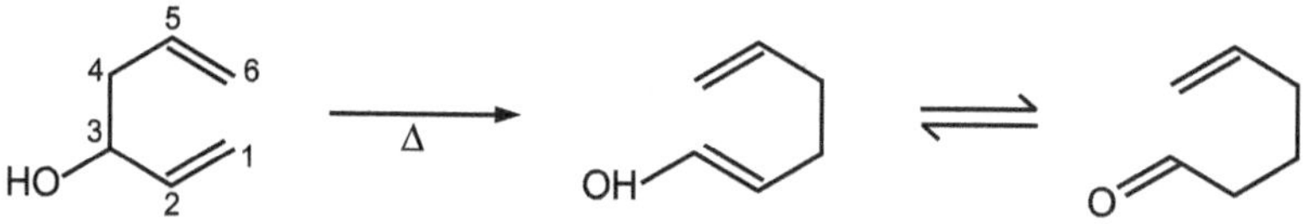

3-hydroxy 1,5-hexadiene

The above reaction is not reversible as 3-hydroxy-1, 5-dienes because the product tautomerizes to the ketone or aldehyde.

Example: 3-methyl -1, 5 hexadiene $\xrightarrow[(300°C)]{\Delta}$ 1, 5 heptadiene.

$$\underset{}{CH = CH - \underset{\overset{|}{CH_3}}{CH} - CH_2HC = CH_2} \longrightarrow CH_2 = CH - CH_2 - CH_2 - HC = CH - CH_3$$

Cope reaction:

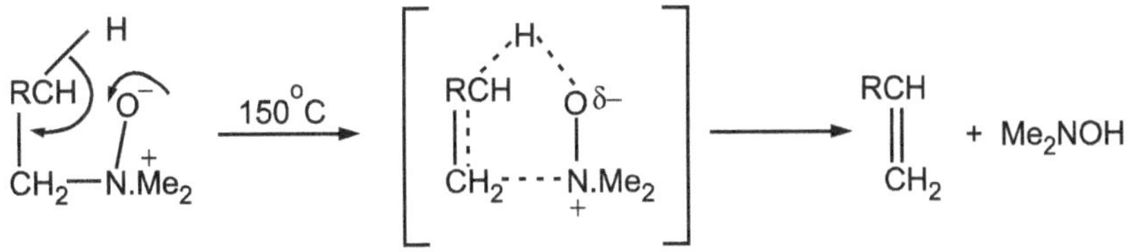

Free Radical Rearrangement:

1.

Transition

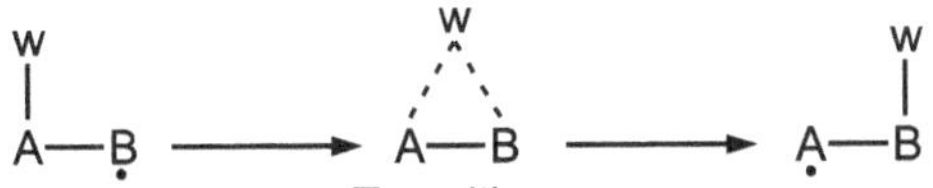

The free radical energy state of transition can be shown as:

↑ (antibonding)

↑↓ (bonding)

The overlap of these orbitals give rise to three new orbitals, 2 or more electrons can be accommodated. There must be generation of free radical which is possible by irradiation or peroxides and then actual migration in which migrating group moves with one electron. The new free radical must stabilize by itself by immediate further reaction. Free radical migration does not occur at ordinary temperatures.

Example 1:

Cyclopropane (Diradical formation) Propene

Example 2:

tri-chloro prop-1-ene

1,2-dibromo, 2,3-dichloro propane

Example 3:

Diradical of But-1-ene

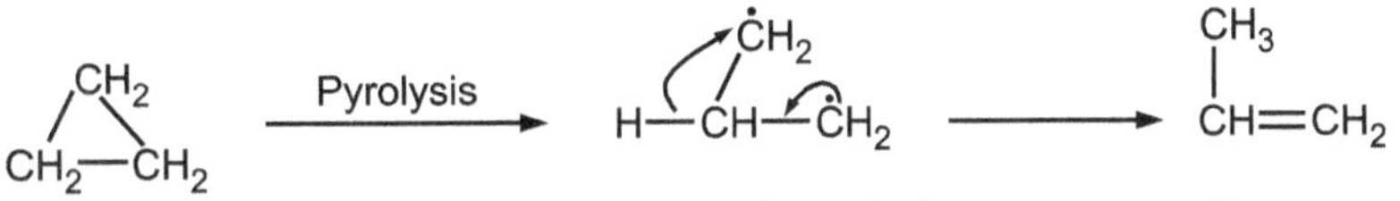

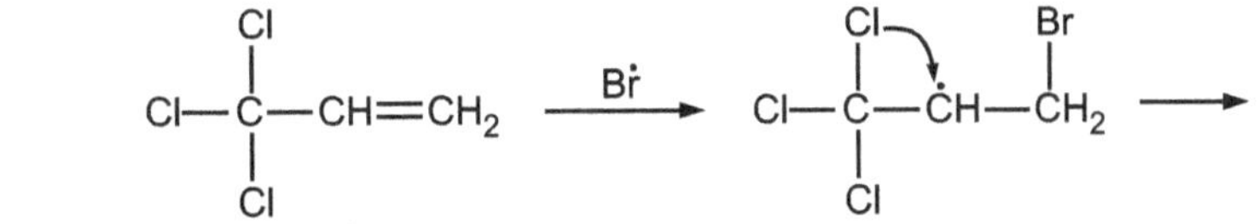

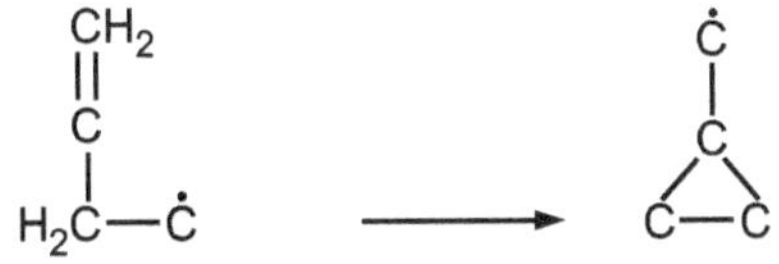

Example 4:

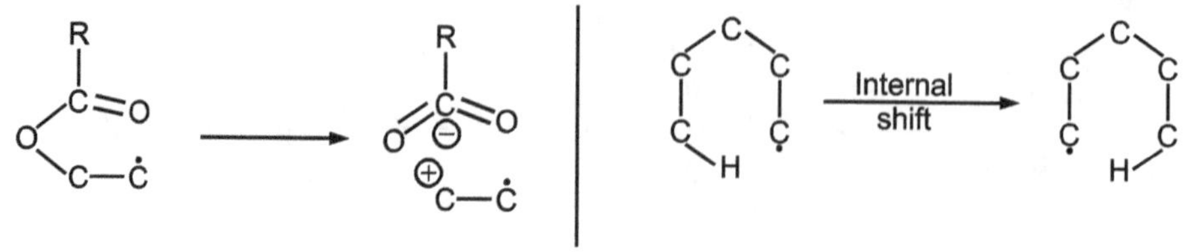

2. Free radicals, unlike carbocations, seldom rearrange. The rearrangement is generally possible in the 3° free radicals.

Example 1:

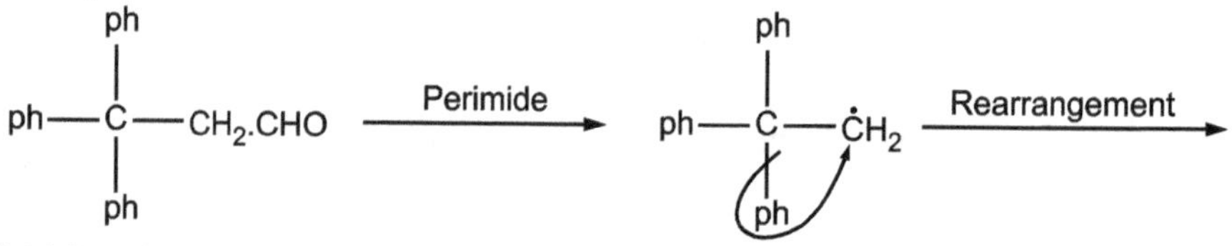

3,3,3-triphenyl propanal   Triphenyl ethyl radical

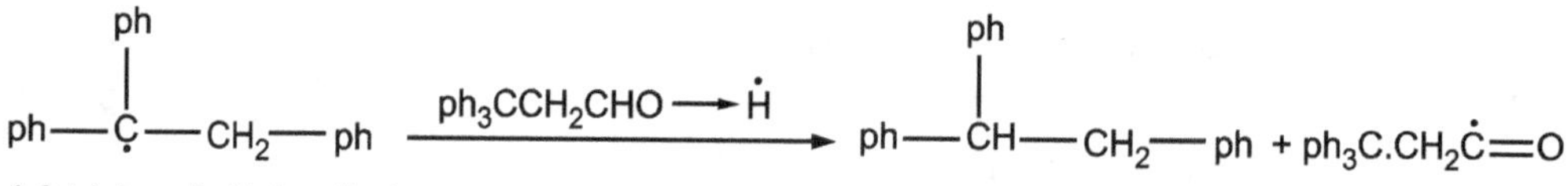

1,1,2-triphenyl ethyl radical   1,1,2-triphenyl ethane

Example 2:

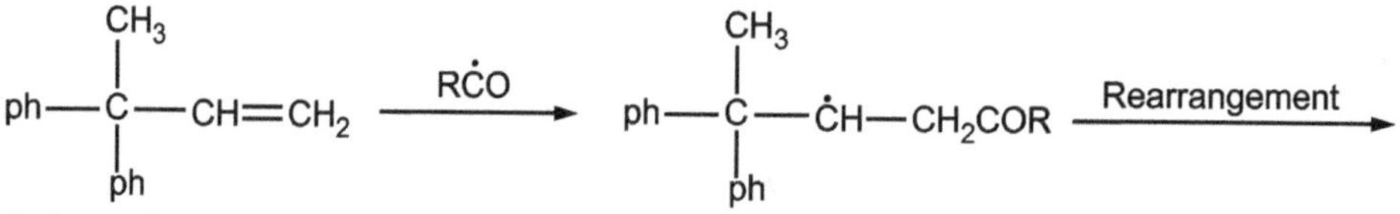

2,2-diphenyl, but-1-ene

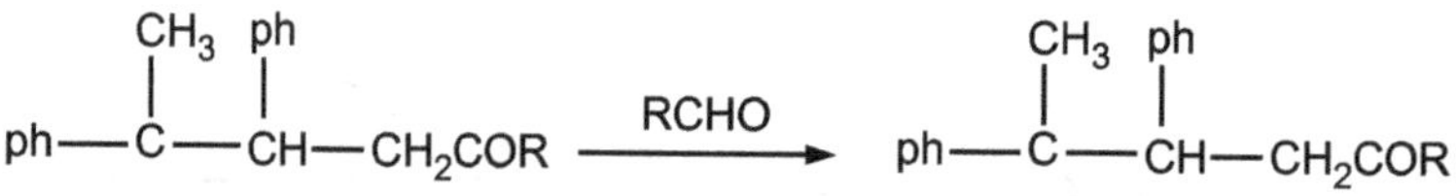

2.22 PERICYCLIC REACTIONS

Definition: "Pericyclic reaction is a type of organic rearrangement reaction wherein the transition state of the molecules has a cyclic geometry and the reaction progresses in a concerted fashion i.e. the electronic rearrangements involved in bond-making/braking proceed simultaneously in a one step process.

Pericyclic reactions remain unaffected by polar reagents, solvent changes, radical initiator etc. but these are influenced by **heat** or **light**.

Mechanism and stereochemistry of pericyclic reactions: Woodword, "Hoffmann and others have shown that in pericyclic reactions, the contrasting results (poor yield and good idea) can be explained by the principle of conservation of **orbital symmetry** which predicts that certain reactions are symmetry allowed and others are symmetry forbidden. (Symmetry forbidden reaction is that for which the concerted mechanism is very difficult.)

The orbital symmetry rules (also called the Woodward-Hoffmann rules) apply only to concerted reactions. There are several ways of applying the orbital-symmetry principle, of which the Frontier orbital method is the most common.

Frontier orbitals and orbital symmetry:

Just as the outer shell of electrons of an atom is regarded as especially significant in determining the chemistry of that atom, so it is reasonable that, for a molecule, it is the highest occupied molecular orbital (Homo) which is the key to determining reactivity and this (HomO) is termed as the **Frontier orbital.**

The theory is based upon two principles:

(i) Since the ground state of almost all molecules has a pair of electrons in the Homo, bonding interaction between two molecules or between two atoms in the same molecule cannot involve only the Homo of each because this would lead to an orbital occupancy greater than two which is contrary to Pauli's principle. The Homo of one reactant needs therefore to interact with an unoccupied molecular orbital of the second. Now since the bonding interaction between two orbitals increases as the energies of the two become more nearly equal, it is expected that the Homo of one reactant would interact efficiently with the **lowest unoccupied molecular orbital (Lumo)** of the second.

(ii) The shaded (+ve) lobe overlaps only with the shaded (+ve) lobe of another orbital and an unshaded (−ve) lobe only with the unshaded (−ve) lobe of another orbital. Overlap of unlike phase results repulsion.

Types: The major classes of pericyclic reactions are:

		Bond changes	
		σ	P
1.	Electrocyclic reaction	+1	−1
2.	Cycloaddition reaction	+2	−2
3.	Sigmatropic reaction	0	0
4.	Group transfer reaction	+1	−1
5.	Chelotropic reaction	+2	−2
6.	Dyotropic reaction	0	0

1. **Electrocyclic reaction: Definition:** These are intramolecular pericyclic reactions which involve either the formation of a ring, with the generation of one new σ-bond and the consumption of one π-bond or ring is broken with opposite consequence i.e. one signal bond is converted into π-bond or vice-versa (Bond change = σ = +1 and π = −1).

Examples:

1.

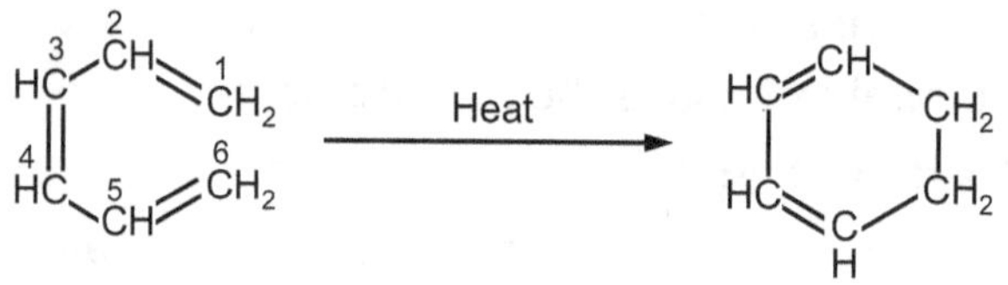

1,3,5 - Hexatriene   1,2 - Dihydrobenzene (1,3 - Hexadiene)

2.

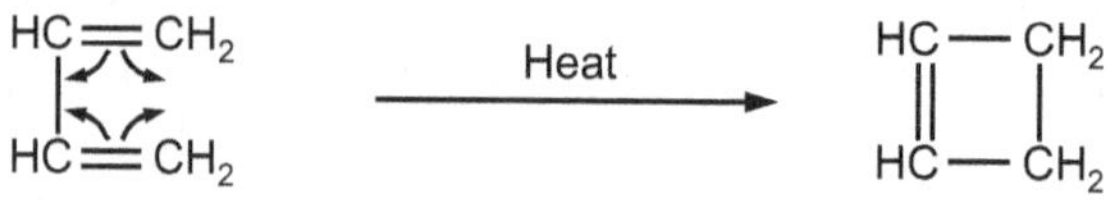

1,3 - Butadiene   Cyclobutene

3.

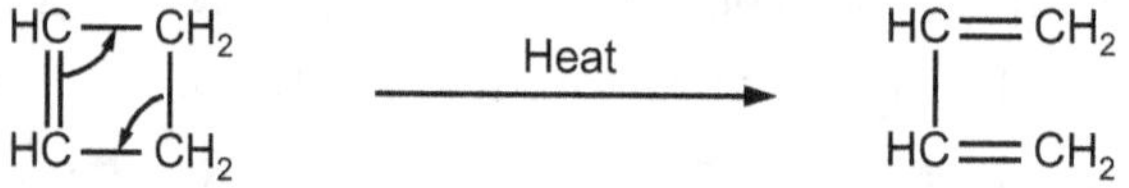

Cyclobutene   1,3 - Butadiene

2.23 WOODWARD-HOFFMANN RULES FOR ELECTROCYCLIC REACTIONS

Number of π electrons	Reaction	Motion
4n	Thermal	Conrotatory
4n	Photochemical	Disrotatory
4n+2	Thermal	Conrotatory
4n+2	Photochemical	Disrotatory

The electrocyclic reactions are completely stereospecific and the exact stereochemistry depends upon two factors viz.

(a) The number of double bonds in the polyene.

(b) Whether the reaction is thermal or photochemical.

According to Woodward-Hoffmann rule, the orbital symmetry of the highest energy occupied molecular orbital (Homo) must be considered and the rotation occurs to permit overlap of two shaded (or unshaded) lobes of the p-orbitals to form the σ-bond.

1. Thermal cyclization of 1, 3-butadiene to form cyclobutene:

As per Woodward-Hoffmann rule and orbital symmetry, the homo of a conjugated diene which is involved in cyclisation is ψ_2.

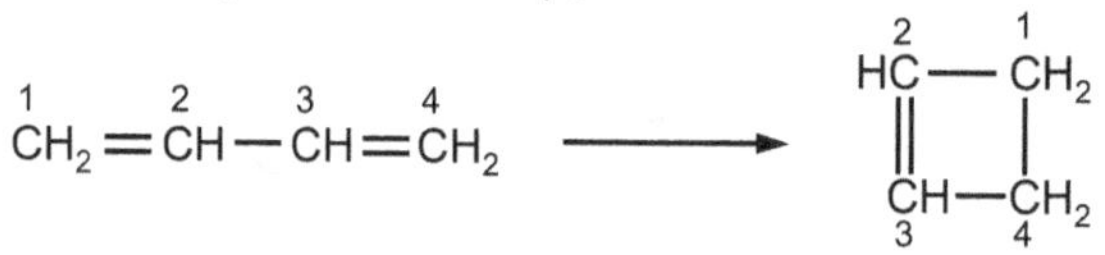

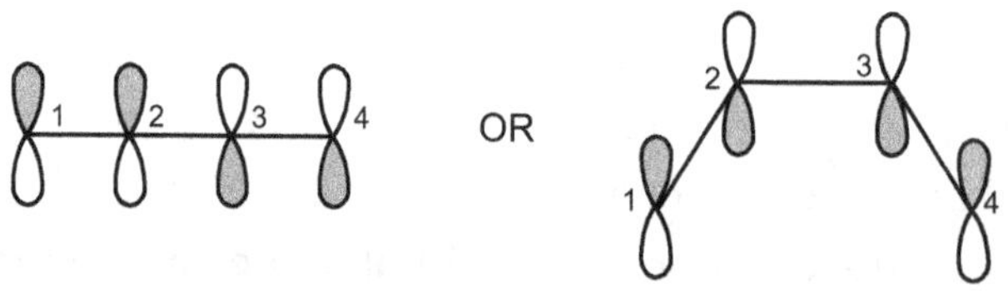

HOMO of ground state (ψ_2) of a conjugated diene

Bond formation between C_1 and C_4 required for cyclization can take place only when the lobes of C_1 and C_4 are in overlapping position i.e. when the shaded (or unshaded) lobe or C_1 faces the shaded (or unshaded) lobe of C_4. We see that these lobes can come in overlapping position only when there is rotation about two bonds $C_1 - C_2$ and $C_3 - C_4$.

Rotation of these two bonds can take place in the same direction i.e. conrotatory motion or in opposite direction i.e. disrotatory motion.

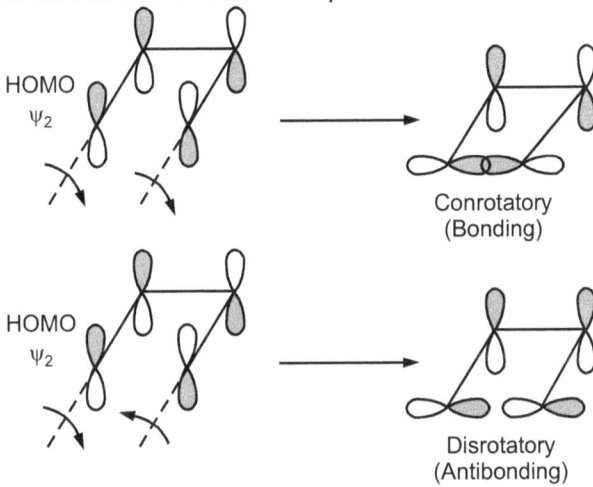

Here the conrotatory motion brings together lobes of same phase and hence overlapping occurs and the **bond** is formed. On the contrary, disrotatory motion brings together lobes of opposite phase leading for antibonding interaction.

Thus, it is evident that in thermal cyclization of conjugated dienes, conrotatory motion takes place and thus the observed stereochemistry of the product must be that which is produced by this motion.

Photochemical cyclization of 1, 3-butadiene to form cyclobutene:

It is important to note that the photochemical cyclization of a disubstituted conjugated dienes gives stereochemistry opposite to that produced during thermal cyclization. This can be explained on the basis of following two facts:

(a) In presence of light, butadiene absorbs light with the result one of the electrons from ψ_2 goes to ψ_3 i.e. here the Homo is ψ_3 and not ψ_2. In other words, the excited state of Homo is ψ_3 whose terminal carbons have symmetry opposite to that in ψ_2.

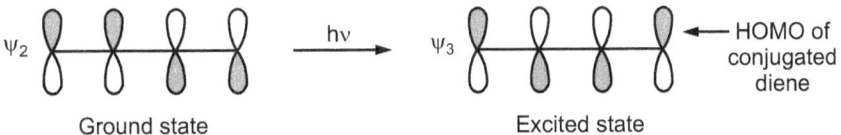

2. Cycloaddition reaction:

A reaction in which two unsaturated molecules combine to form a cyclic compound with π-electrons being used to form two new σ-bonds is known as cycloaddition reaction. (Bond change $\sigma = +2$ and $\pi = -2$).

Example:

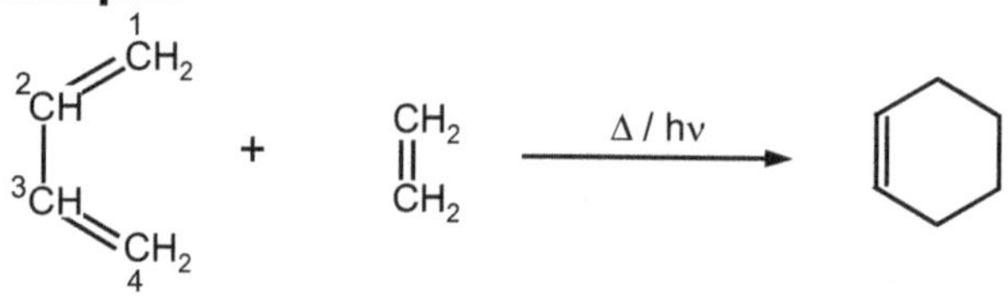

1,3 - Butadiene   Ethylene   Cyclohexene

Types: These are of two types depending upon the number of π-electrons in two compounds:

(i)   (2 + 2) cycloaddition

(ii)   (4 + 2) cycloaddition

(i) **(2 + 2) cycloaddition reaction:** When both the unsaturated molecules have 2π electrons each.

Example:

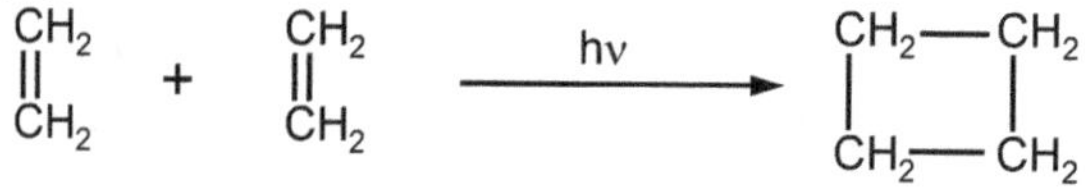

Ethylene   Ethylene   Cyclobutane

(ii) **(4 + 2) cycloaddition reaction:** When one of the systems has 4π electrons and the other has 2π electrons.

Example:

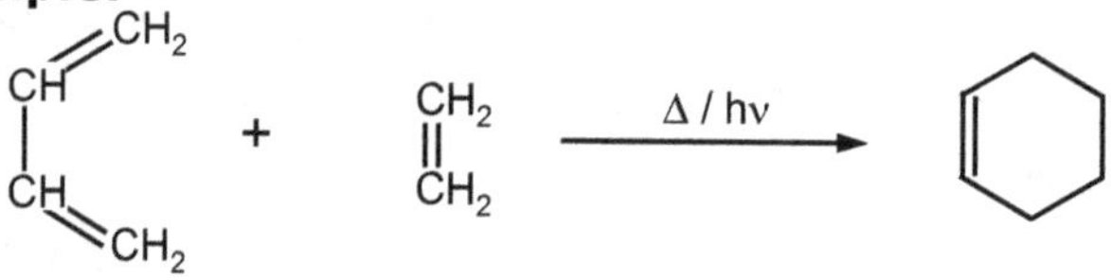

1,3 - Butadiene

Reaction mechanism of (4 + 2) cycloadditions:

The best $(4\pi + 2\pi)$ cycloaddition is the Diel's-Alder reaction of which the simplest possible example is the reaction between 1, 3-butadiene and ethylene to form six-membered ring i.e. cyclohexene.

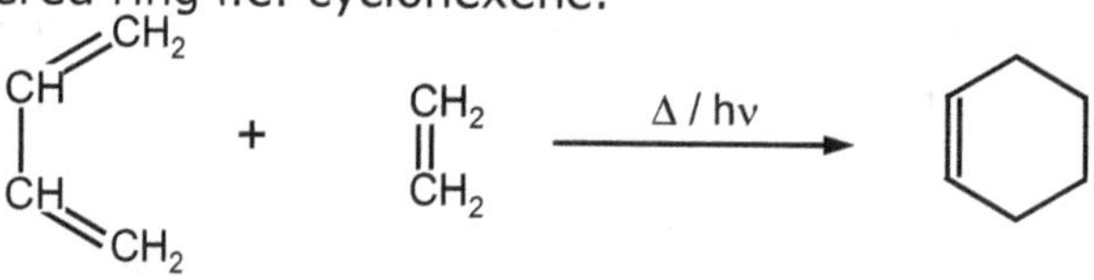

1,3 - Butadiene   Cyclohexene

For this reason, we have to study the electronic configuration of 1, 3-butadiene and ethylene.

Electronic configuration of 1, 3-butadiene:

$$CH_2 = CH - CH = CH_2$$

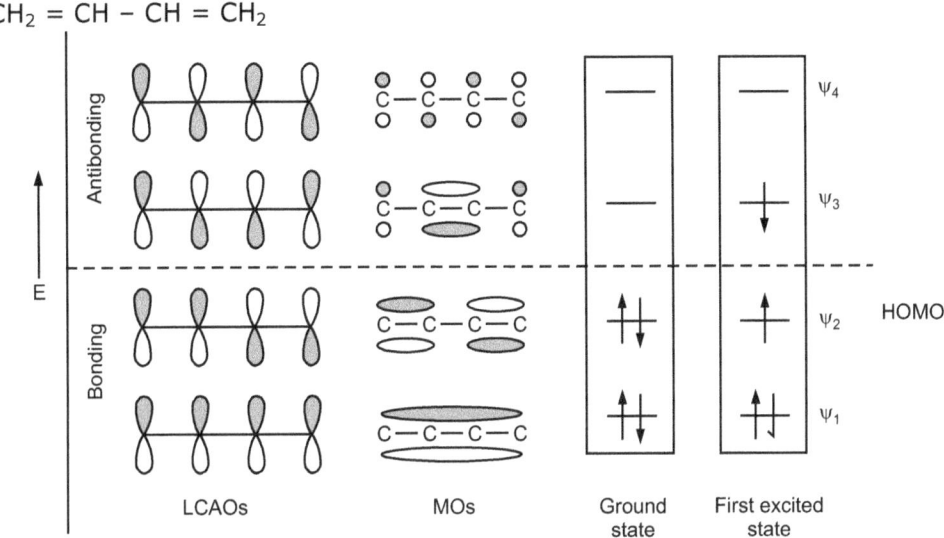

For the four component p orbitals, there are four π MOs (two bonding ψ_1, ψ_2 and two antibonding ψ_3, ψ_4). Thus in the ground state, butadiene has $\psi_1^2 \cdot \psi_2^2$ configuration i.e. there are two electrons in each of the two bonding orbitals (ψ_1, ψ_2). Orbital ψ_1 encompasses all four carbons, this delocalisation provides the net stabilization of the conjugated system and hence this configuration has the minimum energy. The higher ψ_2 orbital resembles two isolated π-orbitals. off course it has somewhat lower energy than the isolated π-orbitals. Absorption of light of the right frequency raises one electron of ψ_2 orbital to ψ_3. Then ψ_3 has one electron in the first excited state although it is vacant in the ground state. Note that it has somewhat higher energy than the ψ_2 but less than ψ_4. Thus the energy of the completely filled orbital of highest energy (HOMO) which is to participate in the bond formation is near to the LUMO (lower unoccupied molecular orbital) and thus these orbitals of comparable energy can overlap.

Electronic configuration of ethylene: The two π-electrons of ethylene are distributed as below:

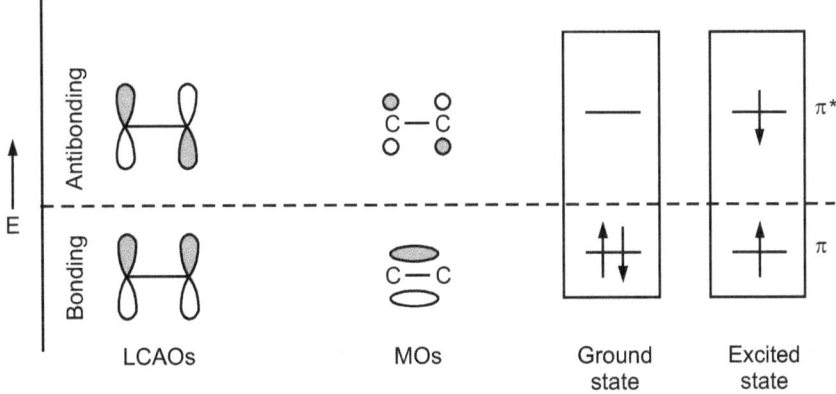

From the symmetry of the MOs of butadiene and ethylene, it is apparent that the symmetries of HOMO of butadiene (ψ_2) and the LUMO of ethylene (π^x) or LUMO of butadiene (ψ_3) and the HOMO of ethylene (π) are such that when the reactants approach each other with their molecular planes parallel, two new C – C σ-bonds can be formed at the same time to give the product i.e. cyclohexene.

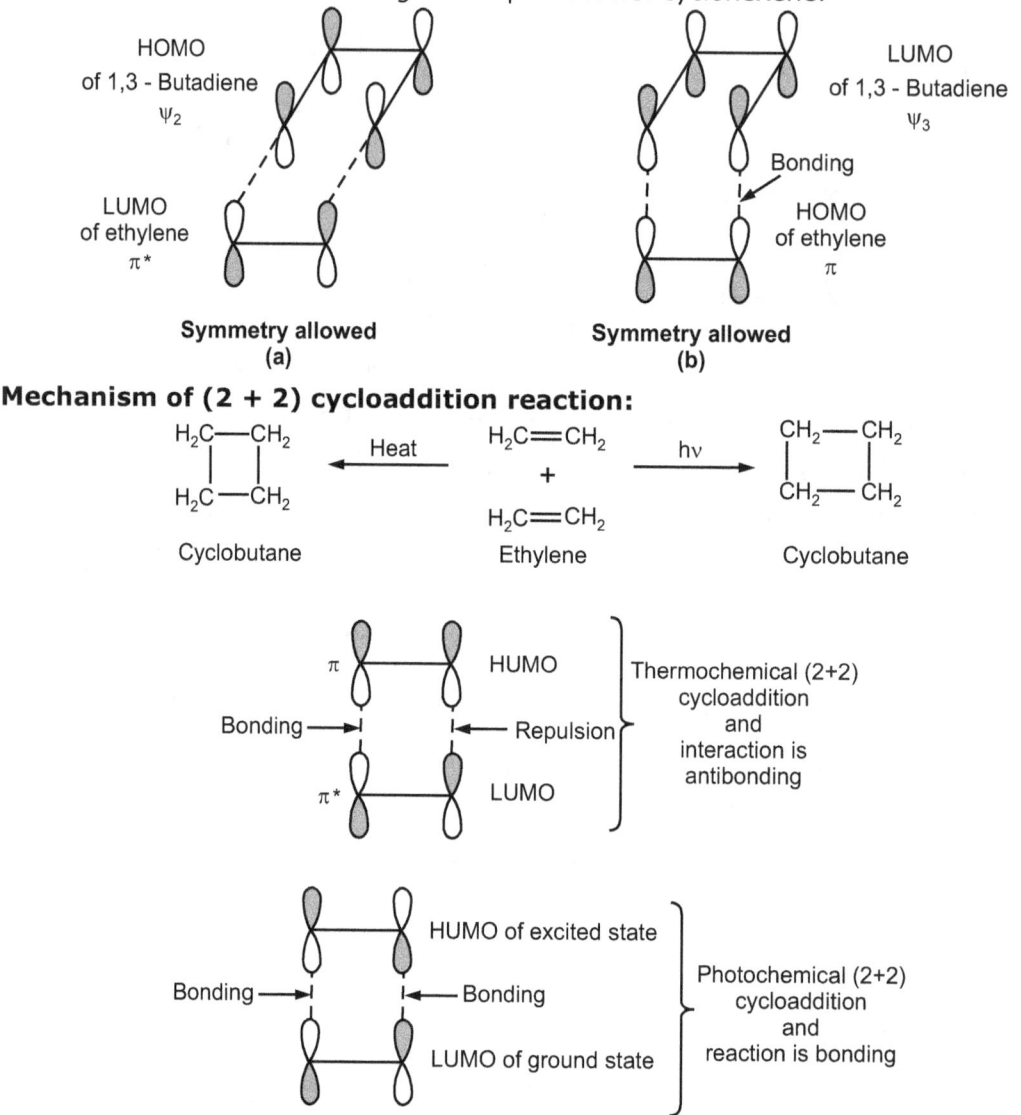

Mechanism of (2 + 2) cycloaddition reaction:

Conversion of ethylene to cyclobutane is very difficult and not very common.

However, the photochemical conversion is easy whereas thermal reaction is difficult.

The thermal reaction is difficult because, in presence of heat the dimerization of ethylene would involve overlap of the HOMO, π of one molecule with LUMO, π^* of the other. Now since, π and π^* are of opposite symmetry, lobes of opposite phase would approach each other. Hence interaction is antibonding and repulsive and concerted reaction does not occur due to symmetry forbidden overlapping.

However, photochemical [2 + 2] cycle addition are symmetry allowed. The simplest interpretation of this is as follows.

When an olefin molecule absorbs a quantum of light, an electron is promoted from the HOMO to the LUMO, so that there are two singly occupied molecular orbitals [SUMO]. The excited HOMO therefore has the symmetry of the ground state LUMO i.e. π^* and consequently the two can now interact and overlap to give the product i.e. cyclobutane.

Thus, the photochemical symmetry allowed overlapping leads to give the product easily in (2 + 2) cycloaddition reaction.

3. Sigmatropic Rearrangement:

Definition: A sigmatropic rearrangement is defined as an uncatalysed intramolecular process in which the σ-bond adjacent to one or more π-systems migrates to a new position in the molecule.

(**Note:** The overall number of π and σ-bonds remain separately unchanged.)

Examples:

1.

A [1,3] sigmatropic rearrangement

2.

A [1,5] sigmatropic rearrangement

The order of a sigmatropic rearrangement is expressed by two numbers placed in bracket. These numbers can be determined by counting the atoms over which each end of the σ-bond has moved.

Example: Consider the simplest example of this type of reaction, [1, 3] sigmatropic rearrangement.

Imaginary transition
state

Symmetry allowed
migration of H

I
Antarafacial

II
Suprafacial

Antarafacial migration: When the hydrogen moves across the π-system, from top to bottom or vice-versa, it is called antarafacial migration.

Suprafacial migration: When the hydrogen moves along the top or bottom face of the π system, it is called suprafacial migration.

In the sigmatropic rearrangement, the main transition state, a three-centre bond is required and this must involve overlap between the s-orbital of the hydrogen and lobes of p-orbitals of the two terminal carbons. Further the rule governing sigmatropic migration of hydrogen is that the hydrogen must move from shaded (or unshaded) to a shaded (or unshaded) lobe, of the HOMO, it cannot move from shaded to unshaded orbital.

Example: In (1, 3) sigmatropic rearrangement, the transition state involves the overlapping of an allyl radical and a hydrogen atom. Of the 3 possible molecular orbitals of allyl radical, we are concerned with the HOMO, I. In this state, overlapping between the s orbital of the hydrogen atom and lobes of 'p' orbitals of two terminal carbons can take place if the migration is antarafacial. Consequently, the rule predicts that antarafacial thermal (1, 3) sigmatropic rearrangements are allowed but the suprafacial pathway is forbidden. However in a photochemical reaction, promotion of an electron means, the HOMO of allyl radical is represented by II. Now the suprafacial pathway is allowed and the antarafacial pathway forbidden.

QUESTIONS

1. What are molecular rearrangement reactions?
2. Give the difference between intramolecular and intermolecular rearrange-ment.
3. Explain the mechanism of Nucleophilic rearrangement.
4. Describe the mechanism of pinacol-pinacolone rearrangement.
5. Give the features of pinacol rearrangement.

6. Describe the reaction mechanism and principle features of Wagner-Meerwein rearrangement.

7. Describe the reaction mechanism of Lossen rearrangement.

8. Explain the reaction mechanism of Schmidt reaction.

9. Write the product and explain the mechanism of following reactions:

(a) 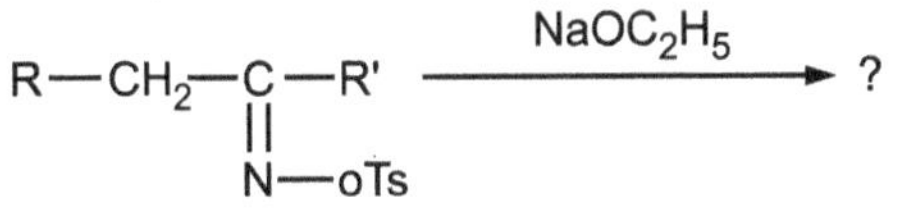 $R-CH_2-\underset{\underset{N-oTs}{||}}{C}-R' \xrightarrow{NaOC_2H_5}$?

(b) $\underset{R'}{\overset{R}{>}}C=N-OH \xrightarrow{Conc. H_2SO_4}$?

(c) $R-\overset{O}{\overset{||}{C}}-R + R'C_3OH \xrightarrow{H^{\oplus}}$?

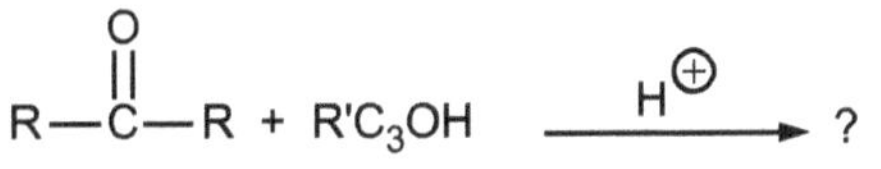

(d) 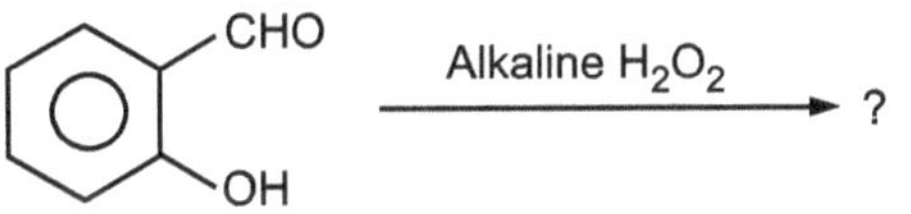 [benzene ring with CHO and OH substituents] $\xrightarrow{Alkaline\ H_2O_2}$?

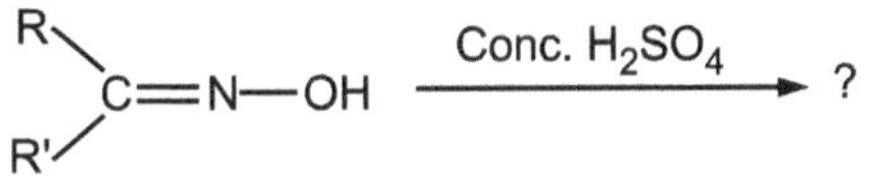

(e) 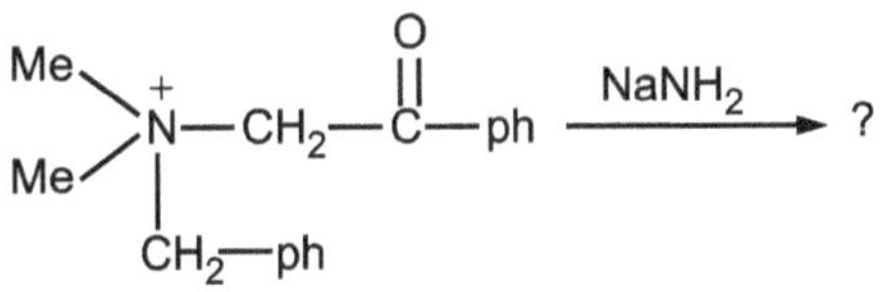 $\underset{Me}{\overset{Me}{>}}\overset{+}{\underset{\underset{CH_2-ph}{|}}{N}}-CH_2-\overset{O}{\overset{||}{C}}-ph \xrightarrow{NaNH_2}$?

(f) 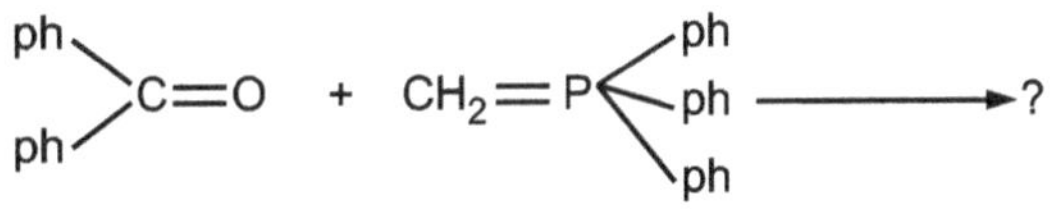 $\underset{ph}{\overset{ph}{>}}C=O + CH_2=P\underset{\underset{ph}{}}{\overset{ph}{<}}ph \longrightarrow$?

(g) 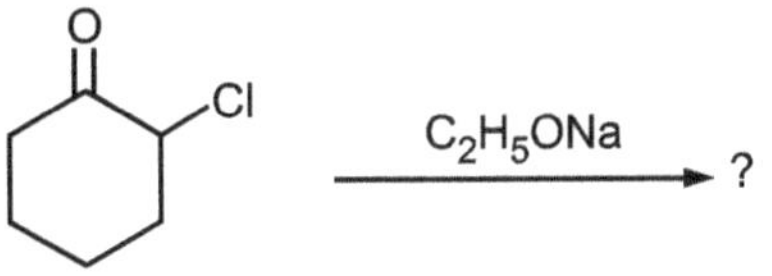 [cyclohexanone ring with Cl substituent] $\xrightarrow{C_2H_5ONa}$?

10. What is Quasi-Favorskii rearrangement.

11. Describe the reaction mechanism of Orton rearrangement.

12. Explain the reaction mechanism of Claisen rearrangement.

13. Give the applications and salient features of Claisen rearrangement.

14. Give one example of each type of the three possible rearrangements involving electron deficient atoms.

15. Describe the reaction mechanism of Fries rearrangement.

16. Write notes on:

   (a) Photo Fries reaction

   (b) Willegerdot reaction and

   (c) Cope rearrangement

17. Explain in brief the Free Radical rearrangement.

18. Why do carbonium ion rearrangements take place far more readily than those involving either a free radical or carbanion?

19. Is there inversion at the migration origin in a 1, 2-shift? Explain this by considering the conversion of camphene hydrochloride to isobornyl chloride.

20. Write the steps involved in the following reaction:

$$R - CONH_2 \xrightarrow[\text{H}_2\text{O}]{\text{Br}_2 \text{ / NaOH}} R - NH_2$$

21. Discuss the mechanism of the following transformation:

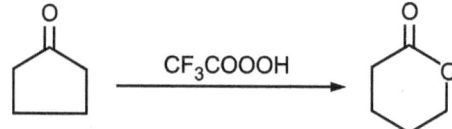

22. Rearrangement of phenolic esters in the presence of $AlCl_3$ yields ortho or para hydroxy ketones. What is the mechanism of this reaction? Is it one step or two step process?

23. Is Claisen rearrangement an intramolecular process? It has been observed that the migrant allyl group moves to ortho/para position, but never to a meta position. How do you explain this observation?

■■■

Chapter 3

CHEMISTRY OF
AMINO ACIDS AND PROTEINS

Syllabus ......

Classification and Structures of Natural Amino Acids, Iso Electric Point, General methods of preparation of Amino Acids, Peptide bonds and Proteins.

AMINO ACIDS

3.1 DEFINITION

"Amino acids are the compounds having one or more amino (–NH₂) groups and one or more carboxyl (–COOH) groups in the same molecule". They are usually classified into α, β, γ etc. according to the relative position of the two functional groups. But only the α-amino acids constitute the protein molecule, the term amino acid is generally used instead of the α-amino acid in reference to proteins.

$$\underset{\alpha\text{-amino propionic acid}}{\overset{NH_2}{\underset{\alpha}{CH_3-CH-COOH}}} \qquad \underset{\beta\text{-amino propionic acid}}{\overset{NH_2}{\underset{\beta}{CH_2-CH_2-COOH}}} \qquad \underset{\gamma\text{-amino butyric acid}}{\overset{NH_2}{\underset{\gamma}{CH_2-CH_2-CH_2-COOH}}}$$

The general structure of α-amino acid is

$$\overset{NH_2}{\underset{H}{R-C-COOH}}$$

However, other amino and carboxylic groups may be present; 'S' may also be present in certain acids and lastly the structure may be a cyclic one.

3.2 CLASSIFICATION OF AMINO ACIDS

Nearly 25 amino acids have been obtained from the hydrolysis of proteins. Except two (proline and hydroxy proline) all are amino acids, while the exceptional to proline and hydroxy proline are imino acids.

Amino acids are classified on the basis of nature of 'R' group as aliphatic amino acids and aromatic amino acids. Further 'R' group of some amino acids consist only of C and H. While in other 'R' group contains C, H, [O], N and S. The 'R' group may be neutral, acidic or basic. The classification is most widely used. Table 3.1 lists some common amino acids. It is important to note that, the "common names of amino acids are in prevalent usage and for convenience the common names are assigned" Three letter abbreviations in showing the structure of proteins".

Table 3.1: Common Amino Acids

Sr. No.	Common Name	Abbreviation	Structure
1.	Glycine	Gly	$H\!-\!\overset{\overset{H}{\mid}}{C}\!-\!COOH$ with NH_2 below
2.	Alanine	Ala	$CH_3\!-\!\overset{\overset{H}{\mid}}{C}\!-\!COOH$ with NH_2 below
3.	Valine	Val	$\begin{smallmatrix}CH_3\\CH_3\end{smallmatrix}\!\!\diagdown\!\!CH\!-\!\overset{\overset{H}{\mid}}{C}\!-\!COOH$ with NH_2 below
4.	Leucine	Leu	$\begin{smallmatrix}CH_3\\CH_3\end{smallmatrix}\!\!\diagdown\!\!CH\!-\!CH_2\!-\!\overset{\overset{H}{\mid}}{C}\!-\!COOH$ with NH_2 below
5.	Isoleucine	Ile	$CH_3\!-\!CH_2\!-\!\overset{\overset{CH_3}{\mid}}{CH}\!-\!\overset{\overset{H}{\mid}}{C}\!-\!COOH$ with NH_2 below
6.	Proline	Pro	pyrrolidine ring with N–H and –COOH

contd. ...

7.	Phenylalanine	Phe	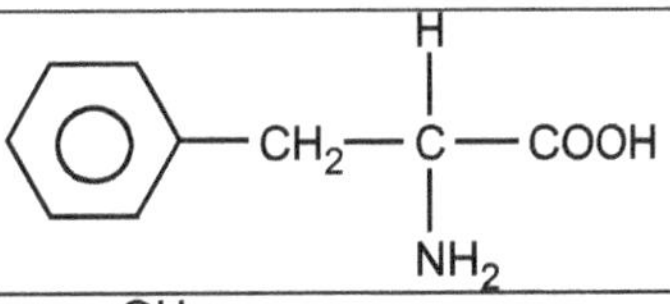
8.	Hydroxyproline	Hyp	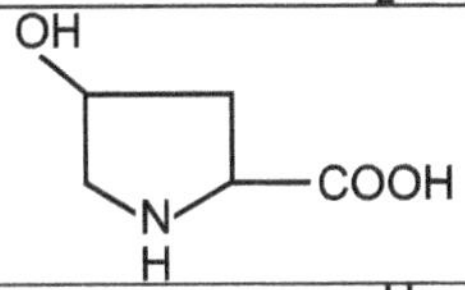
9.	Tyrosine	Tyr	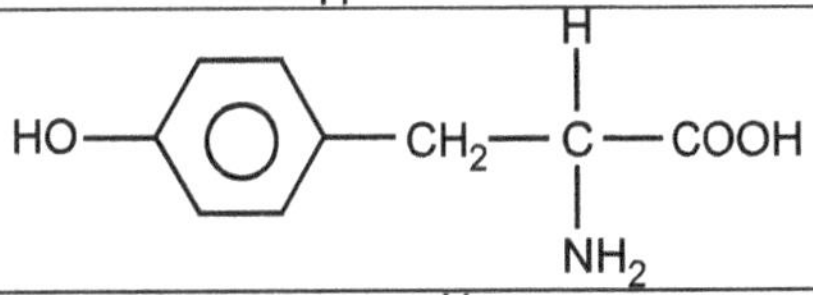
10.	Threonine	Thr	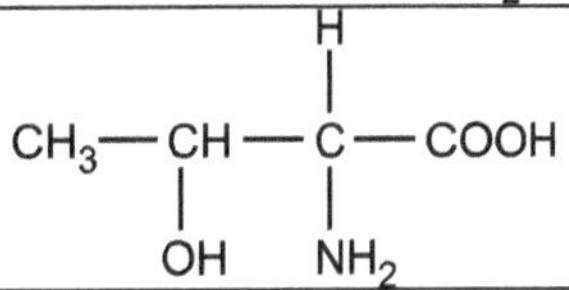
11.	Serine	Ser	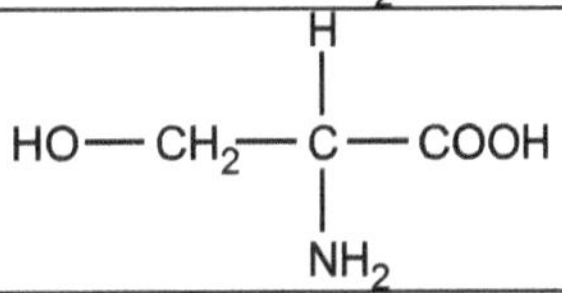
12.	Tryptophan	Try	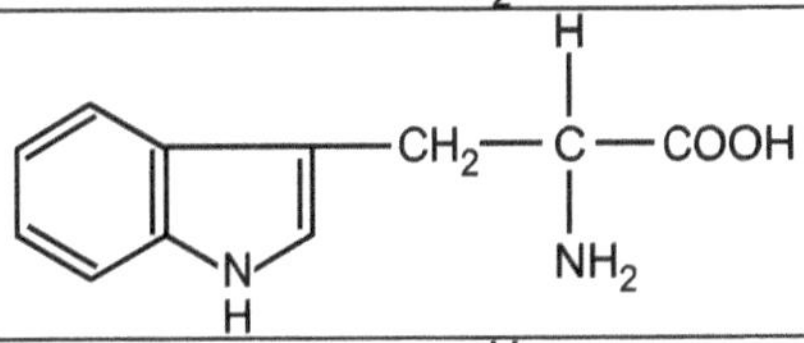
13.	Histidine	His	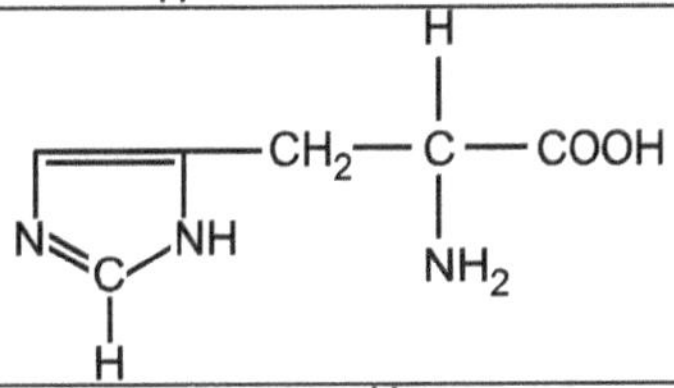
14.	Cysteine	cys or cys - SH	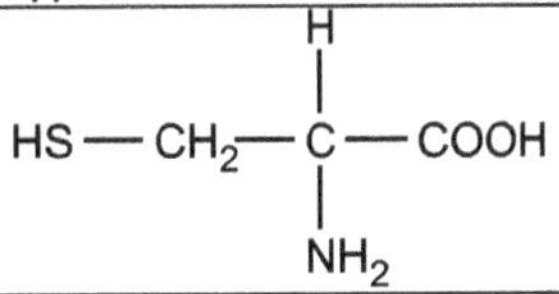
15.	Cystine (Dicysteine)	cys – cys or cys – S – S – cys	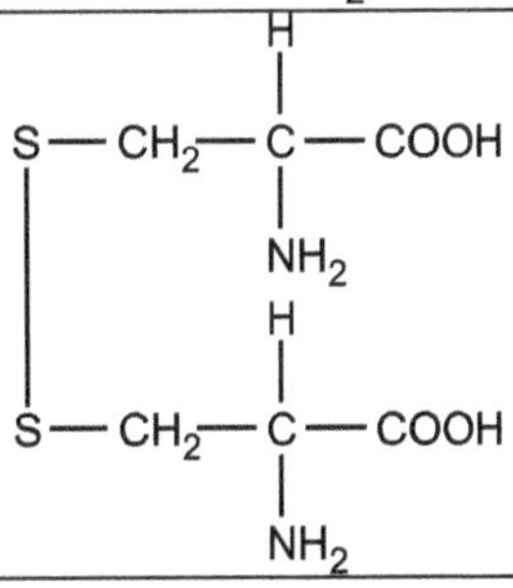

contd. ...

16.	Methionine	Met	$CH_3-S-CH_2-CH_2-\overset{\overset{\displaystyle H}{\vert}}{\underset{\underset{\displaystyle NH_2}{\vert}}{C}}-COOH$

Acidic Amino Acids (Monoamino Dicarboxylic Acids)

1.	Aspartic acid	Asp or Asp–NH$_2$	$HOOC-CH_2-\overset{\overset{\displaystyle H}{\vert}}{\underset{\underset{\displaystyle NH_2}{\vert}}{C}}-COOH$
2.	Glutamic acid	Glu or Glu–NH$_2$	$HOOC-CH_2-CH_2-\overset{\overset{\displaystyle H}{\vert}}{\underset{\underset{\displaystyle NH_2}{\vert}}{C}}-COOH$

Amides of Acidic Amino Acids

1.	Asparagine	Asn	$H_2NOC-CH_2-\overset{\overset{\displaystyle H}{\vert}}{\underset{\underset{\displaystyle NH_2}{\vert}}{C}}-COOH$
2.	Glutamine	Gln	$H_2NOC-CH_2-CH_2-\overset{\overset{\displaystyle H}{\vert}}{\underset{\underset{\displaystyle NH_2}{\vert}}{C}}-COOH$

Basic Amino Acids (Diamino Monocarboxylic Acids)

1.	Lysine	Lys	$H_2N-(CH_2)_4-\overset{\overset{\displaystyle H}{\vert}}{\underset{\underset{\displaystyle NH_2}{\vert}}{C}}-COOH$
2.	Hydroxy lysine	Hyl	$H_2N-CH_2-\overset{\overset{\displaystyle H}{\vert}}{\underset{\underset{\displaystyle OH}{\vert}}{C}}-CH_2-CH_2-\overset{\overset{\displaystyle H}{\vert}}{\underset{\underset{\displaystyle NH_2}{\vert}}{C}}-COOH$
3.	Arginine	Arg	$H_2N-\overset{\overset{\displaystyle NH}{\Vert}}{C}\cdot NH-CH_2-CH_2-CH_2-\overset{\overset{\displaystyle H}{\vert}}{\underset{\underset{\displaystyle NH_2}{\vert}}{C}}-COOH$

From the nutritional point of view, amino acids are of two types:

1. Non-essential amino acids (Dispensable)
2. Essential amino acids (Indispensable).

1. **Non-essential amino acids** are those which can be synthesized in the body and hence are not requisite components of the diet.

2. **Essential amino acids** are those which cannot be synthesized by the animal organism from substances ordinarily present in the diet at a speed of commensurate with normal growth and hence they are always supplied to organism in the form of dietary proteins.

The list of essential amino acids varies somewhat for different animals, however for man the following amino acids are essential.

Amino acid	Minimal daily requirement (gm)	Recommended daily intake (gm)
1. L-Tryptophan	0.25	0.50
2. L-Phenylalanine	1.10	2.20
3. L-Lysine	0.80	1.60
4. L-Threonine	0.50	1.00
5. L-Valine	0.80	1.60
6. L-Methionine	1.10	2.20
7. L-Leucine	1.10	2.20
8. L-Isoleucine	0.70	1.40

Blocking of amino acid metabolism in man may lead to certain diseases, which are then passed from generation to generation.

For example, a body that is unable to oxidize **phenyl alanine** and its metabolic product **phenyl pyruvic acid** will store these compounds in blood and urine which causes **phenylketonuria,** of which **mind feebleness** is one of the characteristics and hence **phenylketonuria**, of which **mind feebleness** is one of the characteristics and hence phenylketonuria have been found to possess intelligence quotient below 50. The initiative of the disease in some cases has been retarded by minimizing the amount of phenylalanine in the protein diet.

Sodium salt of glutamic acid which is manufactured from beet sugar residue by a microbial fermentation is used as a condiment and food flavour enhancer.

3.3 CHARACTERISTICS OF AMINO ACIDS

3.3.1 Physical Properties

Amino acids are colourless, crystalline compounds, generally soluble in water, acids, alkalies but sparingly soluble in organic solvents. Due to presence of basic and acidic groups in the same molecule they may be regarded as salts and hence most of them either possess higher M.P. or melt with decomposition. Except **glycine** all of the amino acids contain atleast one **chiral** center and hence they are **optically active** and can exist in 'd' and 'l' forms.

But it is very important to note that in nature they never exist in racemic form i.e. in nature they are always present in **optically active** forms. Further, all of the amino acids obtained from proteins are configurationally related to L(−) glyceraldehyde and are thus assigned L-series. But however, a few of the D-amino acids have been found in few sources, e.g. D-phenylalanine occurs in the polypeptide antibiotic **gramicidin-S'** discovered by a Russian scientist. Lastly, it should be remembered that in the synthetic amino acids only those belonging to L-series are found to possess biological activity.

Due to the presence of an acidic and a basic group in the same molecule, the amino acids exist largely as **dipolar** or **Zwitterions** or **inner salts** in which proton from carboxyl group has been transferred to the amino group and thus a dipolar ion contains both +ve and −ve charges.

$$NH_2 \qquad\qquad\quad {}^+NH_3$$
$$| \qquad\qquad\qquad |$$
$$R - CH - COOH \rightleftharpoons R - CH - COO^-$$

Amino acid   Zwitter ion

Isoelectric point: "The pH at which there is no net charge on the amino acid molecule and which does not migrate to any electrode under the influence of electric current is known as isoelectric point".

The isoelectric point of each amino acid is constant and as described earlier, an amino acid at pH values lower than that of its isoelectric point exists mainly as the anion II. While at pH values higher than that of its isoelectric point exists mainly as a cation-III.

Isoelectric Points of Amino Acids:

Amino acid	Isoelectric point	Amino acid	Isoelectric point
1. Glycine	6.0	13. Lysine	9.6
2. Alanine	6.0	14. Cysteine	5.1
3. Serine	5.7	15. Cystine	5.0
4. Threonine	5.6	16. Methionine	5.7
5. Valine	6.0	17. Phenylalanine	5.5
6. Leucine	6.0	18. Tyrosine	5.7
7. Isoleucine	6.0	19. Tyroxine	5.7
8. Aspartic acid	2.8	20. Proline	6.3
9. Asparagine	5.4	21. Hydroxyproline	5.7
10. Glutamic acid	3.2	22. Tryptophan	5.9
11. Glutamine	5.7	23. Histidine	7.5
12. Arginine	11.2		

Differences in isoelectric point are used for identification, isolation and purification of amino acids as well as proteins. Just by changing the pH of solution, we can precipitate different amino acids.

The amino acids at the isoelectric point are least soluble. Therefore, the order of precipitation can be varied by changing the pH of the solution. If the solution of amino acids is placed in an electric field, no migration takes place to either electrode because the negative charge exactly balances the positive charge.

At a pH greater than the isoelectric point, the amphoteric electrolyte has excess negative charge, moves towards anode and vice-versa.

Electrophoresis: The mixture of amino acids, peptides or proteins can be separated as they migrate in one direction and at different rates depending upon their isoelectric point and the pH of the solution. This process is called as **electrophoresis**.

Some amino acids like Tryptophan, Tyrosine and Phenylalanine absorb UV rays at 260-290 mμ. This property enables the identification of not only these amino acids but also the proteins which contain them.

3.3.2 Chemical Properties

I. Due to the carboxyl (– COOH) group:

1. Reaction with alcohols: Ethers are formed:

$$\underset{\overset{|}{\underset{\overset{|}{NH_2}}{R - CH - COOH}}}{} + R' - OH \longrightarrow R\ CH_2 - O - R' + NH_3 + CO_2$$

2. Action with NH₃: Corresponding amides are formed:

$$\begin{array}{l} CH_2 - COOH \\ | \\ CH - NH_2 - COOH \end{array} + NH_3 \longrightarrow \begin{array}{l} CH_2\ CONH_2 \\ | \\ CH - NH_2 - COOH \end{array} + H_2O$$

Aspartic acid

3. Decarboxylation:

$$\underset{\overset{|}{\underset{\overset{|}{NH_2}}{R - CH - COOH}}}{} \xrightarrow[\Delta]{Ba(OH)_2} RCH_2NH_2 + BaCO_3 + H_2O$$

Histidine   Histamine

In the presence of foreign protein introduced into the body, very large quantities of histamine are produced in the body and allergic reactions become evident. In extreme cases, shock may result. The physiological effects of histamine may be neutralized or minimized by the use of chemical compounds known as **antihistamines**.

II. Reactions due to $-NH_2$ group:

1. Alkylation:

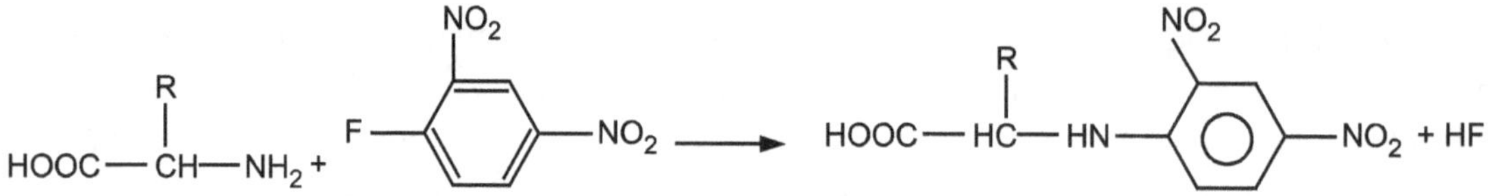

2. Action with HNO_2:

$$\underset{\underset{R-CH-COOH}{|}}{NH_2} + HONO \longrightarrow \underset{\underset{R-CH-COOH}{|}}{OH} + N_2 \uparrow + H_2O$$

III. Reactions due to Amino and Carboxyl group:

1. Action with Ninhydrin: Complex reaction → Brilliant blue colour.

But proline and hydroxy proline give yellow colour.

2. Formation of peptide bond:

$$\underset{\underset{HOOC-CH-NH_2}{|}}{R} + \underset{\underset{HOOC-CH-NH_2}{|}}{R'}$$

$$\longrightarrow \underset{\underset{HOOC-CH-NH-CO-CH-NH_2}{|\hspace{3.2cm}|}}{R\hspace{3.2cm}R'} + H_2O$$

Dipeptide

3. Formation of Diketopiperazine:

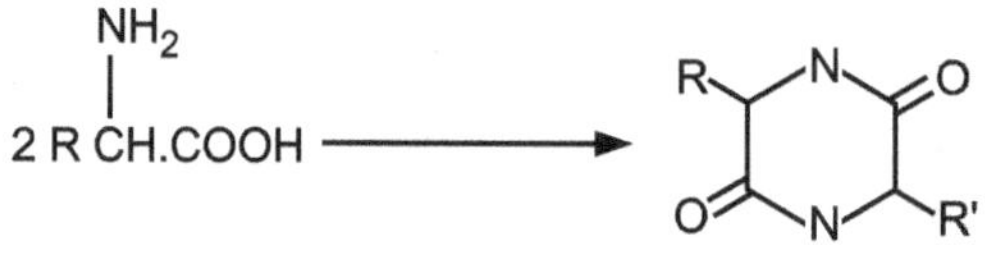

$$2\ R\ \overset{\overset{NH_2}{|}}{C}H.COOH \longrightarrow$$

3.4 METHODS OF PREPARATION OF AMINO ACIDS

1. Amination of α-Halogenated Acids:

(a) By action of NH_3: α-chloro and β-bromo acids, obtained by direct halogenation of carboxylic acid or by bromination of the corresponding malonic acids can be aminated by alcoholic, aq. or liquid NH_3. Generally, the bromo compounds show greater reactivity.

$$RCH_2COOH + X_2 \xrightarrow{\ PX_3\ } \underset{\underset{RCH-COOH}{|}}{X} + HX$$

$$\underset{\underset{R-CH-COOH}{|}}{X} + NH_3(excess) \longrightarrow \underset{\underset{R-CH-COOH}{|}}{NH_2} + NH_4X$$

For example, bromination of acetic acid in the presence of phosphorous tribromide gives α-halocarboxylic acid.

On amination of an α-halocarboxylic acid gives protein - Glycine.

$$CH_3 - \overset{\overset{O}{\|}}{C} - OH \xrightarrow[\text{(Bromination)}]{Br_2 / PBr_3} Br - CH_2 - \overset{\overset{O}{\|}}{C} - OH \xrightarrow[\text{(Excess)}]{NH_3}$$

Acetic acid   (Bromination)   α-halocarboxylic acid (Excess)

$$NH_2 - CH_2 - \overset{\overset{O}{\|}}{C} - OH$$
Glycine

This method is mainly used for the preparation of glycine, alanine, serine, threonine, valine, leucine and non-leucine.

The main precaution in this method is that a large excess of ammonia is required. If insufficient ammonia is used, formation of secondary or tertiary amines is a serious side reaction. In order to prevent the formation of 1° and 2° amines, ammonia (NH_3) may be replaced by hexamethylene-tetramine, hydrolysis of initial product is then necessary.

(b) Gabriel's phthalimide synthesis (1889): Due to side reactions, the above method is not suitable. However, better yields are obtained by using Gabriel's phthalimide synthesis. In this method, an **α-halogenated acid ester** is treated with **potassium phthalimide** to yield a substituted **phthalimide ester.** The latter compound yields the desired amino acid either by drastic hydrolysis or better in two steps by treatment first with hydrazine or 4 N alkali followed by acid hydrolysis.

Potassium phthalimide α-Bromo ethyl propionate

2. Strecker's Synthesis:

In Strecker's synthesis, an aldehyde is converted into an amino nitrile by the action of HCN and NH_3. Then the resulting amino nitrile is hydrolysed with an acid. The inconvenience of using HCN as a reagent is avoided, and the yields are frequently improved by use of ammonium salts and alkali cyanides instead of NH_3 and HCN respectively and by preceding conversion of the aldehyde into its bisulphite addition compound.

$$CH_3 - CH_2 - \underset{\underset{COOH}{|}}{\overset{\overset{NH_2}{|}}{C}} - CH_2CH_3$$

Remark: It is important to describe the condition, name of the chemical used, reaction condition, intermediate rms and initial and final product obtained for serving the purpose as a proper textbook, then one actual example should also be solved.

Except for alanine (R = CH₃), relatively poor yields are obtained by this classical procedure. However, a substantial improvement was found by Bucherer. In this method, the cyanohydrins are heated with urea or better ammonium carbonate in alcoholic solution to yield higher percentage of the corresponding 5-substituted hydantoins. The latter compounds on hydrolysis with alkali or conc. acid yield the desired amino acids.

Practical large-scale synthesis of glycine, alanine, serine, valine, methionine, glutamic acid, leucine, isoleucine and phenylalanine have been based on Strecker and Bucherer synthesis.

Example 2: Strecker synthesis:

Benzaldehyde   Sodium   Ammonium   Benzimine
               cyanide   chloride

$$C_6H_5 - \underset{\underset{COOH}{|}}{\overset{\overset{NH_2}{|}}{CH}}$$

Benza-amino acid

Example 3:

$$(CH_3CH_2)_2C = O + NaCN + NH_4Cl \xrightarrow{H_2O}$$

3-pentanone   Sodium cyanide   Ammonium chloride

$$(CH_3CH_2) - \overset{\overset{\displaystyle NH_2}{|}}{C} - CN \xrightarrow[(\Delta)]{H_3O^+} CH_3 - CH_2 - \overset{\overset{\displaystyle NH_2}{|}}{\underset{\underset{\displaystyle COOH}{|}}{C}} - CH_2 - CH_3$$

3-amino-3-pentanoic acid

Example: Synthesis of lysine.

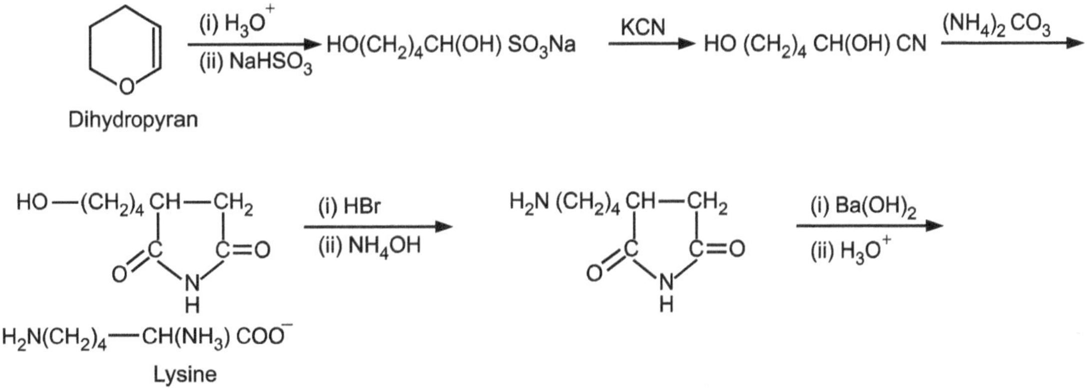

Dihydropyran

$$\xrightarrow[(ii) NaHSO_3]{(i) H_3O^+} HO(CH_2)_4CH(OH) SO_3Na \xrightarrow{KCN} HO (CH_2)_4 CH(OH) CN \xrightarrow{(NH_4)_2 CO_3}$$

$$HO-(CH_2)_4 CH-CH_2 \xrightarrow[(ii) NH_4OH]{(i) HBr} H_2N (CH_2)_4 CH-CH_2 \xrightarrow[(ii) H_3O^+]{(i) Ba(OH)_2}$$

$$H_2N(CH_2)_4-CH(NH_3) COO^-$$

Lysine

3. Malonic Ester Synthesis:

Malonic ester

$$CH_2 \Big\langle \begin{matrix} COOC_2H_5 \\ COOC_2H_5 \end{matrix} \xrightarrow[RX]{C_2H_5ONa} RCH (COOC_2H_5)_2 \xrightarrow[(ii) HCl]{(i) KOH} RCH (COOH)_2 \xrightarrow[- HBr]{Br_2}$$

$$R-CBr (COOH)_2 \xrightarrow{\Delta} R CHBr COOH \xrightarrow{NH_3} R CH (NH_2) COOH$$

4. Albertson Method:

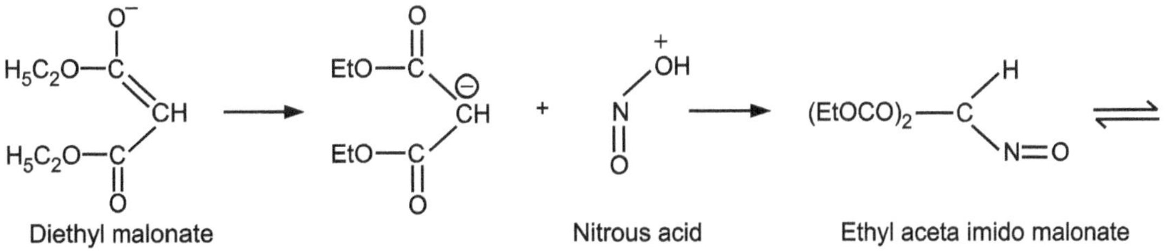

Diethyl malonate   Nitrous acid   Ethyl aceta imido malonate

$$(EtOCO)_2C = NOH \xrightarrow[\text{or } H_2/Ni]{H_2 \text{ (Pt)}} (EtOCO)_2CHNH_2 \xrightarrow{(CH_3CO_2)} (EtOCO)_2CN\,NH\,COCH_3$$

$$\xrightleftharpoons[B^{H+}]{B} (EtOCO)_2\bar{C}NHCOCH_3 \xrightarrow[-X]{RX} (EtOCO)_2 - \overset{\overset{\displaystyle R}{|}}{C}NHCOCH_3 \xrightarrow{H_3O^+}$$

$$(HOCO)_2 C(R)NHCOCH_3 \xrightarrow{-CO_2} HOCOCH(R)\,NHCOCH_3 \xrightarrow{H_3O^+} HOCOCH(R)\,NH_3{}^+$$

5. Curtius Reaction:

By this method, the amino acids like glycine, alanine, phenylalanine and valine can be prepared.

$$CH_2(COOC_2H_5)_2 \xrightarrow[RX]{C_2H_5ONa} RCH(COOC_2H_5)_2 \xrightarrow{KOH} RHC\overset{\displaystyle COOK}{\underset{\displaystyle COOC_2H_5}{\diagdown}} \xrightarrow{N_2H_4}$$

$$RHC\overset{\displaystyle COOK}{\underset{\displaystyle CONHNH_2}{\diagdown}} \xrightarrow{HNO_2} RHC\overset{\displaystyle COOH}{\underset{\displaystyle CON_3}{\diagdown}} \xrightarrow{EtOH} RHC\overset{\displaystyle COOH}{\underset{\displaystyle NHCOOC_2H_5}{\diagdown}} \xrightarrow{HCl} RCH(NH)_2COOH$$

Acid azide

6. Hoffmann's Degradation Method:

$$RHC\overset{\displaystyle COOC_2H_5}{\underset{\displaystyle CONH_2}{\diagdown}} \xrightarrow{Br_2/KOH} RHC\overset{\displaystyle COOC_2H_5}{\underset{\displaystyle NH_2}{\diagdown}} \xrightarrow{HOH} RHC\overset{\displaystyle COOH}{\underset{\displaystyle NH_2}{\diagdown}}$$

7. Darapsky Synthesis:

$$RCHO + H_2C\overset{\displaystyle CN}{\underset{\displaystyle COOC_2H_5}{\diagdown}} \xrightarrow[Ni]{H_2} RCH_2HC\overset{\displaystyle CN}{\underset{\displaystyle COOC_2H_5}{\diagdown}} \xrightarrow[\text{(ii) } HNO_2]{\text{(i) } N_2H_4}$$

$$R\,CH_2HC\overset{\displaystyle CN}{\underset{\displaystyle CON_3}{\diagdown}} \xrightarrow{C_2H_5OH} R\,CH_2HC\overset{\displaystyle CN}{\underset{\displaystyle NHCOOC_2H_5}{\diagdown}} \xrightarrow{HCl} RCH_2CH(NH_2)COOH$$

8. By reducing α-ketonic acids or their derivatives:

$$R-\overset{\overset{\displaystyle O}{||}}{C}-COOH + NH_3 \xrightarrow{H_2/Pd} \left[R\,\overset{\overset{\displaystyle}{\underset{\underset{\displaystyle NH}{||}}{C}}}{}-COOH \right] \longrightarrow RCH(NH_2)\,COOH$$

α-ketonic acid   Ammonia   Alkyl imido acid   Alkyl amino acid

9. Schmidt Reaction:

$$CH_3COCHR\,COOC_2H_5 + NH_3 \xrightarrow[-N_2]{H_2SO_4} CH_3CONHCHRCOOC_2H_5 \xrightarrow{H_2O}$$

Alkylacetoacetic ester $RCH(NH_2)COOH$

10. Erlenmeyer Azlactone Synthesis:

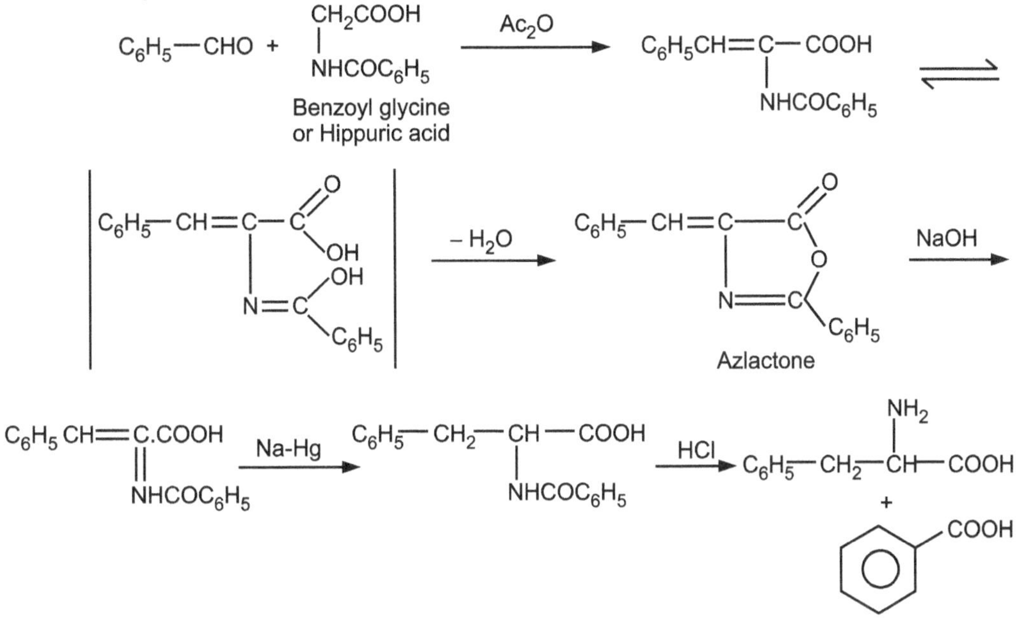

$$C_6H_5-CHO + \begin{matrix} CH_2COOH \\ | \\ NHCOC_6H_5 \end{matrix} \xrightarrow{Ac_2O} \begin{matrix} C_6H_5CH=C-COOH \\ | \\ NHCOC_6H_5 \end{matrix} \rightleftharpoons$$

Benzoyl glycine
or Hippuric acid

$$\left| \begin{matrix} C_6H_5-CH=C-C \\ \end{matrix} \right| \xrightarrow{-H_2O} C_6H_5-CH=C-C \xrightarrow{NaOH}$$

Azlactone

$$\begin{matrix} C_6H_5\,CH=C.COOH \\ \| \\ NHCOC_6H_5 \end{matrix} \xrightarrow{Na-Hg} \begin{matrix} C_6H_5-CH_2-CH-COOH \\ | \\ NHCOC_6H_5 \end{matrix} \xrightarrow{HCl} \begin{matrix} NH_2 \\ | \\ C_6H_5-CH_2-CH-COOH \end{matrix}$$

$$+$$

COOH

11. Hydantoin's synthesis:

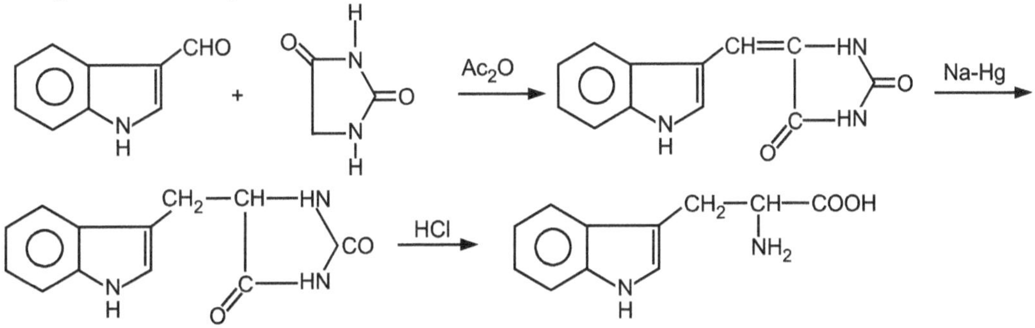

12. Bucherer's Hydantoin Synthesis:

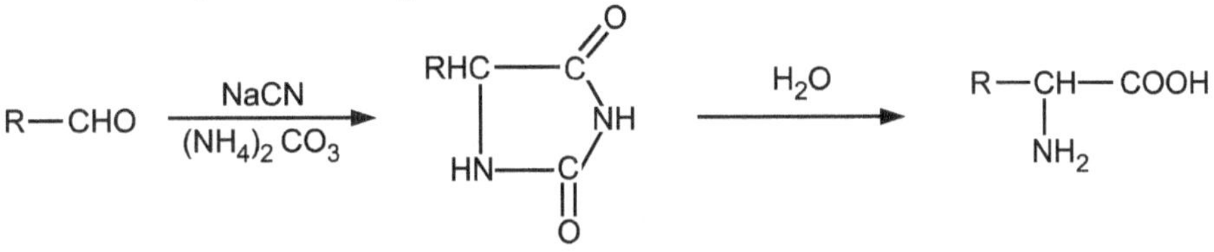

$$R-CHO \xrightarrow[\text{(NH}_4)_2\,CO_3]{NaCN} \begin{matrix} RHC-C \\ | \quad \backslash NH \\ HN-C \end{matrix} \xrightarrow{H_2O} \begin{matrix} R-CH-COOH \\ | \\ NH_2 \end{matrix}$$

13. Synthesis via Diketopiperazine:

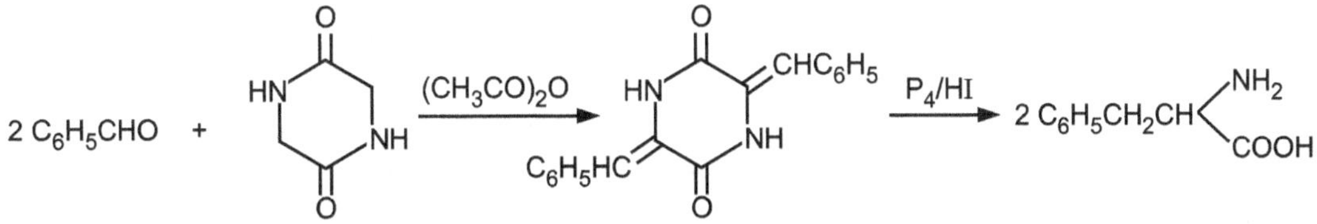

$$2\,C_6H_5CHO + \text{[Diketopiperazine]} \xrightarrow{(CH_3CO)_2O} \text{[intermediate]} \xrightarrow{P_4/HI} 2\,C_6H_5CH_2CH \begin{matrix} NH_2 \\ \backslash \\ COOH \end{matrix}$$

Benzaldehyde   Diketopiperazine

3.5 PEPTIDES

A peptide is composed of two or more amino acids joined through peptide bonds. The term peptide bond is applied to the amide link between amino acid residues.

$$-\overset{O}{\overset{\|}{C}} - \overset{H}{\overset{|}{N}} -$$

When two amino acids combine to form a dipeptide, a water molecule is removed from the α-carboxyl group of one amino acid and α-amino group of other.

Dipeptides:

Example 1: Glycylalanine (gly. ala.):

Glycine   Alanine   Peptide linkage

Example 2:

N-terminal residue   C-terminal residue

Glycylalanine
(gly. ala.)
(Dipeptide)

A tripeptide glycine, alanine and phenylalanine, where glycine is the N-terminal amino acid and phenylalanine is the C-terminal amino acid.

Similarly, tripeptides are formed by the linkage of 3 amino-acids, tetrapeptides by linkage of 4 amino acids and so on. When many amino acids are joined together, the compound is called a **polypeptide**.

The number of peptide bonds in a peptide is one less than the number of amino acid residues. By convention, a peptide chain is drawn with the amino-acid residue containing the free ammonium group (the N-terminal amino acid residue) on the left hand side and the residue containing the free carboxylate group (the C-terminal amino acid residue) on the right hand side.

Peptides generally show IR bands near 3300, 3100 cm^{-1} and 1650, 1550 cm^{-1}. The bands near 3300 and 3100 cm^{-1} are characteristic of hydrogen bonded N-H group whereas bonds near 1650 and 1550 cm^{-1} are characteristic of $>C = O$ group.

3.5.1 Naturally Occurring Peptides

Name of peptide	Biological significance	Number of amino acid residues
1. Adrenocorticotropic Hormone (ATCN)	Stimulator cortex of adrenal gland	39
2. Glutathione	Biological reducing agent	03
3. Bacitracin	Antibiotic	12
4. Gramicidin A.	Antibiotic	10

3.5.2 Synthesis of Peptides

General principles of Polypeptide Synthesis:

For the synthesis of polypeptide, one should keep the following points in view:

1. Protection of the amino group
2. Protection of the carboxyl groups
3. Protection of the side chains of amino acids
4. Activation of the carboxyl group

1. Protection of the Amino Group:

A good protecting group must exhibit the following characteristics.

(a) It should be easily introduced in the amino group without causing racemization of an optically active acid.

(b) It should be removable under sufficiently mild conditions without affecting the peptide linkage or sensitive functional groups which are present on the amino acid side chains. For example, the sulphur containing the groups of cysteine, cystine and methionine.

(c) It must remain inert during the formation of a peptide bond.

Some amino group protecting agents are:

(i) Benzyloxy carbonyl (carbobenzyloxy) – $C_6H_5CH_2OCOCl$

(ii) t-Butyloxycarbonyl (BOC: Carbo-t-butyloxy) – $(CH_3)_3COCONHCHRCOOH$

(iii) Phthaloyl group

(iv) Tosyl group (p-toluene sulphonyl chloride) – $CH_3C_6H_4SO_2Cl$

(v) Trityl group (Triphenylmethyl chloride (trityl chloride)) – $(C_6H_5)_3CCl$.

(vi) o-Nitrophenyl sulphonyl group:

2. Protection of the Carboxyl groups:

Numerous examples are available in the literature in which there is no need for protecting the carboxyl group. In such cases, the formation of the peptide bond has to be carried out in aqueous alkaline solution.

In general, the usual method for protecting a carboxyl group is esterification.

$$RCH(NH_2)COOH + R'OH \text{ (excess)} \xrightarrow{H^+} RCH(NH_2)COOR'$$

3. Protection of side chains of Amino Acids:

Sulphahydryl groups: The sulphahydryl group (i.e. Thiol group) in the side chain of cysteine is a powerful nucleophile especially in the anionic form. Therefore, it must be protected during peptide synthesis. The S-benzyl is generally used as the masking group for the cysteine. S-Benzyl cysteine is prepared by treating cysteine in the form of a sodium salt in liq. NH_3 with benzyl chloride.

Guanidine groups: The guanidine group in the side chain of arginine is strongly basic. The protection of arginine side chain is best done by nitration of the amino acid with a mixture of concentrated HNO_3 and fuming H_2SO_4. The N-nitro group can be removed by hydrogenolysis, although the reaction is usually slow and requires a high concentration of catalyst.

4. Activation of the Carboxyl group:

The carboxyl group needs activation which can be done by converting the – OH of the carboxyl acid to a better leaving group.

For example, if OH is replaced by X such as in acid chlorides the reaction is facilitated.

The other activating groups are:

1. Acid chlorides
2. Esters
3. Mixed anhydrides
4. Acid azides
5. DCC: (N, N'-Dicyclohexylcarbodiimide).

3.5.3 Some Methods for Synthesis of Polypeptides

(a) Bergmann's Synthesis (1932):

In this method, benzyloxy carbonyl chloride is used as an amino protecting group which is readily prepared by the action of carbonyl chloride on benzyl alcohol in toluene solution.

$$C_6H_5CH_2OH + COCl_2 \xrightarrow{\text{Toluene}} C_6H_5CH_2OCOCl + HCl$$

From benzyloxy carbonyl chloride, polypeptide is prepared as:

$$C_6H_5CH_2OCOCl + R_1 - CH - COOH \xrightarrow{OH^-} C_6H_5CH_2OCONH - \overset{\overset{\displaystyle R_1}{|}}{CH} - COOH \xrightarrow{PCl_5}$$

$$\underset{|}{\overset{}{}}$$
$$NH_2$$

$$C_6H_5CH_2OCONHCHR_1COCl \xrightarrow{R_2CH(NH_2)COOH}$$

$$C_6H_5CH_2 OCO NHCH R_1CONH CHR_2COOH \xrightarrow{H_2 - Pd}$$

$$H_2N - CHR_1CONHCHR_2COOH + C_6H_5CH_3 + CO_2 \uparrow$$

Toluene

Catalytic reduction cannot be used if the amino acid contains sulphur which poisons the catalyst. In such a case, the blocking group i.e. benzyloxy carbonyl group may be removed by using sodium in liquid NH_3.

(b) Azide Method:

In this method, acyl azides have been employed as reagents for synthesizing peptides. The azide synthesis is not accompanied by racemisation and this explains the continued popularity of the method. The main disadvantage of this method is that it involves too many steps:

$$C_6H_5CH_2OCOCl + R_1CH(NH_2)COOH \xrightarrow{OH^-} C_6H_5CH_2OCONH CH R'COOH \xrightarrow{CH_3OH}$$

$$C_6H_5CH_2OCONHCHR_1COOCH_3 \xrightarrow{N_2H_4} C_6H_5CH_2OCONHCHR_1CONH - NH_2 \xrightarrow{HNO_3}$$

$$C_6H_5CH_2OCONHCHR_1CON_3 \xrightarrow{NH_2CHR_2COOCH_3}$$

$$C_6H_5CH_2OCONH CHR_1CONH \cdot CHR_2COOCH_3 \xrightarrow{Acid}$$

$$C_6H_5CH_2OCONHCHR_1CHNH \cdot CH R_2COOH \xrightarrow{H_2 \cdot Pd} H_2N \cdot CHR_1CONHCHR_2COOH$$

(c) Trityl Method:

In this synthesis, trityl reagent is used as an amino protecting group. This group may be removed by heating in acetic acid or catalytically H_2-Pd.

$$(C_6H_5)_3CCl + NH_2CHR_1COOCH_3 \xrightarrow{Et_3N} (C_6H_5)_3CNHCHR_1COOCH_3 \xrightarrow[\text{(ii) } CH_3COOH]{\text{(i) NaOH}}$$

Trityl chloride

$$(C_6H_5)_3CNHCHR_1COOH \xrightarrow[\text{(ii) } NH_2CHR_2COOH]{\text{(i) } SoCl_2} (C_6H_5)_3CNHCHR_1CONHCR_2COOH$$

$$\xrightarrow{CH_3COOH} NH_2CHR_1CONHCHR_2COOH + (C_6H_5)_3COOCH_3$$

(d) Sheehan's Method (1940):

In this method, phthaloyl group is used as an amino protecting group.

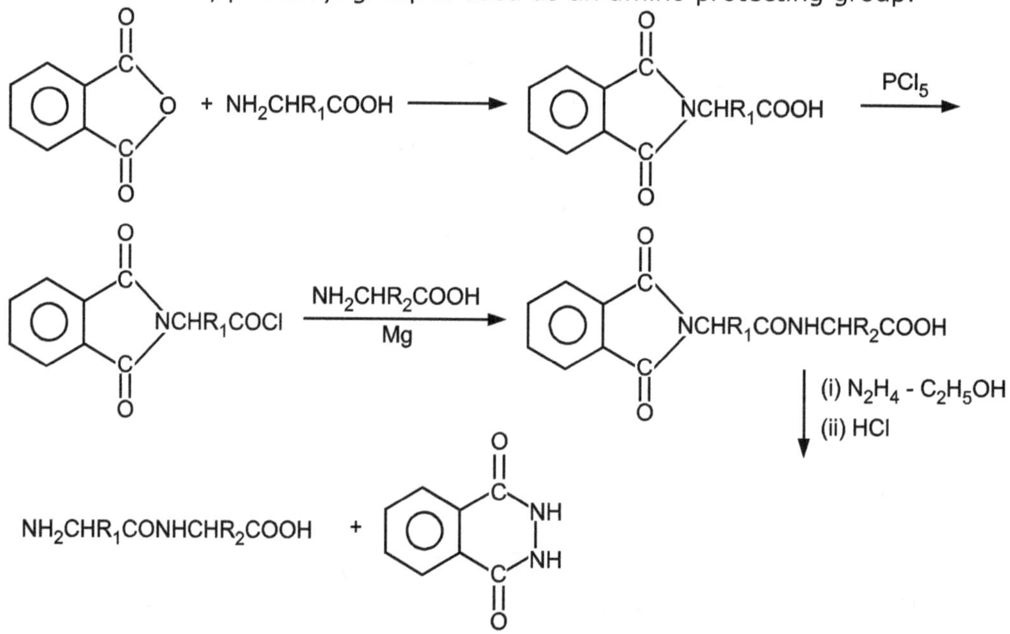

If the temperature does not exceed above 150°C, phthalolylation occurs without racemisation.

(e) Fischer Method (1919):

In this method, tosyl chloride is employed as an amino protecting group. In this synthesis, no racemisation occurs.

$$TsCl + NH_2CHR_1COOH \xrightarrow[\text{(ii) } CH_3COOH]{\text{(i) NaOH}} TsNHCHR_1COOH \xrightarrow{SoCl_2}$$

$$TsNHCHR_1COCl \xrightarrow{NH_2CHR_2COOH} TsNHCHR_1CONHCHR_2COOH \xrightarrow{Na/liq.\ NH_3}$$

$$NH_2CHR_1CONHCHR_2COOH.$$

(f) Anhydride Method:

This method involves the following steps:

$$PhCH_2OH + COCl_2 \longrightarrow PhCH_2OCOCl + HCl$$

$$PhCH_2OCOCl + R_1CH(NH_2)COOH \xrightarrow{OH^-} PhCH_2OCONHCHRCOOH \xrightarrow{PCl_5}$$

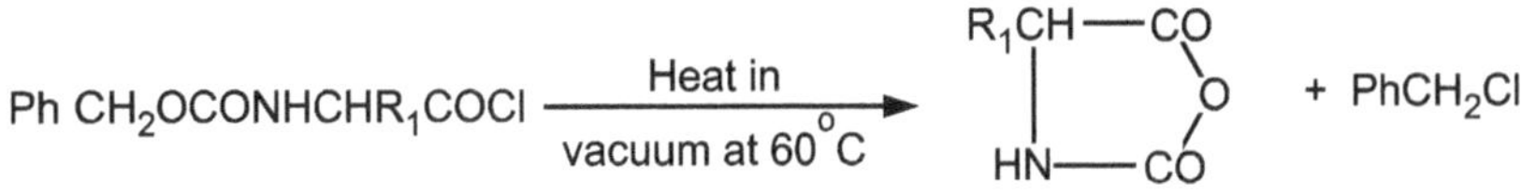

N-Carboxy anhydride (NCA)

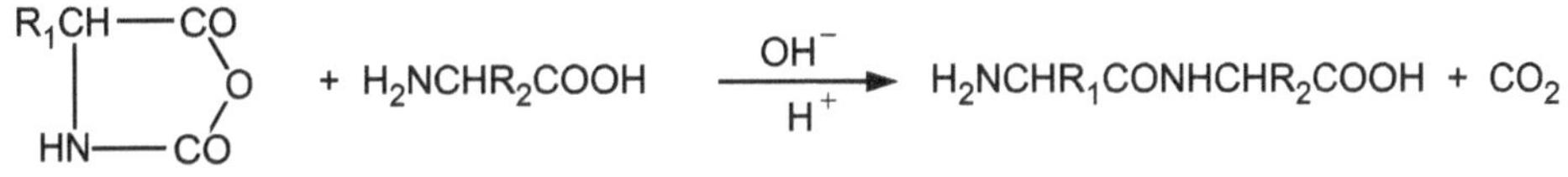

(g) Ethoxyacetylene Method:

Addition of carboxylic acid component to ethoxyacetylene yields acylal-acetate which undergo nucleophilic attack by the amino component to form peptide and ethyl acetate.

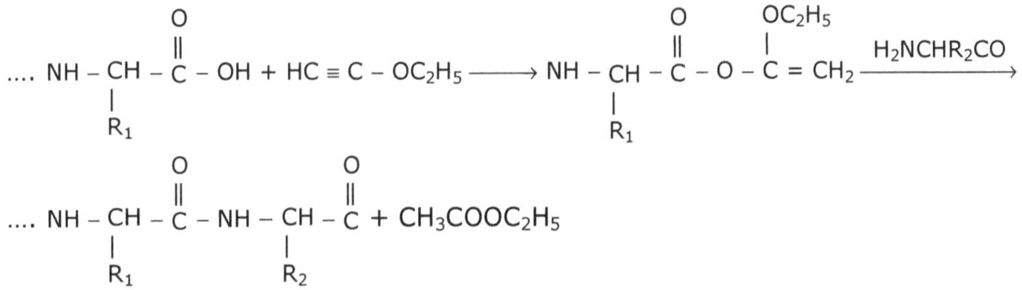

3.5.4 Synthesis of Peptides on a Solid Support

The usual methods employed for the synthesis of peptides suffer from the following disadvantages:

1. It has became a very laborious and time consuming operation because the formation of each peptide bond requires the preparation of an appropriately protected amino acid, coupling and deprotection steps.

2. For each peptide synthesis, reaction condition have to be investigated and optimised with great care to obtain adequate yield and to avoid side reactions.

3. The isolation and separation of peptide formed at the end of reaction require considerable skill and experience.

Synthesis of Peptide: Glycylalanine (Gly. Ala)

Step 1: The amino group of glycine is protected by treatment with benzyl chloroformate.

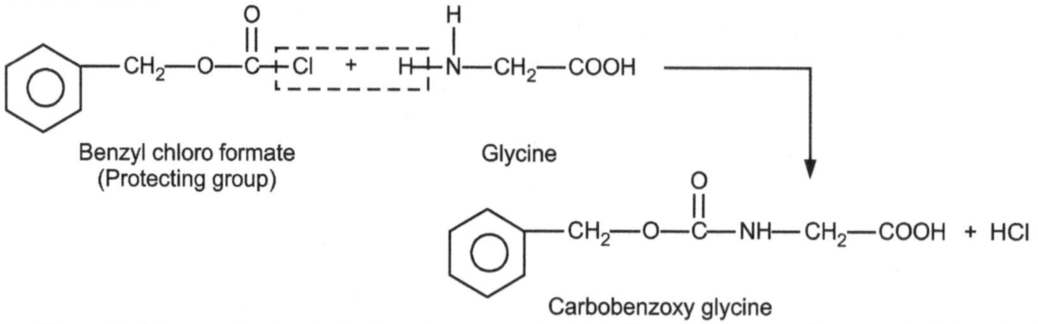

Benzyl chloro formate
(Protecting group)

Glycine

Carbobenzoxy glycine

Step 2: The protected glycine is converted to the corresponding acid chloride by treatment with thionyl chloride.

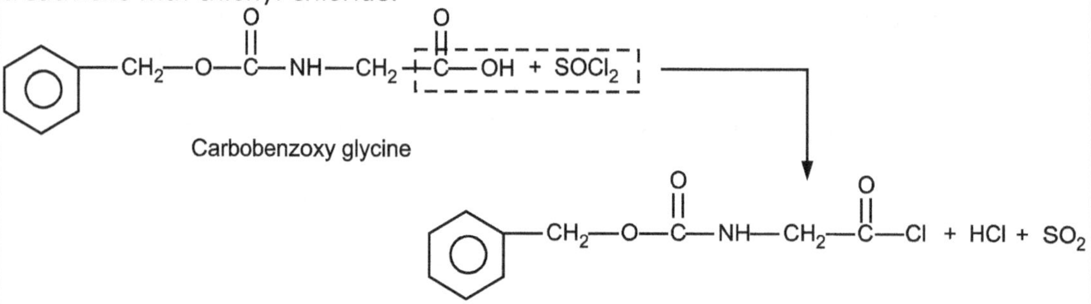

Carbobenzoxy glycine

Step 3: The acid chloride is condensed with alanine.

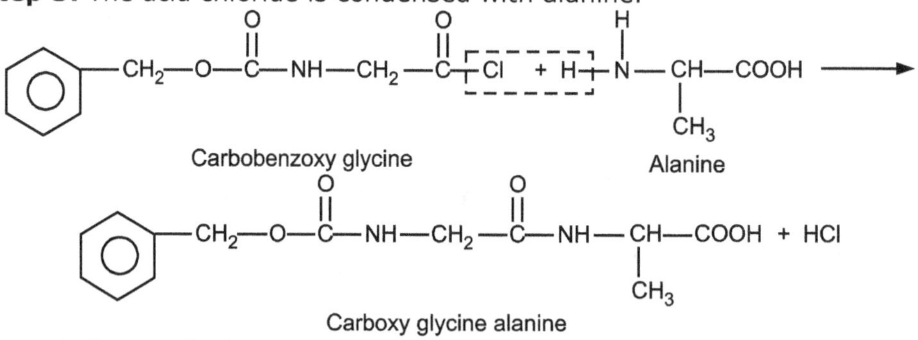

Carbobenzoxy glycine

Alanine

Carboxy glycine alanine

Step 4: Removal of protecting group:

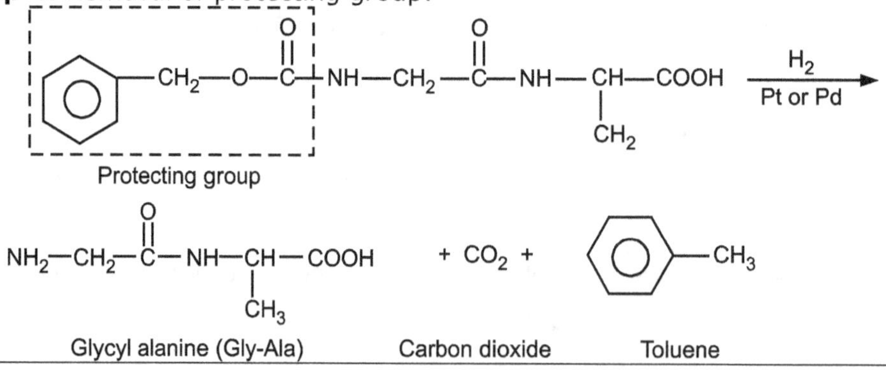

Protecting group

Glycyl alanine (Gly-Ala)

Carbon dioxide

Toluene

Due to above disadvantages, Merrifield (1965) introduced the **solid phase procedure**.

In Merrifield's method, an amino acid or peptide is covalently linked to an insoluble synthetic resin as a support for the peptide and then the chain is build up, one amino acid residue at a time. As soon as the desired peptide has been synthesized, it is liberated from the solid support.

The resin is a copolymer of styrene and DVB in which some of the aromatic rings are chloromethylated and nitrated(I). A suitable N-acyl (e.g. t-butyloxy carbonyl) derivative of the C-terminal amino acid of the peptide to be synthesized is heated under reflux with the resin and $3°$ base in a suitable solvent to convert it into an insoluble benzyl ester derivative (II). The N-acyl group is removed by acid hydrolysis in the presence of triethyl amine to yield the product (III). Then, a dipeptide derivative (IV) is formed, by coupling an N-acyl amino acid using N, N'-dicyclohexylcarbodiimide. By following this procedure, the polypeptide chain is extended. When the desired peptide has been synthesized the ester bond linking it to the resin may be split up by dry HBr in trifluoroacetic acid.

The advantages are:

(i)   As insoluble solid support is used in this process, there is no need for purification of the product.

(ii) This gives high yield.

(iii) The time consumed is considerably of short duration.

PROTEINS

3.6 DEFINITION

Proteins are biopolymers of high molecular weight containing large number of amino acids joined to each other by peptide bonds. These are complex nitrogenous substances which are found in the protoplasm of all animal and plant cells. Most of the proteins were found to contain 46-55% carbon, 12-30% hydrogen, 10-32% nitrogen and 0.2-0.3% sulphur.

3.7 CLASSIFICATION OF PROTEINS

(A) On the basis of Solubility:

1. Fibrous proteins: These are insoluble in common solvents but are soluble in concentrated acids and alkalies. These are highly resistant to digestion by proteolytic enzymes. These proteins appear as fibres made of linear molecules that are arranged roughly parallel to the fibre axis. The long linear protein chains are held together by intermolecular hydrogen bonds.

e.g. silk, wool, skin, hair, horn, nails, hoofs, quills, connective tissue and bone.

2. Globular proteins: These are soluble in water and in dilute acids, alkalies and salts. These proteins are more highly branched and **cross-linked condensation products** of basic or acidic amino acids. The polypeptide chains in this topic of proteins are held together by cross-linked groups or in an aggregate state. Such aggregates may also be folded to 3-dimensional structures by weak non-covalent bonds.

For example, enzymes, oxygen carrying proteins, hormones etc.

(B) On the basis of increasing complexity into their structures:

1. Simple proteins
2. Conjugated proteins and
3. Derived proteins.

1. Simple proteins:

These are such proteins which upon hydrolysis yield amino acids or their derivatives. These include the following groups:

(a) **Albumins:** These are soluble in water, coagulated by heat and precipitated by saturated salt solution like ammonium sulphate. These are usually low or deficient in glycine.

For example, lactalbumin, serum albumin and egg albumin.

(b) **Globulins:** These are soluble in dilute solution of strong acids and bases. These are insoluble in pure water or in moderately concentrated salt solution. These are coagulated by heat. These are precipitated by half saturating their solution with ammonium sulphate. They generally contain glycine.

For example, serum globulin, tissue globulin and vegetable globulin.

(c) Glutelins: These are soluble in dilute acids and alkalies, insoluble in neutral salts coagulated by heat, rich in arginine, proline and glutamic acid.

For example, wheat glutenin and oyrzenin from rice.

(d) Prolamines: These are soluble in 70-90% ethanol, insoluble in absolute alcohol, water and other neutral solvents. These contain large amount of proline but are deficient in lysine.

For example, zein from maize, gladin from wheat and hordein from barley.

(e) Albuminoids (Scleroproteins): These are insoluble in all neutral solvents in dilute acids and alkalies. These are the proteins of supportive tissues.

For example, keratin from hair, hoof, etc. and fibroin from silk. These are, attacked by enzymes.

Albuminoids are further subdivided into two types: (i) Collagens and (ii) Elastins.

(i) Collagens: More than half the total protein in the mammalian body is collagen. When collagens are boiled with water, a water soluble protein gelatin is obtained. The collagens appear to be unique in their high content of hydroxyprolines and it containing hydroxy lysine. They are poor in sulphur since, cysteine and cystine are absent and contain no tryptophan. Collagens are found in skin, tendons and bones. They are attacked by pepsin or trypsin.

(ii) Elastins: These are present in tendon, arteries and other elastic tissues. Although similar to collagens in many respect, they cannot be converted into gelatin and are attacked slowly by trypsin.

(f) Basic proteins: These are strongly basic and are further divided into two subclasses i.e. (i) Histones and (ii) Protamines.

(i) Histones: These are basic proteins which are soluble in water or dil. acids but are insoluble in dil. NH_3. These are not coagulated by heat. These are rich in basic amino acids like histidine and arginine but deficient in tryptophan and contains little cystine or methionine. These are readily hydrolysed by pepsin and trypsin. These can be extracated in large amount from certain glandular tissues such as thymus and pancreas. Most histones are combined with nucleic acids, haemoglobins etc.

(ii) Protamines: These are more basic than histones. These have a simpler structure of relatively low molecular weight. These are soluble in water or in NH_4OH. These are not coagulated by heat. They contain no 'S' but have a high nitrogen content (25-30%) due to the presence of large quantities of arginine. Tyrosine and tryptophan are absent, protamines are hydrolysed by enzymes like trypsin, papain but not by pepsin.

For example, salmine from salmon sperm, protamins of egg cells.

2. Conjugated proteins:

These are the proteins which contain same non-protein substance called **prosthetic group**. This group may be separated from protein by hydrolysis very carefully.

Types:

(a) Nucleoproteins: In these proteins, the prosthetic group is a nucleic acid.

For example, Nuclein.

(b) Chromoproteins: Here prosthetic group is a chromophoric group called coloured prosthetic group.

For example, Haemoglobin, Hemocyanin, Cytochrome, Flavoproteins.

(c) Glycoproteins: These proteins have carbohydrate as prosthetic group.

For example, egg albumin and serum albumin and globulins.

(d) Phosphoproteins: In these proteins, the prosthetic group is phosphoric acid.

For example, Caesin.

(e) Lipoproteins: In these proteins, the prosthetic groups are phospholipid and cholesterol.

For example, lipoproteins of serum.

(f) Metalloproteins: These are conjugated proteins, that contain a metal which is an integral part of the structure. Metals found in metalloproteins are generally Fe, Mg, Cu and Mn.

For example, Haemoglobin and Chlorophyll.

3. Derived proteins:

When proteins are hydrolysed by acids, alkalies or enzymes, the degradation products obtained from them are called derived proteins.

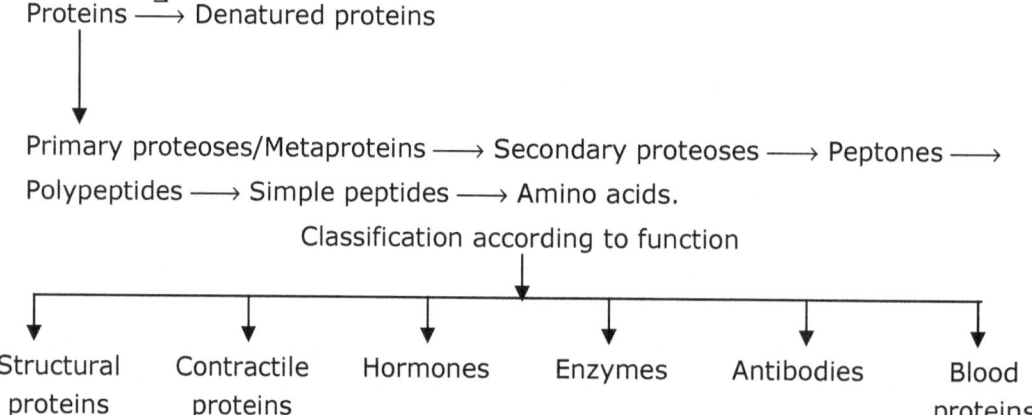

Proteins $\xrightarrow{\Delta}$ Denatured proteins

Primary proteoses/Metaproteins $\longrightarrow$ Secondary proteoses $\longrightarrow$ Peptones $\longrightarrow$ Polypeptides $\longrightarrow$ Simple peptides $\longrightarrow$ Amino acids.

Classification according to function

| Structural proteins | Contractile proteins | Hormones | Enzymes | Antibodies | Blood proteins |

1. **Structural proteins:** These are fibrous proteins, such as collagens which comprise half of man's total protein in the form of skin, cartilage and bone.

2. **Contractile proteins:** They are found in muscles such as myosin and actin.

3. **Hormones:** Proteins of this group serve as a catalyst for the chemical reactions in living organisms, rendering specificity and control to these reactions. For example, pepsin and trypsin.

4. **Antibodies:** When the body is invaded by infectious species that release foreign proteins or antigens, antibodies are produced by our body to destroy the invading species. For example, gamma globulins.

5. **Enzymes:** Proteins of this group serve as a catalyst for the chemical reactions in living organisms, rendering specificity and control to these reactions. For example, pepsin and trypsin.

6. **Blood Proteins:** There are three major protein constituents of the blood namely albumins, haemoglobin and fibrinogen. They maintain osmotic pressure, oxygen transport and blood coagulation respectively.

3.8 STRUCTURE OF PROTEINS

3.8.1 Primary Structure of Proteins

The primary structure of a protein is mainly referred to the number, nature and sequence of amino acids along the peptide chains.

The various steps for establishing the primary structure for proteins are as follows:

1. Isolation of proteins

2. Separation and purification of proteins

3. Number of peptide chains

4. Determination of amino acid composition

5. Determination of C-terminal amino acid

6. Determination of N-terminal amino acid

7. Determination of disulphite bond

8. Determination of the sequence of amino acids

9. Mass spectrometry

1. Isolation of proteins:

The extraction of proteins from disintegrated cells is achieved with water or dilute solution of salts as a sodium chloride. The extraction is generally carried out at a controlled pH by using buffer solution. Having crudely extracted a protein from tissue material, the next step is to precipitate it preferentially from solution at isoelectric pH. The precipitated protein sample is freed from salts by dialysis or gel filtration.

2. Separation and purification of proteins:

This is done by:

(i) Electrophoresis

(ii) Chromatography

(iii) Dialysis

(iv) Crystallisation etc.

3. Determination of number of peptide chains:

The protein consists of a single peptide chain or composed of number of subunits. If it contains number of subunits, these are separated and each chain is examined separately.

4. Determination of amino acid composition:

The constituent amino acids and their nature and amounts are determined by complete hydrolysis of the protein. From the relative amount of each of the amino acid present in a molecule, the empirical formula in terms of amino acids of the proteins can be deduced. The minimum molecule weight of the protein is determined from the empirical formula. The molecular weight of protein is also determined by a physical method.

5. Determination of C-terminal amino acid:

(a) Hydrazinolysis: This is the most widely used method introduced by Akabori. et. al. (1956). In this method, the peptide/protein is heated with anhydrous **hydrazine** at 100°C when all the amino acids except the C-terminal one are converted into amino acid hydrazides. The mixture of products obtained is allowed to pass on a column of a strong cation exchange resin. When eluted, the strongly basic hydrazides are retained on the resin whereas the free amino acid is eluted and can be identified.

Disadvantage: Cystine and tryptophan are completely destroyed whereas arginine is converted into ornithine and methionine is oxidized to its sulphoxide.

$$........\ NHCHR_1CONHCHR_2CONHCHR_3COOH \xrightarrow{N_2H_4}$$

$$........ + H_2NCHR_1CONHNH_2 + H_2NCHR_2CONHNH_2 + H_2NCHR_3COOH$$

(b) Reduction method: In this method, the peptide or protein is reduced with LiAlH$_4$. This converts the free terminal carboxyl group to a 1° alcohol group. The reduced product on hydrolysis yields a mixture of amino acids and an amino alcohol. The amino alcohol is separated and identified by paper chromotagraphy.

$$.....\ NHCHR_1CONHCHR_2CONHCHR_3COOH \xrightarrow{LiAlH_4}$$

$$.....\ NHCHRCONHCHR_2CONHCH_3R_3CH_2OH \xrightarrow{Hydrolysis}$$

$$.....\ + H_2NCHR_1CONHNH_2 + H_2NCHR_2CONHNH_2 + H_2NCHR_3CH_2OH$$

Amino alcohol

(c) Schlack and Kumpf's method: In this method, first of all free amino group is protected by benzylation. Then the C-terminal amino acid of the benzoylated product is converted into thiohydantoin. Finally, the latter product is hydrolysed in the same manner as in Edman method.

$$H_2NCHR_1CONHCHR_2CONHCHR_3COOH \xrightarrow{\ C_6H_5COCl\ }$$

$$C_6H_5CONHCHR_1CONHCHR_2CONHCHR_3COOH \xrightarrow[\text{NH}_4\text{CNS and Ac}_2\text{O}]{\text{Heat with}}$$

$$C_6H_5CONHCHR_1CONHCHR_2CON\!\!-\!\!CHR_3 \quad \xrightarrow{\text{NaOH}}$$

(with ring: $S{-}C{-}N(H){-}CO$)

$$C_6H_5CONHCHR_1CONHCHR_2COOH + HN\!\!-\!\!CHR_3 \xrightarrow{\text{Ba(OH)}_2} H_2NCH\!\!-\!\!COOH$$

(ring: $SC{-}N(H){-}CO$)   (R_3)

Thiohydantoin of	Amino acid (The amino acid so
C-terminal amino acid	formed is identified and procedure is
	repeated on degraded polypeptide)

(d) Carboxypeptidase method (Grassmann et. al. (1930)): Carboxypeptidase enzyme only attacks peptides/proteins only at the end which contains the free α-carboxyl group. When this terminal amino acid residue is liberated, the new terminal free carboxyl group will be attacked by the enzyme.

Suppose there is a peptide .... X, Y, Z. After attacking by carboxy peptidase, a number of successive terminal amino acids will be liberated from this peptide in amounts – Z>Y>X. These amino acids can be identified and quantitatively estimated and in this way their sequence can be established in a peptide.

(e) Racemization method: This is a new method for the identification of C-terminal residues, introduced by the group of Japanese workers (1965, 1972). The procedure involves the racemization of the C-terminal residue and the concurrent selective labelling of that residue with tritium.

In this reaction, peptide is treated with acetic anhydride when acetylation takes place followed by the formation of oxazolone between the C-terminal and adjacent residue. Under the influence of alkaline condition the hydrogen ion is removed from the α-carbon atom of the C-terminal amino acid, resulting an indicated equilibrium. After this the oxazolone is hydrolysed in the presence of tritium oxide which introduces the tritium level on the α-carbon atom. After complete acid analysis, the amino acid in which radioactivity is detected must derive from the C-terminal residue.

This method has been applied successfully to insulin, the hormone angiotensin and several synthetic peptides.

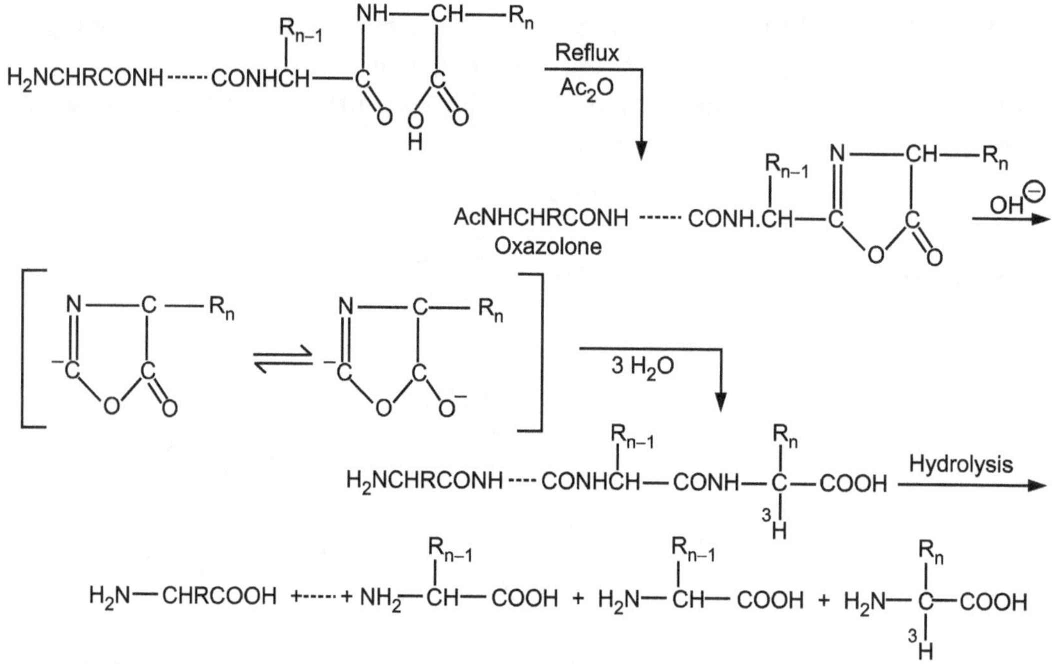

$$\text{H}_2\text{NCHRCONH} \cdots\cdots \text{CONHCH} \underset{\overset{|}{R_{n-1}}}{-} \text{C} \quad \overset{\text{NH}-\text{CH}-R_n}{\underset{|}{\underset{O}{\parallel}}} \text{C} \quad \xrightarrow[\text{Ac}_2\text{O}]{\text{Reflux}}$$

$$\text{AcNHCHRCONH} \cdots\cdots \text{CONH.CH} \underset{\overset{|}{R_{n-1}}}{-} \text{C} \overset{\text{N}-\text{CH}-R_n}{\underset{O}{\parallel}} \text{C} \quad \xrightarrow{\text{OH}^{\ominus}}$$

Oxazolone

$$\left[\quad \rightleftharpoons \quad \right] \xrightarrow{3\,\text{H}_2\text{O}}$$

$$\text{H}_2\text{NCHRCONH} \cdots\cdot \text{CONHCH} \underset{\overset{|}{R_{n-1}}}{-} \text{CONH} \underset{\overset{|}{\underset{H}{\overset{3}{|}}}}{-} \overset{R_n}{\underset{|}{C}} - \text{COOH} \xrightarrow{\text{Hydrolysis}}$$

$$\text{H}_2\text{N}-\text{CHRCOOH} +\cdots\cdot + \text{NH}_2-\overset{R_{n-1}}{\underset{|}{\text{CH}}}-\text{COOH} + \text{H}_2\text{N}-\overset{R_{n-1}}{\underset{|}{\text{CH}}}-\text{COOH} + \text{H}_2\text{N}-\overset{R_n}{\underset{\underset{H}{\overset{3}{|}}}{\underset{|}{C}}}-\text{COOH}$$

6. Determination of N-Terminal Amino Acid:

(a) Phenylthiohydantoin (Edman) Method: This is a widely used method in which the first step is an addition reaction of phenylisothiocyanate with the protein/ peptide to form the phenylthiocarbamyl peptide (PTC) which is cleaved in the presence of anhydrous acetic acid to give thiazolinone intermediate and the liberation of the remainder of the peptide intact. The thiazolinone is hydrolysed by dil. HCl to the PTC-amino acid which is then hydrolysed to form the phenylthiohydantoin derivative of the amino acid. The process can be repeated on the degraded peptide. The PTH-amino acids are extracted with organic solvents and identified by comparison with standard using paper column or TLC.

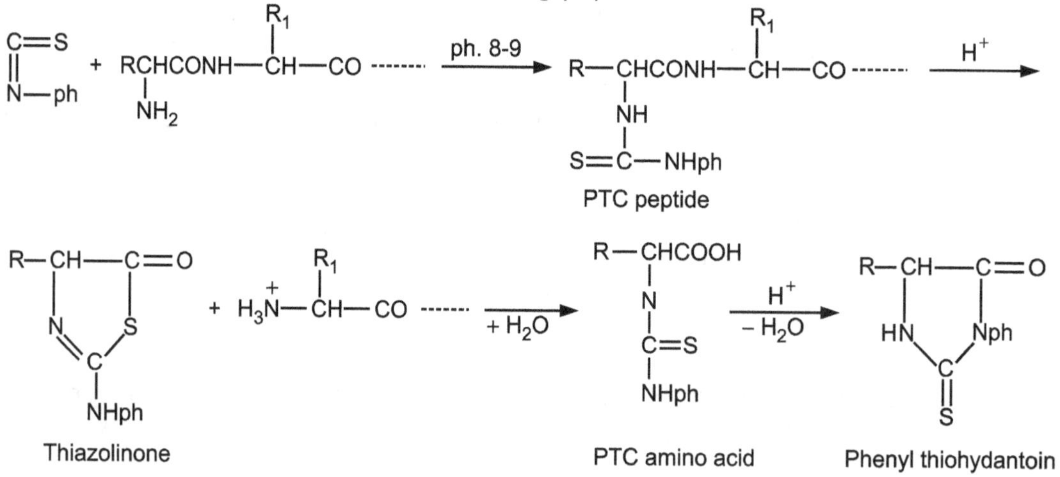

$$\overset{\text{C}=\text{S}}{\underset{\text{N}-\text{ph}}{\parallel}} + \text{RCHCONH}\underset{\overset{|}{\text{NH}_2}}{-}\overset{R_1}{\underset{|}{\text{CH}}}-\text{CO}\cdots\cdots \xrightarrow{\text{ph. 8-9}} \text{R}-\text{CHCONH}-\overset{R_1}{\underset{|}{\text{CH}}}-\text{CO}\cdots\cdots \xrightarrow{\text{H}^+}$$

with NH and S=C—NHph below

PTC peptide

$$\overset{\text{R}-\text{CH}-\text{C}=\text{O}}{\underset{\underset{\text{NHph}}{\overset{|}{\text{C}}}}{\underset{\text{N} \quad \text{S}}{}}} + \text{H}_3\overset{+}{\text{N}}-\overset{R_1}{\underset{|}{\text{CH}}}-\text{CO}\cdots\cdots \xrightarrow[+\text{H}_2\text{O}]{} \overset{\text{R}-\text{CHCOOH}}{\underset{\underset{\text{NHph}}{\overset{|}{\text{C}=\text{S}}}}{\underset{\text{N}}{}}} \xrightarrow[-\text{H}_2\text{O}]{\text{H}^+} \overset{\text{R}-\text{CH}-\text{C}=\text{O}}{\underset{\underset{\text{S}}{\overset{\parallel}{\text{C}}}}{\underset{\text{HN} \quad \text{Nph}}{}}}$$

Thiazolinone   PTC amino acid   Phenyl thiohydantoin

(b) Cyanate Method: This method was developed by **Stark and Smyth** (1963). This method in principle is that of the Edman procedure except that it is not designed to be a degradative one. In it, the hydantoin rather than the phenyl-thiohydantoin is formed, isolated, degraded to the amino acid.

$$NCO^- + NH_2CHRCONHCHR' \text{----} COO^- + NCO^- \xrightarrow{pH\ 8}$$

$$NH_2CONHCHRCONHCHR' \text{----} COO^- \xrightarrow{H^+} \underset{\underset{CO}{HN\quad NH}}{RCH\text{---}CO} \quad + \quad {}^+NH_3CHR'\text{----}COO^-$$

$$\Big\downarrow \begin{array}{l} NaOH\ 0.2\ M \\ or\ HCl\ 6\ M \end{array}$$

$${}^+NH_3CHRCOO^- + NH_3 + CO_2$$

The resultant amino acid obtained by hydrolysis of the isolated hydantoin is quantitated by standard amino acid analysis procedure.

(c) Sanger's Method or DNP Method: This is a useful method for determining the N-terminal residue of a peptide chain and utilises the fact that, 1-fluoro-2, 4-dinitrobenzene (FDNB) reacts smoothly with a terminal α-amino group in bicarbonate-buffered aqueous ethanol to form an N-(2, 4-dinitrophenyl) peptide. The latter compound on hydrolysis with acid yields DNP-amino acid and a mixture of amino acids. As the DNP-amino acids are brilliantly coloured, they may be identified by TLC. The DNP-amino acids are readily located and can be eluted and analysed quantitatively by their absorbance at 360 nm (or 385 nm for DNP-proline). As DNP-amino acid can be determined quantitatively, DNP method may be used to establish the molecular weight of a peptide or protein, if the number of its N-terminal residues can otherwise be established.

DNP-peptide

DNP-amino acid

(d) Dansyl Method: Gray and Hartley (1967) developed a highly sensitive amino-terminal end-group method, called the **Dansyl procedure**. In this method, the amino-terminal analysis is performed with the reagent, 1-dimethyl amino phthalene-5-sulphonyl chloride ((dansyl), DNS-Cl). The method is similar to Sanger's DNP procedure and the reaction of DNS-Cl and peptide produces an acid stable sulphonamide derivative of the free amino terminal residue. The hydrolysis of the DNS-peptide with 6N HCl produces free amino acids and the sulphonamide derivative of amino-terminal residue.

The DNS-amino acid may be identified by paper electrophoresis or by TLC.

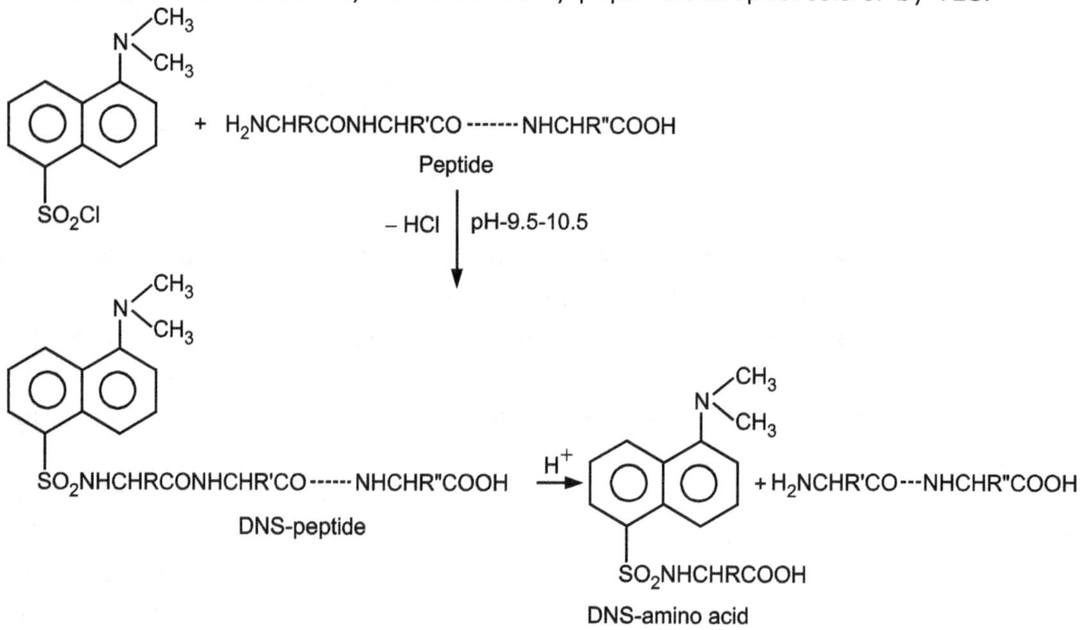

7. Determination of disulphite bond:

If a protein molecule contains the disulphide bond, it must be broken before amino acid sequence analysis is started. The disulphide bond can be broken either by oxidation/reduction. The oxidation is generally carried out with performic acid when there occurs the cleavage of disulphide bonds present in proteins to produce chains containing cysteic acid residues which are stable and assist the separation of the oxidation mixture by ion-exchange methods.

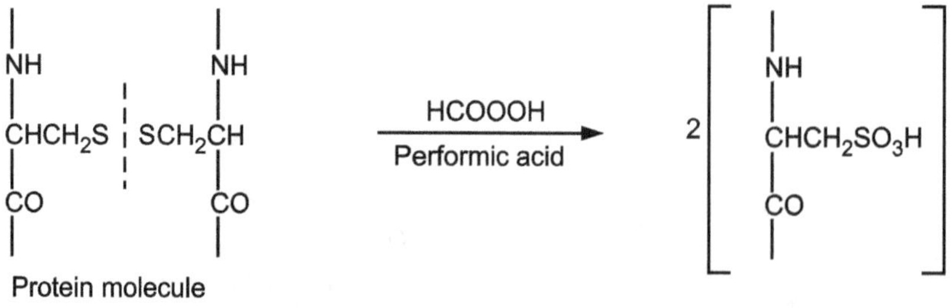

Alternatively the disulphide bond may be reduced to thiol by means of **sodium borohydride**, followed by treatment of products with **iodoacetic acid**.

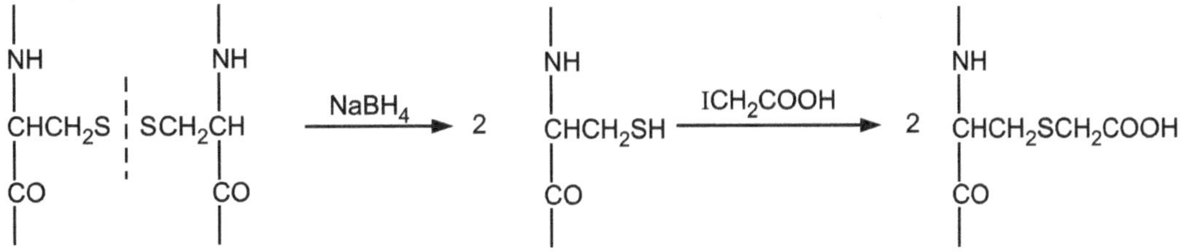

$$
\begin{array}{c}
| \\
\mathrm{NH} \\
| \\
\mathrm{CHCH_2S \cdot SCH_2CH} \\
| \quad\quad | \\
\mathrm{CO} \quad\quad \mathrm{CO} \\
| \quad\quad |
\end{array}
\xrightarrow{\mathrm{NaBH_4}} 2
\begin{array}{c}
| \\
\mathrm{NH} \\
| \\
\mathrm{CHCH_2SH} \\
| \\
\mathrm{CO} \\
|
\end{array}
\xrightarrow{\mathrm{ICH_2COOH}} 2
\begin{array}{c}
| \\
\mathrm{NH} \\
| \\
\mathrm{CHCH_2SCH_2COOH} \\
| \\
\mathrm{CO} \\
|
\end{array}
$$

Protein molecule

The next step is to determine the primary structures of the products obtained in oxidation or reduction and the positions of the disulphide linkages are ascertained from the positions in the sequence of cysteic acid residues or of the carboxymethyl-cysteine residues.

The main disadvantages of oxidation with performic acid are:

(i) Methionine is oxidized to the corresponding sulphone and

(ii) It destroyes tryptophan.

8. Determination of the sequence of amino acids:

This is quite a difficult task because there are many possibilities in which constituent amino acids may be linked in the peptides. Suppose we consider a tripeptide composed of amino acids A, B and C. These can be arranged in 3 or $3 \times 2 \times 1$ or 6 different ways i.e. A.B.C, A.C.B, B.A.C., B.C.A., C.A.B., C.B.A. If N-terminal amino acid (N-T.AA) is determined by some method, the 6 possibilities are grouped into 3 pairs i.e. it is possible to know whether the tripeptide was either one or other of a pair. Similarly, the same possibilities arise if C-terminal amino acid (C-T-AA) is determined by some or other method. Thus:

N-Terminal	C-Terminal
(a) A.B.C. and A.C.B.	(d) B.C.A. and C.B.A.
(b) B.A.C. and B.C.A.	(e) A.C.B. and C.A.B.
(c) C.A.B. and C.B.A.	(f) A.B.C. and B.A.C.

By determining both N and C-terminal groups, it is possible to determine the amino acid sequence of the tripeptide.

For example, if the N-T-AA determination reveals that the tripeptide belongs to group (b) and the C-T-AA determination reveals that the tripeptide belongs to group (d), the tripeptide is therefore B.C.A.

Suppose the application of N and C-T-AA methods to tripeptide say, B-C-A, results in the removal of terminal amino acid. In such a situation, B.C.A. would be left with the following fragments.

(i) N-T-AA first: Fragment C-A.

(ii) C-T-AA first: Fragment B-C.

If either of the above determinations are repeated, then the amino-acid sequence in the tripeptide can be ascertained. It is to be remembered that the sequence of amino acids in a tripeptide may be determined by employing one method twice or by use of each method one.

Final confirmation is done by **Mass Spectrometry**.

3.8.2 Secondary Structure for Proteins

The secondary structure of a protein is concerned with the description of the 3-dimensional arrangement of polypeptide chain. i.e. the conformation of the polypeptide chain. The secondary structural features of proteins have two aspects:

(a)　The way in which the protein is folded and bent.

(b)　The nature of the α-linkages and bonds which stabilize this structure.

The most probable component of the secondary structure of proteins may be either α-helix or β-helix.

α-Helix: This model was proposed by Pauling and Crey in 1951 as one type of secondary structure that should occur in nature due to its inherent stability. The α-helix model is proposed on the basis of the following arguments:

(i)　Peptide bond has a planar structure.

(ii)　There are dihedral angles ϕ and ϕ which are taken about the C_α – C' and the N – C^α bonds respectively. These are close to those corresponding to potential minima in the system.

(iii)　Conformation of the protein is stabilised by hydrogen bonding which is formed between $\rangle$C = O group and an N–H group. The strength of this bond is maximum if the atoms concerned (C = O... H – N) are collinear or failing this ideal condition don't deviate by more than 30° from collinearity.

(iv)　The model to be selected must permit the maximum number of hydrogen bonds.

The α-helix is a spiral arrangement of polypeptide chain, with the chain winding around a central axis and each amino acid residue rising along the spiral in an uniform manner. There are either 3.7 or 5.1 amino acid residues in one complete turn of the helix with a translational distance parallel to the helical axis of 5.4 A°.

Further considerations (largely stereochemical) revealed that a helix with 3.7 residues per turn was more stable than 5.1 or any other. The diameter of the helix has been estimated to be about 10 A°.

In the α-helix every peptide carbonyl oxygen is hydrogen bonded with the amide hydrogen of the 4th amino acid residue further along the helix. This hydrogen bonding prevents free rotation and so the helix is rigid. The overall effect of helical structure and its stabilization by hydrogen bonds is to create a structure that is cylindrical in shape, fairly rigid but capable of undergoing reversible changes in conformation on stretching and bending. Most amino acids are generally accommodated as structural units in the α-helix having the side chains located on the outside and pointing away from the helical axis. The main exception to this is proline which does not fit in a α-helix due to its ring structure. Other exceptions are valine and isoleucine. These are amino acids with bulky side chains which break the helical structure. Amino acids which does not fit into the helix are termed as helix breakers.

The α-helix may be either left or right handed. According to theoretical calculations done by Moffitt it was concluded that the right handed helix (for L-amino acids) is more stable than the left handed helix. Therefore, the right handed helix is the one that would be expected to occur naturally.

α-Helix

β-Conformation: In 1951, Pauling and Corey proposed another type of secondary structure called the **β-conformation or pleated sheet.** In this conformation, polypeptide chains are extended and a number of these are aligned side by side in close contact, and these chains are stabilized by intermolecular hydrogen bonding. In order to have maximum number of hydrogen bonds between the chains, the dimensions of the polypeptide must be slightly shorter than that of a fully extended chain. Due to this the peptide backbone becomes puckered and the conformation resembles a pleated sheet. In the β-conformation, the side chains are situated above and below the plane of the sheet with the direction alternating from one residue to the next.

In β-conformation, there are two types of pleated sheets in which the alignment of the peptide chains may be parallel to one another or antiparallel. In the parallel arrangement, all the chains run in the same direction and in antiparallel arrangement the chains run alternatively in opposite directions.

The existence of the pleated sheet structure in solid proteins has been confirmed by X-ray analysis.

For example, polypeptide chains are parallel in keratin and lysozyme, and polypeptide chains are antiparallel in fibroin, papain and ribonuclease.

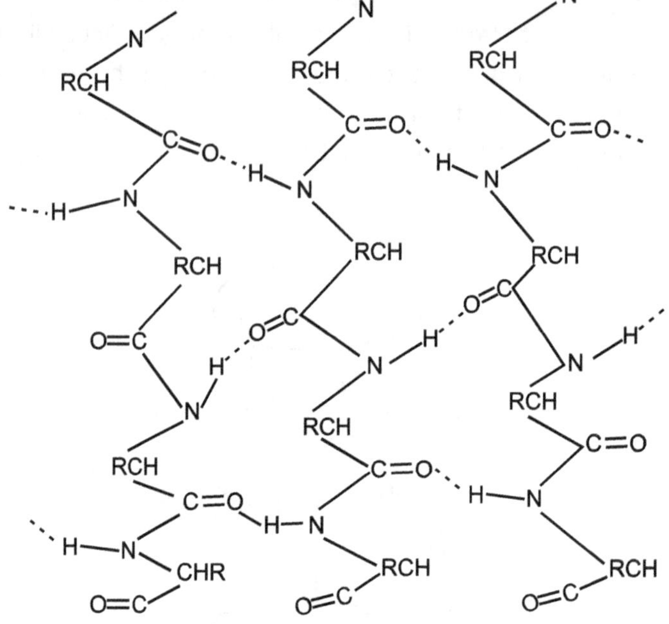

(a) Parallel conformation

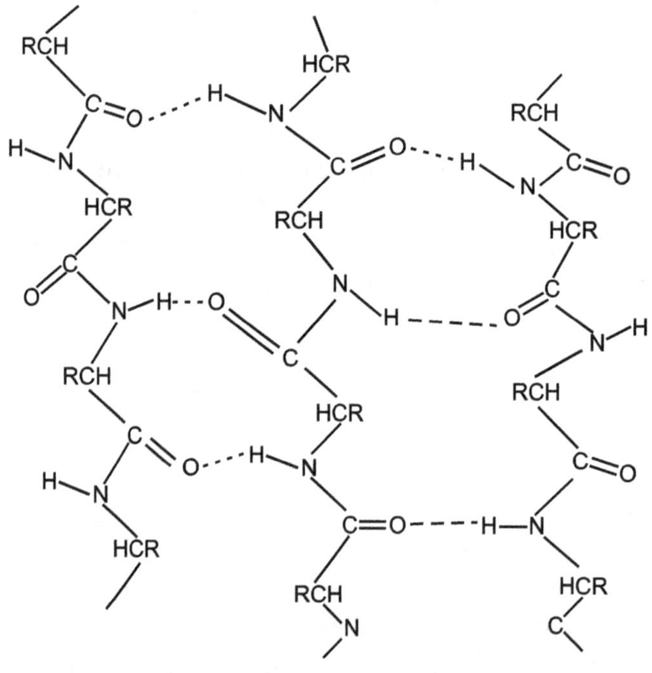

(b) Antiparallel

3.8.3 Tertiary Structures of Proteins

Tertiary structures, as originally defined, refer to the 3-dimensional structure of the polypeptide chain that results from interaction between amino acid residues relatively far apart in the sequence.

The 3° structure of a protein refers to the orientations of the side chains in the folded molecule. The 3° structure that a protein assumes under normal condition, temperature and pH will be in most stable arrangement. Due to this reason, it is generally called the native conformation of that protein. As the 3° structure describes the overall spatial arrangement of the polypeptide chain, it reveals an exact description of molecular shape in most small and medium sized proteins.

For example, structure of chymotrypsin.

3.8.4 Quaternary Structure

The concept of quaternary structure for proteins was initially championed by Sorensen and Svedberg in 1930, but later fell into obscurity only to be resurrected again 30 years later. The unambiguous determination of quaternary structure is possible only by crystallographic methods.

Proteins such as haemoglobin which consist of more than one polypeptide chain are said to possess quaternary structure. Proteins having this type of structure are said to be oligomeric and the individual polypeptide chains are known as protomers/subunits. Each of these subunits is characterized by its own secondary and tertiary structures. The subunits may or may not be identical. When subunits are held together by hydrogen bonds, they may be separated by reagents which do not break covalent bonds.

For example, haemoglobin contains four independent polypeptide chains, two identical α-chains and two identical β-chains/subunits are held together by covalent bonds but by the interaction between the exposed groups of the folded chains. Each of these chains is characterized by its own 2° and 3° structures.

QUESTIONS

1. Define the terms:
   (a) Amino acids
   (b) Isoelectric point
   (c) Peptide
   (d) Polypeptide and
   (e) Protein

2. Give the classification of amino acids.

3. Give the reason of amino acids with the following reagents:

   (a) Alcohols

   (b) Ammonia

   (c) Ninhydrin

   (d) HNO_2

4. Explain the various methods of preparation of amino acids.

5. Explain the general principles of polypeptide synthesis.

6. Explain the various methods for synthesis of polypeptides.

7. Write a note on solid phase support synthesis of peptides.

8. Give the classification of proteins with suitable example.

9. Write a note on primary and secondary structures of proteins.

■■■

Chapter 4...

POLYCYCLIC COMPOUNDS

Syllabus ......

Synthesis and Reactions of Naphthalene, Phenanthrene and Anthracene

4.1 POLYNUCLEAR AROMATIC HYDROCARBONS / FUSED RING HYDROCARBONS

The aromatic hydrocarbons made up of two or more benzene rings fused together are called polynuclear aromatic hydrocarbons.

Examples:

Naphthalene   Phenanthrene   Anthracene

4.2 NAPHTHALENE

Naphthalene is a colourless solid which forms shining flaked-crystals, M.P. = 80.2°C, B.P. = 217.9°C. It has a familiar odour of moth balls. It is volatile and sublimes slowly at room temperature. It is insoluble in water and soluble in ether and benzene. It burns with a smoky flame.

4.2.1 Synthesis of Naphthalene

1. Haworth synthesis (1932):

Benzene   Succinic anhydride   β - Benzoyl propionic acid

γ - Phenyl butyric acid   α - Tetralone   Tetralin

Naphthalene

2. From α-methyl naphthalene (Distillate of petroleum)

α - Methyl naphthalene   Naphthalene

4.2.2 Chemical Reactions

Naphthalene gives the usual aromatic electrophilic substitution reactions. But the α-product always predominates. The mechanism of substitution is the same as for benzene.

Naphthalene   + E—Nu   α - Product (Predominate)   and/or   β - Product   + H—Nu

Why α-product predominate can be explained by resonance structure.

Attack at α-position:

Two resonance forms ∴ More stable

β-attack:

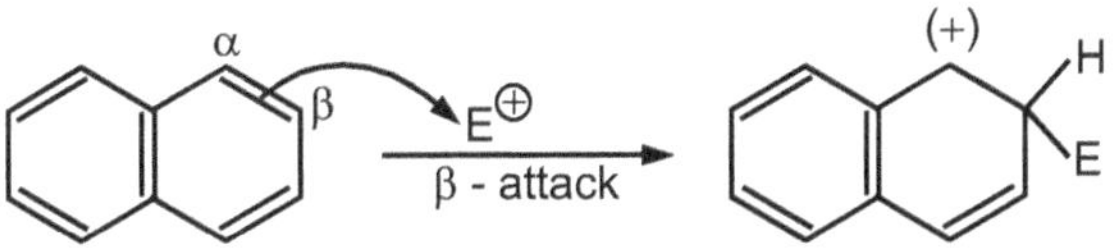

No resonance form ∴ Less stable

Therefore, α-substitution predominates in naphthalene, whereas β-substitution occurs only when the reaction is carried out at high temperature or when bulkier solvents are used.

Therefore, some important chemical reactions of naphthalene are as mentioned below:

1. **Halogenation:** Naphthalene reacts with Cl_2 and Br_2 in CCl_4 solution to form α-chloronaphthalene or α-bromonaphthalene.

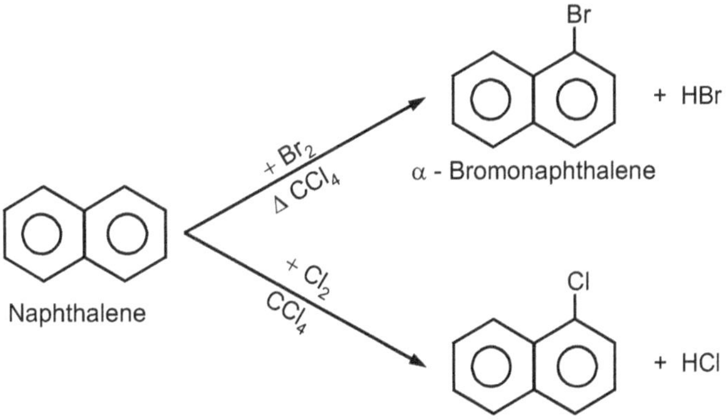

2. **Nitration:**

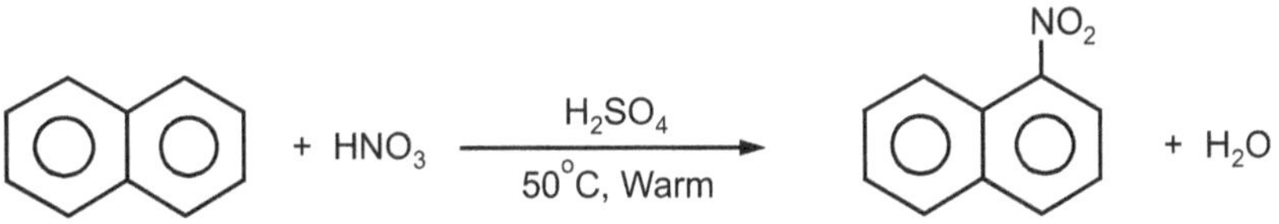

3. **Sulfonation:**

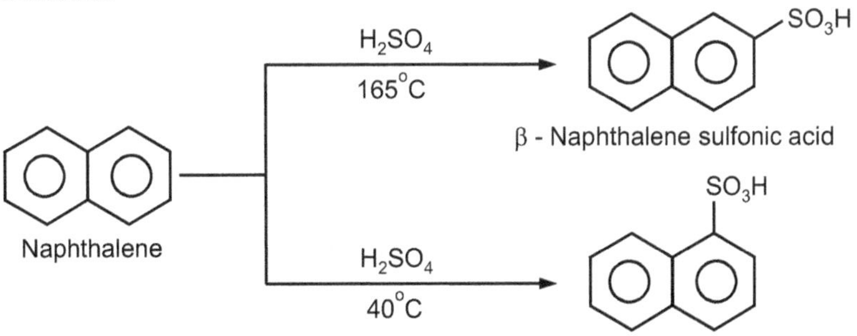

4. Friedel-Craft's Acylation:

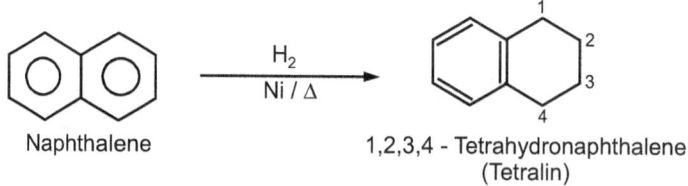

Naphthalene

$CH_3COCl / AlCl_3$
in $CS_2 / -15^{\circ}C$ → α - Acetyl naphthalene (COCH₃)

$CH_3COCl / AlCl_3$
in [nitrobenzene] $NO_2 / 25^{\circ}C$ → β - Acetyl naphthalene (C=O—CH₃)

5. Reaction with acids followed by NaOH:

Naphthalene

H_2SO_4 40°C → (SO₃H) $\xrightarrow[\Delta, 300^{\circ}C]{NaOH}$ (ŌNa⁺) $\xrightarrow[H_2O]{H^+}$ (OH) α - Naphthol

H_2SO_4 165°C → (SO₃H) $\xrightarrow[\Delta, 300^{\circ}C]{NaOH}$ (ŌNa⁺) $\xrightarrow[H_2O]{H^\oplus}$ (OH) β - Naphthol

6. Reduction: Depends on condition and catalyst used as below:

(i) By sodium and alcohol:

Naphthalene + 2[H] $\xrightarrow{Na / C_2H_5OH}$ 1,4 - Dihydronaphthalene

(ii) By H₂ and platinum catalysts:

Naphthalene $\xrightarrow[\Delta / Pt]{5H_2}$ Decahydronaphthalene (Decalin)

(iii) By hydrogen and nickel cation:

Naphthalene $\xrightarrow[Ni / \Delta]{H_2}$ 1,2,3,4 - Tetrahydronaphthalene (Tetralin)

7. Oxidation:

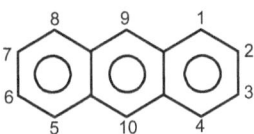

Naphthalene

Air
V_2O_5 / Δ

Phthalic anhydride

CrO_3
CH_3COOH

1,4 - Naphthaquinone

4.2.3 Uses

1. It is used as a moth-repellant in which order it has now been replaced by p-dichlorobenzene.
2. For commercial production of phthalic anhydride.
3. For making α-naphthol (insecticides) and β-naphthol (fungicide agent).
4. For manufacture of dyes, explosives and synthetic resins.

4.3 ANTHRACENE

Anthracene is a colourless solid, M.P. = 217°C, B.P. = 340°. When crystallized from benzene it forms lustrous plates which exhibit a fine blue fluorescence. It is insoluble in water, soluble in alcohol and ether.

4.3.1 Synthesis of Anthracene

1. Haworth synthesis:

Phthalic anhydride   Benzene

$AlCl_3$

o - Benzoyl benzoic acid

Δ / H_2SO_4
$- H_2O$

9,10 - Anthraquinone

Zn dust
Distill

Anthracene

4.3.2 Chemical Reactions

Anthracene is less aromatic than benzene, hence it gives both electrophilic substitution and addition reactions equally well. These reactions preferentially occur at C-9 and C-10 positions as inferred from considerations similar to those given in case of naphthalene.

1. Halogenation:

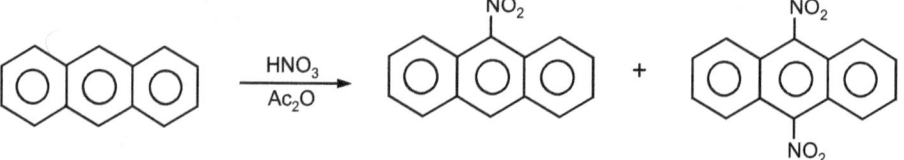

| Anthracene | Anthracene dibromide (Addition product) | 9 - Bromoanthracene (Substitution product) |

2. Nitration:

Anthracene   9 - Nitroanthracene   9,10 - Dinitroanthracene

3. Sulphonation:

Anthracene   conc. H_2SO_4

Low temperature → 1- Anthracene sulfonic acid

High temperature → 2- Anthracene sulfonic acid

4. Reduction:

Anthracene

Na / C_2H_5OH or H_2 / Pd

9,10 - Dihydroanthracene

5. Oxidation:

Anthracene   + [O]

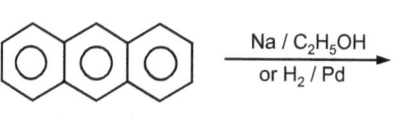

$\dfrac{Na_2Cr_2O_7}{H_2SO_4}$

9,10 - Anthraquinone (Anthraquinone)   + H_2O

$+ \dfrac{3}{2} O_2$

$V_2O_5 / \Delta , 400°C$

Anthraquinone   + H_2O

4.3.3 Uses

1. It is used for manufacture of anthraquinone.
2. For making dyes life Alizarin.
3. Used in smoke screens.

4.4 PHENANTHRENE

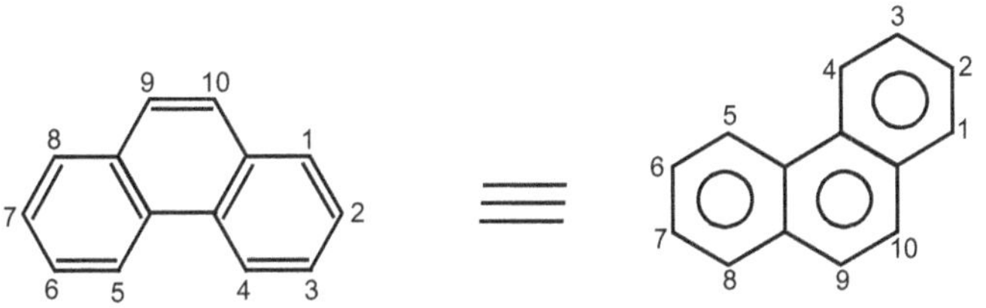

It is a colourless solid, M.P. = 100°C. It is insoluble in water, but dissolves in benzene and ether. It gives blue fluorescene in benzene solution.

4.4.1 Synthesis of Phenanthrene

1. Haworth synthesis:

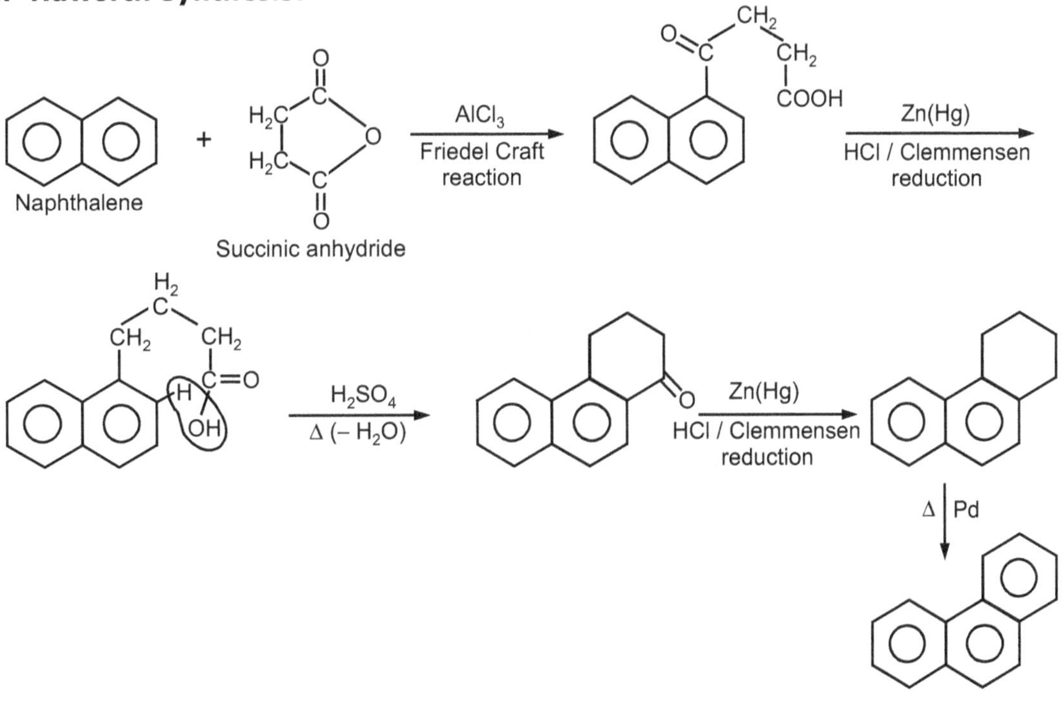

Phenanthrene

4.4.2 Chemical Reactions

Like anthracene, phenanthrene undergoes oxidation addition and electrophilic substitution reactions at C-9 and C-10 positions.

Some of the important reactions of phenanthrene are as described below:

1. Halogenation:

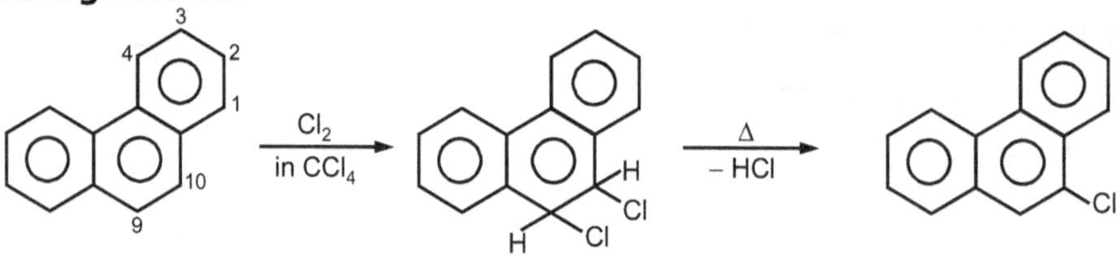

| Phenanthrene | 9,10 - Dichloro-
9,10 - Dihydrophenanthrene | 9 - Chlorophenanthrene |

2. Nitration:

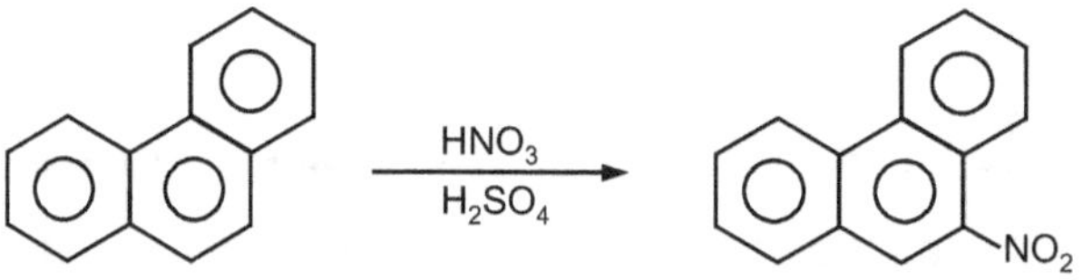

Phenanthrene   9 - Nitrophenanthrene

3. Sulphonation:

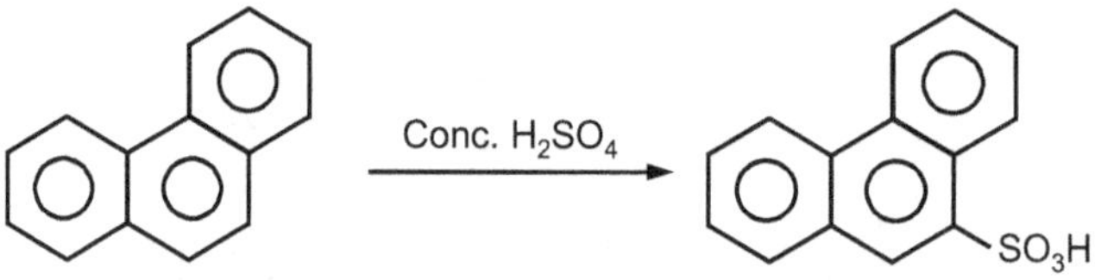

Phenanthrene   9 - Phenanthrene
sulphonic acid

4. Friedel-Craft's acylation:

4.4.3 Uses

It is of little industrial importance. But this ring system is found widely in carcinogenic hydrocarbons, bile acids, sex hormones, morphite, alkaloids and cholesterol.

QUESTIONS

1. What are polycyclic compounds? Give example.
2. Discuss in detail the methods of preparation of Naphthalene.
3. Give the various chemical reactions of Naphthalene.
4. Give the different methods of preparation of Phenanthrene.
5. Explain the various chemical reactions of Phenanthrene.
6. Give the different methods of preparation of Anthracene.
7. Explain the various chemical reactions of Anthracene.
8. Draw the structure and numbering of Naphthalene.
9. Draw the structure and numbering of Phenanthrene.
10. Draw the structure and numbering of Anthracene.

■■■

Chapter 1...

HETEROCYCLIC COMPOUNDS

Syllabus ......

Structures, Numbering and Corresponding drugs of the following Heterocyclic compounds: Furan, Thiophene, Pyrrole, Pyrazole, Thiazole, Imidazole, Oxazole, Isoxazole, Hydantoin, Pyridine, Pyridazine, Pyrimidine, Indole, Benzfuran, Benzthiazole, Benzimidazole, Benzoxazole, Quinoline, Isoquinoline, Quinazoline, Cinnoline, Purine, Xanthine, Pteridine and Coumarin. Synthesis and Reactions of following compounds: Furan, Pyrrole, Indole, Imidazole, Pyridine and Quinoline.

1.1 DEFINITION

The cyclic compounds in which one or more carbon atoms are replaced by the hetero atom like nitrogen (N), sulphur (S), oxygen (O) etc. are termed as Heterocyclic compounds.

When the hetero atom forms a part of an aromatic ring, the compound is referred to as aromatic heterocyclic compound or aromatic heterocycle.

Example:

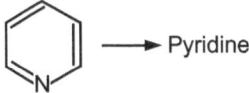 Pyridine

1.2 IUPAC NOMENCLATURE OF HETEROCYCLIC COMPOUNDS

For a monocyclic ring the proper nomenclature is derived by combining an appropriate prefix and suffix to a given system according to following rules.

The heterocyclic name consists of following skeleton.

Prefix – Stem – Suffix.

1. The names of the monocyclic compounds are derived by a prefix (prefixes) indicating the nature of the hetero atom present and introducing the 'a' wherever necessary.

Example: Oxygen – oxa

Sulphur – thia

Nitrogen – aza

When two or more of the same hetero atoms are present, then the prefix di, tri, tetra etc. are used.

Example: Two oxygen – dioxa

Two 'N' – diaza

When two or more different atoms are present, they are named in the order of O > S > N > P > Si

Note: O and S = Divalent, N and P = Trivalent, Br = Tetravalent.

Example: System containing O and N → Oxaza

System containing S and N → Thiaza

System containing O and S → Oxathia

2. The size of the ring is denoted by the appropriate *stem* and the degree of unsaturation is specified in the *suffix* as given in the table and it is important to note that the suffix is slightly modified when there is presence or absence of 'N' in the ring.

Ring size	Stem	Rings with 'N'		Rings without 'N'	
		Unsaturated	**Saturated**	**Unsaturated**	**Saturated**
3	– ir –	– irine	– iridine	– rene	– irane
4	– et –	– ete	– etidine	– ete	– etane
5	– ol –	– ole	– olidine	– ole	– olane
6	– in –	– ine	– A –	– in	– ane
7	– ep –	– epine	– A –	– epin	– epane
8	– oc –	– ocine	– A –	– ocin	– ocane
9	– on –	– onine	– A –	– onin	– onane
10	–ec –	– ecine	A	– ecin	– ecane

A – expressed by prefixing "perhydro" to the name of the corresponding unsaturated compound.

3. The numbering of monocyclic heterocyclic compound containing hetero atoms; the numbering of the ring begins with the heteroatom of highest priority (O > S > N > P > S) and proceeds around the ring so as to give other hetero atoms or substituents the lowest possible number.

Example:

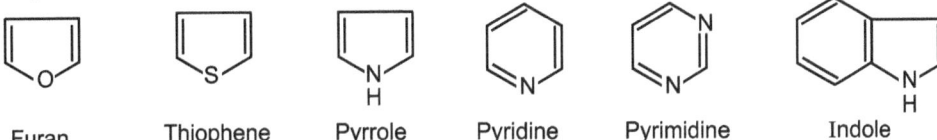

$\Longrightarrow$ 3-Methyl oxepin

4. Many of the common heterocyclic ring systems have acquired trivial names, which are retained in systematic nomenclature.

Examples:

Furan   Thiophene   Pyrrole   Pyridine   Pyrimidine   Indole

1.2.1 Polycyclic Heterocyclic Compounds

1. In polycyclic heterocycles, the ring containing heteroatom is chosen as the parent compound and the name of the fused ring is attached as prefix.

Example:

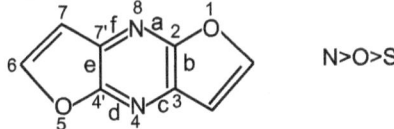

2,3-Benzopyridine   4,5-Benzothiazole
or Benzo (b) pyridine

In selecting the parent ring when two or more hetero rings are present, a nitrogen containing ring is given preference over an oxygen containing ring and oxygen over sulphur. However in numbering the polycyclic compound, an oxygen heteroatom if present is given the least possible number. In numbering omit ring junction.

Example:

N>O>S

Difuro [2,3-b, 4'7'-e] pyrazine

Sometimes, preference is given to the largest hetero ring system which has a simple name.

Example:

Benzoquinoline
(But not Naphthoquinoline)

The above structure is not fully identified by the name, benzoquinoline. For this, it is necessary to indicate in the name the position of ring junction. To do this the sides of the parent ring of quinoline are named as a, b, c etc. Starting as the 1-2 bond the benzo grouping is found fused to bond 'g' and this is so indicated in the name i.e. Benzo (g) quinoline.

1.2.2 IUPAC Names of some Heterocyclic Compounds

Structure	Name	Structure	Name
1.	Aziridine	17.	3-Methyloxepin
2.	Azirine	18.	4-Ethyloxacane
3.	Oxirene	19.	Benzo (b) pyridine or 2, 3-benzopyridine
4.	Oxirane	20.	4,5-benzothiazole
5.	Oxetane	21.	Difure (2, 3-6, 5, 6, 6') pyrazine
6.	Azetidine	22.	Benzo (g) quinoline
7.	Oxole		
8.	Oxolane		
9.	Thiole		

contd. ...

Structure	Name
10. Thiolane	Thiolane
11. Azole (Pyrrole)	Azole (Pyrrole)
12. Azolidine	Azolidine
13. Oxin (Pyran)	Oxin (Pyran)
14. Oxane (Tetra-hydro pyran)	Oxane (Tetra-hydro pyran)
15. Azine	Azine
16. Perhydroazine (Piperidine)	Perhydroazine (Piperidine)

STRUCTURE AND NUMBERING OF HETEROCYCLIC DRUGS

1.3 FURAN / HETEROCYCLIC DRUG CONTAINING FURAN NUCLEUS

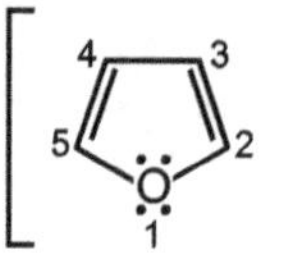

(Oxole)

(a) Nitrofurantoin:

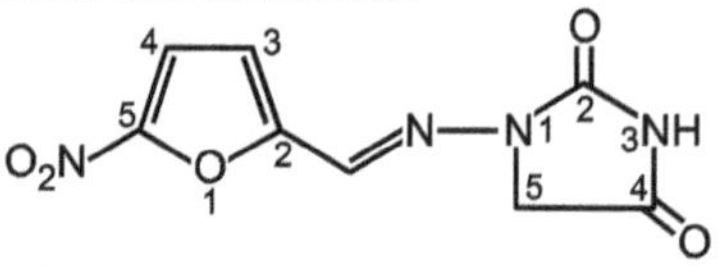

1[(5-Nitro-2-furyl) methylidene amino] imidazolidine-2, 4-dione.

Use: As an antibiotic for the treatment of cystitis.

(b) Nitrofurazone:

$C_6H_6N_4O_4$

2-[(5-nitro-2-furanyl)methylene] hydrazine carboxamide

(c) Streptomycin:

$C_{21}H_{39}N_7O_{12}$

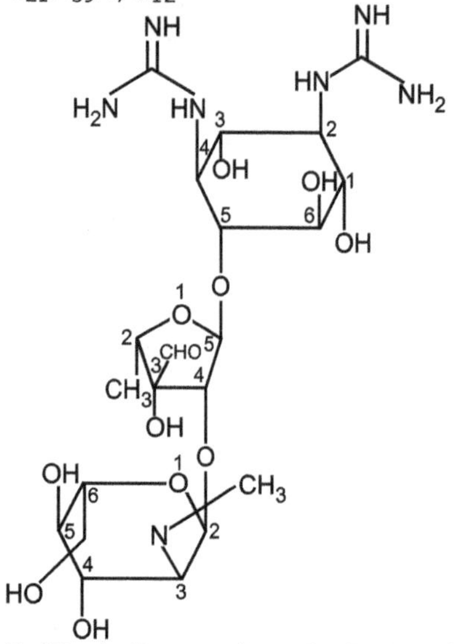

5–(2, 4-diguanidino-3, 5, 6-trihydroxy-cyclohexoxyl-4-[4, 5-dihydroxy-6-(hydroxymethyl)-3-methylamino-tetrahydropyran-2-yl]
oxy-3-hydroxy-2-methyl- tetrahydrofuran-3-carbaldehyde.

(d) Ascorbic acid:

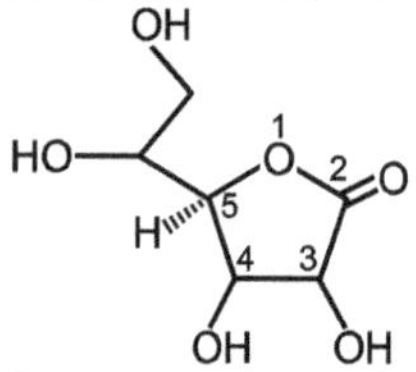

2-oxo-L-threo-hexano-1, 4-lactone-2, 3-enediol.

or

(R) – 3H-dihydroxy-5-(S)-1, 2-dihydroxy-ethyl furan-2(5H)-one

1.4 THIOPHENE

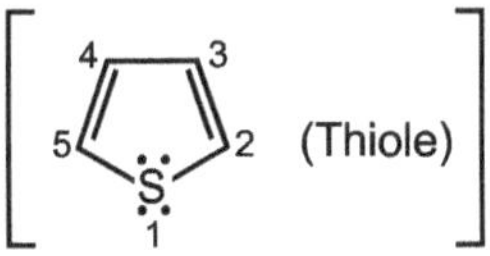

(Thiole)

Chlorothen

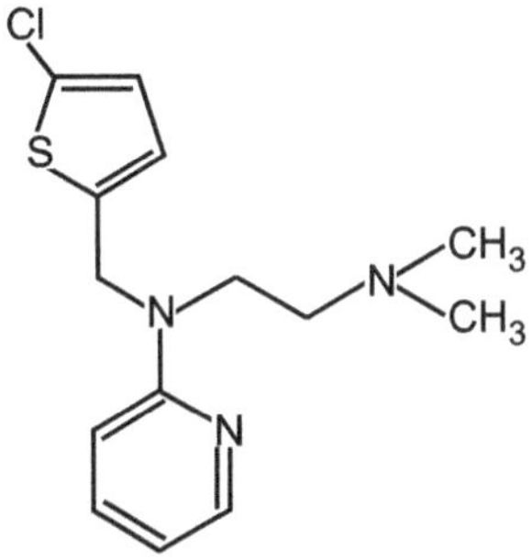

1.5 PYRROLE

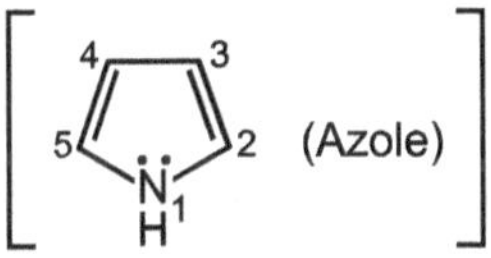

(Azole)

Pyrvinium Pamoate (Brand name: Vanquin): $C_{75}H_{70}N_6O_6$

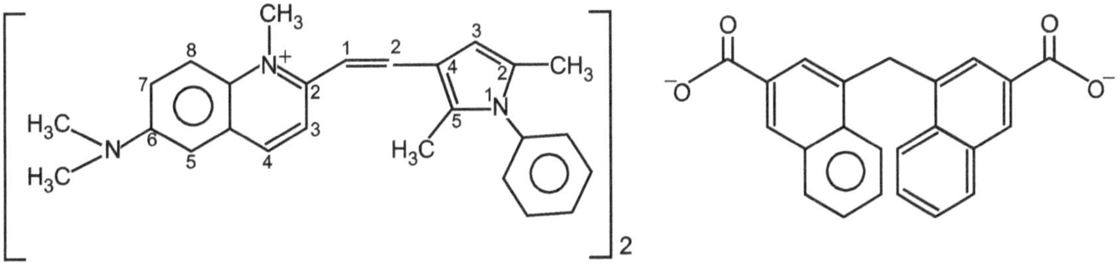

Quinolinium -6-(dimethylamino)-2-[2-(2,5-dimethyl-1-phenyl-1H-pyrrol-3-yl) ethenyl]-1-methyl-salt with 4, 4'-methyl-enebis[3-hydroxy-2-naphthaline carboxylic acid] [2: 1]

1.6 PYRIDINE

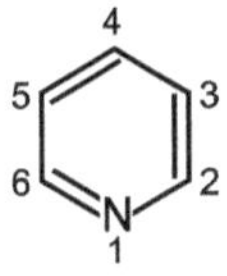

(Azine)

Niacinamide:
or
Nicotinamide

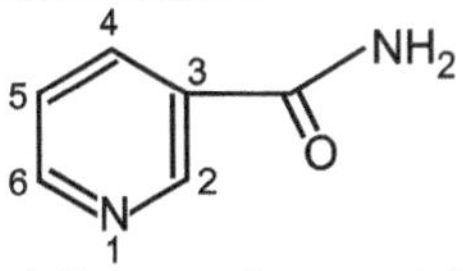

3-pyridine carboxamide

Propyliodone:

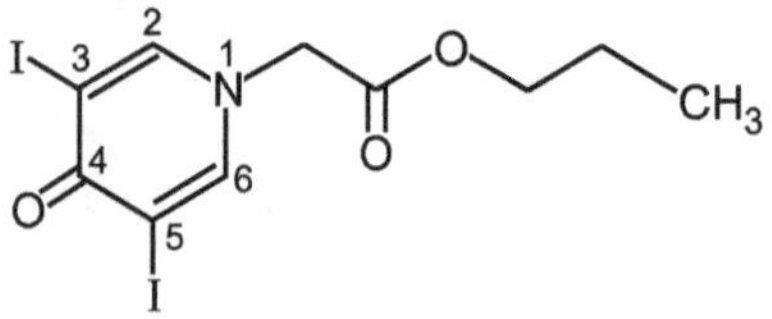

1(4H)-pyridineacetic acid, 3, 5-diiodo-4-oxo-propylester

or   propyl-3, 5-diiodo-4-oxo-1(4H) pyridineacetate.

Doxylamine succinate:

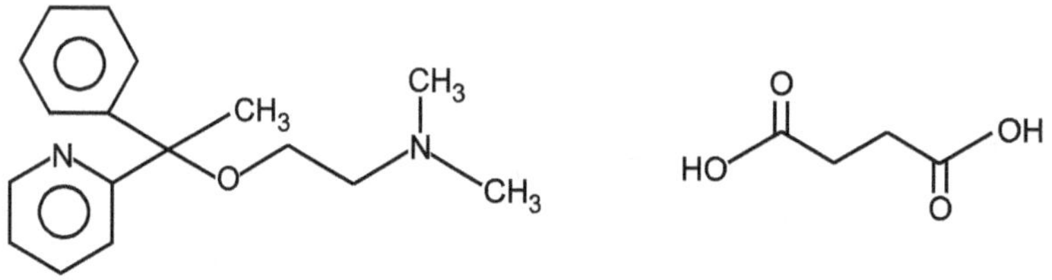

2-[α-[2-(Dimethylamino) ethoxy]-α-methylbenzyl] pyridine succinate (1: 1)

or   Ethanamine, N, N-dimethyl-2-[1-phenyl-1-(2-pyridinyl) ethoxy]

butanedioate (1: 1)

1.7 PYRIMIDINE

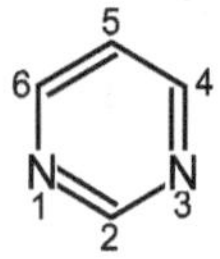

(1,3-Diazine)

(a) Pyrimethamine:

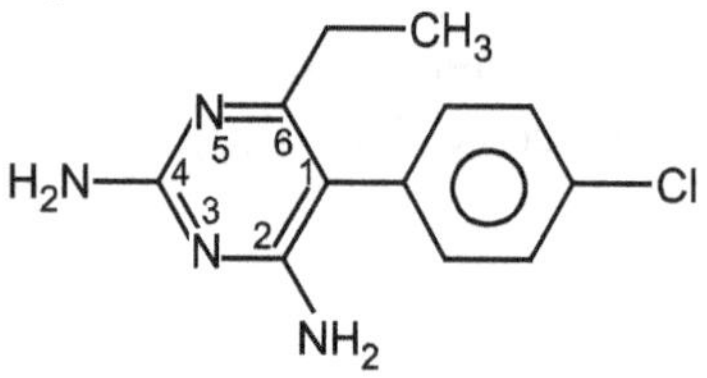

2, 4-pyrimidinediamine, 5-(4-chlorophenyl)-6-ethyl-

[2, 4-Diamino-(p-chlorophenyl)-6-ethyl pyrimidine]

(b) Sulfadiazine:

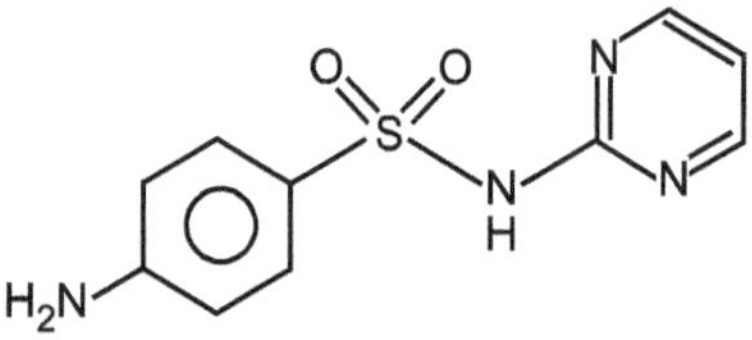

Benzene sulfonamide, 4-amino-N-2-pyrimidinyl-N'-2-pyrimidinyl sulfanilamide.

(c) Idoxuridine:

Uridine, 2'-deoxy-5-iodo-2'-Deoxy-5-iodouridine

(d) Propylthiouracil:

4(1H) – pyrimidinone, 2, 3-dihydro-6-propyl-2-thioxo-6-propyl-2-thiouracil

(e) Primidone:

4,6(1H, 5H)-pyrimidinedione-5-ethyldihydro-5-phenyl

[5-Ethyldihydro-5-phenyl-4, 6(1H, 5H)-pyrimidinedione]

1.8 PYRIDAZINE

Sulfachlorpyridazine

N'(6-chloro-3-pyridazinyl) sulfanilamide

1.9 PYRAZOLE

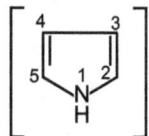

(a) Antipyrine:

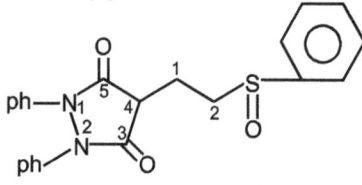

1, 2-Dihydro-1, 5-dimethyl-2-phenyl-3H-pyrazol-3-one
or [2, 3-Dimethyl-1-phenyl-3H-pyrazolin-5-one]

(b) Phenylbutazone:

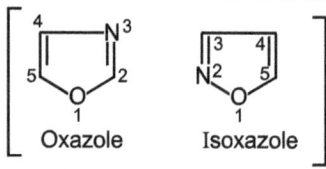

3, 5-pyrazolidinedione, 4-butyl-1, 2-diphenyl [4-Butyl-1, 2-Diphenyl-3, 5-pyrazolidine dione]

(c) Sulfinpyrazone:

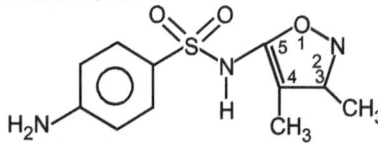

3, 5-pyrazolidinedione-1, 2-diphenyl-4-[2-(phenylsulfinyl) ethyl].
or [1, 2-Diphenyl-4-[2-(phenylsulfinyl)ethyl]-3, 5-pyrazolidinedione]

1.10 OXAZOLE AND ISOXAZOLE

Oxazole   Isoxazole

Sulfisoxazole:

Benzenesulfonamide, 4-amino-N-(3, 4-dimethyl-5-isoxazolyl)-
[N'-(3,4-Dimethyl-5-isoxazolyl) sulfanilamide]

Cycloserine:

3-Isoxazolidinone-4-amino(R) – [(+)-4-Amino-3-Isoxazolidine]

1.11 THIAZOLE

(a) Thiabendazole:

[2-(4-Thiazolyl) benzimidazole]

(b) Thiamine HCl:

Thiazolium, 3-[(4-amino-2-methyl-5-pyrimidinyl)] methyl]-5-(2-hydroxy ethyl)-4-methyl-chloride, monodihydrochloride
or Thiamine monohydrochloride

1.12 IMIDAZOLE (IMINAZOLE, GLYOXALINE)

Histamine

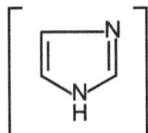

1H-Imidazole-4-ethanamine

Pilocarpine:

2(3H) Furnone-3-ethyldihydro-4-[(1-methyl)]-1H-imidazol-5-yl]-[3S(i)]

Antazone:

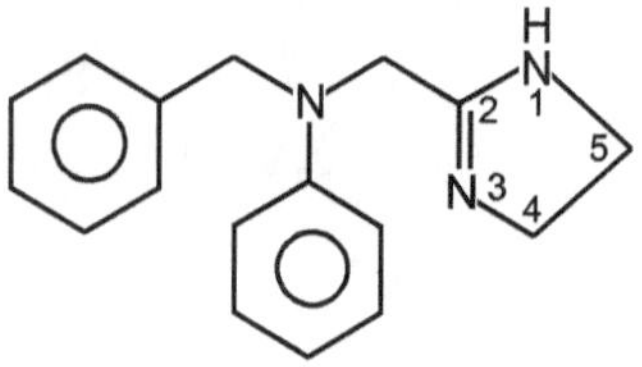

1H-Imidazole-2-methanamine, 4,5-dihydro-N, Pheny-N-(phenylmethyl) [2[(n-Benzylaniline) methyl]-2-imidazoline].

Phentolamine:

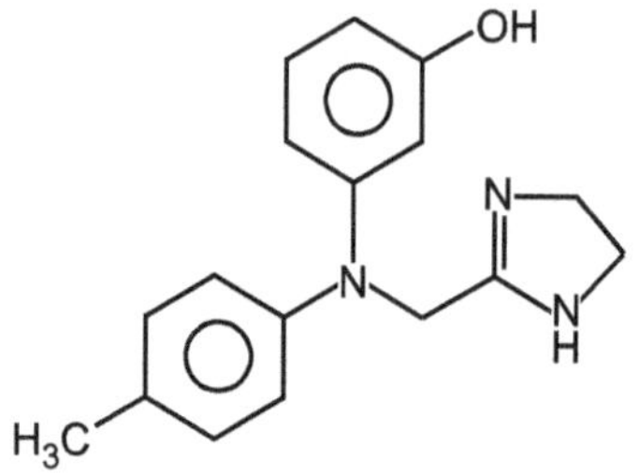

Phenol-3-[(((4,5-dihydro-1H-imidazol-2-yl) methyl) (4-methyl-phenilamine)

or

m-[N-(2-Imidazolin-2-yl methyl)-p-toluidine]phenol

1.13 INDOLE (BENZOPYRROLE)

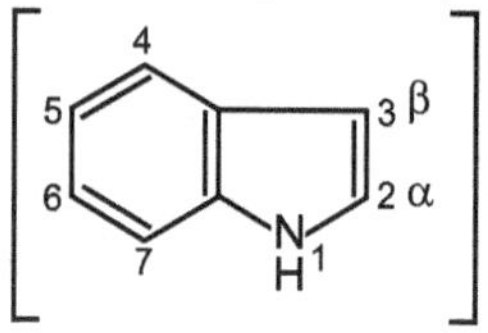

(a) Indomethacin:

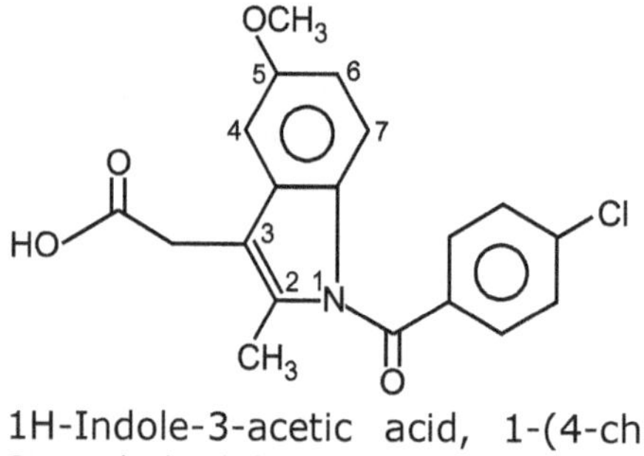

1H-Indole-3-acetic acid, 1-(4-chlorobenzoyl)-[5-methoxy-1-(p-chlorobenzoyl)-2-methylindole-3-acetic acid]

(b) Chlorthalidone:

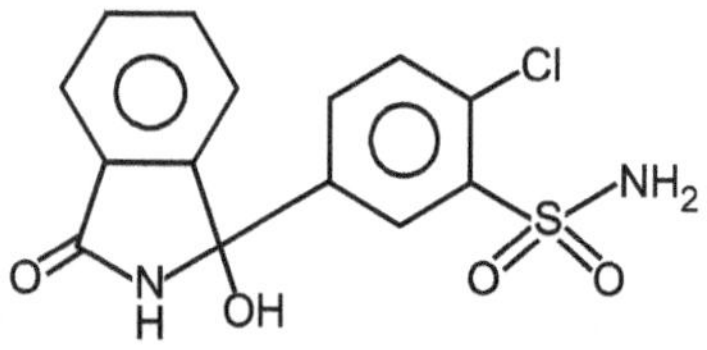

Benzenesulfonamide,2-chloro-5-(2,3-dihydro-1-hydroxy-3-oxo-1H-isoindol-1-yl) 2-chloro-5(1-hydroxy-3-oxo-1-isoindolinyl) benzene sulfonamide.

1.14 BENZOFURAN

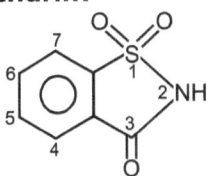

Griseofulvin:

Spiro[benzofuran-2(3H), 1'-[2] cyclohexene]-3, 4'-dione, 7-chloro-2', 4, 6-trimethoxy-6'methyl-(1's – trans).

or   [7-chloro-2', 4, 6-trimethoxy-6', β-methylspiro[benzofuran-2-(3H), 1'-[2] cyclohexene]-3,4'-dione]

1.15 BENZOTHIAZOLE

Saccharin:

1, 2-Benzisothiazol-3(2H)-one, 1, 1-dioxide

[1, 2-Benzisothiazolin-3-one 1, 1-dioxide]

1.16 BENZIMIDAZOLE

(a) Thiabendazole:

1H-Benzimidazole-2-(4-thiazolyl)-[2-(4-thiazolyl)benzimidazole].

(b) Droperidol:

2H-Benzimidazol-2-one, 1-[1-[4-(4-Fluorophenyl)-4-oxobutyl]-1, 2, 3, 6-tetrahydro-4-pyridinyl]-1, 3-dihydro.

1-[1-[3-(P-Fluorobenzoyl) propyl] – 1, 2, 3, 6-Tetrahydro-4-pyridyl]-2-benzimidazolinone.

1.17 BENZOXAZOLE

1.18 QUINOLINE

(a) Chloroquine:

1, 4-pentanediamine, N^4-[7-chloro-4-quinolinyl]-N', N'-diethyl

[7-chloro-4-[[4-(diethylamino)-1-methylbutyl]amino] quinoline]

(b) Quinine sulfate:

Cinchonan-9-ol, 6'-methoxy-(8α, 9R)-sulfate (2 : 1) salt dihydrate.

1.19 ISOQUINOLINE

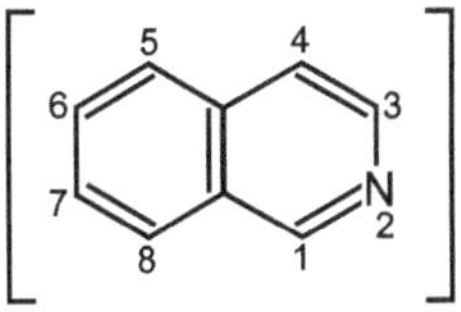

(a) Papaverine HCl:

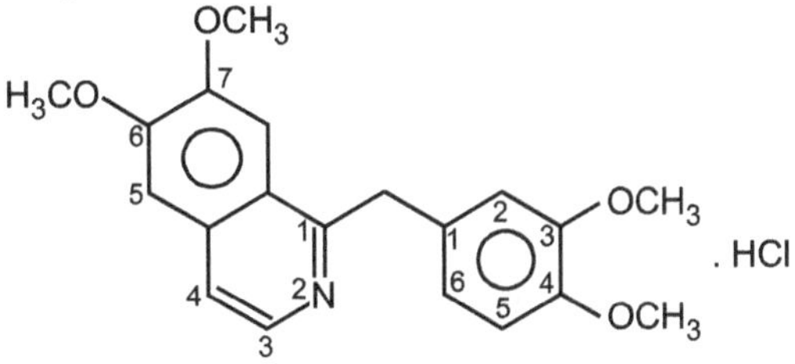

. HCl

Isoquinoline 1-[(3, 4-dimethoxyphenyl)methyl]-6, 7-dimethoxy.HCl

6, 7-Dimethoxy-1-veratrylisoquinoline. HCl

6, 7-Dimethoxy-1-[1-(3, 4-dimethoxyphenyl) methyl] isoquinoline

(b) Primaquine:

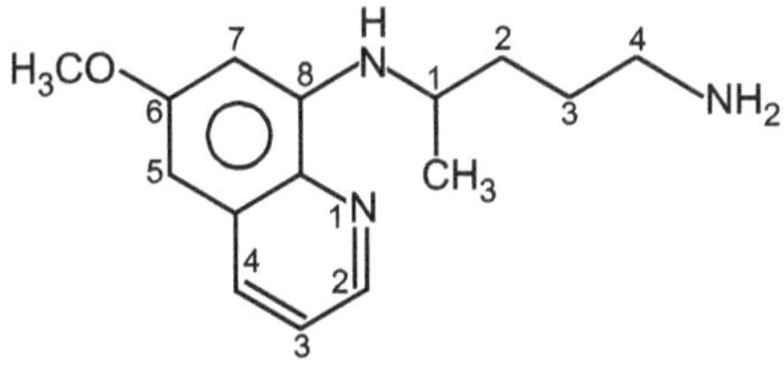

1, 4-pentanediamine, N-(6-methoxy-8-quinolinyl)–(±)

or   [(±) – 8 – [(4-Amino-1-methyl butyl) amino]-6-methoxyquinoline]

(c) Emetine:

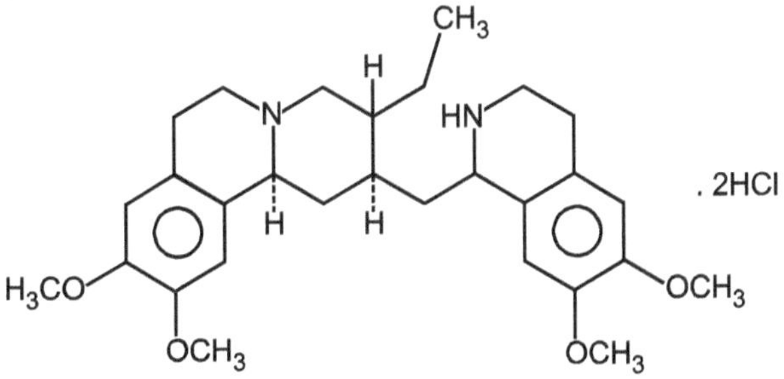

. 2HCl

Emetan, 6', 7', 10, 11-tetramethoxy.2HCl

1.20 CINNOLINE

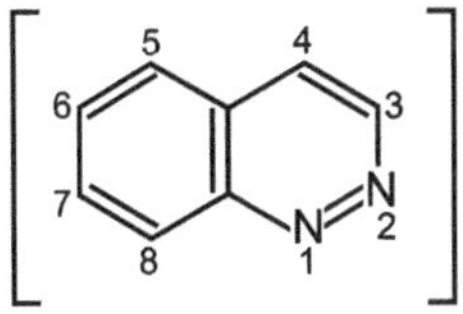

1.21 PURINE

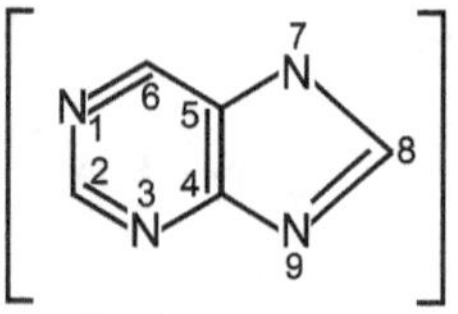

(a) Caffeine:

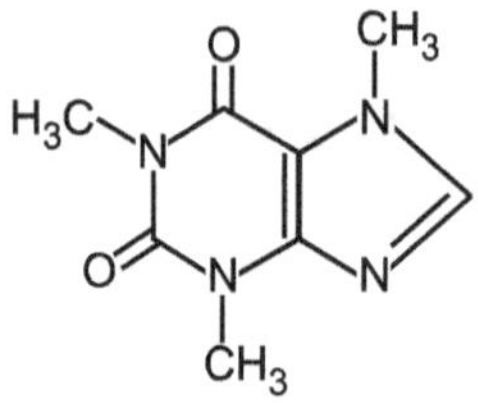

1H-purine-2, 6-dione-3, 7-dihydro-1, 3, 7-trimethyl

or 1, 3, 7-trimethylxanthine

1, 3, 7-trimethyl-3, 7-dihydro purine 2, 6-dione

(b) Dimenhydrinate:

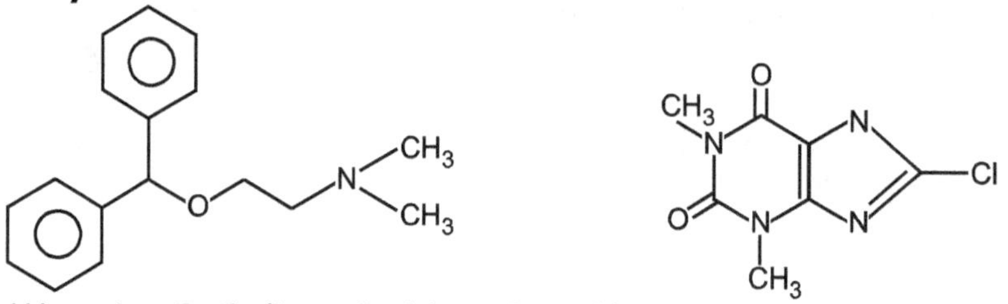

1H-purine-2, 6-dione-8-chloro-3, 7-dihydro-1, 3-dimethyl compound with 2-(diphenylmethoxy)-N, N-dimethylethanamine (1: 1)

or 8-Chlorotheophylline compound with 2-(diphenylmethoxy)-N, N-dimethyl ethylamine (1: 1).

1.22 XANTHINE

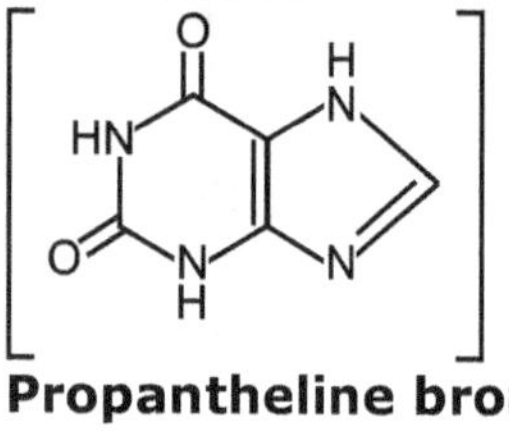

(a) Propantheline bromide:

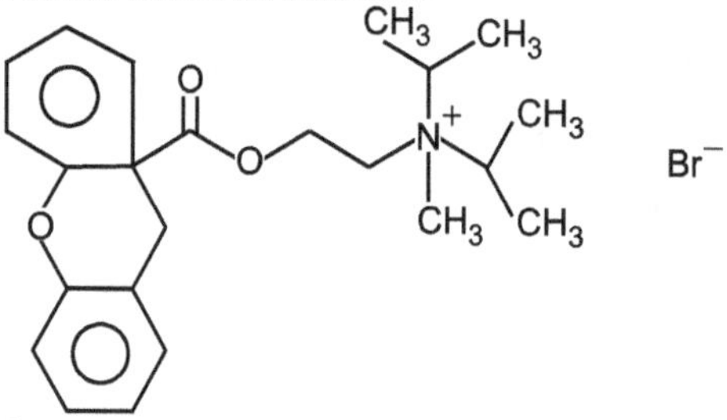

2-propanaminium-N-methyl-N-(1-methylethyl)-N-[2-[[(9H-xanthene-9-Gylcarbonyl) oxy] ethyl]-bromide

or (2-Hydroxyethyl) diisopropylmethylammonium bromide xanthene-9 carboxylate.

(b) Thiothixene:

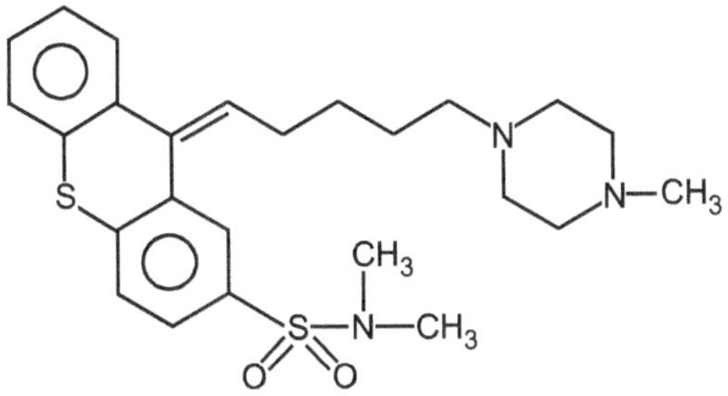

9H-thioxanthene-2-sulfonamide N, N-dimethyl-9-[3-(4-methyl)-1-piperazinyl] propylidene-(2)

1.23 PTERIDINE

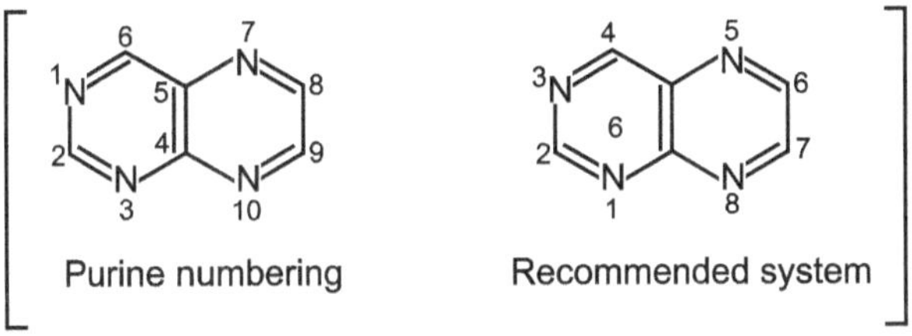

Purine numbering   Recommended system

(a) Folic acid:

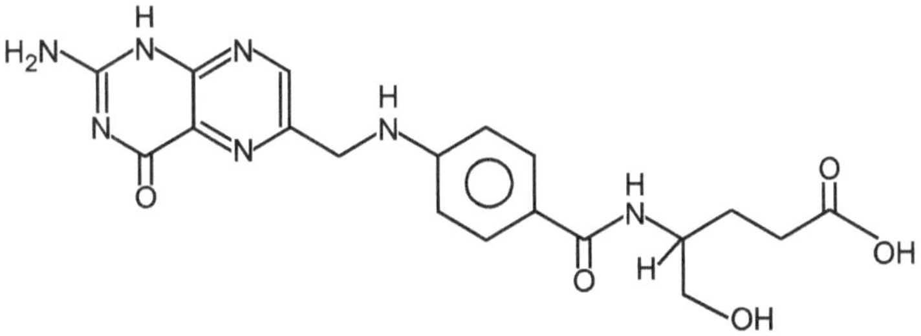

L-Glutamic acid, N-[4-[[(2-amino-1, 4-dihydro-4-oxo-6-pteridinyl]methyl] amino] benzel] folic acid

or   N-[P-[[(2-amino-4-hydroxy-6-pteridinyl)methyl]amine] – benzoyl]-L-glutamic acid

(b) Methotrexate:

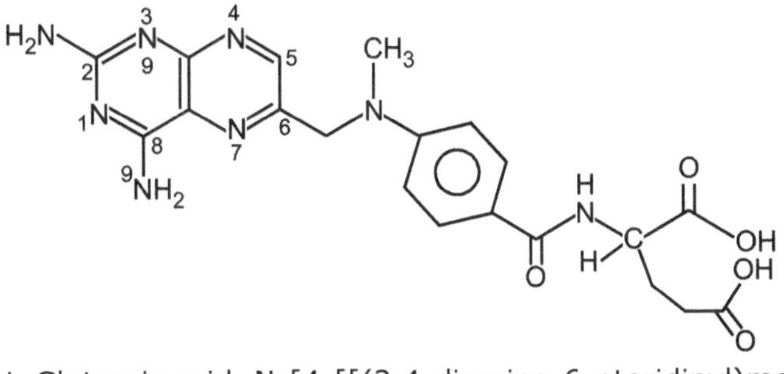

L-Glutamic acid, N-[4-[[(2,4-diamino-6-pteridinyl)methyl]-methylamine]benzoyl] L(+)-N-[P[(x,y-Diamino-6-pteridinyl]methyl]methylamino]benzoyl]glutamic acid

1.24 COUMARIN

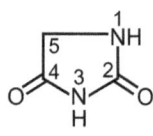

1.25 QUINAZOLINE

1.26 HYDANTOIN

Hydantoin   5,5-Diphenyl hydantoin

SYNTHESIS AND REACTIONS OF FOLLOWING DRUGS
1.27 FURAN

Furan

Furan is a colourless liquid (B.P. = 31.4°C). It has odour of chloroform. It is slightly soluble in water but completely soluble in all organic solvents.

1.27.1 Synthesis

1. From mucic acid:

Mucic acid on dry distillation gives furoic acid which on decarboxylation in the presence of quinoline in copper powder yields furan.

Mucic acid $\xrightarrow[\text{−3H}_2\text{O, −CO}_2]{\text{Dry distillation}}$ Pyromucic acid or Furoic acid $\xrightarrow[\substack{\text{Decarboxylation in the} \\ \text{presence of quinoline in} \\ \text{Cu-powder, − CO}_2}]{\Delta}$ Furan $+ CO_2 \uparrow$

2. From an Aldopentose (Industrial preparation):

Aldopentose is obtained by distillation of maize cobs or rice husk with dil. H_2SO_4. Aldopentose on dry distillation gives furfural which on heating in the presence of oxide catalyst at 400°C gives furan.

Aldopentose $\xrightarrow[\Delta]{- 3H_2O}$ Furfural $\xrightarrow[\substack{\text{Oxide catalyst} \\ (-CO)}]{\text{Steam, 400}^\circ\text{C}}$ Furan

3. Preparation of Derivatives of Furan:

(a) 2, 5-derivatives of Furan (From 1, 4-dicarbonyl compound):

Enolizable 1, 4-dicarbonyl compound is heated with dehydrating agent such as P_2O_5 to get corresponding 2, 5 derivatives of furan.

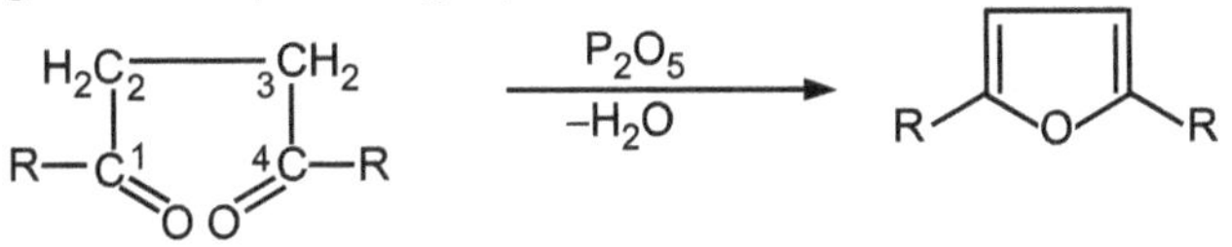

(b) 2, 3, 5-derivatives (Feist-Benary Synthesis):

α-haloketone reacts with β-ketoester in the presence of pyridine to form corresponding 2, 3, 5 derivative of furan which is called Feist-Benary synthesis.

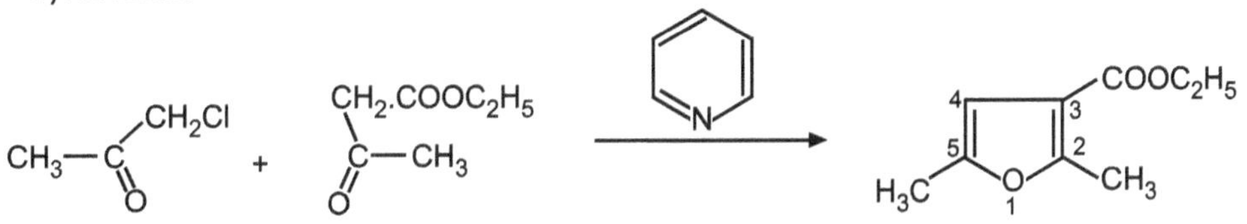

α-chloroacetone   β-ketoester (EAA)   2,5-Dimethyl-3-ethyl furanoate

(c) 2, 3, 4, 5 derivatives (From ethylacetoacetate):

Ethyl acetoacetate reacts with sodium hydroxide to form its salt, which in the presence of iodine forms 1, 4-dimethyl-1, 4-dioxo-2, 3-dimethyl, acetate which on further enolization followed by acidification to give corresponding 2, 3, 4, 5 derivatives of furan.

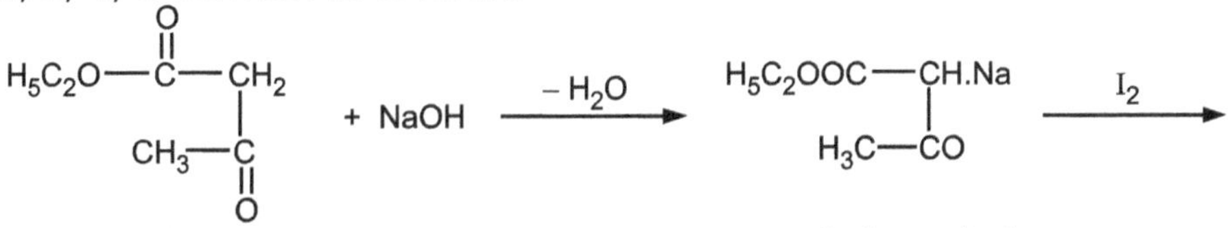

EAA
(Ethyl aceto acetate)

Sodium salt of
ethyl aceto acetate

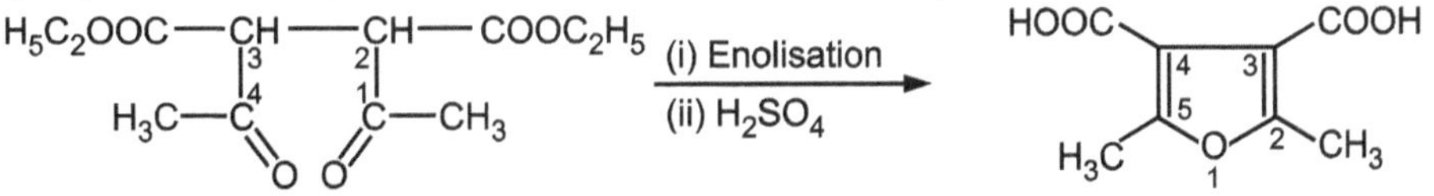

(1,4-dimethyl, 1,4-dioxo-2,3-dimethyl acetate)   (2,5-dimethyl furan 3,4-dicarboxylic acid)

1.27.2 Chemical Reactions

Resonance structures of furan

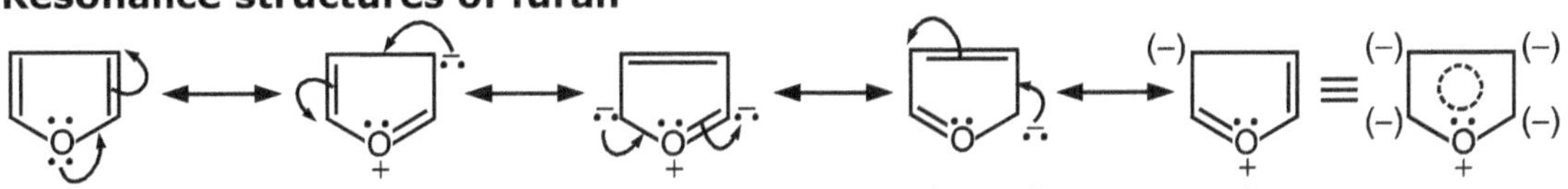

The aromatic properties of furan may be interpreted in terms of M.O.T. But since the oxygen atom in furan accommodates +ve charge less readily than 'N' of pyrrole, therefore, furan is less reactive than pyrrole, just as phenol is less reactive than aniline.

It undergoes electrophilic substitution reaction at 2 or 5 position.

1. Electrophilic Substitution:

Furan undergoes electrophilic substitution at 2 or 5 position.

(a) Halogenation: At room temperature, furan reacts rapidly with halogens and the liberated halogen acids cause polymerization. Hence halogeno-furans are generally prepared by either of the methods given below:

(i)

Furan   + Cl_2 $\xrightarrow{-40\,^{\circ}C}$ 2,5-Dichloro furan   +   2-Chloro furan

(ii)

Furoic acid   COOH $\xrightarrow{Br_2}$ Bromo furoic acid $\xrightarrow[-CO_2]{\Delta}$ Bromo furan

(iii)

Furan $\xrightarrow[CH_3COONa]{HgCl_2}$ Furyl mercuric chloride (HgCl) $\xrightarrow[Demercuration]{I_2}$ Iodo furan (I)

However, chlorination of furan at 40°C gives 2-chloro and 2, 5-dichloro products. Similarly, 2-bromofuran can be produced by action of Br_2 in dioxan or furan at 0°C.

(b) Nitration:

Furan $\xrightarrow[(Nitroacetate)]{CH_3COONO_2}$ 2-Nitro furan (HgCl)   + CH_3COOH Acetic acid

Furan + HNO_3 (Nitric acid) + $CH_3-\overset{\overset{O}{\|}}{C}-O-\overset{\overset{O}{\|}}{C}-CH_3$ (Acetic anhydride) $\longrightarrow$ 2-Nitro furane ($-NO_2$) + 2 $CH_3-\overset{\overset{O}{\|}}{C}-OH$

(c) Sulphonation: Furan can be sulphonated by heating with sulpho-pyridine or conc. H_2SO_4 or sulphur trioxide in pyridine at 70°C to yield furan-2-sulphonic acid.

Furan $\xrightarrow{}$ Furan-2-sulphonic acid (SO_3H)

Sulpho pyridine
pyridine sulphonic acid
or H_2SO_4

(d) Acylation (Friedel-Craft's Reaction):

(i) Furan can be acetylated with acetic anhydride in the presence of BF_3 or $SnCl_4$ at $0°C$ to give 2-acetyl furan.

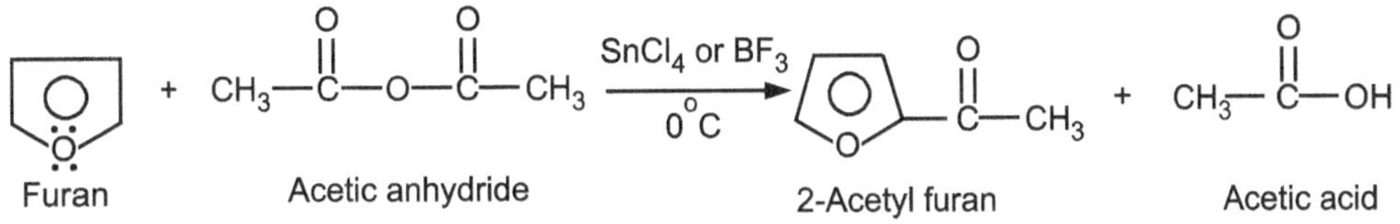

Furan   Acetic anhydride   2-Acetyl furan   Acetic acid

(ii)

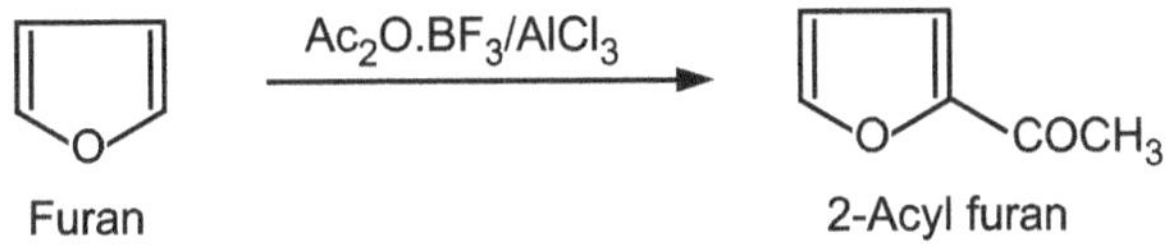

Furan   2-Acyl furan

(e) Formylation:

(i) Gattermann reaction: When furan is treated with HCN, HCl and $ZnCl_2$ or $Zn(CN)_2$ and HCl or HCN and $ZnCl_2$ to give rise to formylated furan.

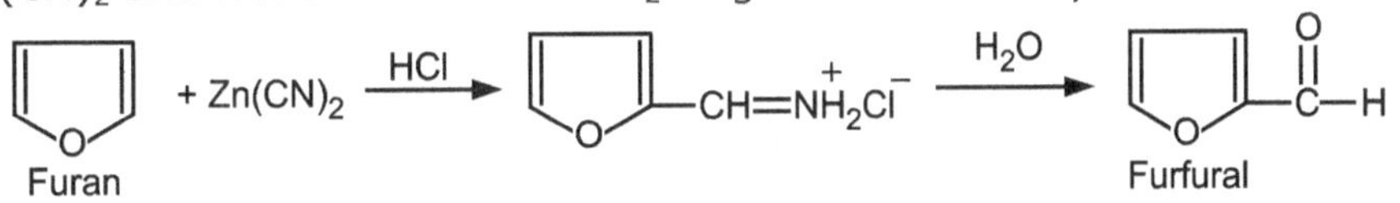

Furan   Furfural

(ii) Vilsmeyer reaction: Furan react with dimethyl formamide and phosphorous oxychloride to formylate furan.

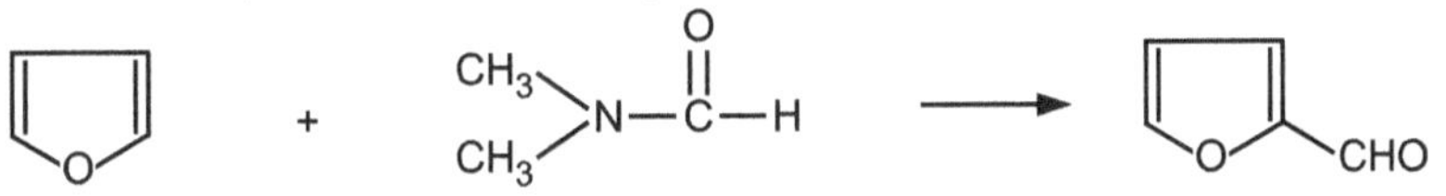

2. Reaction with diazonium salts (Gomberg reaction):

Furan on heating with phenyl diazonium chloride gives corresponding phenyl furan.

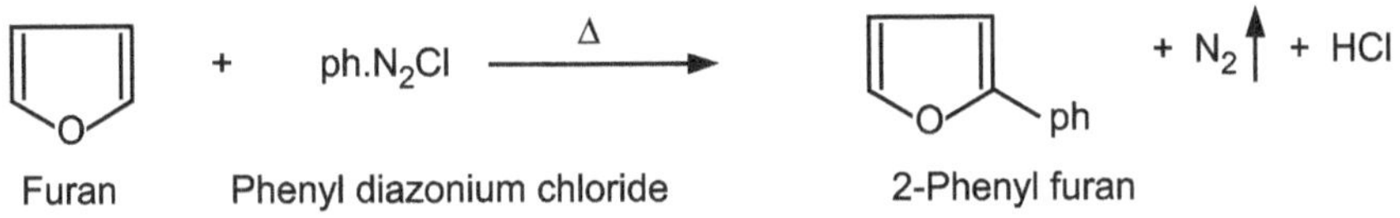

Furan   Phenyl diazonium chloride   2-Phenyl furan

3. Reaction with Organic Lithium (R-Li/Ar-Li):

Furan reacts with n-butyl lithium in ether to give 2-furan lithium.

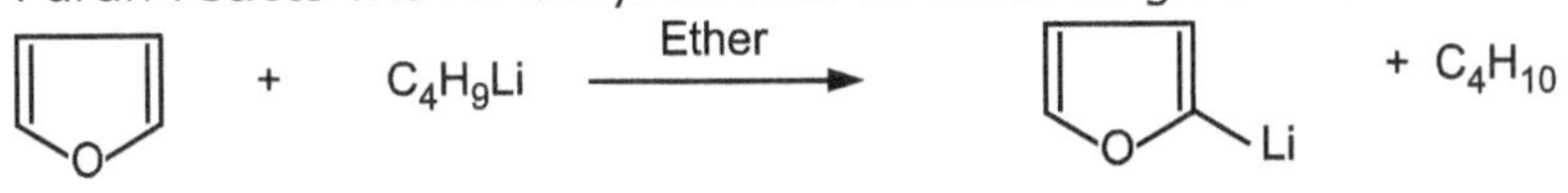

2-Litho furan (2-Furan lithium)
(Important synthetic compound)

2-furan lithium undergoes many of the usual reactions of organolithium compounds. It combines with carbon dioxide to form furoic acid (furan-2-carboxylic acid).

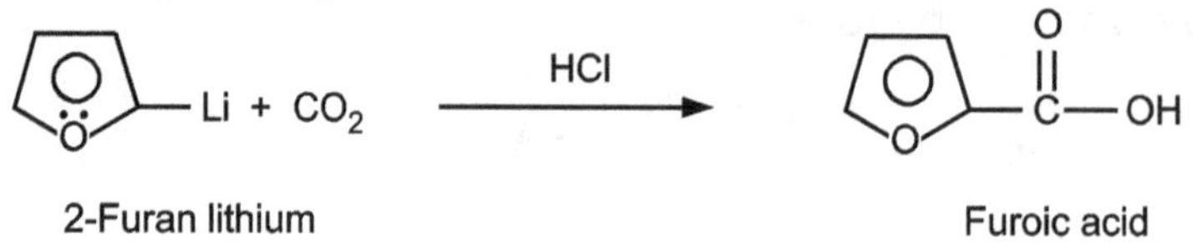

2-Furan lithium   Furoic acid

4. Diels-Alder Reaction (Reaction with maleic anhydride):

Diels-Alder reaction consists of addition of a conjugated diene to a second unsaturated molecule generally called as dienophile resulting in the formation of cyclic compound commonly known as Diels-Alder Adduct.

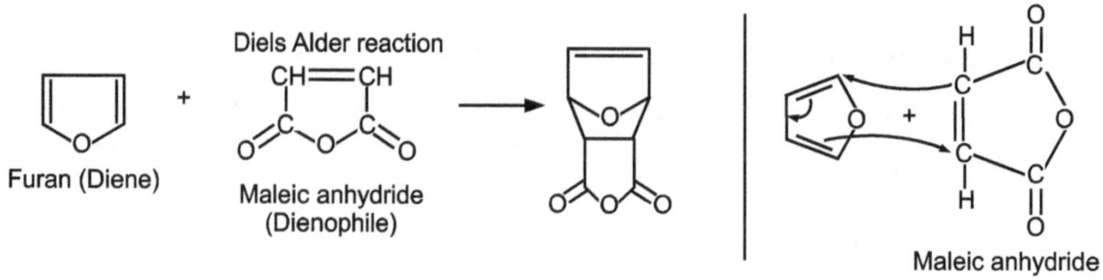

Furan (Diene)   Maleic anhydride (Dienophile)   Maleic anhydride

5. Reduction and Oxidation:

Reduction: Furan is reduced by hydrogen in the presence of nickel to produce tetrahydrofuran.

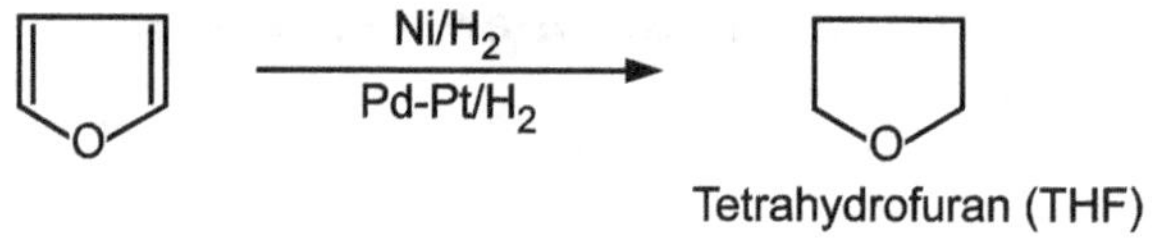

Tetrahydrofuran (THF)

Oxidation:

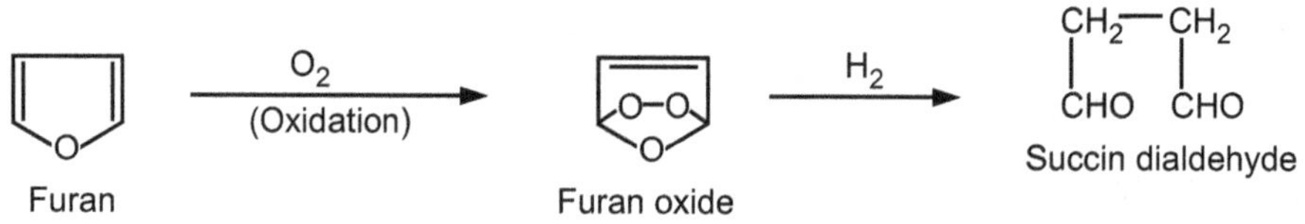

Furan   Furan oxide   Succin dialdehyde

1.28 PYRROLE

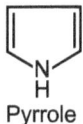

Pyrrole

Pyrrole occurs in coal tar and in bone oil, the latter is obtained by dry distillation or pyrolysis of animal by-products such as horns, hooves and bones.

Pyrrole is a colourless liquid having B.P. = 131°C, turns brown in air. The vapours with HCl give red colour. It is most important among the 5 membered ring because its nucleus occurs in many important natural products e.g. Chlorophyll, Haemin, Bilirubin, alkaloid, vit. B_{12} etc.

1.28.1 Isolation

It occurs in coal tar and bone oil. Bone oil on fractional distillation by boiling with potassium hydroxide, the fraction between 100°C - 150°C containing pyrrole is collected.

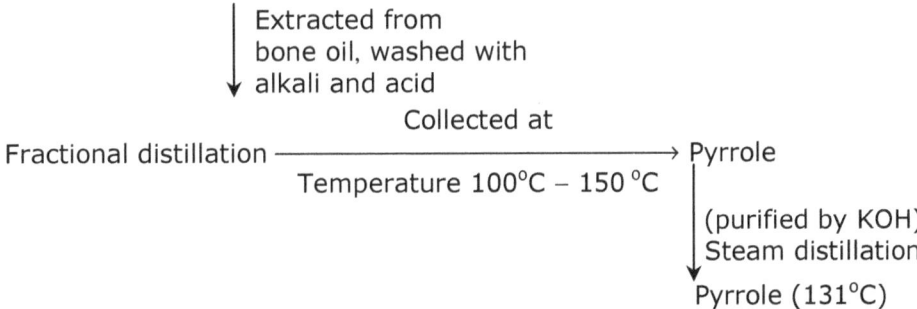

1.28.2 Synthesis

1. **From acetylene and ammonia:** By passing a mixture of acetylene and ammonia through a red hot tube.

    CH≡CH + CH≡CH + HNH H → (Red hot tube, Δ) → Pyrrole + H₂↑

2. **From furan and NH₃:** By passing a mixture of furan, ammonia and steam over aluminium oxide catalyst at 480° – 490°C. This is a commercial method of producing large scale of pyrrole in industry.

    Furan + NH₃ → (Al_2O_3, 480-490°C) → Pyrrole + H_2O

3. Synthesis of pyrrole derivatives:

(i) Pall-Knorr Synthesis (2, 5-derivatives): This method consists of the condensation of 1, 4-dicarbonyl compounds with NH_3 or $1°$ amine when succinaldehyde (i.e. R = R' = H) pyrrole itself is obtained.

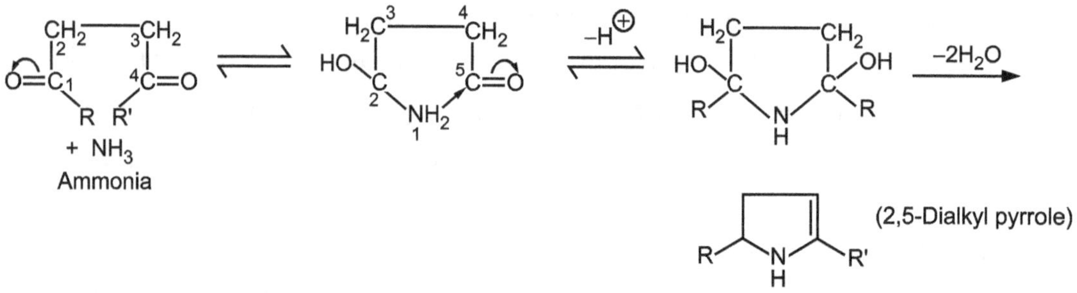

(2,5-Dialkyl pyrrole)

(ii) Knorr synthesis (2, 3, 4 derivatives): This is the most general method for the synthesis of pyrrole and involves the condensation of an α-amino ketone or α-amino-β-ketoester with another ketone having an active methylene group such as acetoacetic ester/ethyl aceto acetate.

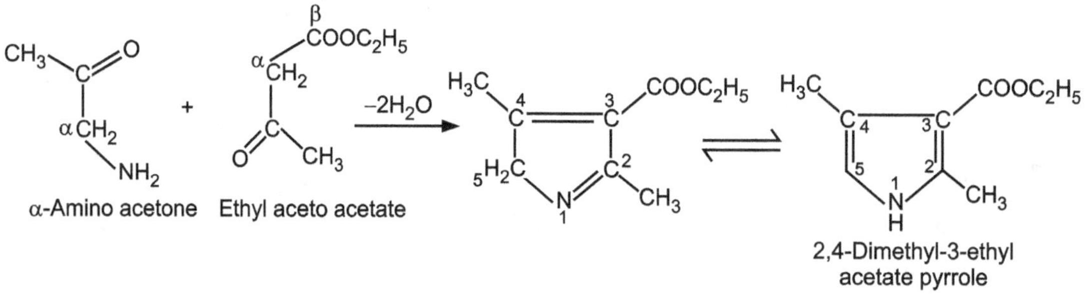

α-Amino acetone   Ethyl aceto acetate

2,4-Dimethyl-3-ethyl acetate pyrrole

(iii) Hantzsch synthesis (2, 3, 5 derivatives): This method involves the condensation of a β-ketoester and α-chloroketone in the presence of ammonia or $1°$ amine. But this method suffers from the fact that some furan derivative is also formed.

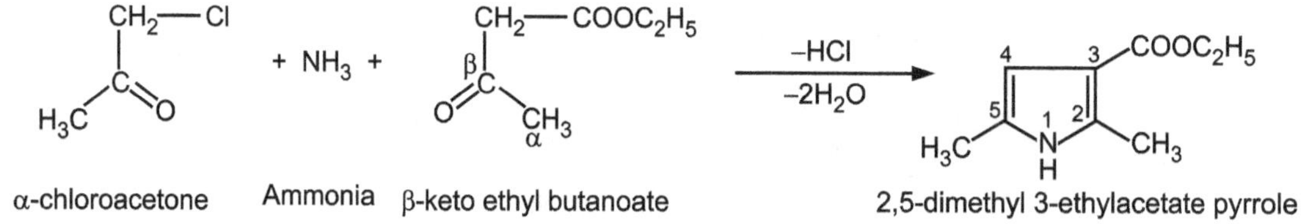

α-chloroacetone   Ammonia   β-keto ethyl butanoate   2,5-dimethyl 3-ethylacetate pyrrole

1.28.3 Basic and Acidic Character of Pyrrole

Basic character: From the resonating structure we see that the lone pair of electrons on the nitrogen atom is not readily available for protonation and hence pyrrole behaves as a weak base.

Acidic character: Pyrrole is a weakly acidic compound due to the presence of iminohydrogen atom. The acidic character of pyrrole can be explained on the basis of the following two facts.

(a) Due to greater 'S' character (sp hybridization) of the N-H bond in pyrrole the bonding electrons of the bond are held more strongly to the pyrrole 'N' and hence hydrogen is eliminated as a proton.

(b) Once the pyrryl anion is formed, it is stabilized due to resonance.

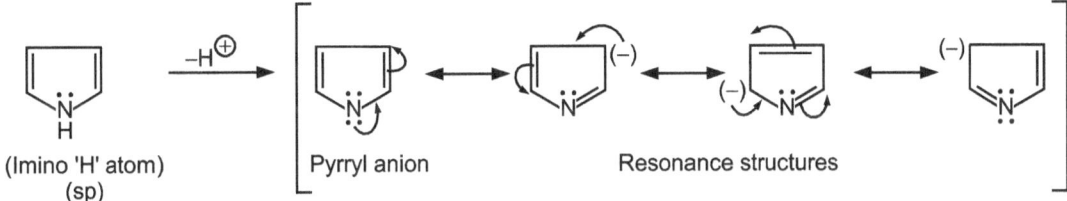

(Imino 'H' atom)   Pyrryl anion   Resonance structures
(sp)

However, the stabilization of pyrryl anion does not mean that pyrrole is a strong acid. It is important to note that alkali metal derivatives of pyrrole resemble phenol, it undergoes Kolbe and Reimer-Tiemann reaction.

1.28.4 Chemical Reactions

Resonance structures of pyrrole:

Pyrrole is the most reactive among thiophene, furan, benzene and pyridine towards electrophilic substitution reagent and its reactivity is comparable to that of aromatic amines and phenols.

The electrophilic substitution of pyrrole occurs preferentially at 2nd position followed by 3rd. The predominance of 2nd substituted product over 3 is because of the fact that the positive charge in the transition state of the former is delocalized over 3rd atom as compared to 2nd atom in the latter. Thus, the intermediate from α-attack (2-substituted) has less energy (more stable) than the intermediate from β-attack (3-substituted).

1. C-2 Substitution:

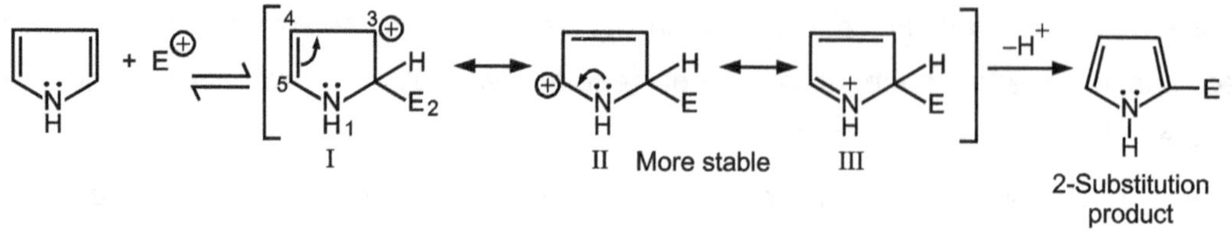

I   II More stable   III

2-Substitution product

2. C-3 Substitution:

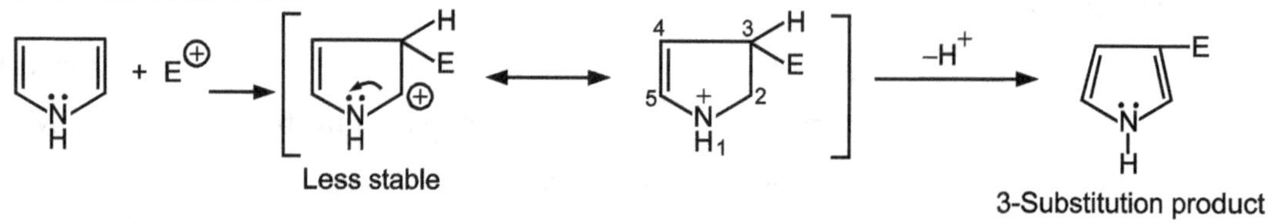

Less stable

3-Substitution product

Thus position 3 is attacked only when both of the 2-positions are blocked.

1. Pyrrole Reactions: Electrophilic substitution reactions in pyrrole.

(a) Halogenation:

(a) Chlorination of pyrrole is carried out with sulphuryl chloride in ether at 0°C. Tetra chloropyrrole is obtained.

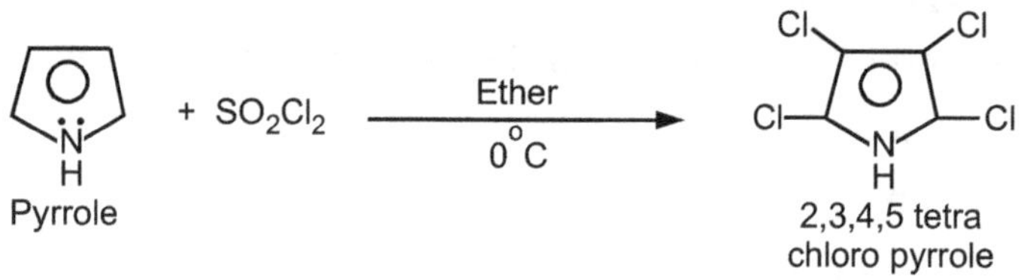

Pyrrole   + SO_2Cl_2 $\xrightarrow[0°C]{Ether}$

2,3,4,5 tetra chloro pyrrole

(b) Bromination of pyrrole is done with bromine in ethanol at 0°C. Tetra bromo pyrrole is obtained.

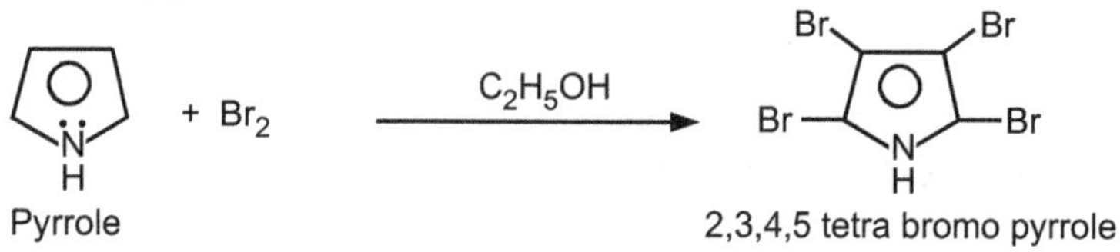

Pyrrole   + Br_2 $\xrightarrow{C_2H_5OH}$

2,3,4,5 tetra bromo pyrrole

(c) Iodination with iodine in an aqueous solution of potassium iodide produces tetraiodo pyrrole.

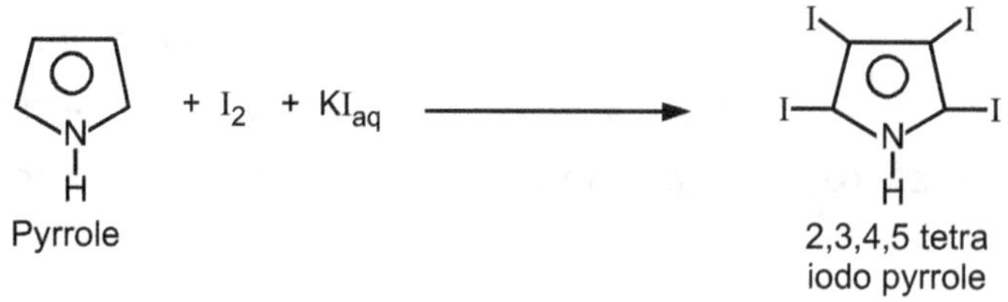

Pyrrole   + I_2 + KI_{aq} $\longrightarrow$

2,3,4,5 tetra iodo pyrrole

(b) Nitration: Pyrrole can be nitrated by taking cold solution of nitric acid in acetic anhydride to give 2-nitropyrrole.

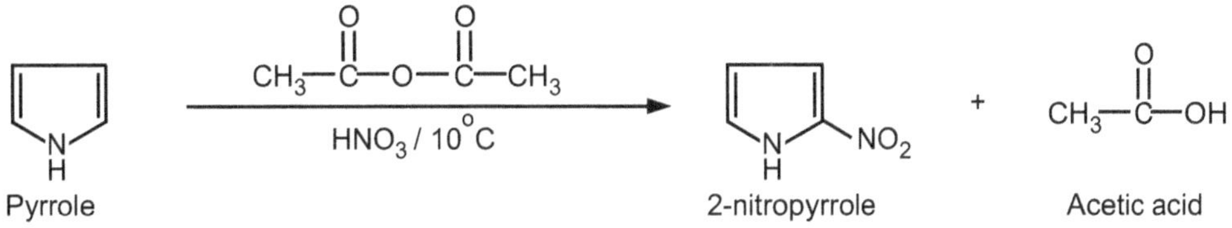

Pyrrole   2-nitropyrrole   Acetic acid

(c) Sulphonation: Pyrrole may be sulphonated with sulphur trioxide in pyridine at 100°C to give pyrrole-2-sulphonic acid.

Pyrrole   Pyrrole-2-sulphonic acid

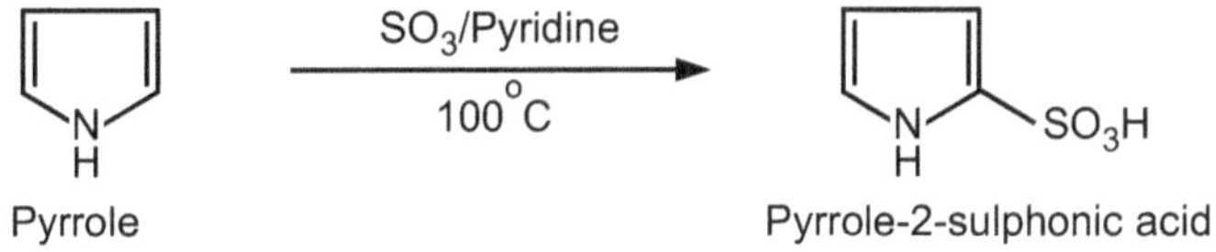

(d) Acetylation:

(i) **Friedel-Craft reaction:** Pyrrole reacts with acetyl chloride and tin chloride or acetic anhydride and boron trifluoride and undergoes Friedel-Craft reaction to form 2-acetopyrrole.

Pyrrole   2-Acetopyrrole

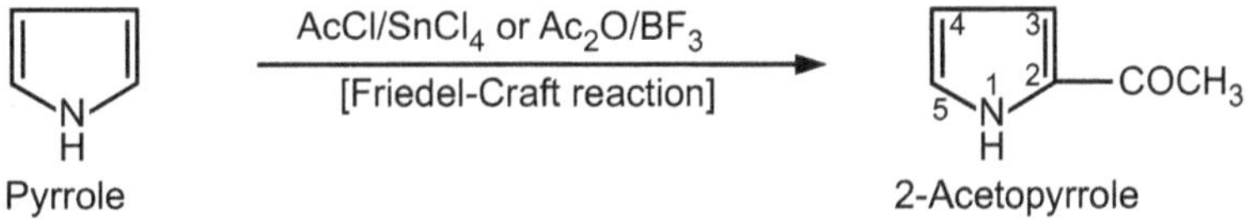

(ii) **Houben-Hoesch synthesis:** Pyrrole when treated with methyl cyanide in the presence of zinc chloride (acidic) and the product obtained on acidification to form 2-acetopyrrole.

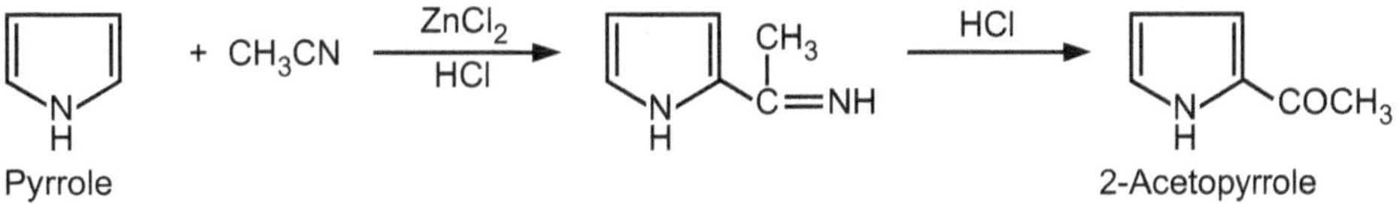

Pyrrole   2-Acetopyrrole

(iii)

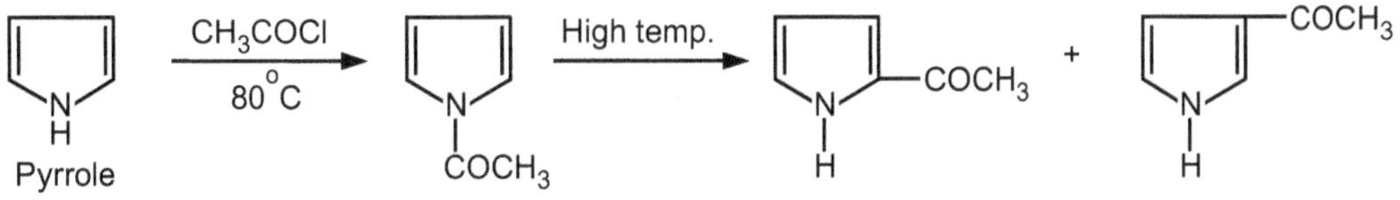

Pyrrole

(e) Formylation:

(i) Gattermann reaction: Pyrrole reacts with hydrogen cyanide and hydrochloric acid followed by hydrolysis to form pyrrole-2-aldehyde.

Pyrrole   (i) HCN—HCl   (ii) H_2O Pyrrole-2-aldehyde

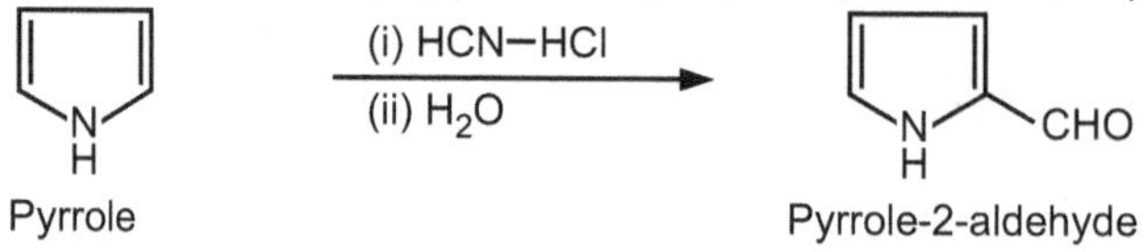

(ii) Vilsmeyer reaction: Pyrrole reacts with dimethyl amino formaldehyde and oxyphosphorous chloride to form pyrrole-2-aldehyde.

$Me_2NCHO—POCl_3$

Pyrrole   Pyrrole-2-aldehyde

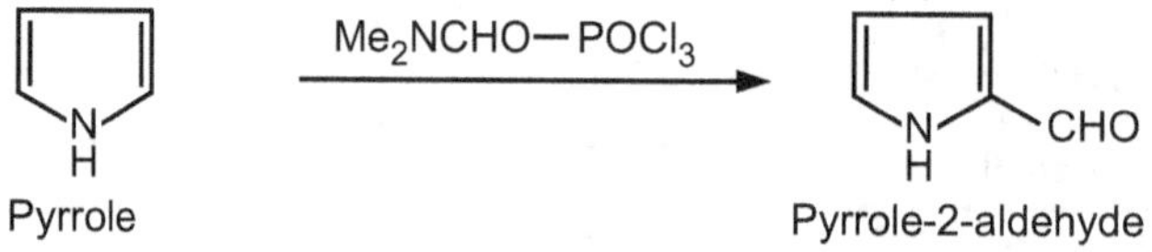

(iii) Reimer-Tiemann reaction: Pyrrole reacts with chloroform, aqueous potassium hydroxide and hydrochloric acid to form pyrrole-2-aldehyde and 3-chloro pyridine.

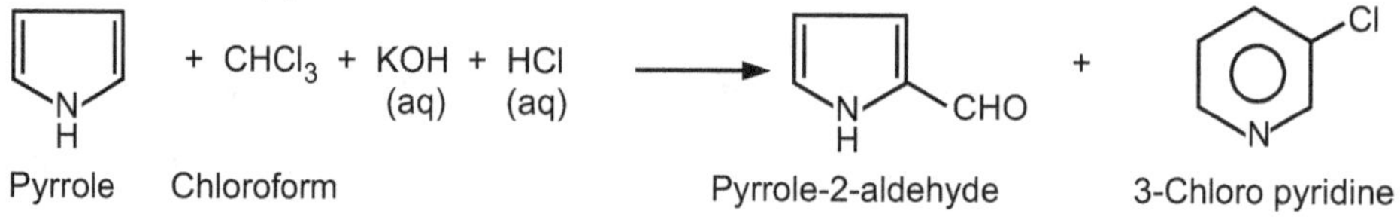

$+ CHCl_3 + KOH + HCl$
(aq)   (aq)

Pyrrole   Chloroform   Pyrrole-2-aldehyde   3-Chloro pyridine

(f) Alkylation:

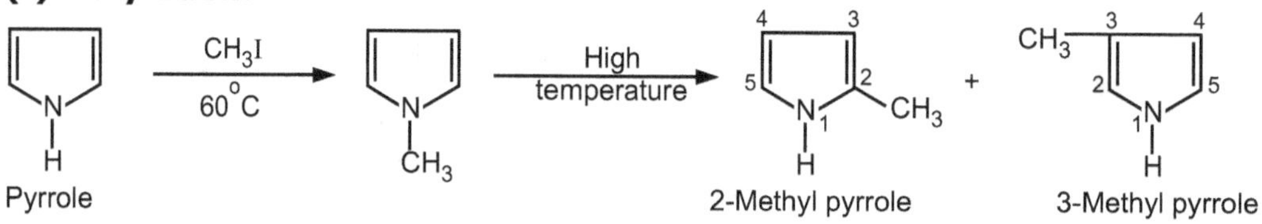

Pyrrole CH_3I $60°C$ High temperature   2-Methyl pyrrole   3-Methyl pyrrole

1. Carboxylation:

(i) Kolbes-Schmidt reaction: Pyrrole on heating with carbon dioxide at 120°C, 6 atm. pressure followed by hydrolysis to form 2-pyrrolic acid.

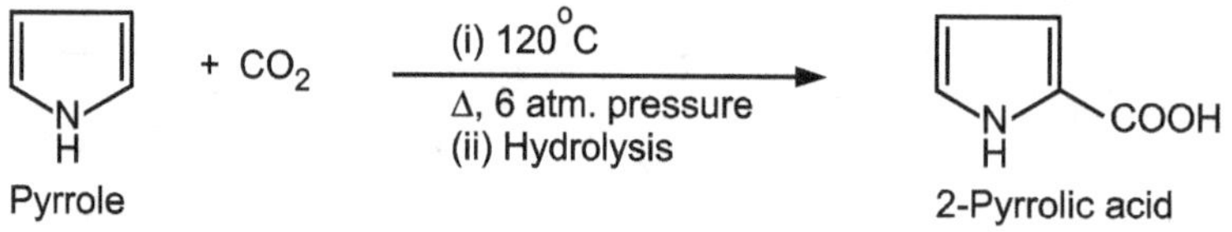

Pyrrole $+ CO_2$ (i) $120°C$ Δ, 6 atm. pressure   (ii) Hydrolysis   2-Pyrrolic acid

(ii) Carboxylation: Pyrrole reacts with carbon tetrachloride and potassium hydroxide to form 2-pyrrolic acid.

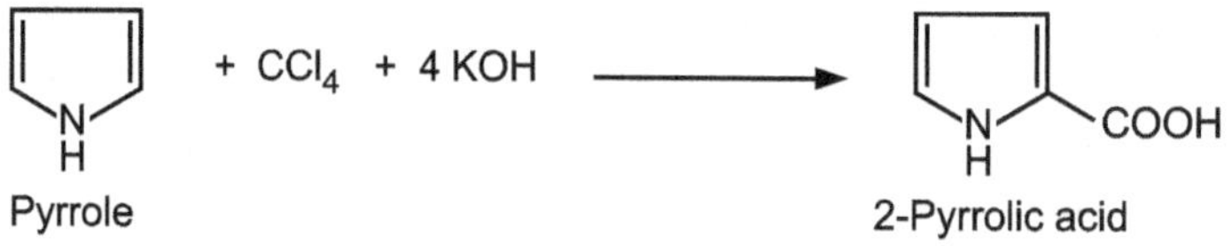

Pyrrole $+ CCl_4 + 4 KOH$ 2-Pyrrolic acid

3. Reaction with diazonium salt:

Pyrrole reacts with phenyl diazonium chloride in the presence of sodium acetate to form 2 (phenylazo) pyrrole.

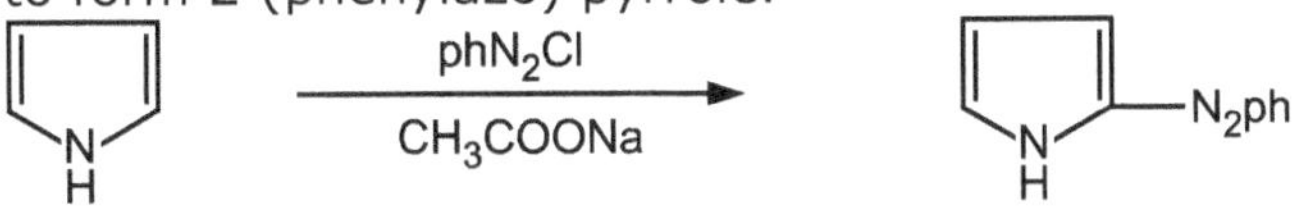

Pyrrole — $\xrightarrow[\text{CH}_3\text{COONa}]{\text{phN}_2\text{Cl}}$ — 2 (Phenylazo) pyrrole ($-N_2$ph)

4. Reaction with Grignard reagent:

Pyrrole reacts with methyl magnesium bromide to form pyrrole magnesium bromide.

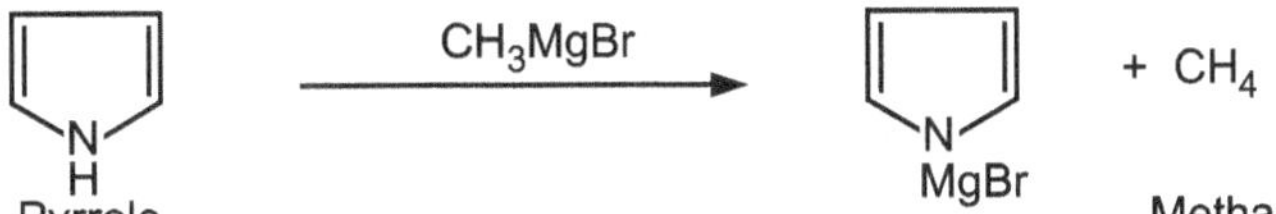

Pyrrole — $\xrightarrow{\text{CH}_3\text{MgBr}}$ — MgBr + CH_4 Methane

5. Mannich reaction:

Aromatic compound when treated with formaldehyde, ammonia, $1°$ amine or $2°$ amine in the presence of HCl forms corresponding β-amino compound.

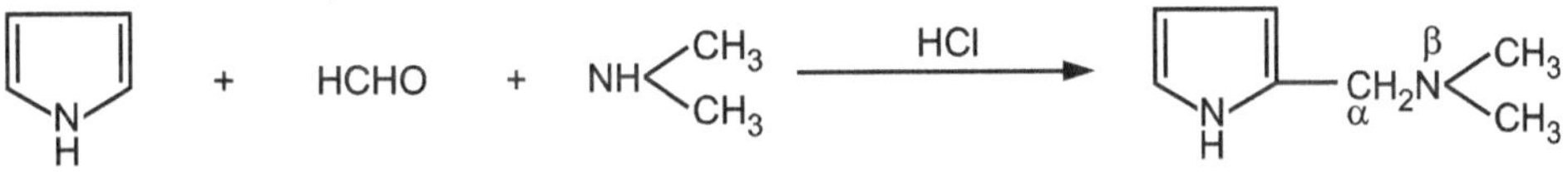

Pyrrole + HCHO (Formaldehyde) + $NH\begin{smallmatrix}CH_3\\CH_3\end{smallmatrix}$ (N,N-Dimethyl amine) $\xrightarrow{\text{HCl}}$ β-dimethyl amino methyl pyrrole ($-CH_2N\begin{smallmatrix}\beta\,CH_3\\\alpha\,CH_3\end{smallmatrix}$)

6. Reaction with maleic anhydride:

Pyrrole reacts with maleic anhydride to form pyrrole-2-maleic anhydride which on hydrolysis forms 2-pyrrole succinic acid.

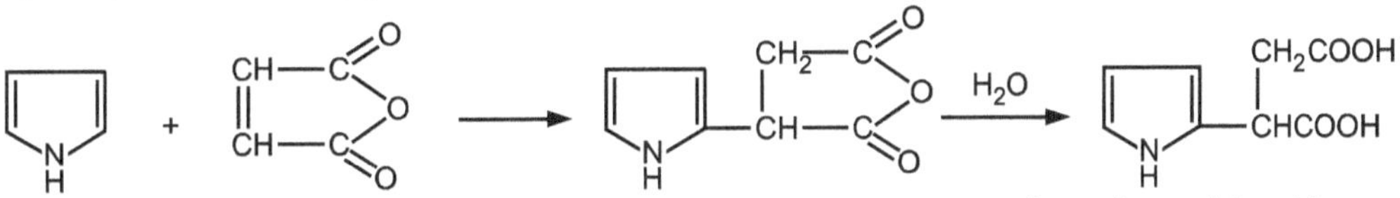

Pyrrole + Maleic anhydride → (pyrrole-2-maleic anhydride) $\xrightarrow{H_2O}$ 2-pyrrole succinic acid

7. Condensation with aldehyde:

Two moles of pyrrole condense with formaldehyde to form dipyrrylmethane.

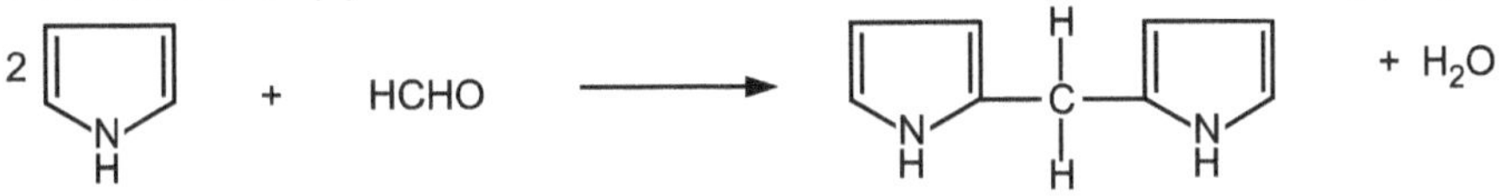

2 Pyrrole + HCHO (Formaldehyde) → Dipyrrylmethane + H_2O

8. Reduction:

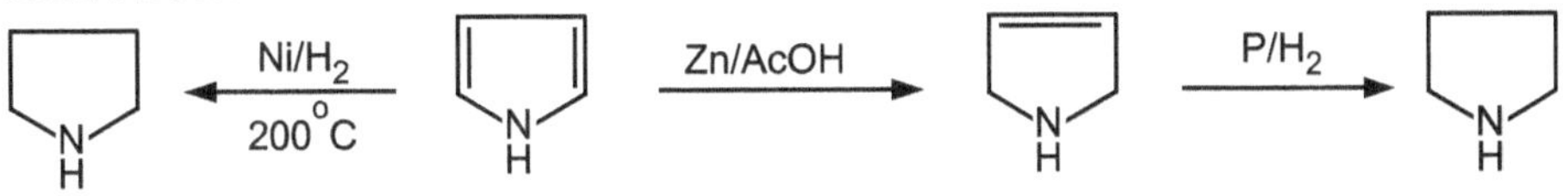

Pyrrolidine ($88°$C) $\xleftarrow[200°C]{\text{Ni/H}_2}$ (131°C) $\xrightarrow{\text{Zn/AcOH}}$ Pyrroline ($91°$C) $\xrightarrow{\text{P/H}_2}$ Pyrrolidine

1.29 PYRIDINE

Pyridine and methyl pyridine were discovered by 'Anderson' in 1849 from bone oil. Pyridine also occurs (0.1%) in the oil fraction of coal tar and is generally isolated from this source by extraction with dil. H_2SO_4 when pyridine forms pyridine sulphate. The free base is then obtained by neutralizing the acid layer with NaOH followed by fractional distillation of the liquid.

Pyridine is hygroscopic colourless liquid, b.p. = 115°C with an unpleasant smell. It is soluble in water as well as organic solvents. Long exposure of pyridine leads to impotency.

1.29.1 Synthesis

1. **From acetylene and HCN:** By passing a mixture of acetylene and hydrogen cyanide through red hot tube.

2. **From aldehyde / ketone and NH₃:**

   (a)

   $4\ CH_3CHO + 2NH_3 \xrightarrow[\Delta]{230°C}$ 2-Methyl-5-ethyl pyridine + 2-Methyl pyridine (α-picoline)

   Acetaldehyde   Ammonia

   (b)

   Glutaconic aldehyde $\xrightarrow[-2H_2O]{NH_3}$ Pyridine

3. **From pentamethylene diamine HCl:**

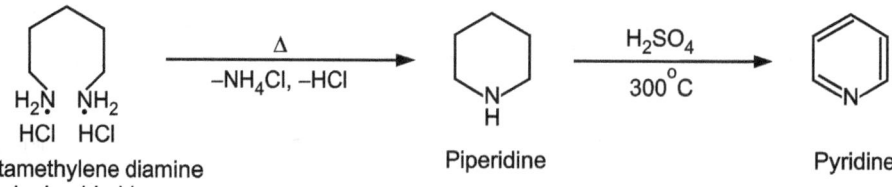

   Pentamethylene diamine hydrochloride $\xrightarrow[-NH_4Cl,\ -HCl]{\Delta}$ Piperidine $\xrightarrow[300°C]{H_2SO_4}$ Pyridine

4. Derivative preparation:

(i) 2, 4/2, 4, 6 derivative (Hantzsch synthesis): This is widely used method for the synthesis of symmetrically substituted pyridine. The method consists of condensation of the two molecules of β-ketoester and one molecule of aldehyde in the presence of NH_3 to give dihydropyridine which is then oxidized with HNO_3. On the other hand if two molecules of aldehyde and one molecule of β-ketoester are used, 2, 4-derivative is obtained.

(a)

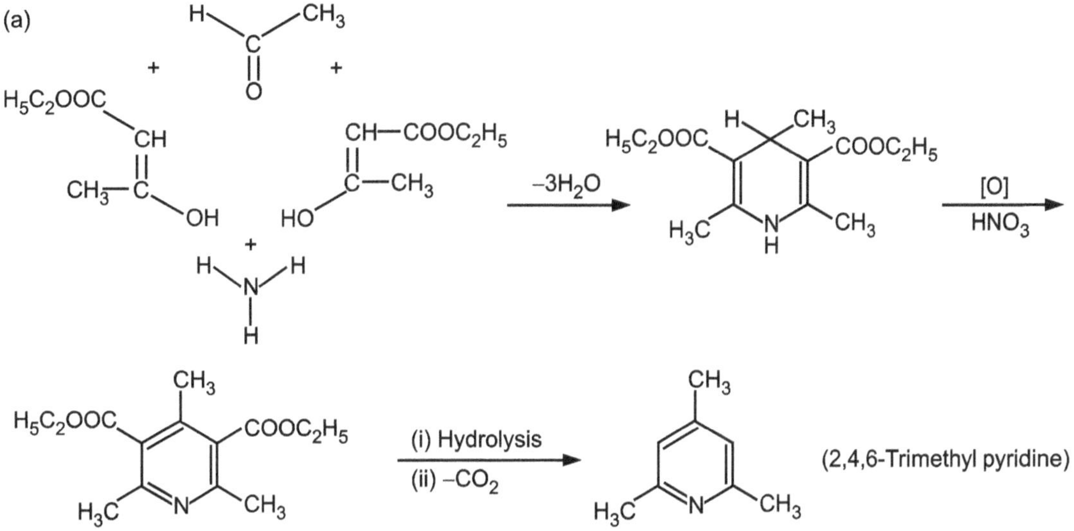

(2,4,6-Trimethyl pyridine)

(b)

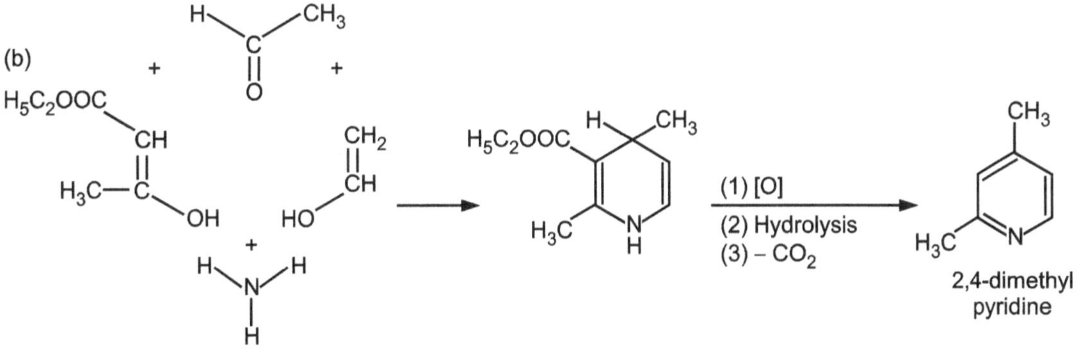

2,4-dimethyl pyridine

(ii) 2, 5-derivative:

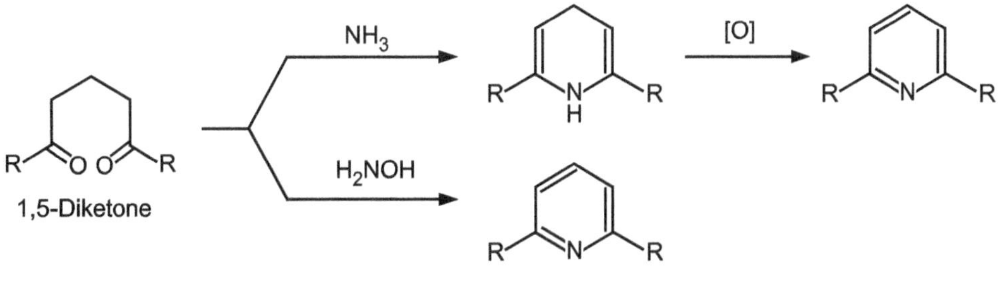

1,5-Diketone

(iii) 3-derivative (Gaureschi Synthesis):

(a) Treatment of cyanoacetamide with a diketone to yield pyridone which can be converted to pyride as below is called Gaureschi synthesis.

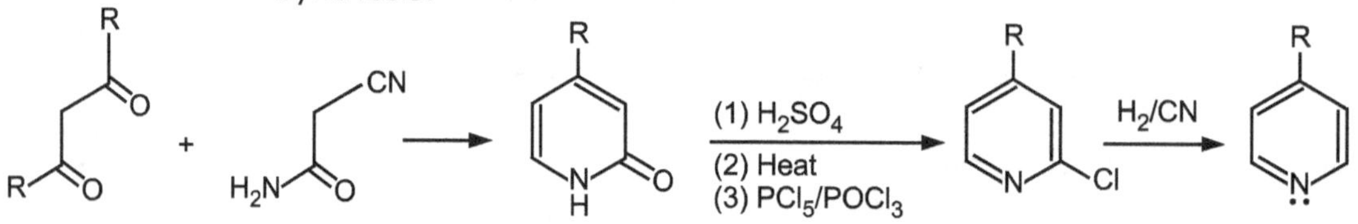

(b) The self condensation of acetoacetic ester to form 2-pyrone dehydroacetic acid which in the presence of H_2SO_4 rearranges to 4-pyrone as extension of Gaureschi synthesis.

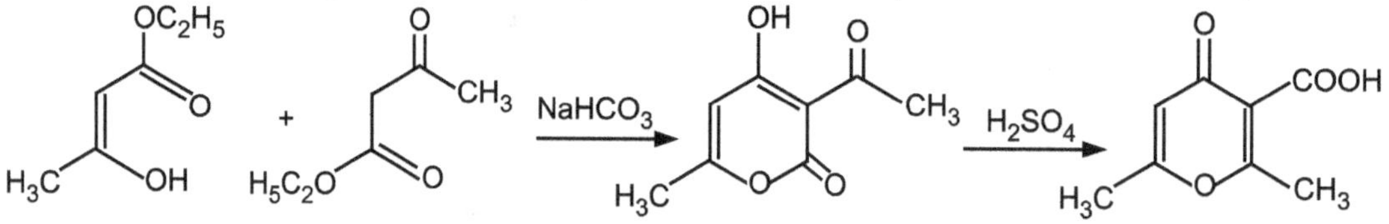

(iv) 2, 3-derivative (from furan):

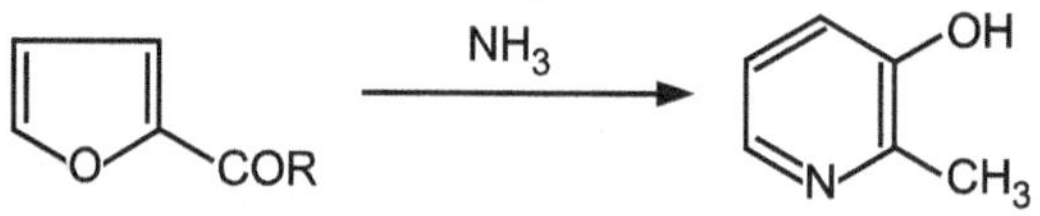

1.29.2 Basic Nature of Pyridine

The basic character of pyridine is due to the presence of a lone pair of electrons on the 'N' atom which can protonate with mineral acids (HCl). It is very interesting to note that, the 'N' atom of pyridine even carrying a lone pair of electrons for protonation is less basic than the alkylamine and also piperidine. One possible explanation for this is that as the 'N' atom of pyridine is sp^2 hybridized (i.e. has more 's' character), it is more electron attracting than the sp^3 (has less 's' character) of $R-NH_2$ and hence the lone pair of electrons on the pyridine 'N' atom is more tightly held or less available for protonation. On the other hand, pyridine is a stronger base than pyrrole because the lone pair of electrons on the 'N' atom in pyridine is not involved in forming aromatic sextet while in pyrrole this pair is involved in aromatic sextet.

The tendency of unshared pair of electrons on 'N' to act as a base has an enormous influence on the behaviour of pyridine towards electrophilic aromatic substitution.

1.29.3 Chemical Reactions

Resonance structure for pyridine:

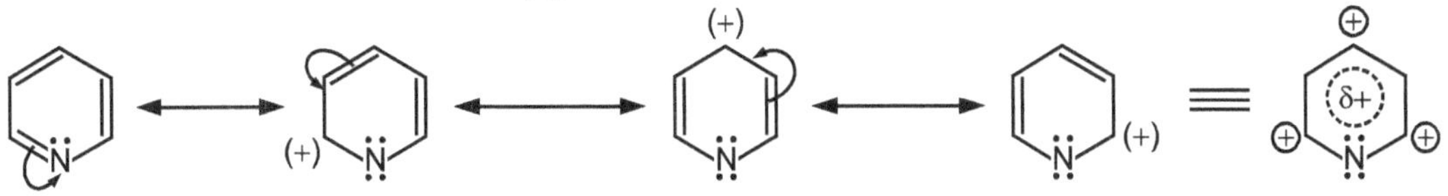

Pyridine is much lesser reactive than benzene towards electrophilic reagents and correspondingly more reactive towards nucleophilic reagents (at 2, 4 and 6). Further the usual electrophiles such as those causing halogenation, nitration, sulphonation and R^+ may react with 'N' atom. Therefore the formation of pyridinium ion deactivates the ring and thus further substitution occurs with difficulty and at position '3'. Hence pyridine may be substituted by electrophiles only under vigorous conditions.

1. Nucleophilic Substitution Reactions:

(a) Amination:

(i)

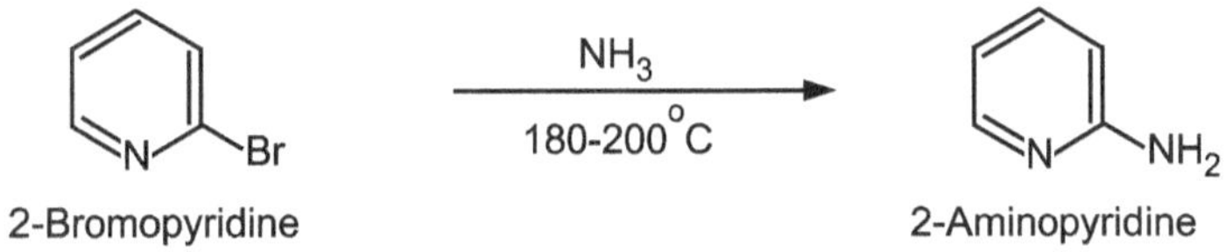

2-Bromopyridine   2-Aminopyridine

(ii)

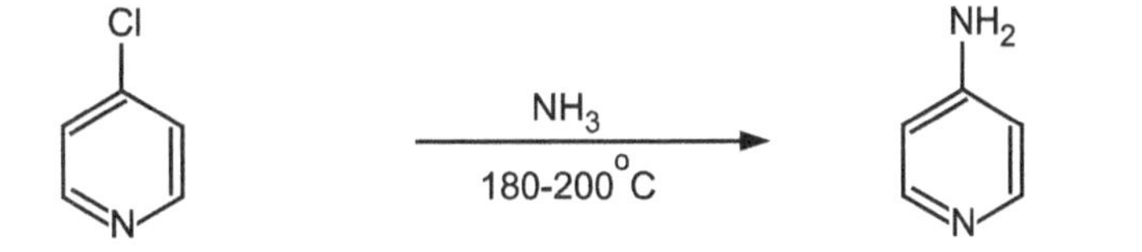

4-chloro pyridine

(iii)   Tschitschibabin / Chichibabin reaction: Direct amination of pyridine occurs on heating it with sodamide in dry toluene at 110°C.

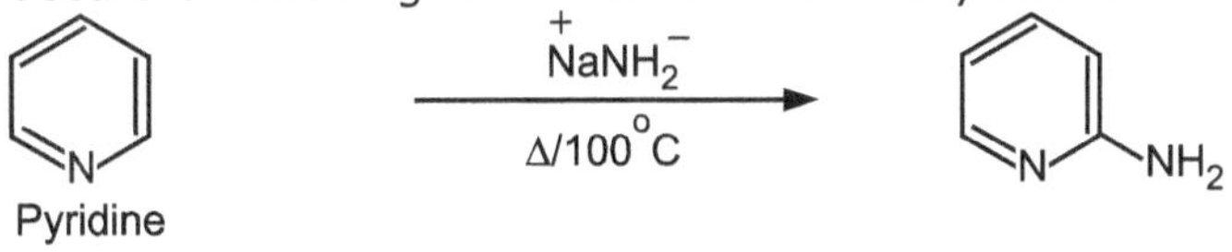

Pyridine

(b) Anilation:

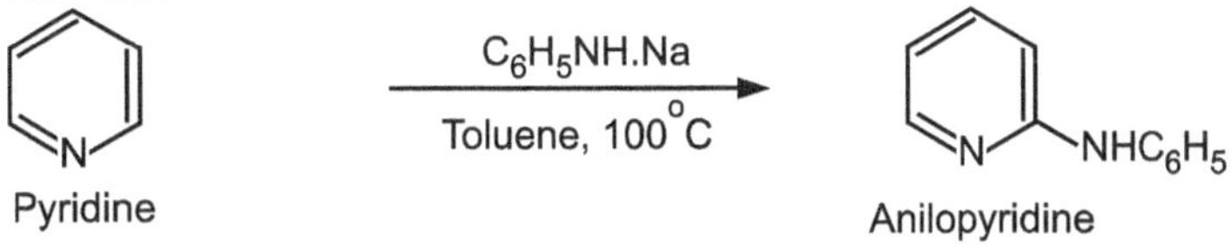

Pyridine   Anilopyridine

(c) Alkylation:

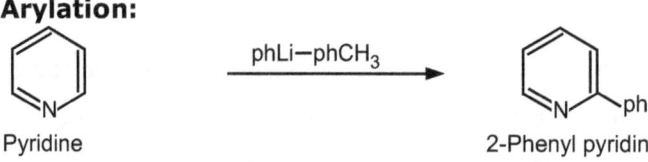

Pyridine $\xrightarrow[100^\circ C]{C_4H_9Li}$ 2-Butyl pyridine

(d) Arylation:

Pyridine $\xrightarrow{phLi-phCH_3}$ 2-Phenyl pyridine

(e) Benzylation – Action with Grignard's reagent:

Pyridine $\xrightarrow{phCH_2MgCl}$ 2-Benzyl pyridine   +   4-Benzyl pyridine

(f) Hydroxylation:

Pyridine $\xrightarrow[320^\circ C]{KOH}$ (pyridine–OK) $\xrightarrow{H^\oplus}$ 2-Hydroxy pyridine

2. Action with sodium:

2 Pyridine $\xrightarrow{2Na}$ Na.N ... N.Na $\xrightarrow{Air/H_2O}$ 4,4'-Dipyridil

3. Electrophilic substitution reactions:

(i) Nitration: Pyridine undergoes nitration with conc. HNO_3 and conc. H_2SO_4 at 300°C to give 3-nitropyridine.

Pyridine $\xrightarrow[300^\circ C]{HNO_3-H_2SO_4}$ 3-Nitropyridine   (Only 5% product)

(ii) Sulphonation: Pyridine undergoes sulphonation with fuming sulphuric acid in the presence of mercuric sulphate at 230°C to give pyridine-3-sulphonic acid.

$$\underset{\text{Pyridine}}{\text{[pyridine]}} \xrightarrow[\text{HgSO}_4,\ 230^\circ\text{C}]{\text{SO}_3\text{-H}_2\text{SO}_4} \underset{\text{Pyridine-3-sulphonic acid (70\%)}}{\text{[pyridine-SO}_3\text{H]}}$$

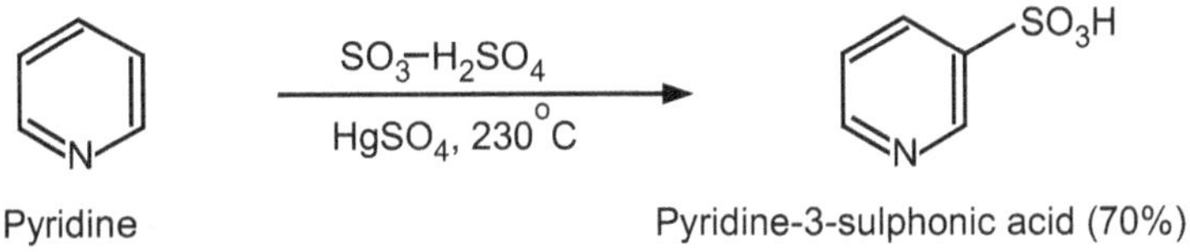

(iii) Bromination: Pyridine can be brominated by passing the vapours of pyridine and bromine over charcoal catalyst at 300°C to give 3-bromopyridine and 3, 5 dibromopyridine and at 500°C it gives 2-bromo pyridine and 2, 6-dibromo pyridine.

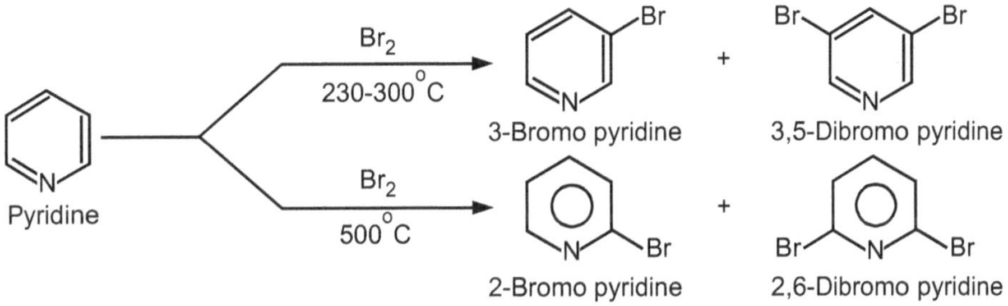

3-Bromo pyridine + 3,5-Dibromo pyridine

2-Bromo pyridine + 2,6-Dibromo pyridine

4. Oxidation:

Oxidation: Addition of oxygen/removal of hydrogen/loss of electron → increases positive character, decreases negative character.

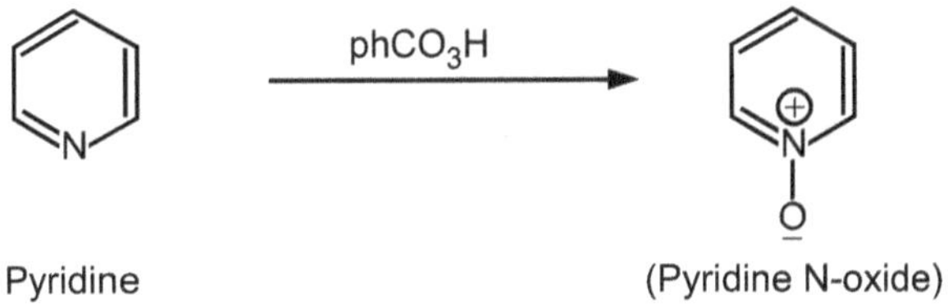

$$\underset{\text{Pyridine}}{\text{[pyridine]}} \xrightarrow{\text{phCO}_3\text{H}} \underset{\text{(Pyridine N-oxide)}}{\text{[pyridine N-oxide]}}$$

Pyridine-N-oxide exists in more resonance forms and is more reactive than pyridine and thus has importance in organic synthesis.

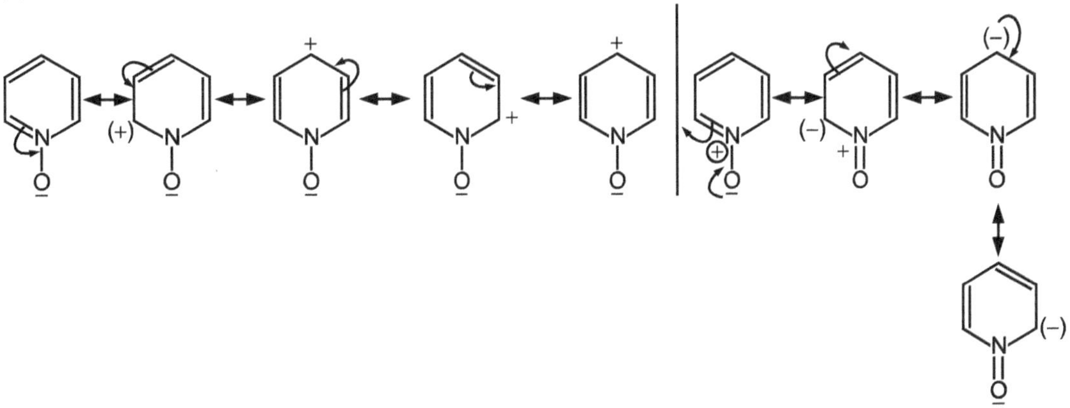

5. Reduction:

Due to lower electron density about the carbon atoms, the pyridine ring is more easily reduced than benzene.

Piperidine
(Hexahydropyridine)

n-Pentane

Dihydropyridine   Tetrahydropyridine

Derivatives of pyridine:

α-Picoline   β-Picoline   γ-Picoline   2,4-Lutidine   2,4,6-Collidine

Picolinic acid   Nicotinic acid   Isonicotinic acid

1.30 IMIDAZOLE

Imidazole, iminazole or glyoxaline is isomeric with pyrazole.

The imidazole nucleus is found in certain natural products viz. histidine, purines and also as a riboside. Imidazoles are weak bases but stronger than the isomeric pyrazoles. Like pyrazole, imidazole exhibits tautomerism as a result of which positions 4 and 5 are equivalent and thus only one C-alkyl derivative corresponding to 4 or 5 alkyl imidazole is obtained.

The imino hydrogen atom of imidazole can be replaced by metals and alkyl groups.

1.30.1 Methods of Preparation

(i) By the action of NH_3 on glyoxal:

$$\begin{matrix} CHO \\ | \\ CHO \end{matrix} + H_2O \longrightarrow HCHO + HCOOH$$

Glyoxal

$$\begin{matrix} CHO \\ | \\ CHO \end{matrix} + \begin{matrix} NH_3 \\ \\ NH_3 \end{matrix} + HCHO \longrightarrow \text{[Imidazole]} + 3H_2O$$

Glyoxal   Ammonia   Formaldehyde   Imidazole

(ii) By treating paraldehyde with bromine in ethylene glycol and heating the resulting product, 2-bromomethyl-1, 3-dioxolan with formamide and NH_3.

$$CH_3CHO \xrightarrow[-HBr]{Br_2} Br.CH_2CHO \longrightarrow \begin{matrix} CH_2OH \\ | \\ CH_2OH \end{matrix} \longrightarrow \text{(dioxolan)} \longrightarrow \begin{matrix} CHO \\ | \\ CH_2Br \end{matrix} \xrightarrow[NH_3]{HCONH_2} \text{[Imidazole]}$$

(iii) Imidazole is best prepared by the action of ammonia on a mixture of formaldehyde and tartaric acid dinitrate and decarboxylating the product.

$$\begin{matrix} COOH \\ | \\ CHO.NO_2 \\ | \\ CHO.NO_2 \\ | \\ COOH \end{matrix} \xrightarrow{-2HNO_2} \begin{matrix} COOH \\ | \\ CO \\ | \\ CO \\ | \\ COOH \end{matrix} \xrightarrow[HCHO]{2NH_3} \text{[HOOC...imidazole...COOH]} \xrightarrow[-2CO_2]{Cu,300^{\circ}C} \text{[Imidazole]}$$

Imidazole

1.30.2 Substituted Imidazole

1. By the action of ammonia and aldehyde on glyoxal of other 1, 2-diketo compounds (analogous to method (i) used).

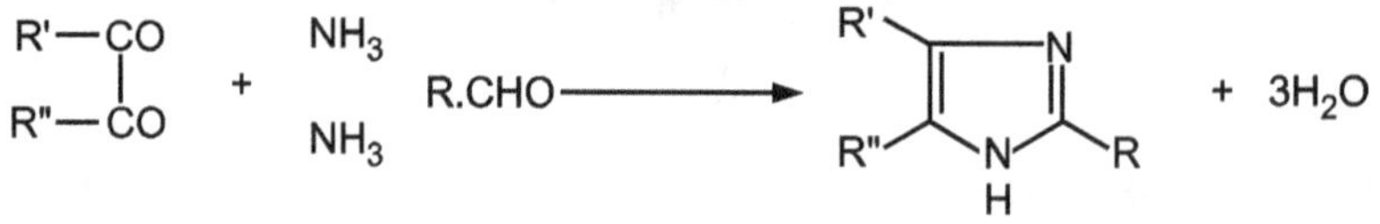

2. By the action of KCN on HCl of an α-amino aldehyde or ketone to form imidazoline thione which may be desulphurised with Raney Ni.

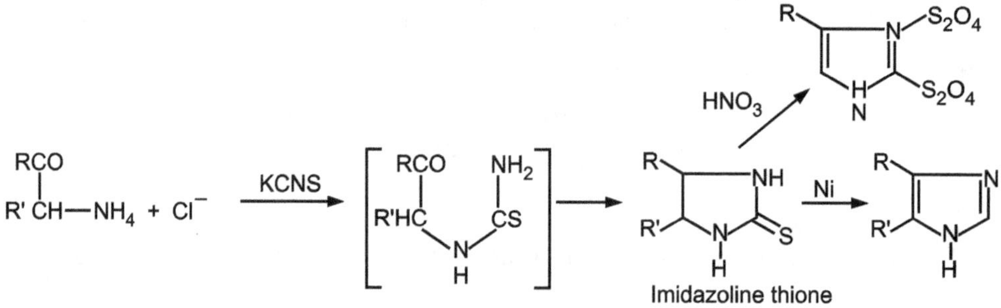

Imidazoline thione

3. By the action of α-bromoketone and an amidine.

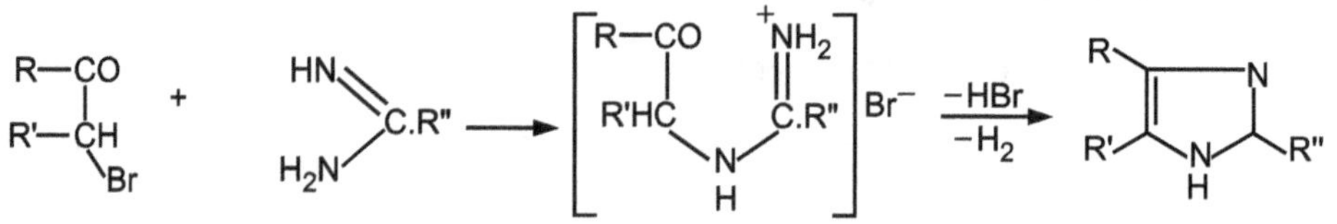

1.30.3 Chemical Reactions

Substitution Reactions:

1. The imino-hydrogen atom of imidazole can be replaced by metals and alkyl groups. N-Alkyl imidazoles isomerise on passing through red hot tube to 2-alkyl imidazole.

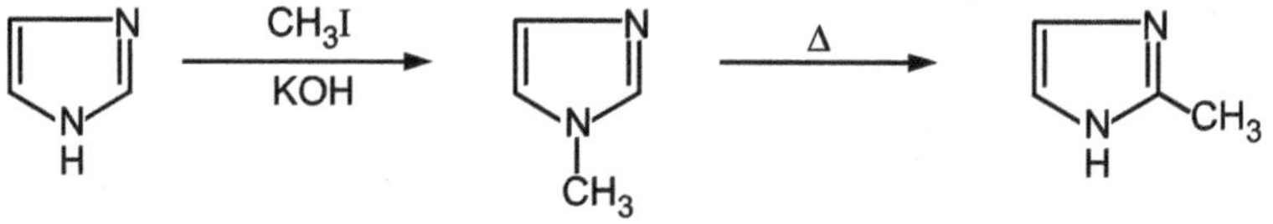

2. Nitration, sulphonation and bromination of imidazole produce the 4(S) derivative. In case positions 4 and 5 are blocked, substitution takes place in position 2.

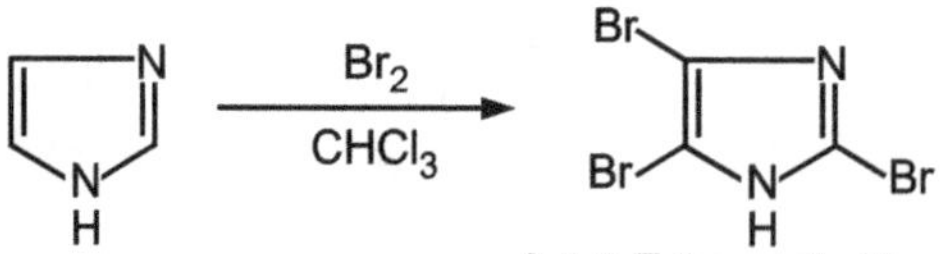

2,4,5-Tribromoimidazole

3. Acetic anhydride and acetyl chloride have no effect on imidazole while benzoyl chloride in the presence of NaOH opens the ring to form di-(benzoylamino) ethylene.

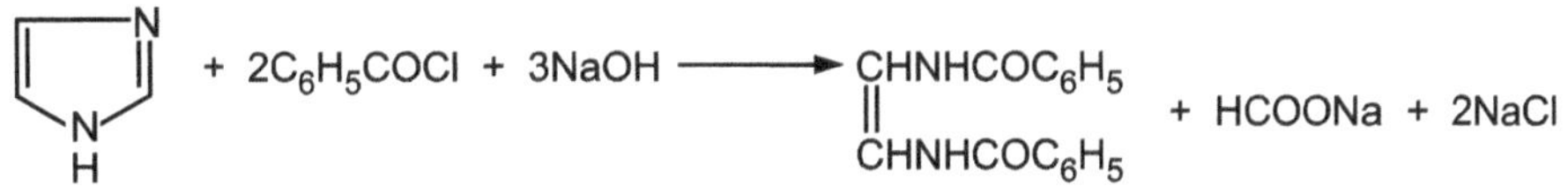

$$\text{Imidazole} + 2C_6H_5COCl + 3NaOH \longrightarrow \begin{matrix} CHNHCOC_6H_5 \\ \| \\ CHNHCOC_6H_5 \end{matrix} + HCOONa + 2NaCl$$

4.

$$\text{Imidazole} \xrightarrow{H_2O_2} \begin{matrix} CONH_2 \\ | \\ CONH_2 \\ \text{Oxamide} \end{matrix}$$

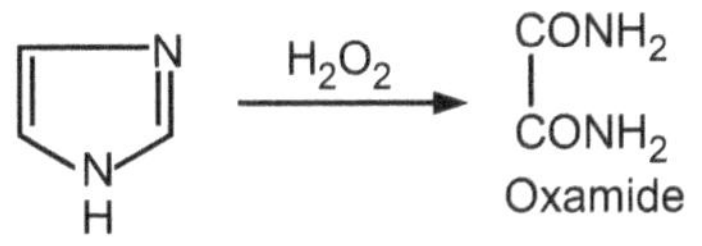

1.31 INDOLE

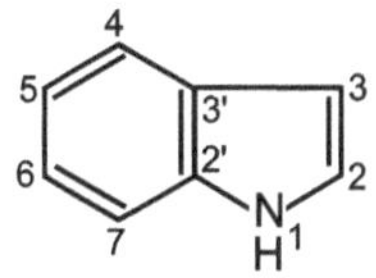

Indole (2,3-Benzopyrrole)

It occurs in coal-tar, jasmine flowers and orange blossoms. The indole crystallizes in colourless leaflets, m.p. = 52°C. It is a weak base and does not form salts with acids, but polymerise to a resin like substance. Like pyrrole it also produces red colour with a pine splint dipped in HCl.

1.31.1 Preparation / Methods of Synthesis

1. The Fischer synthesis:

This is the most important method for the synthesis of indole derivatives. It consists of heating the phenyl hydrazones of aldehydes, ketones or keto acids with $ZnCl_2$, H_2SO_4, BF_3 or polyphosphoric acid to about 180°C.

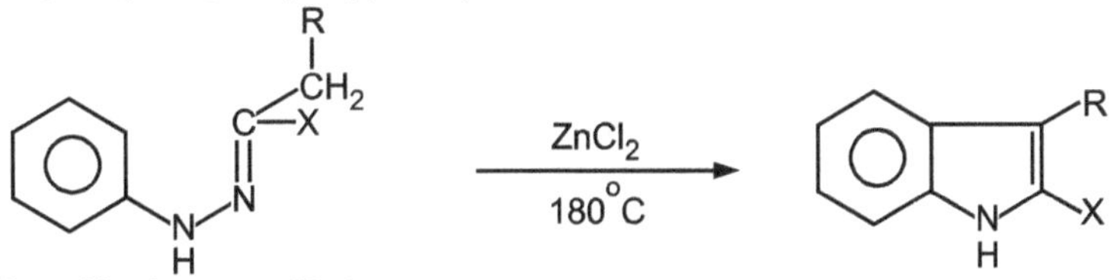

Phenyl hydrazone of ketone

where X = H/alkyl group of COOH group and R = H/alkyl group.

Example:

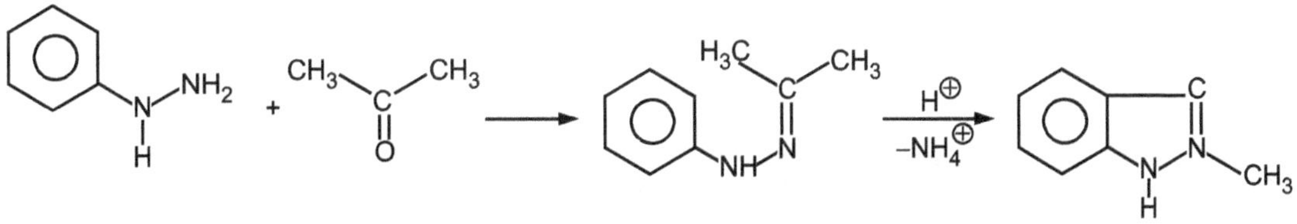

Phenyl hydrazine   Acetone   Acetone phenyl hydrazone   2-Methyl indole

Mechanism:

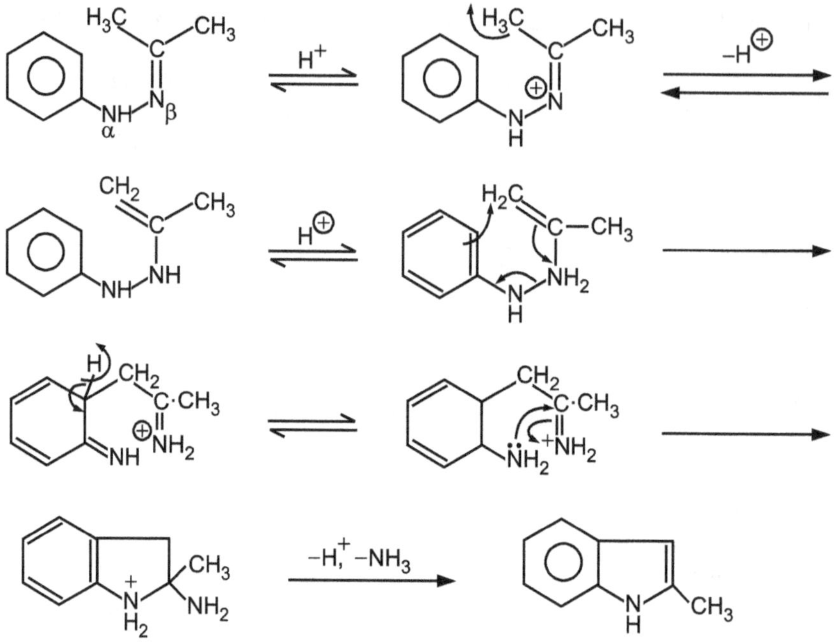

2-Methyl indole

It must be noted that, the mechanism of the reaction is analogous to o-benzidine rearrangement.

The reaction fails with acetaldehyde and hence indole itself cannot be prepared directly. However, indole can be prepared by this synthesis using pyruvic acid (a keto acid) instead of acetaldehyde and decarboxylating the resulting indole-2-carboxylic acid, thermally.

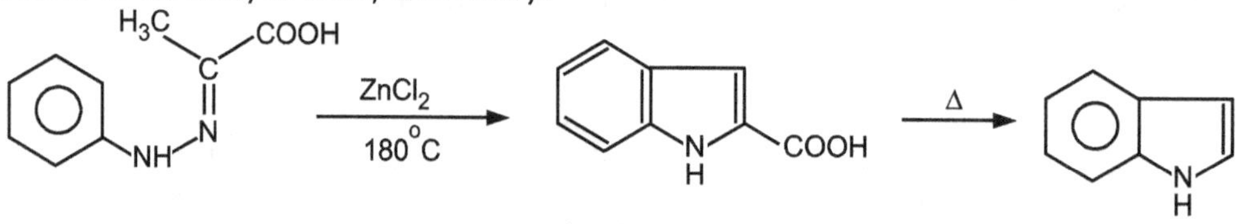

Indole-2-carboxylic acid   Indole

2. Madelung Synthesis:

This method consists of heating an o-acylaminotoluene with a base such as sodium ethoxide, sodamide, potassium-t-butoxide etc. The probable mechanism of the reaction is as follows:

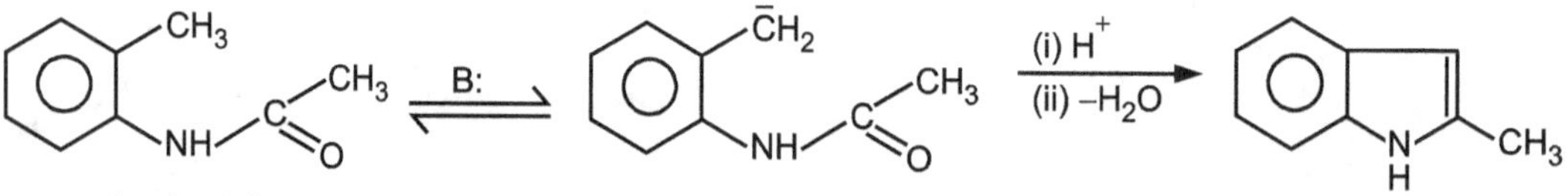

o-acylamino toluene   2-Methyl indole

3. The Bischler Synthesis:

This is the condensation reaction between an α-halo or α-hydroxy ketone with an arylamine in the presence of an acid.

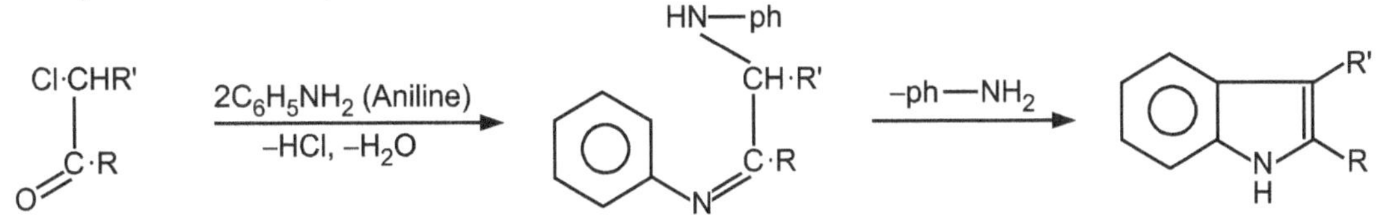

α-Chloro ketone

2,3-Dialkyl indole

4. Reissert Synthesis:

It involves the following steps:

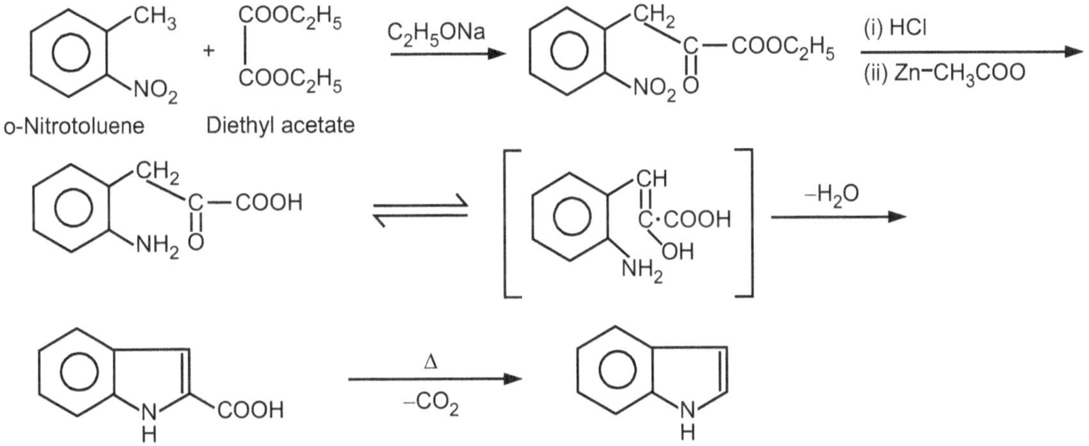

o-Nitrotoluene   Diethyl acetate

Indole-2-carboxylic acid

Indole

5. Baeyer Indole Synthesis:

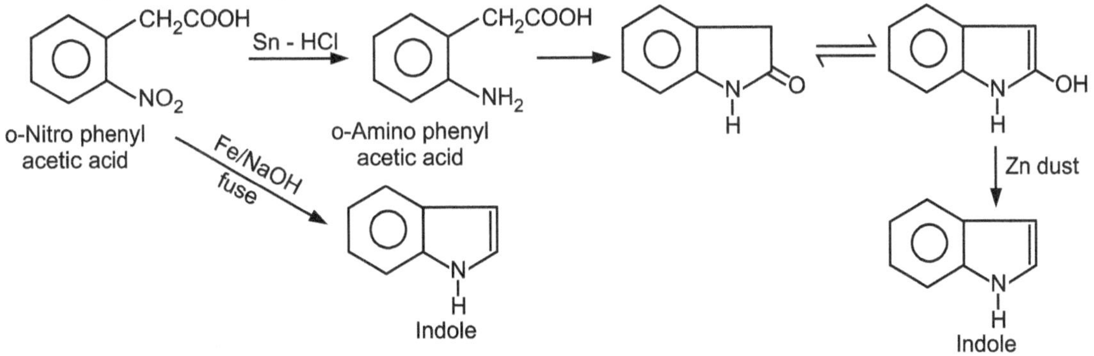

o-Nitro phenyl
acetic acid

o-Amino phenyl
acetic acid

Indole

Indole

1.31.2 Chemical Properties

The chemical properties of indole in general are quite similar to those of pyrrole.

Electrophilic substitution occurs in the 3rd position but if this is already occupied than on the 2nd position. Further if both the 2nd and 3rd positions are blocked then position is occupied by the electrophilic reagent.

Although pyrrole undergoes electrophilic substitution at position-2, the benzopyrrole forms mainly 3-substituted products. It is due to the fact that the transition state of 3-substituted indole is more stable due to benzenoid structure, whereas in the transition state of 2-substituted product the benzenoid system is disrupted.

3-Substitution   2-Substitution

The important electrophilic substitution reactions of indole are as summarized below:

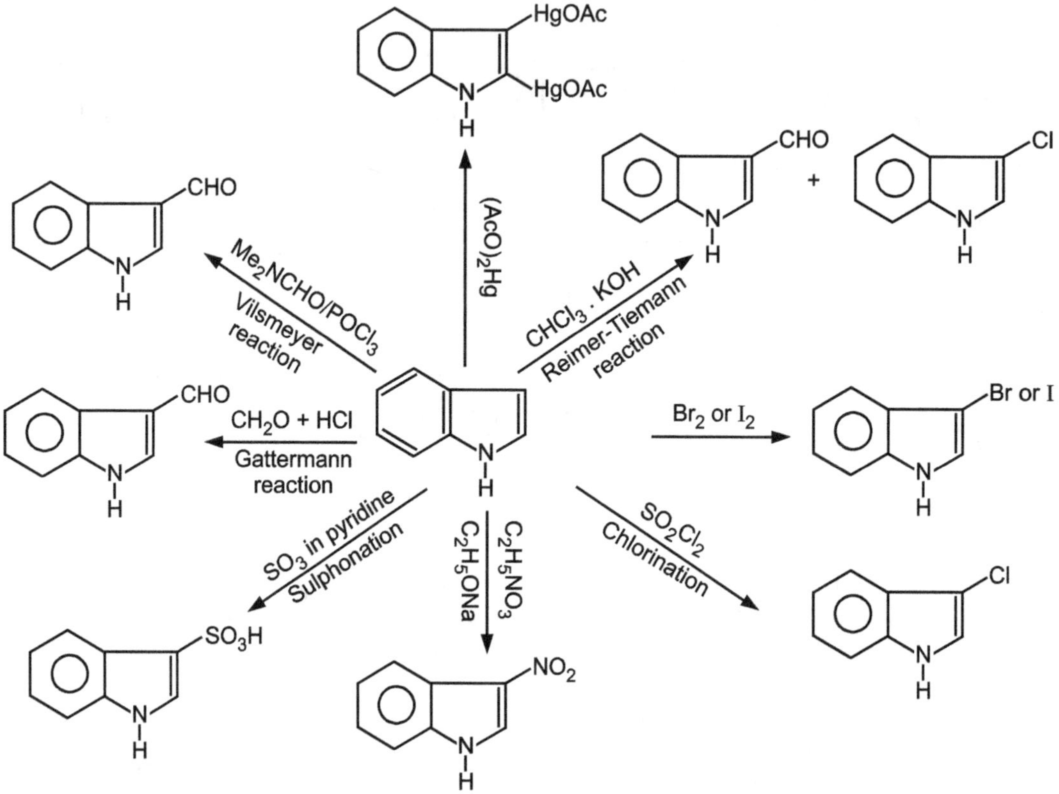

Mannich Reaction:

This is the condensation between a compound containing atleast one active hydrogen atom, formaldehyde and ammonia, a primary or a secondary amine (preferably as the hydrochloride). So the net change, during this reaction is the replacement of the active hydrogen atom by an aminomethyl group or substituted aminomethyl group. In practice the base, commonly known as "Mannich base" is usually isolated as HCl.

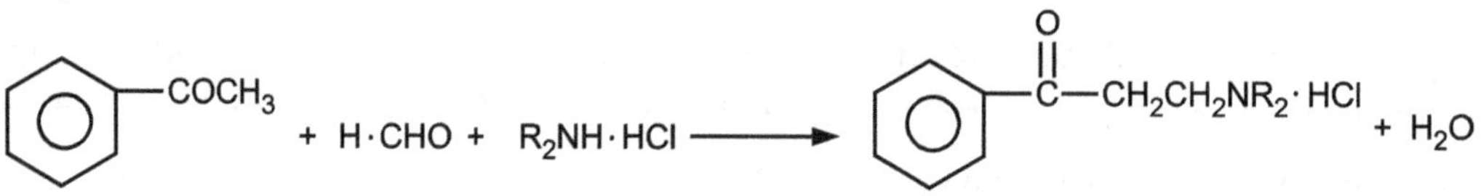

∴ Indole also undergoes Mannich reaction with HCHO and $(CH_3)_2NH$ to form Gramine (3-dimethylamino methyl indole).

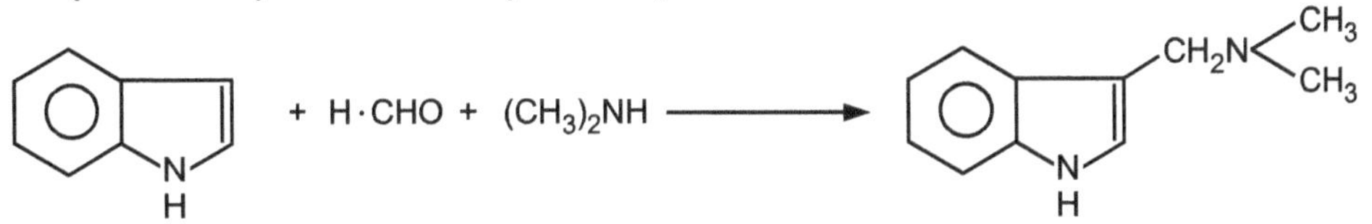

Michael Reaction:

This is the addition reaction between an α, β-unsaturated keto compounds (acceptor) and a compound with an active methylene group (addendum) in the presence of a base.

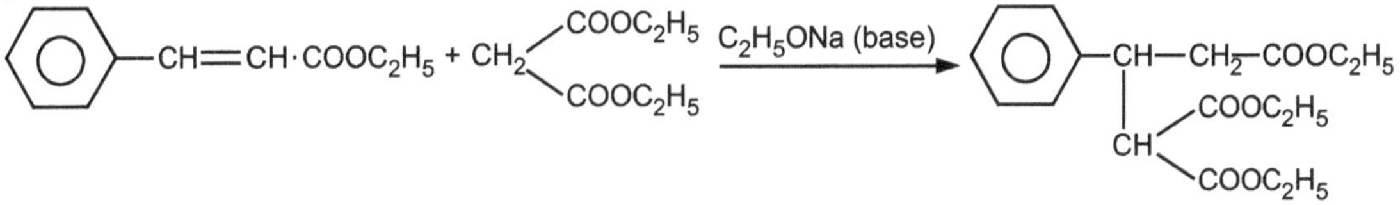

Similarly, indole undergoes Michael reaction to form the corresponding 3-substituted products.

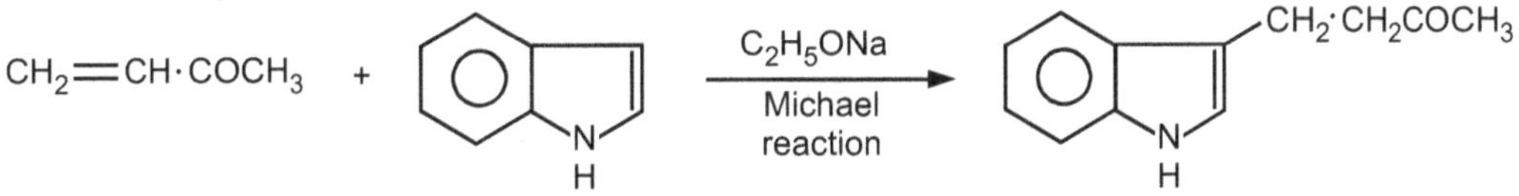

Friedel-Craft reaction:

The reaction of an alkyl halide or acyl halide with benzene in the presence of a Lewis acid generally $AlCl_3$ is known as Friedel-Craft reaction. Further, it can be divided into:

1. Alkylation and

2. Acylation.

1. Alkylation: The alkylation of benzene atleast with primary alkyl halides takes place with the formation of a polar addition compound between $AlCl_3$ and alkyl halide. Thus the function of $AlCl_3$ is to supply the electron deficient species in the following manner.

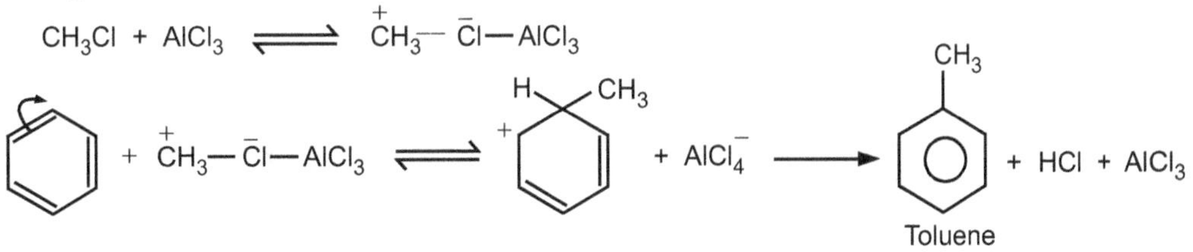

2. Acylation: Acylation of benzene may be brought about with the acid chlorides or anhydrides in the presence of Lewis acids.

$$CH_3COCl + AlCl_3 \longrightarrow CH_3\overset{+}{C}O + AlCl_4^-$$

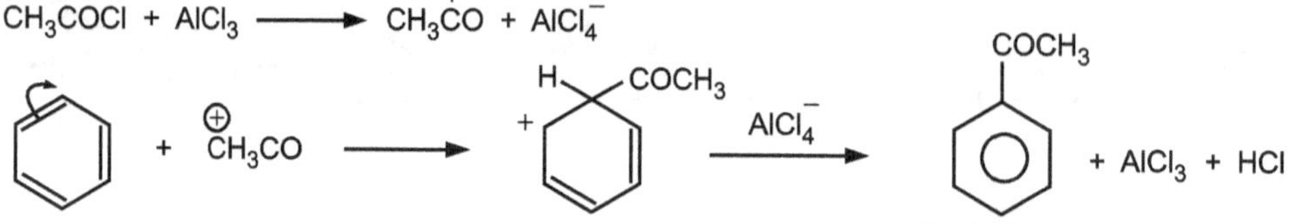

Acetophenone

Similarly, indole undergoes Friedel–Craft reaction to form the corresponding 3-substituted product. When C_3 of indole is blocked, electrophilic attack takes place at C_2 via 3, 3-disubstituted product.

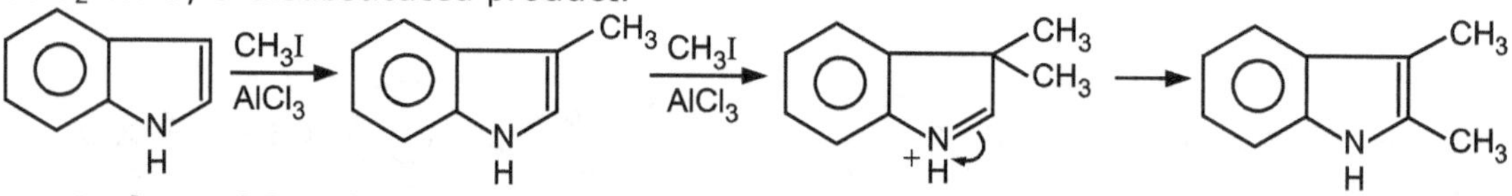

Action with Grignard reagent: Indole reacts with Grignard reagent at the NH group of pyrrole ring to form N-magnesium derivative which is further used for the preparation of substituted indoles. e.g. Heteroauxin.

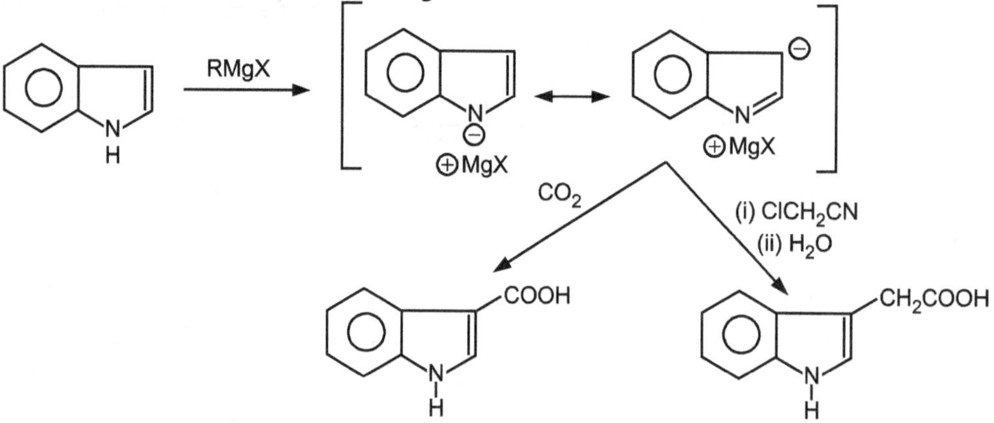

IAA

Heteroauxin

Reduction:

Indole may be reduced to 2, 3-dihydroindole (indoline) by means of acidic (Sn-HCl) electrolytic or catalytic reduction. On the other hand, catalytic reduction in the presence of Raney Ni gives octahydroindole.

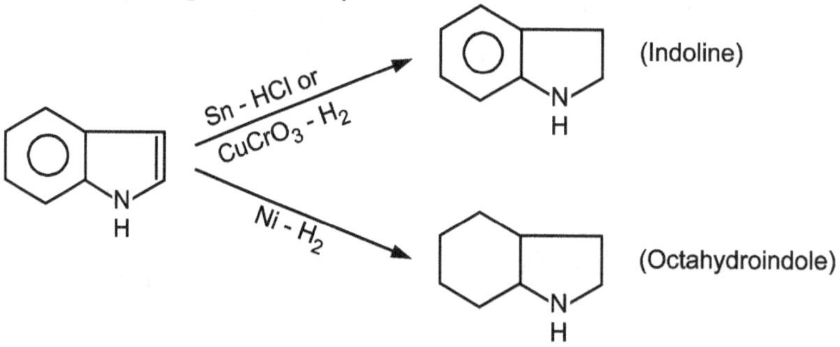

(Indoline)

(Octahydroindole)

1.31.3 Some Important Derivatives of Indole

Oxindole (2-Hydroxyindole):

It is a colourless solid, M.P. = 126 – 127°C. On boiling with aq. $Ba(OH)_2$ solution, it is hydrolysed back into o-amino phenyl acetic acid.

Synthesis:

Baeyer synthesis:

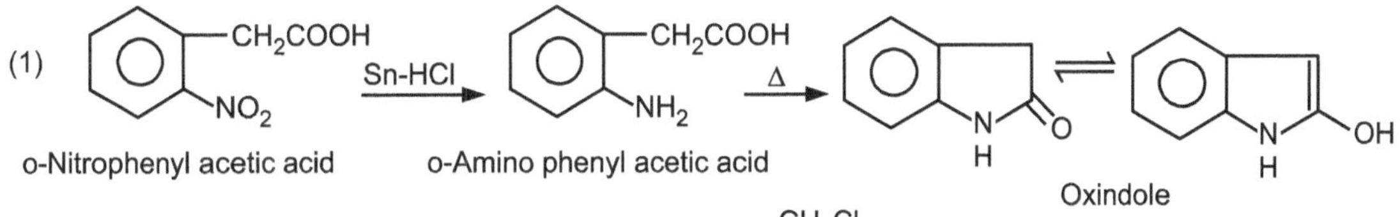

(1)

o-Nitrophenyl acetic acid   o-Amino phenyl acetic acid

Oxindole

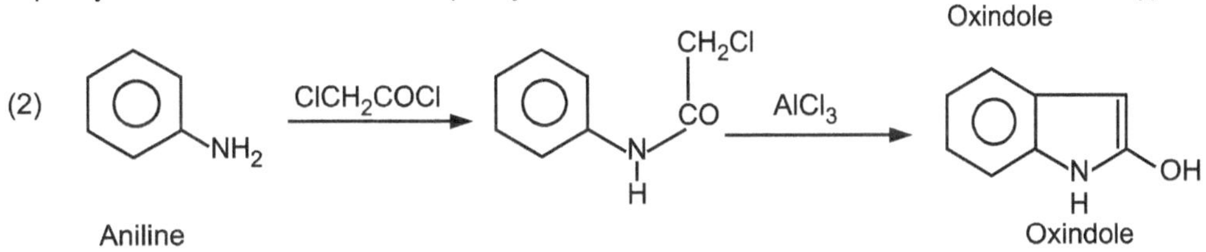

(2)

Aniline   Oxindole

1.32 INDOXYL (3-HYDROXYINDOLE)

Enol form   Keto form

It is a bright yellow solid. M.P. = 85°C. In alkaline solution, it is readily oxidized by air to the dyestuff indigotin.

1.32.1 Synthesis

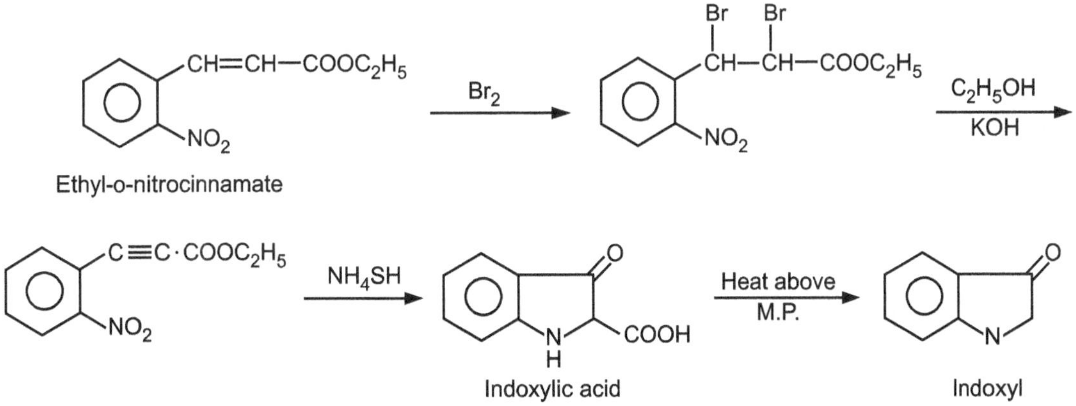

Ethyl-o-nitrocinnamate

Indoxylic acid   Indoxyl

1.32.2 Reaction

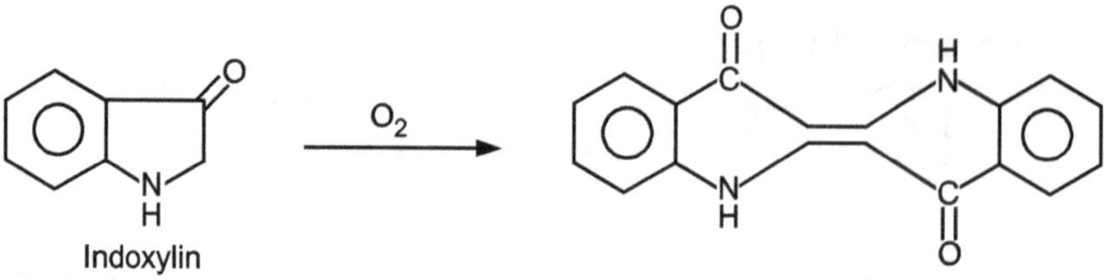

Indoxylin → O_2 → Indigotin (dyestuff)

1.33 ISATIN

Lactam ⇌ Lactim

Isatin is a red crystalline solid. M.P. = 200-201°C. During the study of isatin, it is very interesting to note that isatin was the first compound to exhibit the phenomenon of tautomerism. It is an example of Lactam-Lactim tautomeric system.

1.33.1 Preparation

Isatin was first obtained by the oxidation of indigotin with HNO_3. But now-a-days it is synthesized by condensing aniline with chloral and hydroxylamine in the presence of H_2SO_4, treating the resulting isonitrosoacetanilide with concentrated sulphuric acid and finally hydrolyzing the β-imide linkage with water.

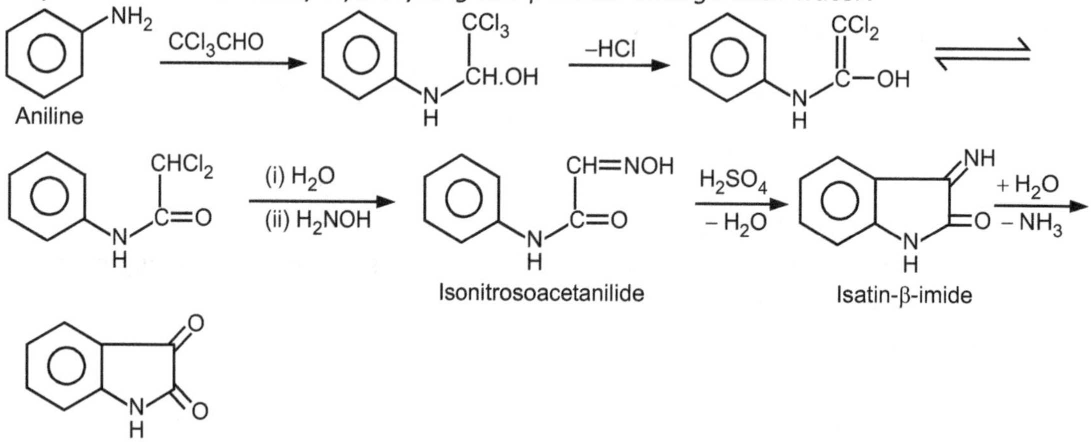

Aniline → CCl_3CHO → (–HCl) → ⇌

Isonitrosoacetanilide → (H_2SO_4, $-H_2O$) → Isatin-β-imide (+H_2O, –NH_3)

Isatin

1.34 CARBAZOLE (DIBENZOPYRROLE)

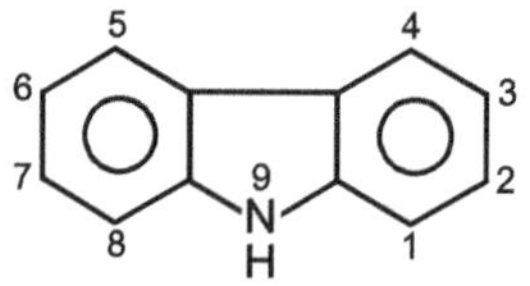

It is found in the anthracene fraction of coal tar. It is a colourless solid. M.P. = 245°C. It is attacked by electrophilic reagents at positions 3 and 6 and in this respect it appears to behave as a typical aniline.

1.34.1 Synthesis

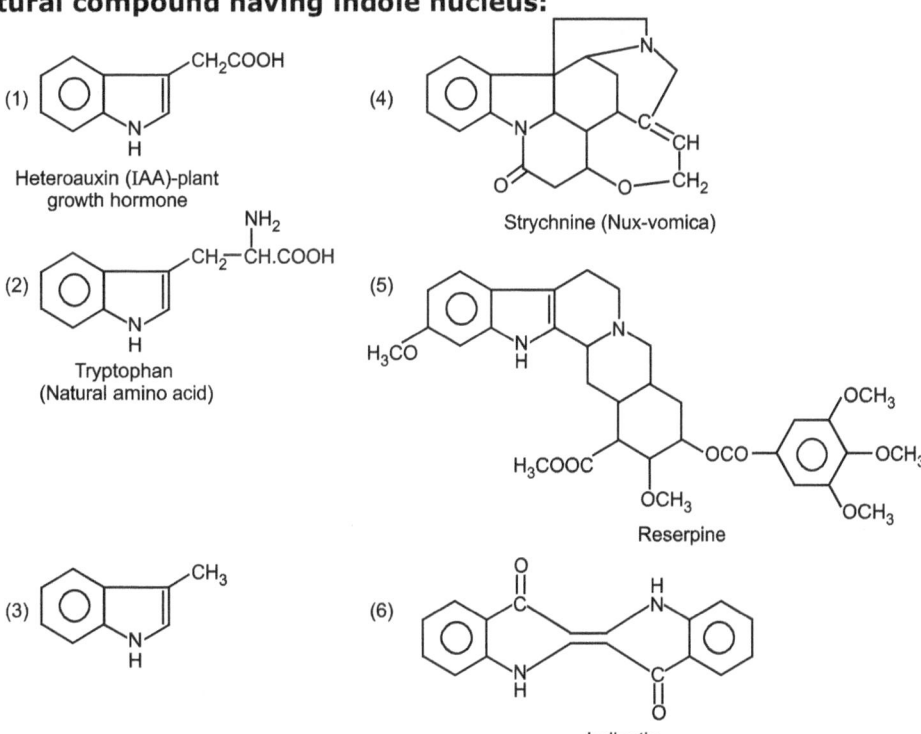

(1) Diphenylamine — Red hot tube → Carbazole

(2) 2,2'-Diaminodiphenyl — H_3PO_4 → Carbazole

Natural compound having indole nucleus:

(1) Heteroauxin (IAA)-plant growth hormone

(2) Tryptophan (Natural amino acid)

(3)

(4) Strychnine (Nux-vomica)

(5) Reserpine

(6) Indigotin

Skatole – Formed by putrifaction of proteins.

It has strong offensive odour and imparts the characteristic odour to faeces.

1.35 QUINOLINE (α, β-BENZOPYRIDINE, 1-AZANAPHTHALENE)

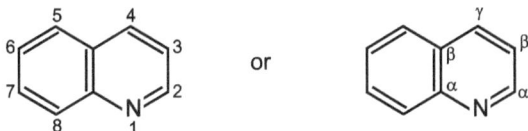

or

Quinoline was first isolated from coal tar (Runge – 1835), but later on in 1842 it was obtained by heating the alkaloid cinchonine or quinine with alkali. It is a colourless liquid, b.p. = 237°C. It has odour of pyridine.

1.35.1 Preparation

1. Skraup's synthesis (1880):

This is the most important method for the synthesis of quinole and consists of heating a mixture of aniline, glycerol, conc. H_2SO_4 and $FeSO_4$ in presence of oxidizing agent such as nitrobenzene, stannic chloride, ferric salts or arsenic acid.

The reaction involves the following steps:

1. Dehydration of glycerol by hot H_2SO_4 to form the unsaturated aldehyde i.e. Acrolein.
2. Nucleophilic addition (Michael type) of aniline to acrolein to form β-(phenylamino) propionaldehyde.
3. Electrophilic attack on the aromatic ring by the electron deficient carbonyl carbon of the protonated aldehyde (cyclization step).
4. Dehydration of the secondary alcohol to form 1, 2-dihydroquinoline by the strong acid.
5. Oxidation of 1, 2-dihydroquinoline by nitrobenzene resulting in the aromatization to form quinoline.

Function of $FeSO_4$ is to moderate the reaction and it may be replaced by boric acid.

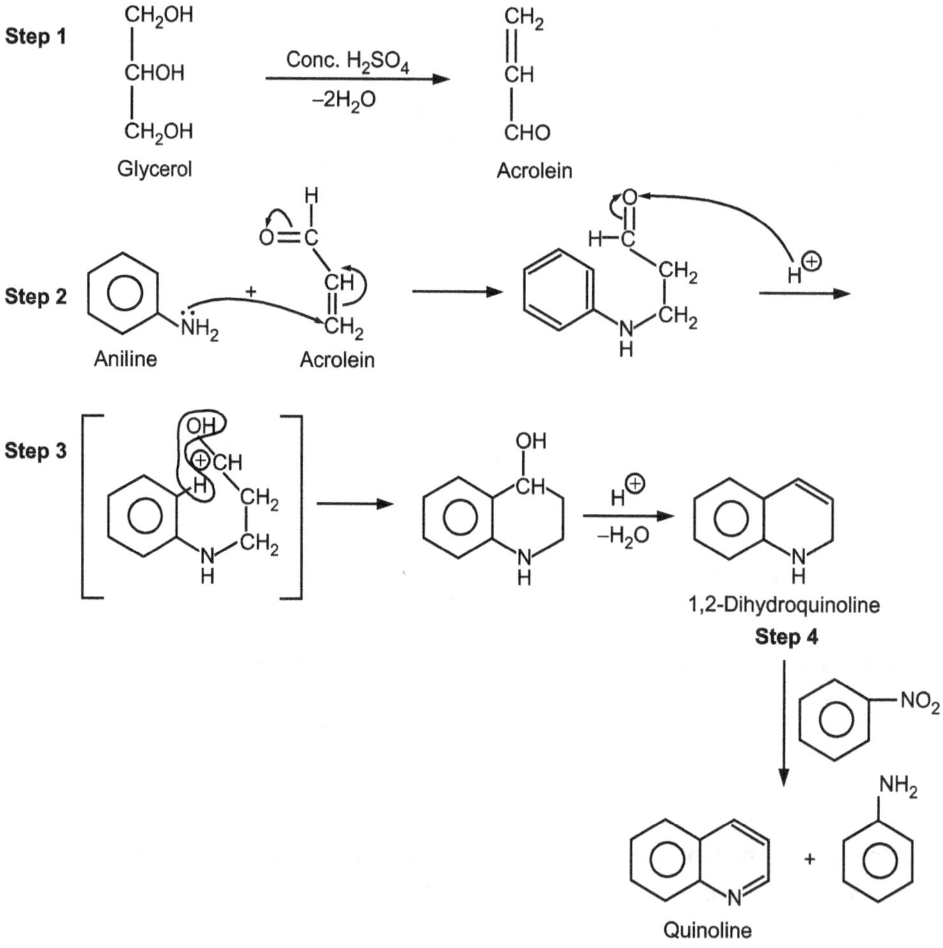

2. Doebner – Von. Miller Synthesis (1881):

This synthesis is closely related to that of Skraup and consists of heating a primary aromatic amine with an aliphatic aldehyde in presence of hydrochloric acid. e.g. Aniline on heating with acetaldehyde gives quinaldine (2-methyl quinoline). In this reaction, acetaldehyde first of all undergoes aldol condensation to give croton-aldehyde which reacts in the same manner as in Skraup synthesis. In this process, since no oxidizing agent is added from outside, the final step (dehydrogenation) is thought to be brought about by hydride transfer for the Schiffs base which is formed by reaction between aniline and the aldehyde or ketone.

$$2\ CH_3CHO \xrightarrow[\text{Aldol condensation}]{H^+:\ -H_2O} CH_3 - CH = CH - CHO$$

Acetaldehyde   Crotonaldehyde

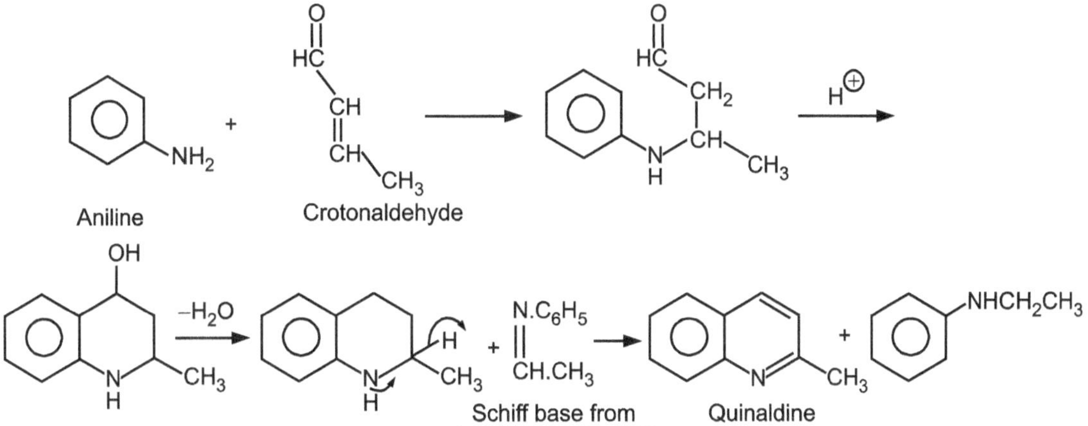

Aniline   Crotonaldehyde

Schiff base from
$C_6H_5NH_2 + CH_3CHO$

Quinaldine

3. Friedlander Synthesis (1879):

o-Amino benzaldehyde reacts with ketone containing active methylene group in the presence of NaOH to form 2, 3-dialkyl quinoline.

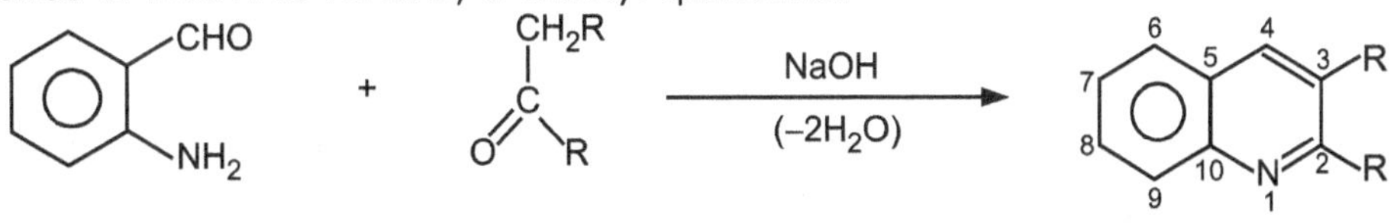

o-Amino benzaldehyde   Ketone containing   2,3-Dialkyl quinoline
                              reactive methylene group

4. Pfitzinger Synthesis (1886):

Isatin reacts with sodium hydroxide to form corresponding sodium salt which on treatment with ketone containing reactive methylene group followed by decarboxylation to form 2, 3 dialkyl quinoline.

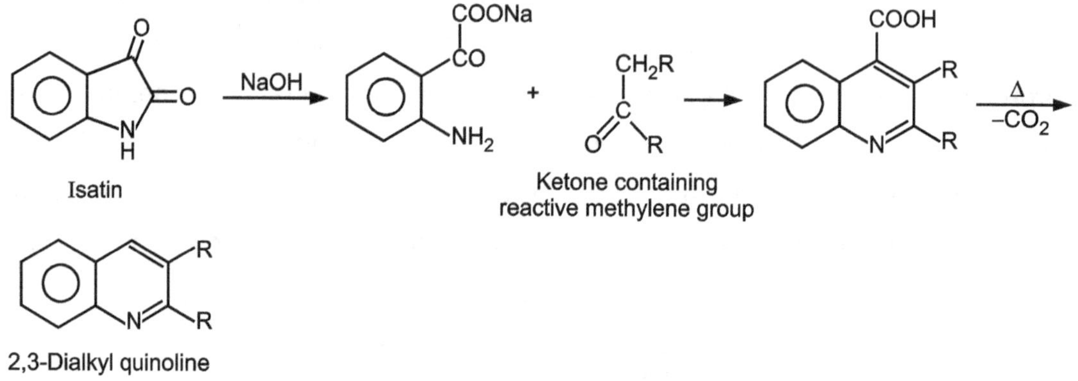

Isatin

Ketone containing reactive methylene group

2,3-Dialkyl quinoline

5. Conardt-Limpach Synthesis (1887):

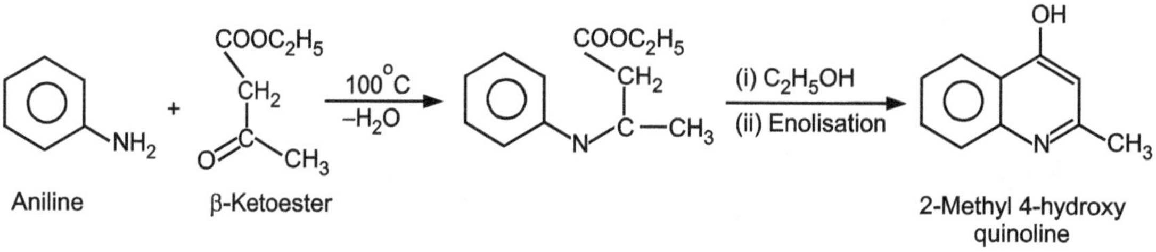

Aniline   β-Ketoester

2-Methyl 4-hydroxy quinoline

6. Knorr Quinoline Synthesis (1886, 1888):

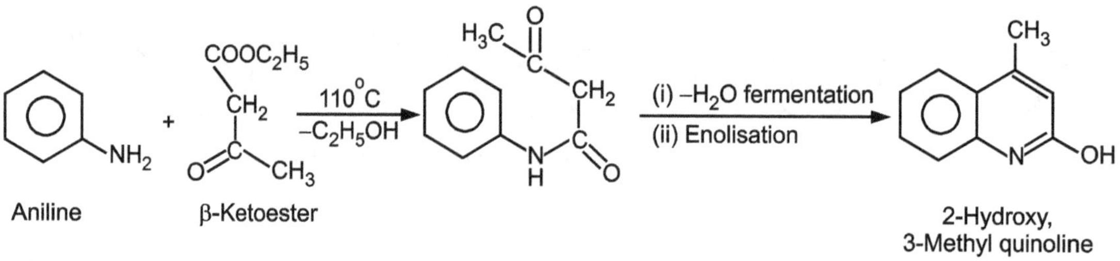

Aniline   β-Ketoester

2-Hydroxy, 3-Methyl quinoline

1.35.2 Chemical Reactions

Like pyridine, the electron-withdrawing properties of 'N' atom deactivate the pyridine ring of quinoline towards electrophilic reagents and hence the electrophilic substitution occurs preferentially in the **benzene** ring whereas the nucleophilic substitution occurs preferentially in the pyridine ring, especially if acidic conditions are used. Furthermore calculation of charge densities show that positions 8, 6 and 5 shall be attacked preferentially by electrophilic reagents and positions 2 and 4 by nucleophilic reagents.

$E^{\oplus}$ Substitution / Electrophilic Substitution Reactions:

1. **Nitration:** Nitration of quinoline with fuming nitric acid in the presence of fuming sulphuric acid to give a mixture of 8-nitroquinoline and 5-nitroquinoline.

Quinoline   5-Nitroquinoline   8-Nitroquinoline

2. **Sulphonation:** Sulphonation of quinoline with fuming sulphuric acid to give 8-sulphoquinoline, which on heating at 300°C to form 6-sulphoquinoline.

Quinoline   8-Sulpho quinoline   6-Sulpho quinoline

$Nu^{\ominus}$ Substitution / Nucleophilic Substitution Reaction

1. **Amination:** Quinoline reacts with sodamide in liquid ammonia at about 100°C to form 4-aminoquinoline.

2-Aminoquinoline   4-Aminoquinoline

2. **Alkylation:** Quinoline reacts with n-butyl lithium to yield 2-n butyl quinoline. Any R–Li or Ar–Li can be added to obtain the respective product.

Quinoline   2-n-Butyl quinoline

Halogenation:

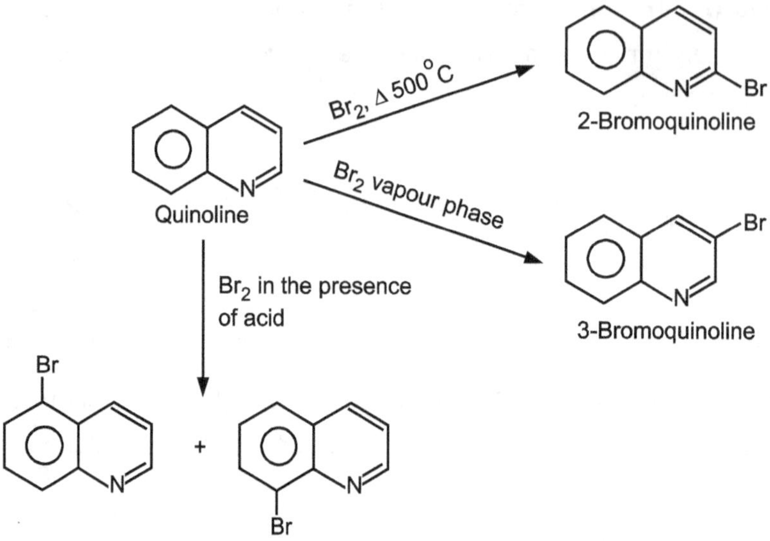

2-Bromoquinoline

3-Bromoquinoline

Quinoline

Br_2, Δ 500°C

Br_2 vapour phase

Br_2 in the presence of acid

5 and 8 Bromoquinolines

This is due to the formation of quinidinium cation with an acid.

Formation of salts:

Like most of the 3°-amines, quinoline forms salts with inorganic acid and quaternary or quinolinium salts with alkyl halide.

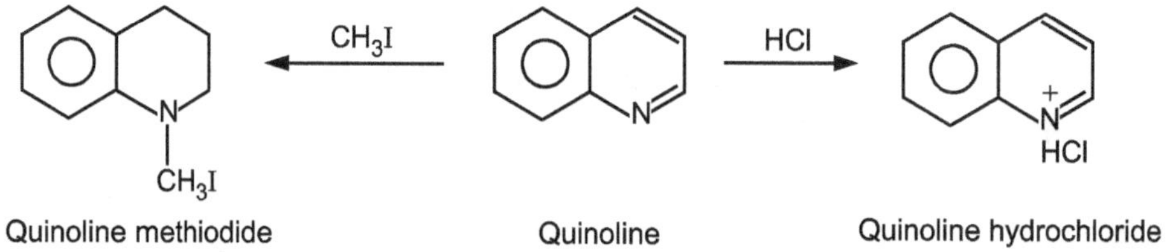

Quinoline methiodide

CH_3I

Quinoline

HCl

Quinoline hydrochloride

Oxidation:

Since oxidation is dependent on electron availability, permanganate oxidation will destroy the benzene ring and leave the π-deficient pyridine ring intact. Thus vigorous oxidation of quinoline oxidizes the benzene ring to form quinolinic acid.

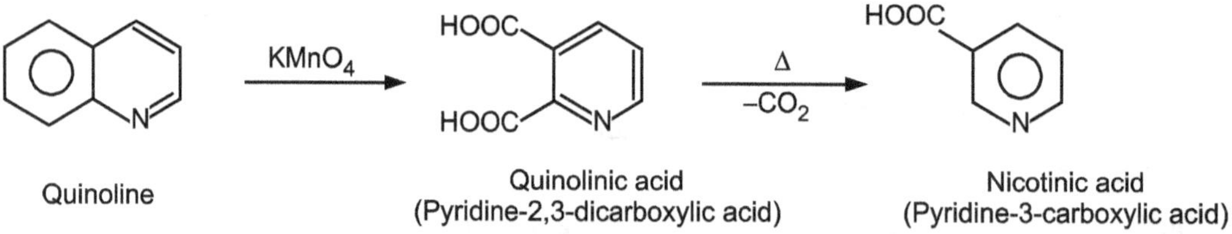

Quinoline

$KMnO_4$

Quinolinic acid
(Pyridine-2,3-dicarboxylic acid)

Δ
$-CO_2$

Nicotinic acid
(Pyridine-3-carboxylic acid)

Reduction: Catalytic reduction attacks preferentially the more electron deficient pyridine ring of quinoline.

Example:

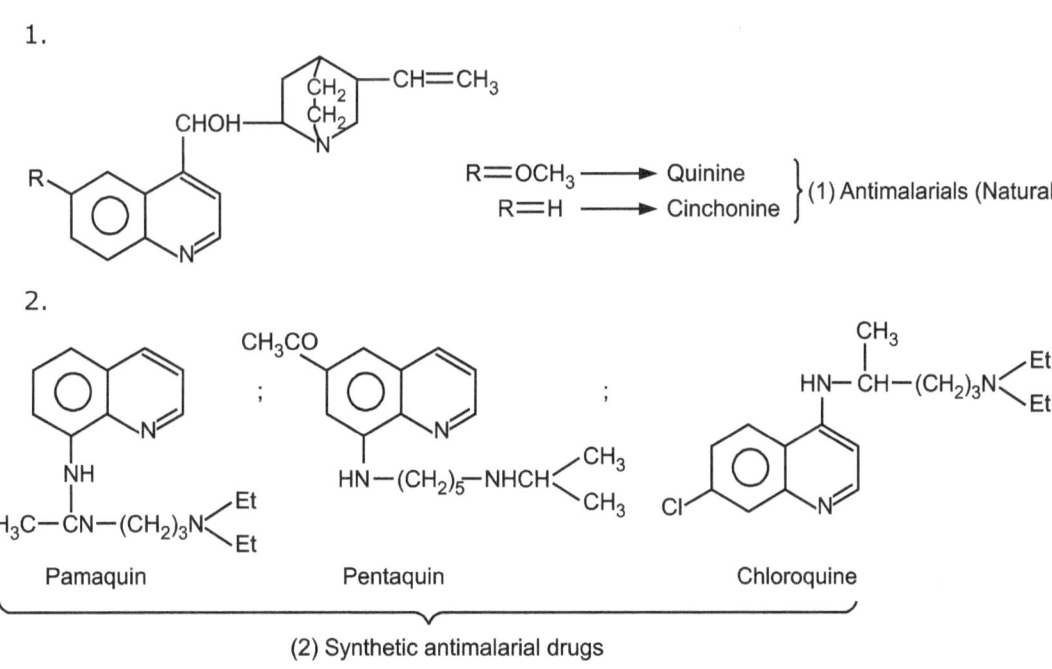

1.35.3 Some Important Quinoline Derivatives

1.

$R=OCH_3 \longrightarrow$ Quinine
$R=H \longrightarrow$ Cinchonine

$\left.\begin{array}{c} \end{array}\right\}$ (1) Antimalarials (Natural)

2.

Pamaquin

Pentaquin

Chloroquine

(2) Synthetic antimalarial drugs

3.

Nupercaine
(a powerful anaesthetic)

4.

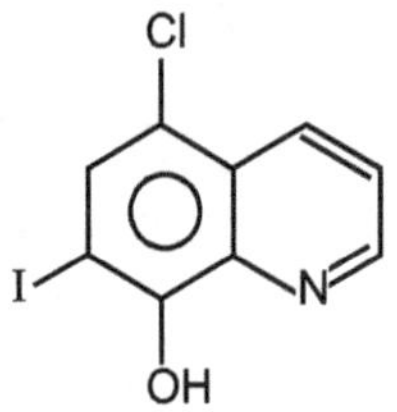

Vioform (Remedy for
gastro-intestinal infection)

5.

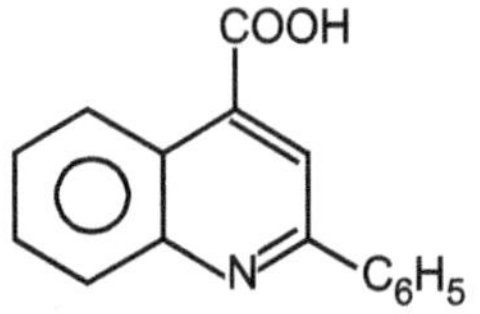

⟶ Atophan (cinchophen) - Remedy for gout

6.

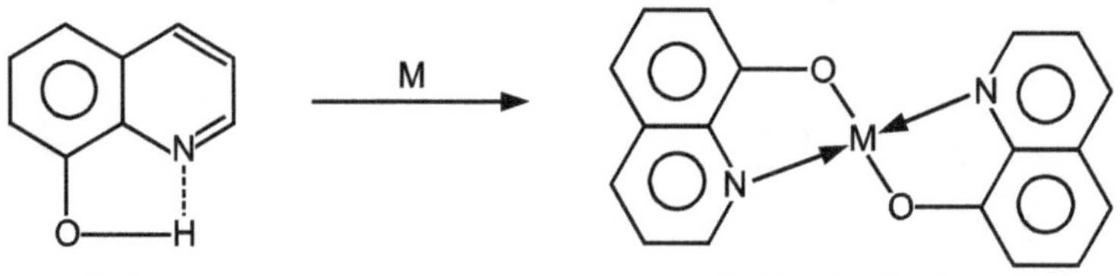

Oxime   Metal salt of oxime
(8-Hydroxy quinoline)

    (i) Used in gravimetric analysis of many metals e.g. Mg. Zn, Cd etc.

    (ii) Used as antiseptic.

7. Quinoline dyes:

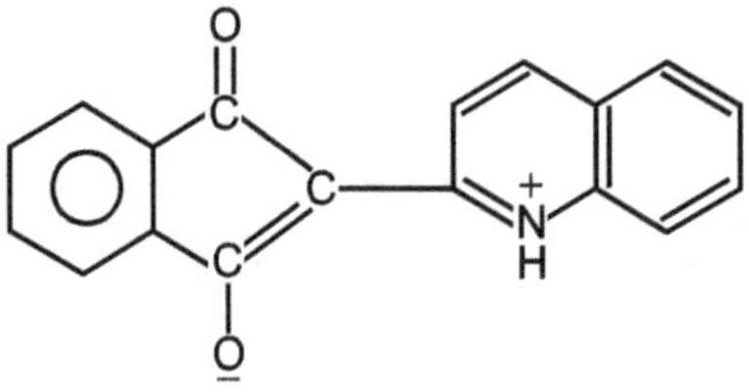

(Quinoline yellow, used as dye for textiles)

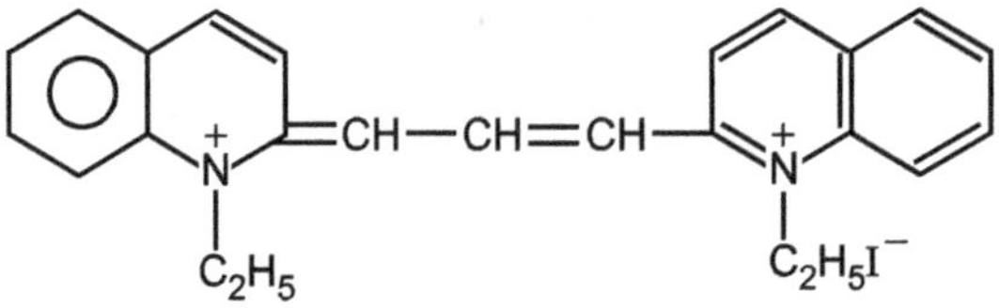

(Sensitor red)

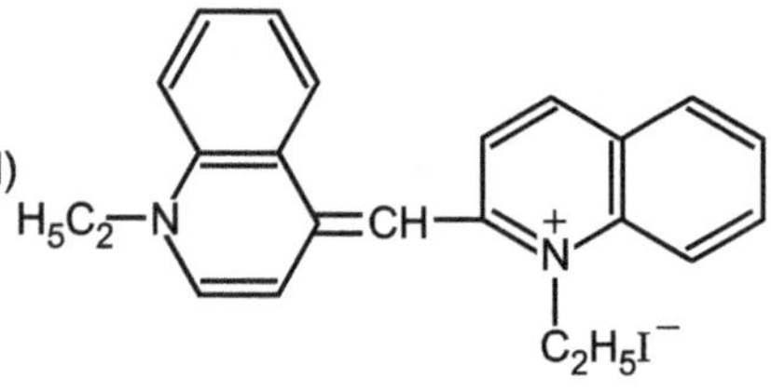

Ethyl red
(Isocyanine dye)

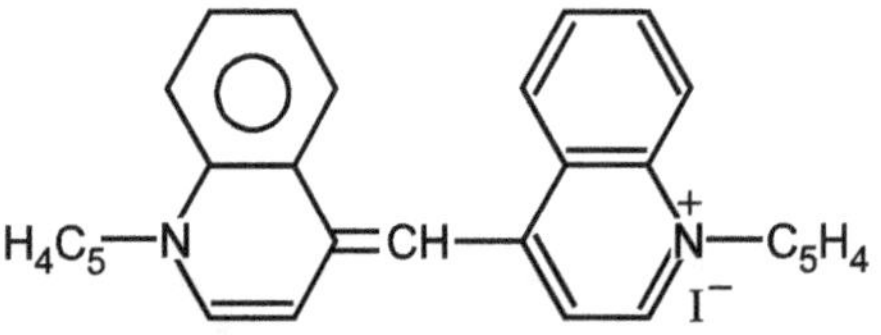

Quinoline blue (cyanine dye)

1.36 ISOQUINOLINE

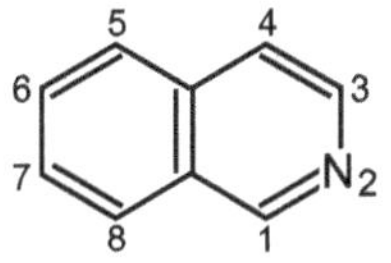

Isoquinoline is a colourless solid. M.P. = 23°C and B.P. = 243°C. It is isomeric with quinoline and always present with quinoline in coal tar and bone oil. The two compounds are separated by the fractional crystallization of their sulphates.

1.36.1 Synthesis

1. By passing benzylidine ethylamine vapours through red hot tube:

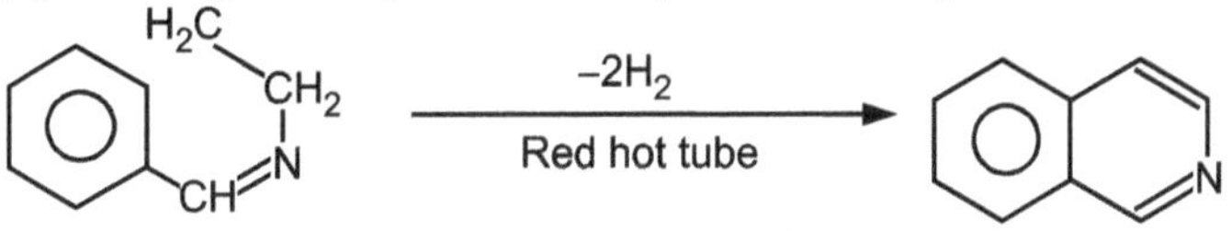

Benzylidine ethylamine   Isoquinoline

2. Gabriel synthesis:

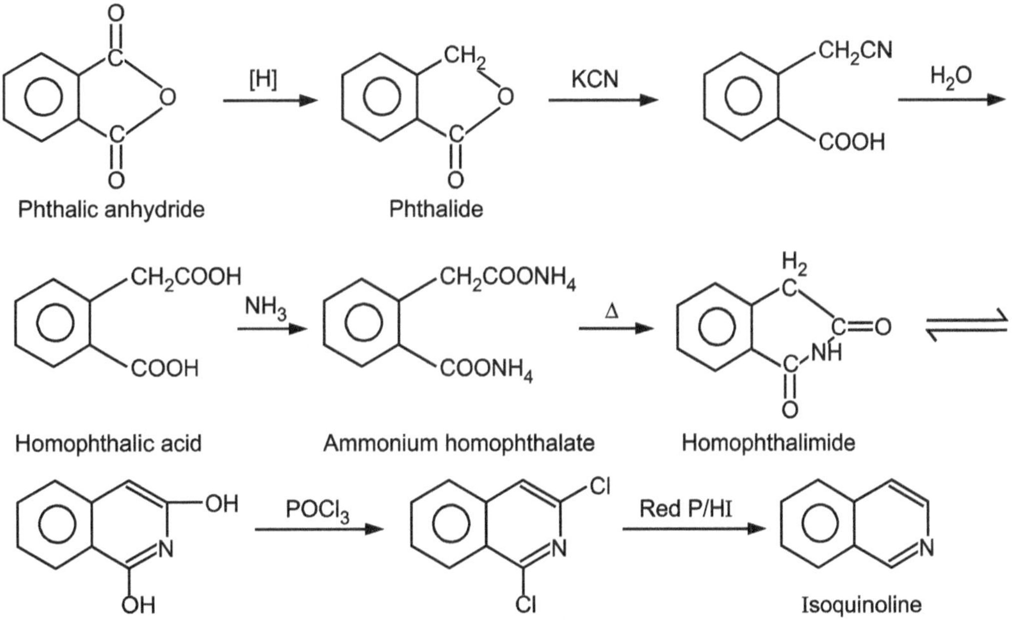

Phthalic anhydride   Phthalide

Homophthalic acid   Ammonium homophthalate   Homophthalimide

Isoquinoline

3. By heating the oxime of cinnamaldehyde with P_2O_5:

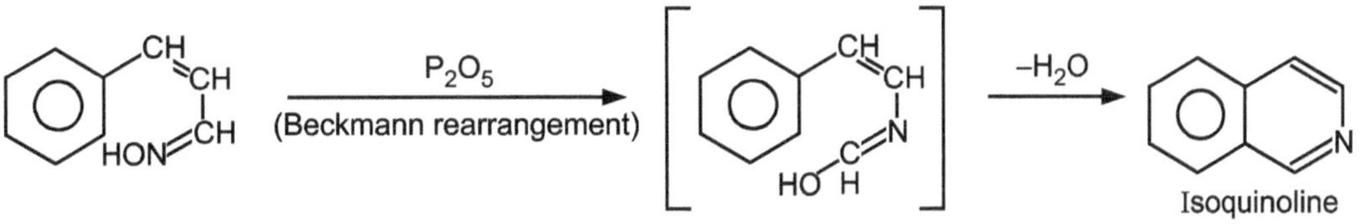

Isoquinoline

4. **Biscbler - Napieralski reaction:** In this method, the β-aryl ethylamides are converted into corresponding dihydro-compounds by heating with an acidic reagent viz. POCl$_3$, PCl$_5$, P$_2$O$_5$, anhydrous ZnCl$_2$ etc. The dihydro compound is then dehydrogenated by means of palladium S or Se into the corresponding isoquinoline. The β-aryl ethyl amides are generally prepared by the condensation of β-aryl ethyl amines with acid chlorides.

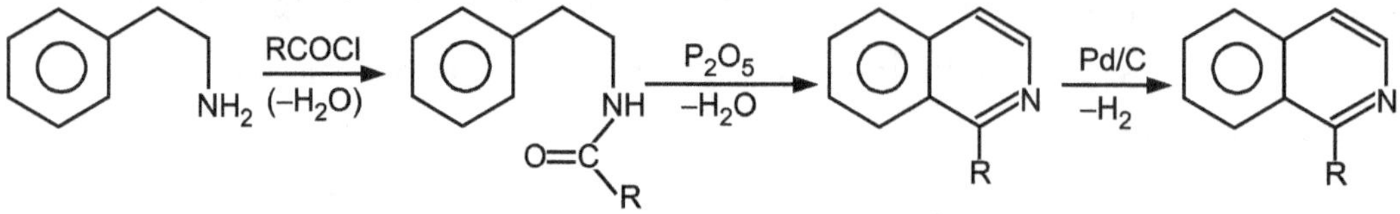

Benzyl ethylamine   Benzyl ethylamide

5. **Pictet - Spengler reaction:** This reaction consists of the condensation of β-aryl ethyl amine with an aldehyde in the presence of dil. HCl to form the tetrahydro isoquinoline which can be dehydrogenated by palladium.

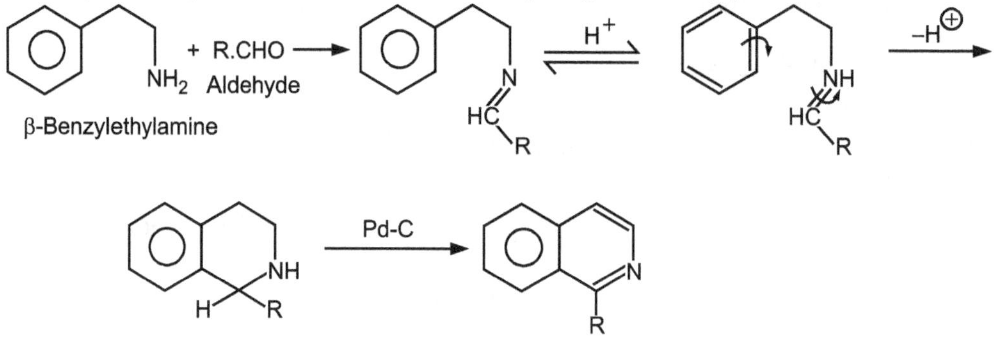

β-Benzylethylamine

Tetrahydroisoquinoline

6. **Pomeranz - Fritsch reaction:** This synthesis is carried out by condensing an aromatic aldehyde with an aminoacetal to form Schiff's base which is then cyclised with H$_2$SO$_4$.

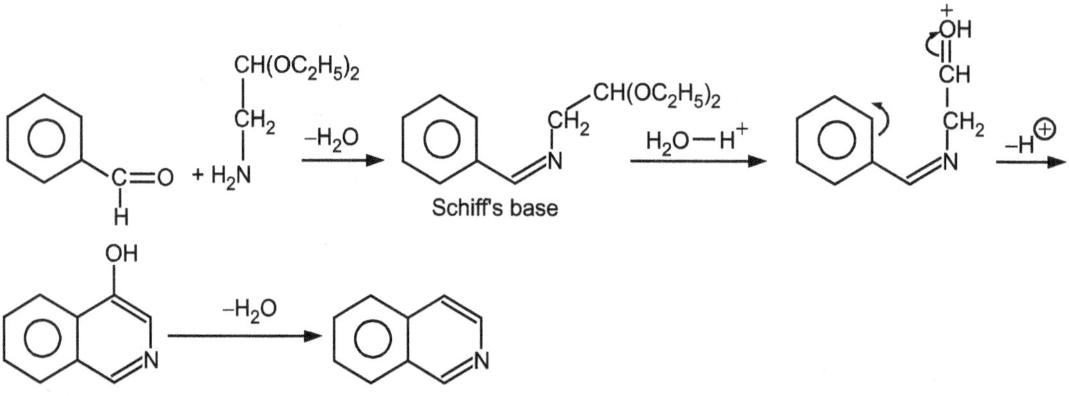

Schiff's base

Isoquinoline

7. **Schlittler - Muller synthesis:** When aromatic ketones are used in the Pomeranz reaction, this is called Schlittler M. reaction. In this reaction, the yield is very poor. However, the yield can be improved by the following route:

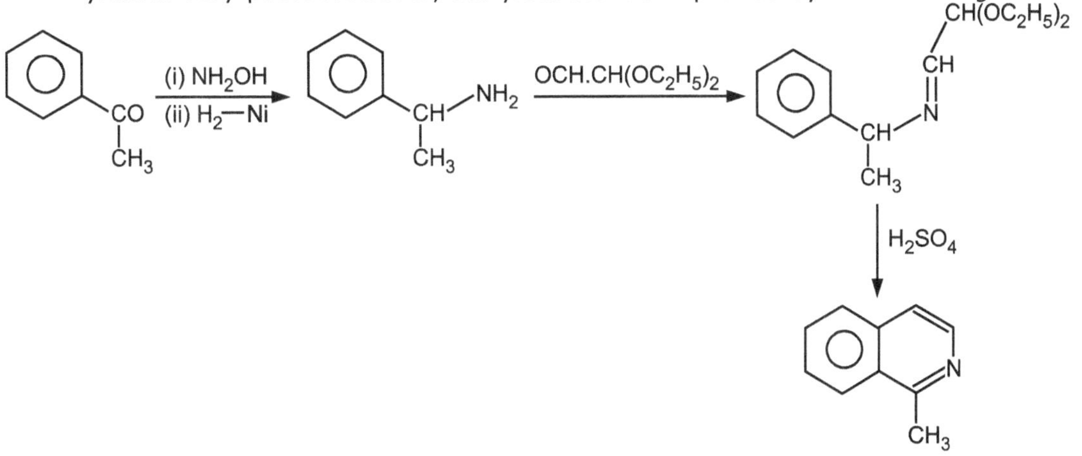

1.36.2 Chemical Reactions

Chemically, isoquinodline resembles with quinoline in most of its reactions e.g. Like quinoline it adds alkyl halides readily and forms the quaternary isoquinolinium salts.

Like quinoline it undergoes electrophilic substitution e.g. Nitration and sulphonation at the 5 and 8 positions. On the other hand, bromination and mercuration occur at position 4.

It also undergoes nucleophilic substitution at position 1.

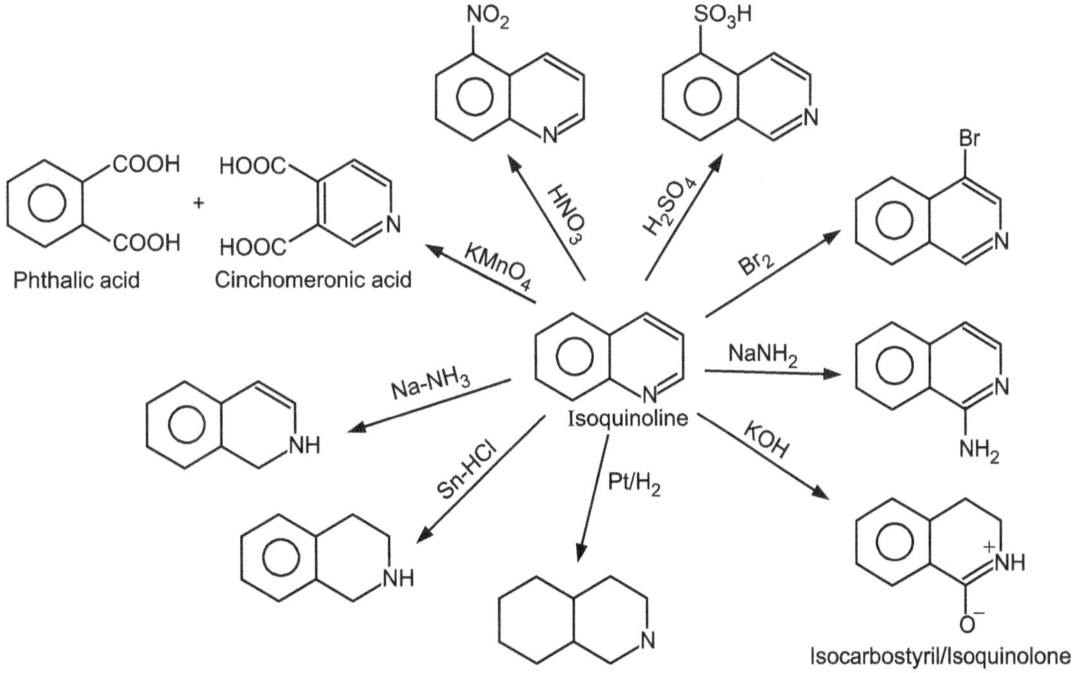

1.36.3 Some Important Isoquinoline Derivatives

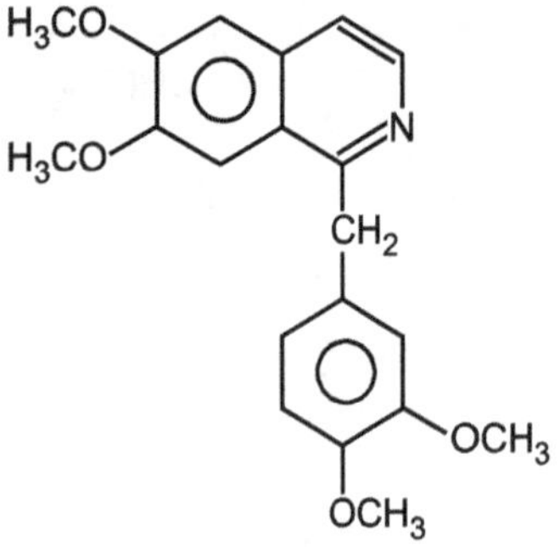

Papaverine

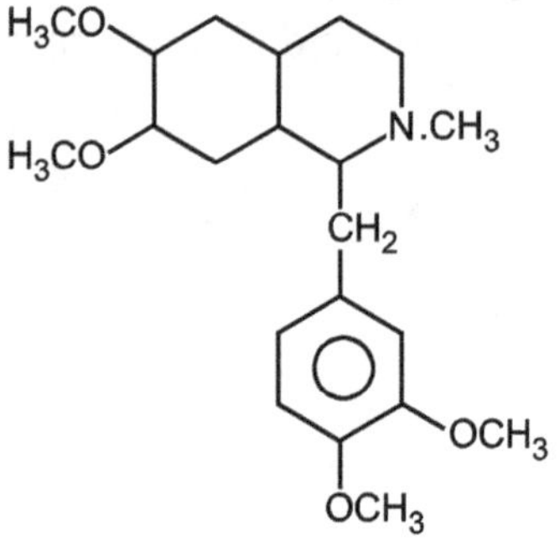

Laudanosine

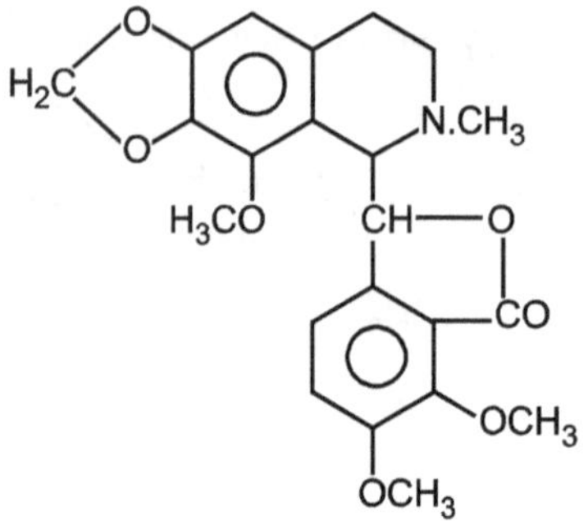

Narcotine

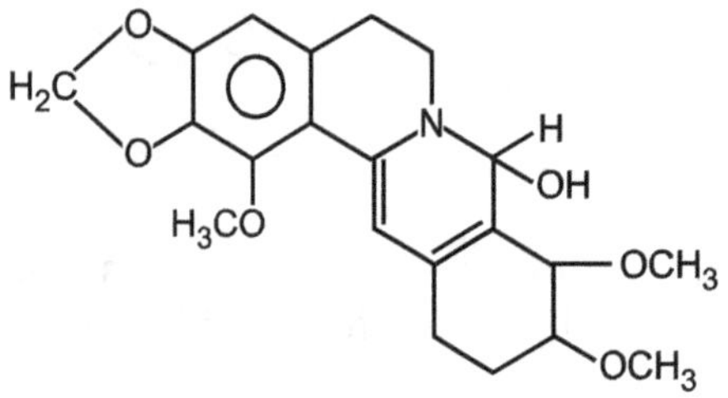

Berberine

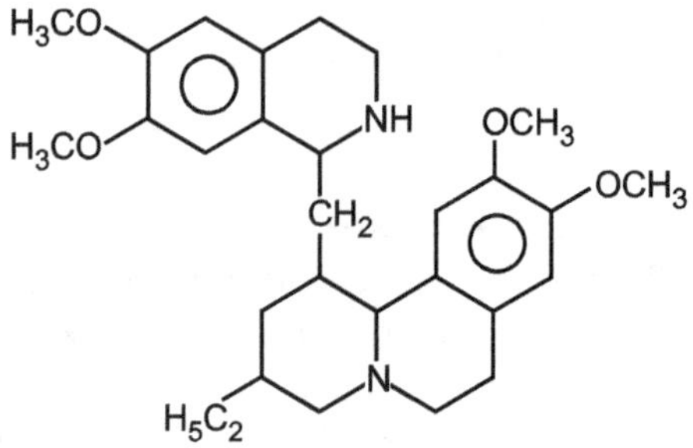

Emetine

QUESTIONS

1. What are heterocyclic compounds? Give example.
2. Explain IUPAC nomenclature for heterocyclic compounds.
3. What are polycyclic Heterocyclic compounds? Give examples.
4. Draw the structure and numbering for following heterocycles.
   (a) Furan
   (b) Thiophene
   (c) Pyrrole
   (d) Pyrazole
   (e) Thiazole
   (f) Imidazole
   (g) Oxazole
   (h) Isoxazole
   (i) Pyridine
   (j) Pyrimidine
   (k) Azirene

(l)   Aziridine

(m) Oxirane

(n)   Azetidine

(o)   Indole

(p)   Quinoline

(q)   Isoquinoline

(r)   Quinazoline

(s)   Cinnoline

(t)   Purine

(u)   Xanthine

(v)   Pteridin

(w)   Coumarin

(x)   Hydantoin

(y)   Benzofuran

(z)   3-Methyl quinolone

(aa) 3-methyloxepin

(bb) Antipyrine

(cc) Caffeine.

5. Give any three methods of synthesis of

(a)   Furan

(b)   Pyrrole

(c)   Imidazole

(d)   Indole

(e)   Quinoline

(f)   Isoquinoline

6. Write a short note on

(a)   Madelung synthesis,

(b)   Baeyer synthesis

(c)   Reissert synthesis

(d)   Fishcher indole synthesis

(e)   Chichibabin reaction

(f)   Pall Knorr synthesis

(g)   Hantzsch synthesis.

(h)   Skraup quinolone synthesis.

7. Draw resonance structures of Furan, Pyrrole and Pyrimidine.

8. Give different chemical reactions of:

   (a) Furan

   (b) Pyrrole

   (c) Imidazole

   (d) Pyrimidine

   (e) Indole and

   (f) Quinoline

■■■

Chapter 2

INTRODUCTION TO COMBINATORIAL CHEMISTRY

Syllabus ......

History, Introduction to Linkers and Solid Supports. Various Techniques used in Combinatorial Synthesis (Mix and Split, Parallel Synthesis), Applications.

2.1 COMBINATORIAL CHEMISTRY

Combichem is an innovative method of synthesizing many different substances quickly and simultaneously.

Combichem is used to synthesize large number of chemical compounds by combining sets of building blocks. Each newly synthesized compound composition is slightly different from the previous one. A traditional chemist can synthesize 100-200 compounds per year. A combinatorial robotic system can produce in a year thousands or millions of compounds which can be tested for potential drug candidates in a high-throughput screening process. In a very short time, the topic has become the focus of considerable scientific interest and research efforts.

Combinatorial chemistry is a technique by which large numbers of structurally distinct molecules may be synthesized in a time and submitted for pharmacological assay. The key of combinatorial chemistry is that a large range of analogues are synthesized using the same reaction conditions, the same reaction vessels. In this way, the chemist can synthesize many hundreds or thousands of compounds in one time instead of preparing only a few by simple methodology. Combinatorial chemistry offers the potential to make every combination of compounds A_1 to A_n with compounds B_1 to B_n.

$$
\begin{array}{ll}
A_1 & B_1 \\
A_2 & B_2 \\
A_3 & B_3 \\
A_4 & B_4 \\
. & . \\
. & . \\
. & . \\
A_n & B_n
\end{array}
\quad \longrightarrow \quad A_1B_1 + A_2B_2 + \text{.......} \, A_nB_n
$$

The range of combinatorial technique is highly diverse and these products could be made individually in a **parallel** or in **mixtures**, using either solution or solid phase technique. Whatever the technique used the common denominator is that productivity has been amplified beyond the levels that have been routines for the last hundred years.

The synthetic methods applied in combinatorial chemistry are used to prepare either large series of individual compounds or mixtures of large number of compounds. Both series compounds and mixtures are termed as **libraries**.

The synthetic methods can be classified into two categories, viz.

1. Real combinatorial synthetic methods,
2. Parallel synthetic methods
1. The real combinatorial methods can produce mixtures containing a very large number of compounds but can be used to make individual compounds too.
2. In parallel synthesis, each product is usually prepared individually in a separate reaction vessel. The real gain in parallel synthesis is in the reaction time. Tens or even hundreds of compounds can be prepared within the time range devoted for making a single substance.

2.2 SPLIT-MIX SYNTHESIS

A combinatorial oligomer library, containing all sequences that can be deduced from three different (white, gray and black) monomers, could be synthesized by conventional methods, following the branches of the combinatorial tree demonstrated in Fig. 2.1. The sequences of the library members can be read by going from the origin along the branches (e.g. white-white-white, black-black-black on the right and left sides respectively). Looking at the combinatorial tree, one can deduce a very important rule, "The combinatorial distribution rule" i.e. *"Each product formed in a given step of a combinatorial process has to be distributed into samples, then react each sample with one of the monomers of the next reaction step".*

The split-mix method realizes the combinatorial distribution rule by mixing the products after each reaction step, then distributing the mixture into equal portions.

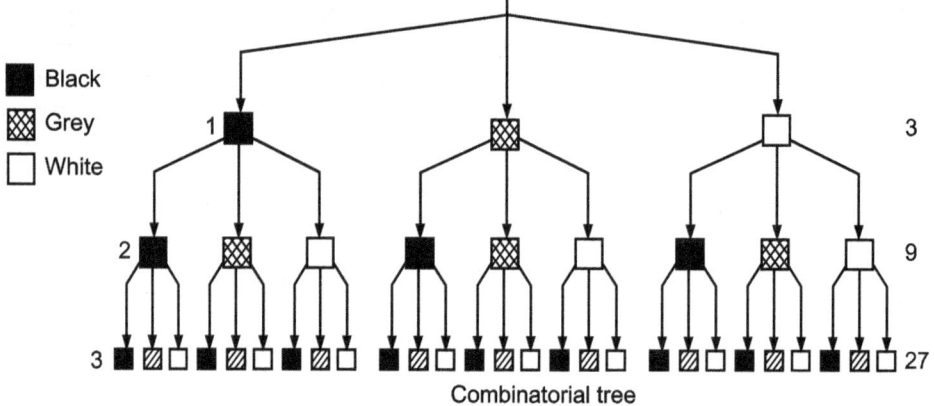

Combinatorial tree

Fig. 2.1

In this, each square in the figure represents a reaction vessel, and their black, gray and white colours symbolize the monomers that are couples in the vessels. The numbers in the left side indicate the number of reaction steps and the order of branches. The numbers on the right side show three things:

1. Number of reaction vessels used in reaction step.
2. The number of executed reaction cycles and
3. The number of products,

The split-mix method was developed for preparing peptide libraries. The method is based on Merrifield's solid phase procedure. Each coupling cycle of the solid phase synthesis is replaced by the following simple operations:

1. Dividing the solid support into equal portions.
2. Coupling each portion individually with only one of the amino acids.
3. Mixing portions.

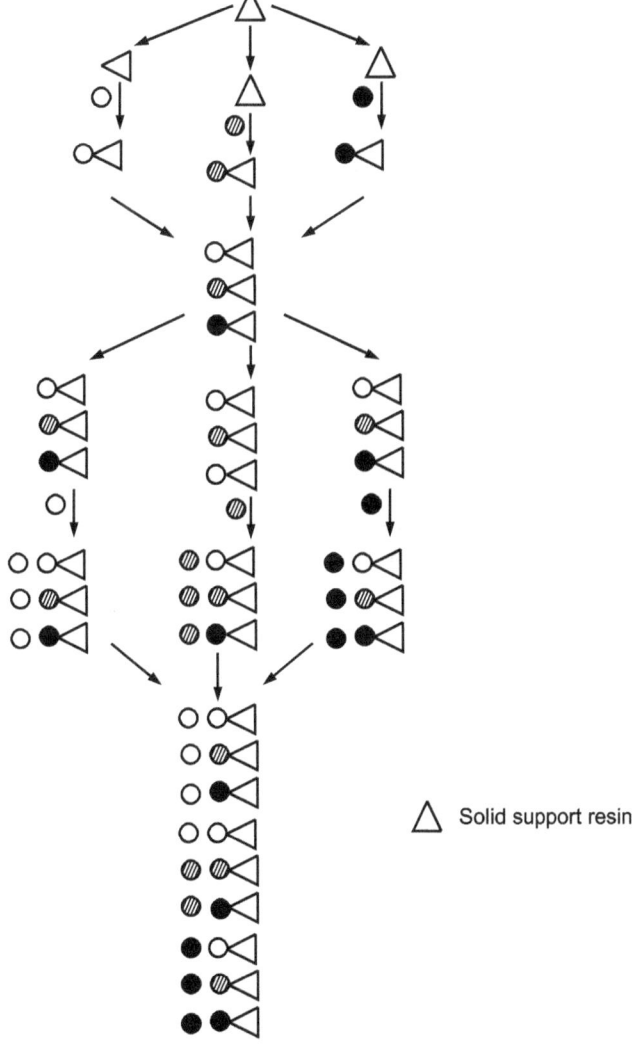

△ Solid support resin

Fig. 2.2

The method is exemplified by the synthesis of a peptide library on solid support, using only three different amino acids. The scheme of the procedure is shown in Fig. 2.2. The amino acids are represented by white, gray or black circles. In the first coupling cycle, the amino acids are coupled to equal portions of the resin. The product after recombining and mixing the portions is the mixture of the three amino acids bound to the resin. In the second cycle, this mixture is again divided into three equal portions and the amino acids are individually coupled to these mixtures. In each coupling step, three different resin-bound dipeptides are formed. As a consequence, the end product-after mixing is a mixture of nine dipeptides. The divergent, vertical and convergent arrows indicate portioning, coupling (with one kind of amino acid) and combining-mixing respectively. If the synthesis is continued after executing a further partioning, coupling and mixing step leads to the formation of mixture of 27 resin-bound tripeptides, and if an additional coupling step is carried out the end product comprises as 81 tetramers.

2.2.1 Liquid Phase Split-Mix Synthesis

In 1995, a liquid phase variant of the split-mix method was described. The synthesis is carried out on polyethylene glycol monomethyl ether (MeoPEG) support. This polymer is soluble in the course of the reaction and the homogeneous phase is advantageous for coupling, but can be precipitated, allowing washing out the excess of the reagents. This method has an additional advantage. The molar ratio of the products is not affected by statistics. The method has, however a disadvantage too, only mixtures can be made. Since there are no beads, the one-bead-one compound feature of the original method is completely lost.

2.3 COMBINATORIAL SOLID SUPPORT SYNTHESIS

Since Merifield pioneered solid phase synthesis back in 1963, work, which earns him a Nobel prize the subject has changed radically.

The use of solid support for organic synthesis relies on three interconnected requirements.

1. A **cross linked**, insoluble polymeric material that is inert to the condition of synthesis – Resins.
2. Some means of linking the substrate to this solid phase that permits selective cleavage of some or all the products from the solid support during synthesis for analysis of the extent of reactions and ultimately to give the final product of interest – Linkers.
3. A chemical protection strategy to allow selective protection and deprotection of reactive groups – protective sp.

Merifield developed a series of chemical reactions that can be used to synthesize proteins. The direction of synthesis is opposite to that used in the cell. The intended carboxyl terminal amino acid is anchored to a solid support. Then the next amino acid is coupled to the first one. In order to prevent further, chain growth at this point, the amino acid which is added, has its amino group blocked. After the coupling step, the block is removed from the primary amino group and the coupling reaction is repeated with the next amino acid. The process continues until the peptide or protein is completed. Then the molecule is cleaved from the solid support and any groups protecting amino acid side chains are removed. Finally, the peptide or protein is purified to remove the partial products and products containing errors.

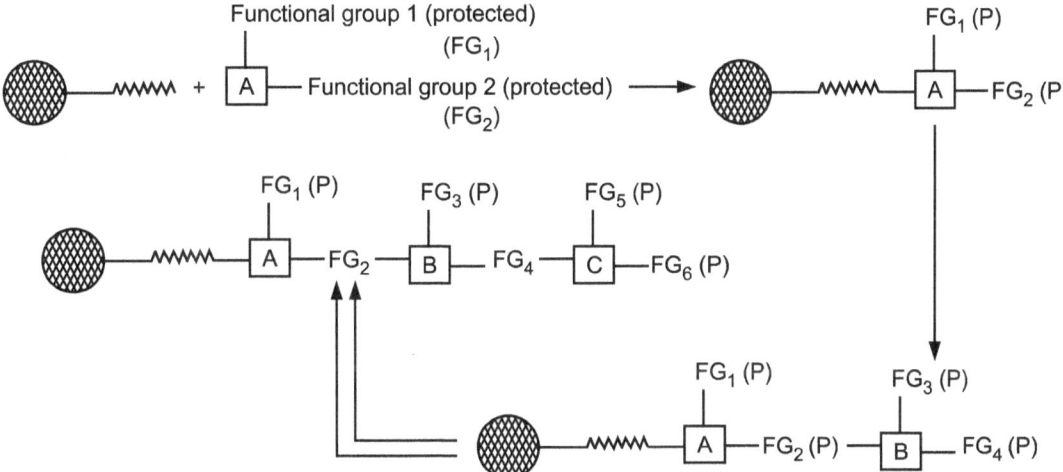

Combinatorial synthesis on solid phase can generate very large number of products, using a method described as **mix and split synthesis.** This technique was pioneered by **Furka** and has been enthusiastically exploited by many others since its first disclosure. For example, Houghten has used mix and split on a macro scale in a **"tea bag"** approach for the generation of large libraties of peptides. The method works as follows:

2.4 TEA BAG APPROACH

A sample of resin support material is divided into a number of equal portions (x) and each of these are individually reacted with a single different reagent. After completion of the reactions and subsequent washing to remove excess reagents, the individual portions are recombined, the whole is thoroughly mixed and may then be divided again into portions. Reaction with a further set of activated reagents gives the complete set of possible dimeric units as mixtures and this whole process may then be repeated as necessary (for a total of n times). The number of compounds obtained arises from the geometric increase in potential products: in this case – X to the power of n.

A simple example of a 3 × 3 × 3 library gives all 27 possible combinations of trimeric products. X, Y and Z could be amino acids in which case the final products would be tripeptides but more generally they could be any type of monomeric units or chemical precursor. It can be seen that the mix and split procedure finally gives three mixtures each consisting of nine compounds each and there are several ways of progressing these compounds to biological screening. Although the compounds can be tested whilst still attached to the bead, a favoured method is to test the compounds as a mixture following cleavage from the solid phase. Activity in any given mixture reveals the partial structure of active compounds within the library as the residue coupled last (usually the N-terminal residue) is unique to each mixture. Identification of the most active compound relies deconvoluting the active mixtures in the library through further synthesis and screening.

In the example where the active structure is YXZ, the mixture of Y at the terminal position will appear as the most active. Having retained samples of the intermediate dimers on resin (so called "recursive" deconvolution) addition of Y to each of the 3 mixtures will give all nine compounds with Y at the terminal position and the second position defined by the mixture. The most active mixture here defines the middle position of the most active trimer to be residue X. Finally, the 3 individual compounds can be independently resynthesized and tested to reveal both the most potent compounds and also some structure-activity relationship data. In contrast, Lam et. al. tested a family of peptides whilst still attached to the resin bead solid phase. Nineteen amino acids were incorporated into pentapeptide to generate a library of almost two and half million compounds. By using a colorimetric array, beads bearing peptide sequences that bound tightly to the protein streptavidin or to an antibody raised against β-endorphin were revealed by visual inspection. Bead picking using micromanipulation isolated the beads and the active peptide structures were determined by micro-sequencing.

A modification of this method has allowed screening of such libraries in solution. Linkers have been devised that allow several copies of the library compounds to be released sequentially. Using this method it is possible to identify an active mixture using a solution array and then return to the beads that produced these compounds and redistribute them into smaller mixtures for retest. By repeatedly reducing the mixture size, ultimately to single compounds, the bead containing the most potent sequence may be identified and the peptide product sequenced.

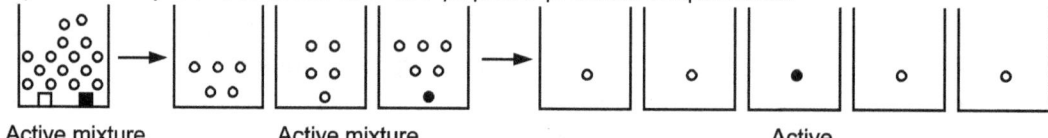

Active mixture   Active mixture   Active

2.5 RESINS FOR SOLID PHASE SYNTHESIS

In solid phase support synthesis, the solid support is generally based on a polystyrene resin. The most commonly used resin supports for sps include:

1. Spherical beads of lightly cross linked gel type polystyrene (1-2% divinylbenzene) and

2. Poly(styrene-oxyethylene) graft copolymers which are functionalized to allow attachment of linkers and substrate molecules. Each of these materials has advantages and disadvantages depending on the particular application.

1. Cross-linked polystyrene:

Lightly cross-linked gel type polystyrene (GPS) has been most widely used due to its common availability and inexpensive cost. GPS beads which are functionalized with chloromethyl, aminomethyl and a variety of linkers are commercially available from a variety of sources. A prominent characteristic of GPS beads is their ability to absorb large relative volumes of certain organic solvents (swelling). This swelling causes a phase change of the bead from a solid to a solvent-swollen gel, and therefore the reactive sites are accessed by diffusion of reactants through a solvent swollen gel network. In solvents, which swell the polymer well, the gel network consists of mostly solvent with only a small fraction of the total mass being polymer backbone. This allows relatively rapid diffusional access of reagents to reactive sites within the swollen bead. In solvents, which do not swell the polymer, the cross-linked network does not expand and the diffusion of the reagents into the interior of the bead is impeded.

GPS has good swelling characteristic in solvents of low to medium polarity ranging from aliphatic hydrocarbons to dichloromethane, polar, protic solvents, such as alcohols and water do not swell. GPS resins and accessibility to all reaction sites may be compromised. Hence GPS supports are most suitable for chemistry performed in solvents of low to medium polarity.

Friedel Craft
CH_3OCH_2Cl
$SnCl_2$

CH_2Cl

CH_2OR

R $=$ H - Merrifield Resin

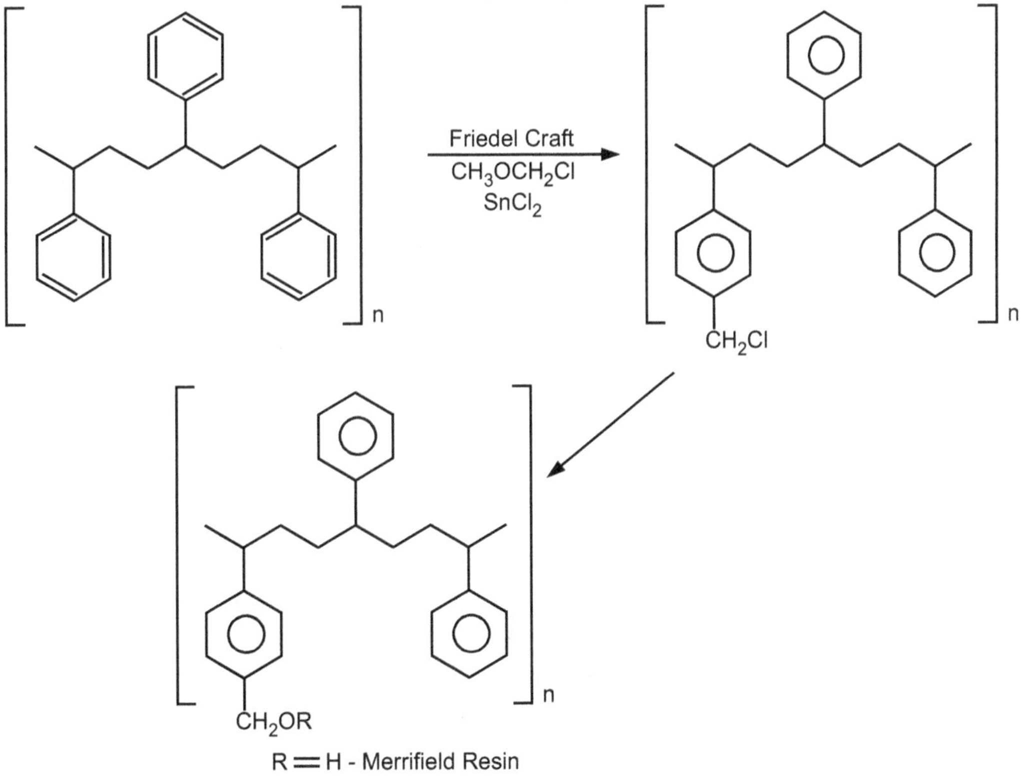

Polyamide Resins:

Sheppard designed polyacrylamide polymers for peptide synthesis, as it was expected that these polymers would more closely mimic the properties of the peptide chains themselves and have greatly improved solvation properties in polar, aprotic solvents (e.g. DMF or N-methyl pyrrolidinone).

Backbone monomer   Cross linked

Backbone monomer with protected functional group

Sheppard also proposed the use of a new protection and linking strategy. The Merrifield approach is depended on a benzyl ester linkage and BOC protection. But a more mild protection/deprotection were sought. The protecting group finally chosen was the fluorenylmethoxycarbonyl (Fmoc) which can be removed by base (usually piperidine).

2. Poly (Styrene-oxyethylene) graft Copolymers:

Poly graft copolymers, first reported by Bayer and Rapp are another class of widely used supports for organic synthesis. As with the polyacrylamide resins, in order to produce a polar reaction milieu that is closer to the solvents generally used by solution synthetic chemists, grafted polymer beads have been prepared. The most pre-eminent of these is **Tenta Gel resin** which consists of polyethylene glycol attached to cross-linked polystyrene through an ether link and combines the benefits of the soluble polyethylene glycol support with the insolubility and handling characteristics of the polystyrene bead. The resin was originally prepared by the polymerization of ethylene oxide on cross-linked polystyrene already derives with tetra-ethylene glycol to give polyethylene glycol chains. Poly (styrene-methylene) graft copolymer beads display relatively uniform swelling in a variety of solvents from medium to high polarity ranging from toluene to water. The polymers are produced by grafting ethylene oxide from the polystyrene backbone creating long flexible chains that terminate with a reactive site specially separated from the more rigid polystyrene backbone.

Some disadvantages of poly graft copolymers support are:

1. Relatively low functional group loading with GPS.

2. The potential instability of polyethylene glycol.

3. The presence of linear polyethylene glycol impurities found in the small molecule products after cleavage from the resin.

4. The tendency for resins to become sticky and difficult to handle as the synthesis progresses.

2.6 LINKERS

The group that joins the substrate to the resin bead is an essential part of solid phase synthesis. The linker is a specialized protecting group, in that much of the time, the linker will tie up a functional group only for it to reappear at the end of the synthesis. The linker must not be affected by the chemistry used to modify or extend the attached compound. And finally the cleavage step should proceed readily and in a good yield. The best linker must allow attachment and cleavage in quantitative yield.

2.6.1 Carboxylic Acid Linkers

The first linking group used for peptide synthesis bears the name of the father of solid phase synthesis, **Merrifield resin**. It is cross-linked polystyrene functionalized with a chloromethyl group. The carbonyl group is attached by the nucleophilic displacement of the chloride with a cesium carboxylate salt in DMF. Cleavage to regenerate the carboxylic acid is usually achieved by hydrogen fluoride.

The second class of linker used for carboxylic acid is **Wang linker**. This linker is generally attached to cross-linked polystyrene Tenta Gel and Polyacrylamide to form wang resin. It was designed for the synthesis of peptide carboxylic acids using the Fmoc-protection strategy and due to the activated benzyl alcohol design, the carboxylic acid product can be cleaved with TFA.

A more acid-labile form of the wang resin has been developed. The SASRIN resin has the same structure as the wang linker but with the addition of a methoxy group to stabilize the carbonium ion formed during acid catalysed cleavage.

2.6.2 Carboxamide Linkers

Chemist developed a linking group that would generate carboxamide in mild acidic condition. The first development was the methylbenzhydrylamine (MBHA) linker on polystyrene for improved synthesis of peptide using the BOC protection strategy. Sieber developed a new linker with greater acid ability. He used a xanthenyl derivative, the acid-labile g-xanthenyl group has been used to protect the amide group of asparagine and glutamine.

As the xanthenyl group is less acid-labile than BOC, an additional $-OCH_2-$ group was introduced between the anchor and polystyrene to increase acid-lability.

An other acid-labile linker was developed in the same time. The rink linker is now preferred for generating primary carboxamide on solid phase. The greater acid sensitivity in this linker is a consequence of the two additional election donating methoxy groups. In the generation of primary carboxamide, the starting material is attached to the linker as a carboxylic acid and after synthetic modification is cleaved from the resin with TFA.

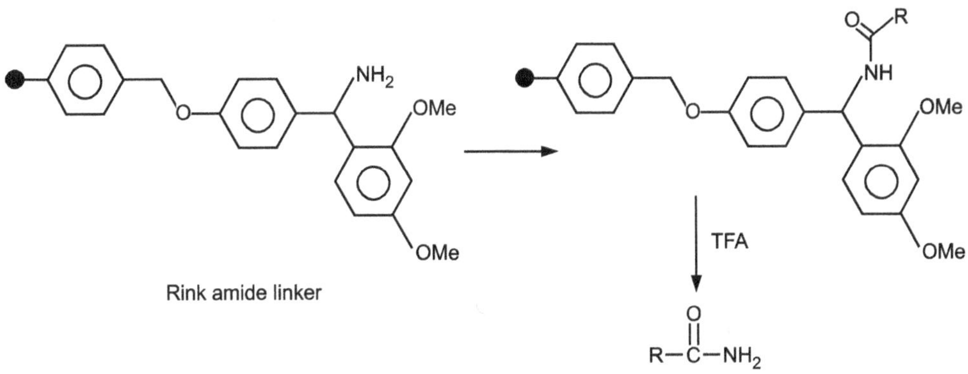

Rink amide linker

TFA

$$R-\overset{O}{\overset{\parallel}{C}}-NH_2$$

2.6.3 Alcohol Linkers

A hydroxy linker based on the tetrahydropyranyl (THP) protecting group has been developed by Thompson and Ellmann. All types of alcohols readily add to dihydropyran and the resulting THP protecting group is stable to strong base, but easily cleaved with acid. This linker is attached to a Merrifield resin.

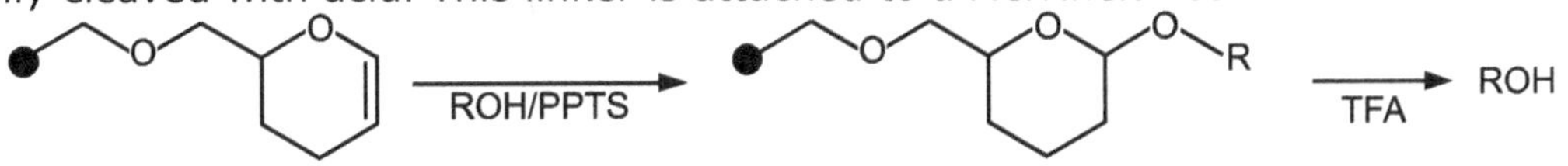

ROH/PPTS   TFA   ROH

The trityl group is a good acid-labile protecting group for a lot of heteroatoms. The trityl group has been used to another alcohols in the synthesis of a library of β-mercaptoketones.

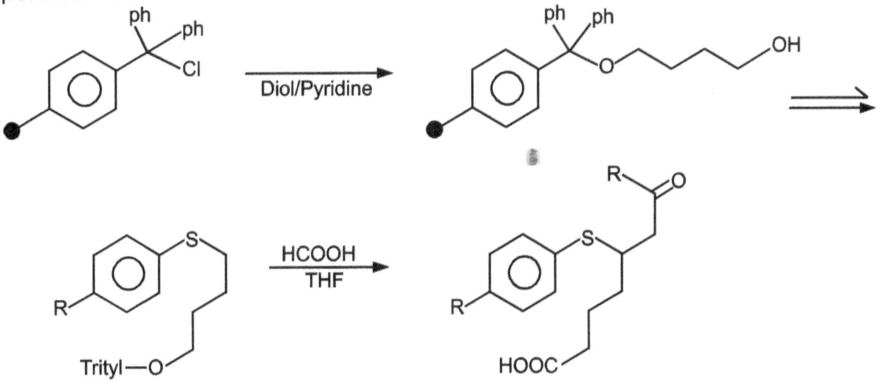

Diol/Pyridine

HCOOH
THF

Trityl—O   HOOC

2.6.4 Amine Linkers

Carbamate Linker has been used for the synthesis of a combinatorial library of 576 polyamines prepared in the search of inhibitors of trypanosomal parasitic infections. Two linkers were investigated. One based on hydroxymethyl benzoic acid 1 and another one as electron-donating group has been added 2. The last one allowed cleavage by TFA while the first one could be cleaved with strong acidic condition.

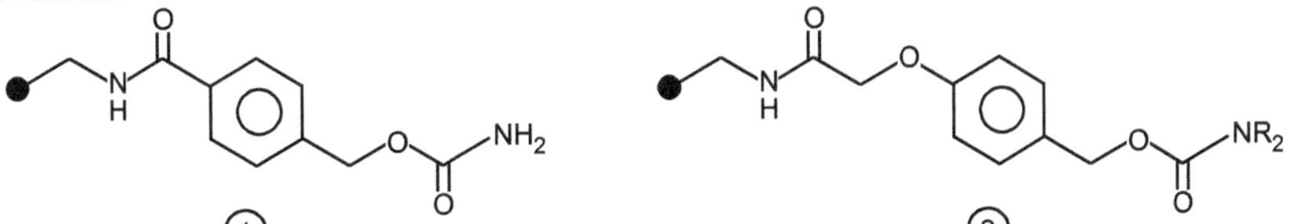

①   ②

A very useful linker has been recently developed for the generation of tertiary amine. $1°$ and $2°$ amines are introduced to the linker by Michae addition. The amine may be alkylated to give a resin-bound quaternary ammonium ion. In mildly basic condition, Hoffmann elimination occurs to give a $3°$ amine of high purity.

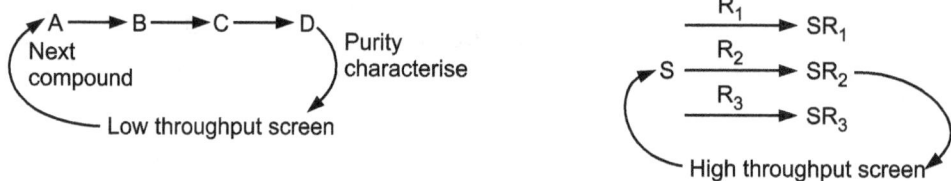

2.7 PARALLEL SOLUTION PHASE SYNTHESIS

Mannual or automated approaches can be used for the parallel preparation of 10-100 of analogues of a biologically active substrate. The products are synthesized using reliable coupling and functional group interconversion chemistry and are progressed to screening after removal of solvent and volatile by-products. Parallel and orthodox synthesis is compared below.

A $\longrightarrow$ B $\longrightarrow$ C $\longrightarrow$ D
Next compound) Purity characterise
$\longrightarrow$ Low throughput screen

$\xrightarrow{R_1}$ SR_1
$S \xrightarrow{R_2} SR_2$
$\xrightarrow{R_3} SR_3$
$\longrightarrow$ High throughput screen

Orthodox analogue synthesis and screening   Parallel analogue synthesis and screening

Orthodox synthesis usually involves a multistep sequence. For example, from A through to the final product D, which is purified and fully characterized before screening. The next analogue is then designed and guided by the biological activity of the previous compound prepared and then screened. This process is repeated to optimize both activity and selectivity.

In contrast parallel analogue synthesis involves reaction of a substrate 'S' with multiple reactants R_1, R_2, R_3 .... R_n to produce a compound library of 'n' individual products SR_1, SR_2, SR_3 ...... SR_n. The library is screened. Usually without purification and with only minimal characterization of the individual compounds using a rapid throughput screening technique.

Panlabs have recently disclosed an interest in making large number of compounds as individual components using parallel reliable solution chemistry. Reactions are pushed to completion by the use of excess quantities of the reactive reagent and are isolated by solvent – solvent extraction. There is no further purification and they prefer to describe these samples as "reaction products".

2.8 APPLICATIONS OF COMBINATORIAL CHEMISTRY

1. **In Pharmaceutical Companies for Drug Designs**
   Transition-State Analog HIV Protease Inhibitors: Extensive efforts towards the rational design of aspartyl protease inhibitors such as renin and HIV have led to the discovery of several transition-states analog mimics. These templates can serve as the central unit around which molecular

diversity can be generated by application of appropriate chemistries. Recently, solid phase synthesis of hydroxyethylamine and 1,2-diol transition-state pharmacophore units and their utility for synthesis of HIV protease inhibitors have been reported by two different groups.

The first instance, bifunctional linkers are used by Wang to serve the dual purpose of protecting the hydroxyl group of these BBs and providing point for attachment on the solid support.

1

Diamino alcohol core unit

(1) PPTS

(2) Pd(PPh$_3$)$_4$, dimedone
(3) DCC, MBHA Resin

(1) Conc. H$^+$ (CAT)

2

Core unit to resin via acetal protected alcohol

3

Diamino diol core unit

(2) H$_2$, Pd/C
(3) Fmoc-OSu
(4) DCC, HMBA Resin

4

Core unit linked to resin via ketal protected diol

2 or 4

1) Piperidine
2) Fmoc-Val-OH, PyBOP
3) Piperidine
4) R-COOH, PyBOP
5) TFA cleavage

(X = H or OH)

Diamino alcohol core unit

Thus, one linker possesses a vinyl ether group at one end and a free carboxylate group at the other. The vinyl ether moiety is reacted with diamino alcohol BB 1 under acid-catalysed conditions to form an acetal protecting group and the carboxylic acid group is used for ester-type linkage to the solid support. The other linker possesses a methyl ketone and carboxylic groups at the two ends, with the ketone group forming a ketal with diol 3. Resulting intermediates 2 and 4 are now well suited for a bi-directional solid phase synthesis strategy for preparing C2 symmetric HIV protease inhibitors. The two terminal amino groups of 2 and 4 are deprotected and reacted with a variety of carboxylic acid, sulfonyl chlorides, isocyanates, and chloroformates to extend the core unit in both directions and generate a wide variety of aspartyl protease inhibitors. The authors claim that a library of 300 discrete analogs was prepared and screened against HIV protease to identify several potent inhibitors.

2. The future of combinatorial chemistry will undoubtedly provide a wealth of pre-clinical lead compounds and potential drugs. Advances thus far in combinatorial techniques will shift drug discovery from the normal time-consuming/labor-oriented synthesis to accelerated synthesis of a multitude of compounds that can be screening and optimized quickly.

3. The first stage is finding promising lead compounds, which is facilitated greatly with the compilation of the combinatorial libraries. The library can also takes the lead compound and derivatize it to give it pharmacological properties that are necessary for a potential drug.

4. The second step - lead development – is where combinatorial chemistry begins to fall short of ideal. As the lead molecule becomes more complex, problems that can arise are difficulties with detaching the structurally diverse molecules from the solid support, unfavorable side reactions, and harmful effects that often occur in the harsh reaction conditions employed by combinatorial syntheses. These problems magnify if the natural product happens to be sensitive and fragile. Solutions to these conditions are being studied in combinatorial biocatalysis which employs enzymatic conditions and microbial transformations on an existing lead instead of the more harsh organic reaction conditions.

5. One of the methods used by the combinatorial chemists in imitating the molecular evolution is trial and error. Another term for the trial and error combinatorial chemistry is dry evolution or development. This method alters the cycles of selection and amplification within the molecules, thereby imitating mutations. Although this method may be quick in the laboratorial setting, it lacks even a minimum amount of environmental selection. Environmental selection is important in that efficacy, potency, stability, and selectivity are evolutionarily designed so that the molecules can withstand many survival challenges. It took 15 years for Eli Lilly to develop ProzacÓ. "We think we are clever when we develop combination drug strategies to attack disorders such as cancer and AIDS. But snails discovered this strategy 15 million years ago." It is through the natural products, which help in finding potential target genes from macromolecules lying along the targeted gene disruption path that we can come to a quick and effective drug discovery.

QUESTIONS

1. Define Combinatorial chemistry.
2. Discuss the history of Combichem.
3. Explain various linkers and solid supports in combinatorial chemistry.
4. Describe various terms used in Combichem.
5. Describe briefly Multiple parallel synthesis.
6. Discuss Mix and split synthesis in combichem.
7. Describe various techniques in solid support synthesis.
8. Give the applications of Combinatorial chemistry.

■■■

Chapter 3

RETRO-SYNTHESIS

Syllabus ......

Introduction to common terms, General Rules and Guidelines involved in Retro-synthesis, Disconnections involving one and two functional groups. The retro-synthesis of following drugs to be covered: Ibuprofen, Propranolol, Ciprofloxacin and Sulfamethoxazole.

3.1 DEFINITION

An analytical operation that breaks a bond and converts a molecule into possible starting materials. It is exactly the reverse of chemical synthesis. Therefore, it is also called as Retrosynthesis.

OR

An analytical approach to organic synthesis in which the target molecule is broken into fragments through a series of logical disconnections to get the best possible and likely starting materials (synthons).

Synthon/Disconnection approach helps devising better and easy synthetic routes for complex molecules.

3.2 TERMINOLOGIES

Disconnection: An operation involving breaking of bond/s between atoms.

Synthon: An idealised fragment, usually an ion or radical obtained by disconnection. (It may or may not be actually employed in actual synthesis).

Reagent: Actual compounds (chemicals) used in practice for a synthesis.

e.g.　　　　　Synthon $= Me^+$

　　　　　　　Reagent $= MeI$ or Me_2SO_4

FGI / FGE: Functional Group Interconversions / Functional Group Equivalents.

Usually written over a double arrow $\Longrightarrow$. This means substitution of a functional group by another equivalent to it.

e.g.

$$-COOH \xrightarrow{\text{FGE}} -CN; \quad --NH_2 \xrightarrow{\text{FGE}} -NO_2 \xrightarrow{\text{FGE}} -H \quad -Cl \xrightarrow{\text{FGE}} -OH$$

Symbols:

TgM　　　:　Target molecule

SM　　　　:　Starting material

$\Rightarrow$: Double arrow .. indicates substitution

$\sim\!\!\!\sim$: Indicates which bond is broken.
Curved arrow on the top indicates which fragment will carry negative charge in a heterocyclic disconnection.

3.3 BASIC RULES

Rule 1:

Disconnection of a bond should be such that stable fragment ions are obtained. e.g. Two modes of disconnection are A and B.

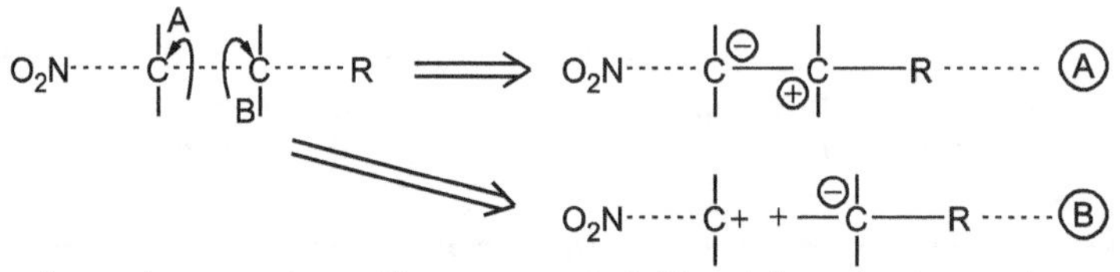

'A' will be preferred as carbocations are stabilized by electron donor groups R, OR etc. and carbanions are stabilized by electron withdrawing groups NO_2, CN, COOR, etc.

Rule 2:

Number of fragments generated through a disconnection should be as minimum as possible.

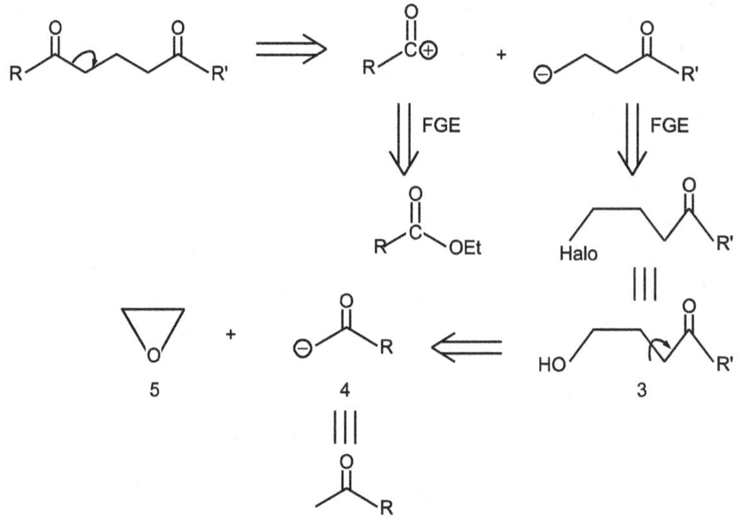

Stepwise 1-5 fragments

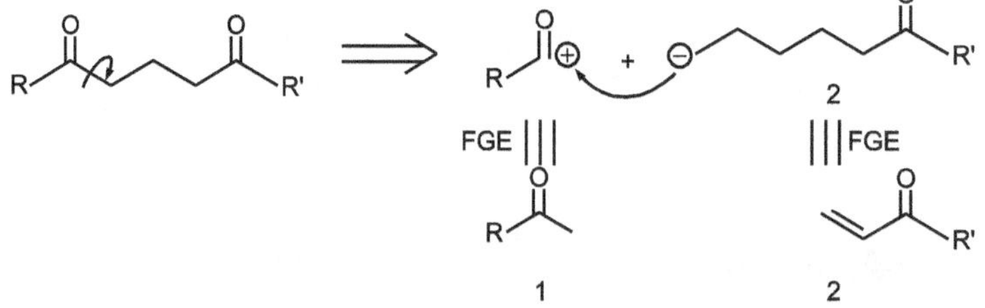

Stepwise 2 fragments

Rule 3:

Always a C-Hetero atom (O, N, S) bond is broken, with the electron pair being transferred to the heteroatom (as heteroatoms are more electronegative than 'C', they can accommodate the electron pair).

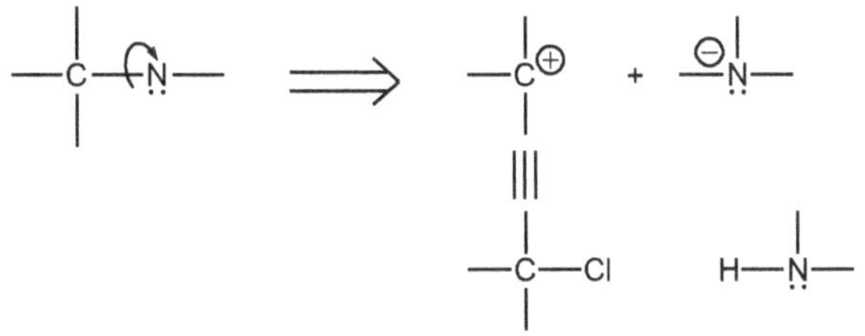

Rule 4:

Sometimes a disconnection does not generate sufficiently stabilized fragments. But such fragments can be obtained using FGC or introducing additional electron withdrawing groups and removing them after the synthesis.

Example 1:

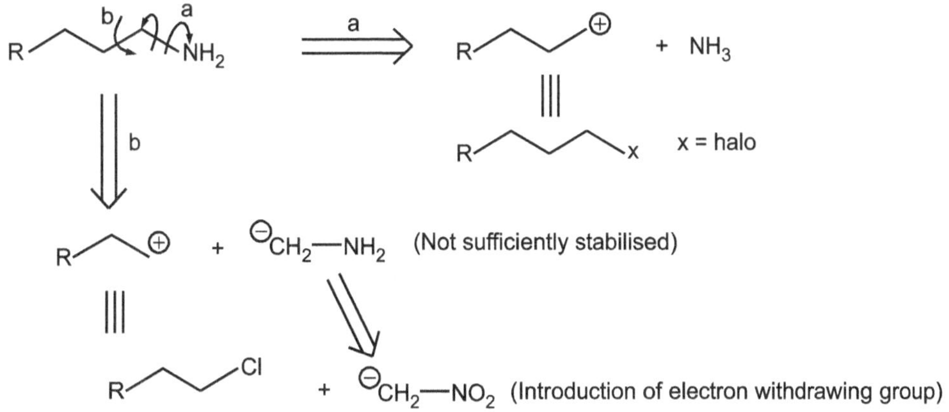

CH_2—NH_2 (Not sufficiently stabilised)

CH_2—NO_2 (Introduction of electron withdrawing group)

Actual synthesis:

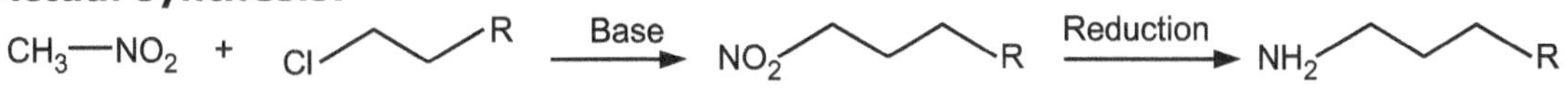

CH_3—NO_2 + Cl~~~R →(Base)→ NO_2~~~R →(Reduction)→ NH_2~~~R

Example 2:

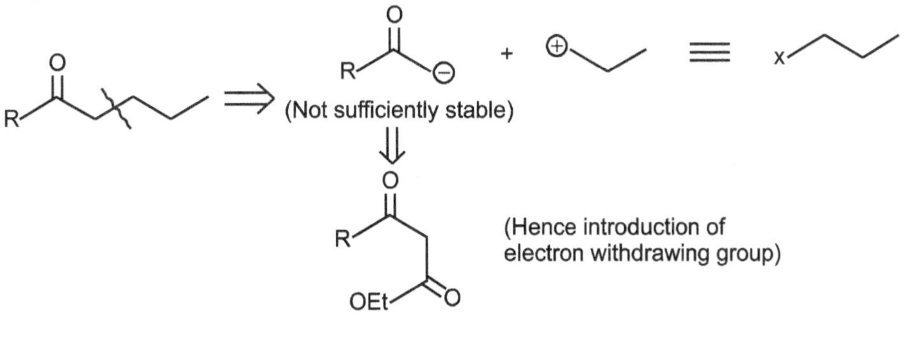

(Not sufficiently stable)

(Hence introduction of electron withdrawing group)

Actual synthesis:

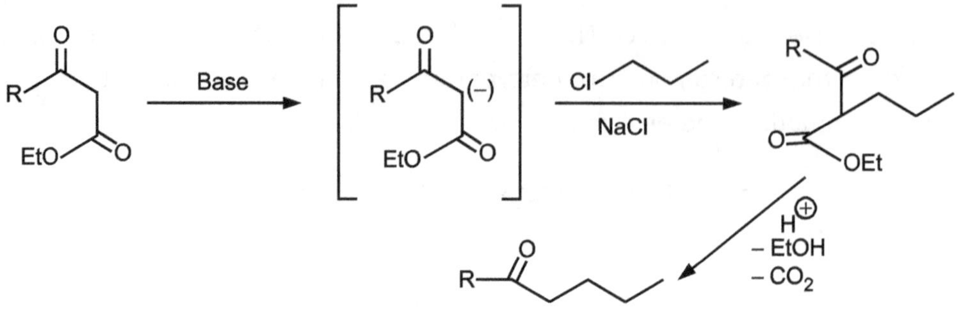

Rule 5:

Equivalence: The +ve and −ve fragments generated by disconnection are replaced by recognizable and meaningful chemical entities.

+ ve fragments

e.g.

$$R - \overset{\oplus}{C}H_2 \equiv R - CH_2 - X \text{ (alkyl halide)}$$

(+vely charged alkyl) $R - CH_2 - OH$ (alcohol)

$$R - CH_2 - OEt \text{ (ether)}$$

$$R - C = \overset{\oplus}{O} \equiv R - CO - X \text{ (acyl halide)}$$

(+vely charged acyl) $R - CO - OH$ (acid)

$$R - CO - OEt \text{ (ester)}$$

$$R - CO - O - CO - R \text{ (anhydride)}$$

− ve fragments

The −vely charged fragments are considered equivalent to their protonated species. Thus,

$$O_2N - \overset{\ominus}{C}H - R \equiv O_2N - CH_2 - R$$

$$R - \overset{\ominus}{O} \equiv R - OH$$

$$R - \overset{\ominus}{N}H = RNH_2$$

$$R - O - CO - \overset{\ominus}{C}H - R \equiv ROCO - CH_2 - R'$$

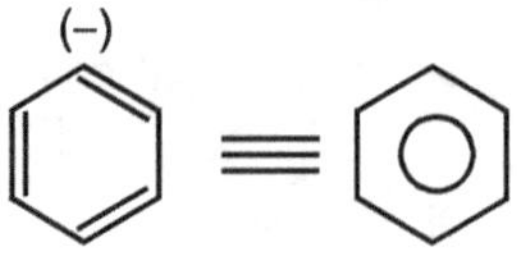

$$(-)$$

Let us apply these rules to the following example:

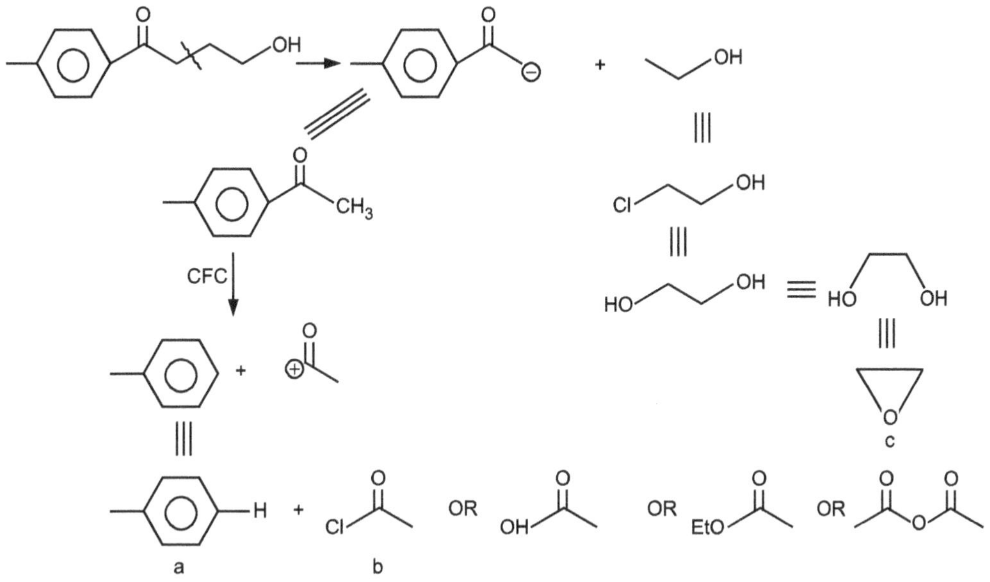

Thus, we have

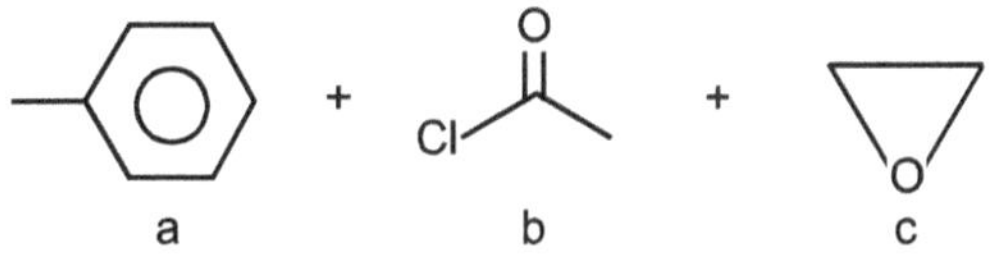

Thus,

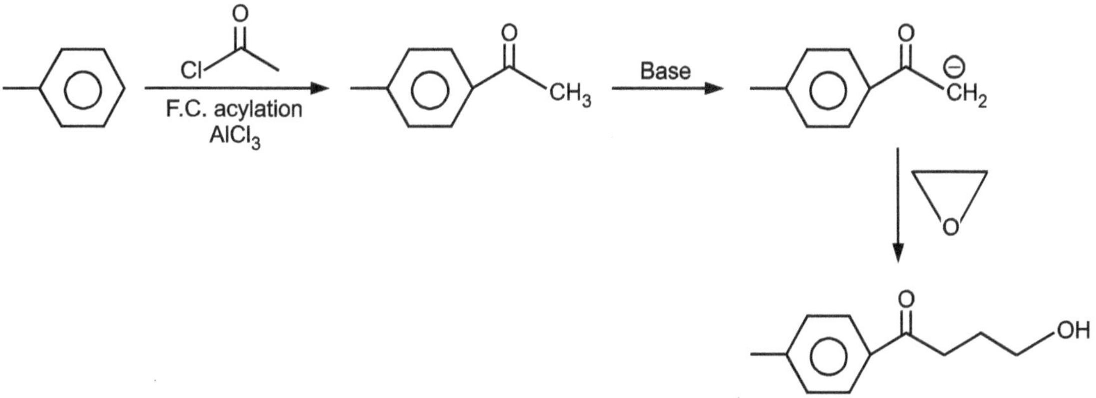

3.4 GUIDELINES (STRATEGIES AND ORDER OF EVENTS)

G-1

Examine the relationship between groups i.e. which group is the proper directing group (disconnect if the last) to get the TgM. Here, thus the order is important.

Analysis:

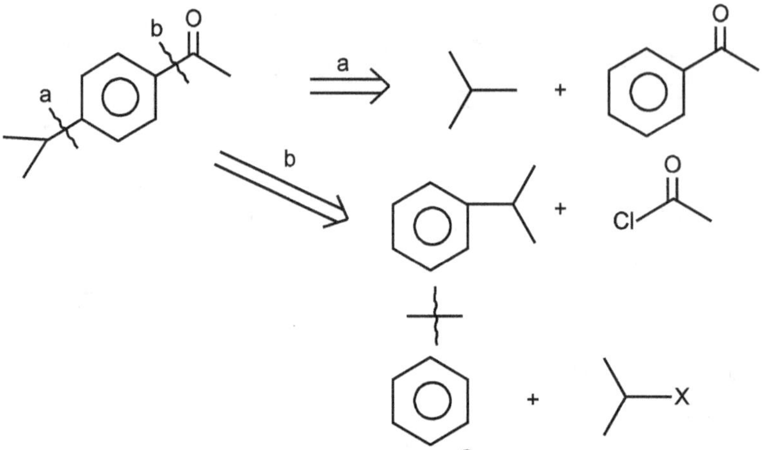

Here b > a, as we cannot start with 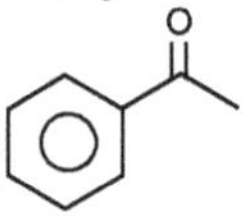 as 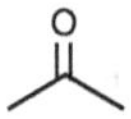 is a m-director (which retards the reaction).

∴   Proceed via 'b'.

∴   **Synthesis:**

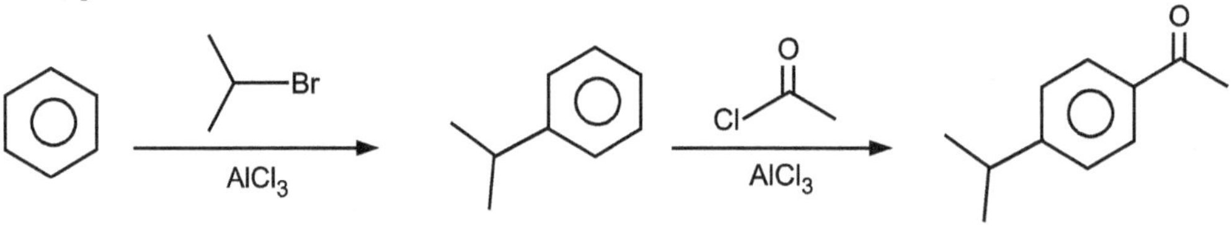

G-2:

The most electron withdrawing group to be disconnected first (i.e. to be added last in the synthesis).

Analysis:

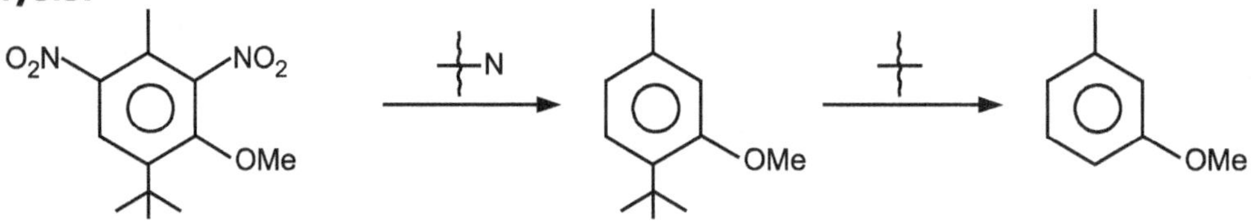

Synthesis:

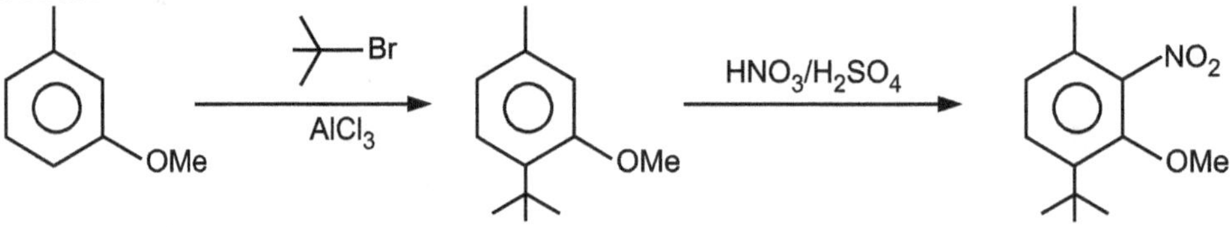

G-3:

If FGI is needed do it at an appropriate stage to get the desired effect on orientation.

Analysis:

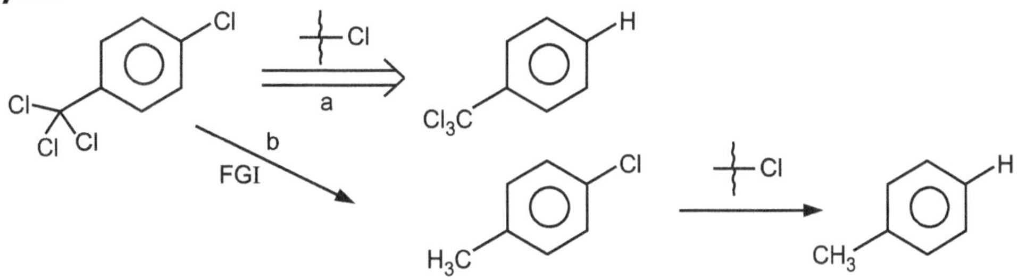

Here CCl_3 is meta director, but its FGI, CH_3 is p-directional. Therefore, do FGI prior to C-Cl disconnection.

Synthesis:

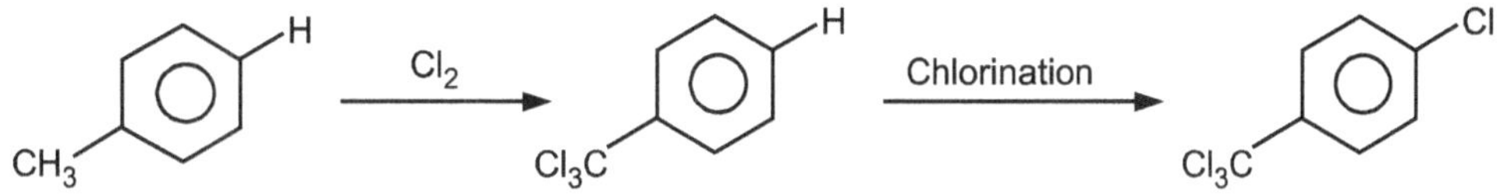

G-4:

Avoid sequences that may lead to unwanted reactions at other sites of the molecules.

Analysis:

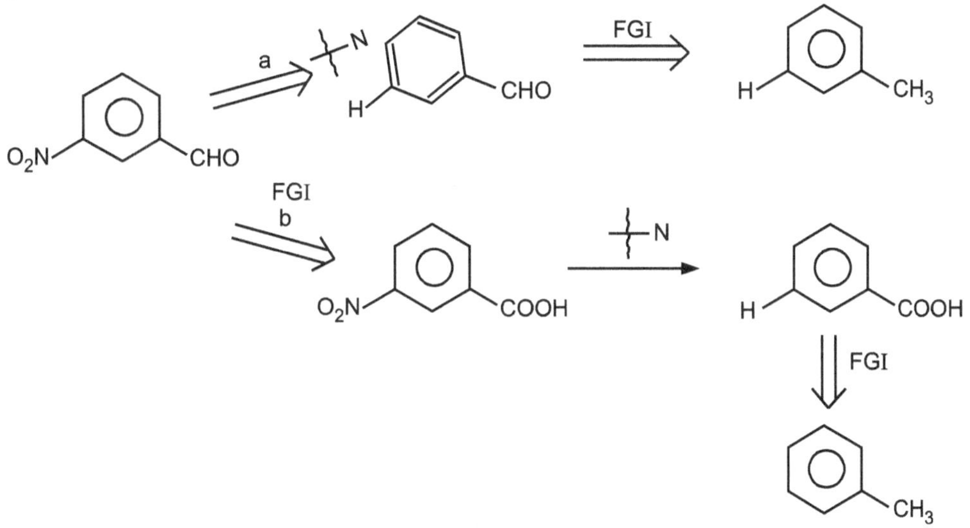

Therefore 'b' to be adopted as nitration of benzaldehyde may lead to side reaction i.e. oxidation CHO → COOH.

∴ **Synthesis:**

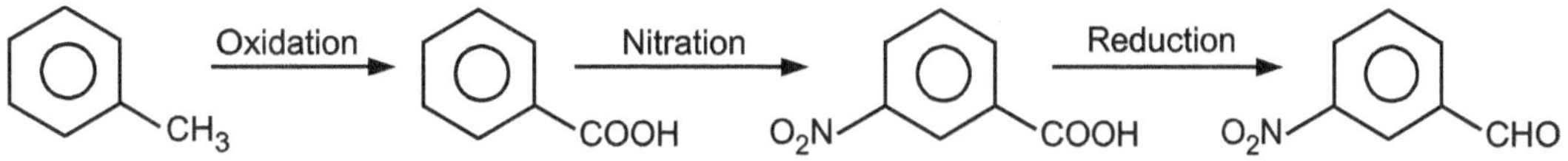

3.5 IMPORTANT TABLES

Table 3.1

X	Reagent	Reaction
CH_2Cl	CH_2O + $ZnCl_2$ + HCl	Chloromethylation
CHO	CH_3Cl + H_2O (OH⁻) OR (Me_2N = CH – $OPCl_2$) Cl OR CO + HCl + $AlCl_3$	Riemer – Tiemann CO-Formylation
R^+ (alkyl group)	RBr + $AlCl_3$ ROH + $H^\oplus$ Alkene + H	F.C. Alkylation
$RCO^\oplus$	RCOCl + $AlCl_3$	F.C. Acylation
$NO_2^\oplus$	HNO_3 / H_2SO_4	Nitration
CC^+	Cl_2 / $FeCl_3$	Chlorination
$+SO_3H$	H_2SO_4	Sulfonation
SO_2Cl	$ClSO_3H$	Chlorosulfonation
$ArN_2^\oplus$	ArN_2^+	Diazocoupling

Table 3.2

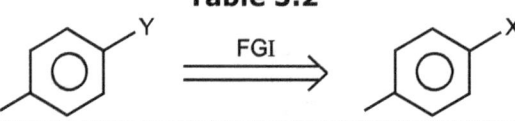

	Y	X	Reagent
Reduction	NO_2 COR COR	NH_2 CH(OH)R CH_2R	H_2/Pd – C, Sn/HCl $NaBH_4$ Zn/Hg, conc. HCl, N_2H_4 / KOH, glycol
Oxidation	CH_2Cl CH_2R, CH_3 COR CH_3 CH_3 CN	CHO COOH OCOR CCl_3 CF_3 COOH	Hexamine, DMSO $KMnO_4$ RCO_3H (peracids) Cl_2, PCl_5 SbF_5 –OH / H_2O

Table 3.3

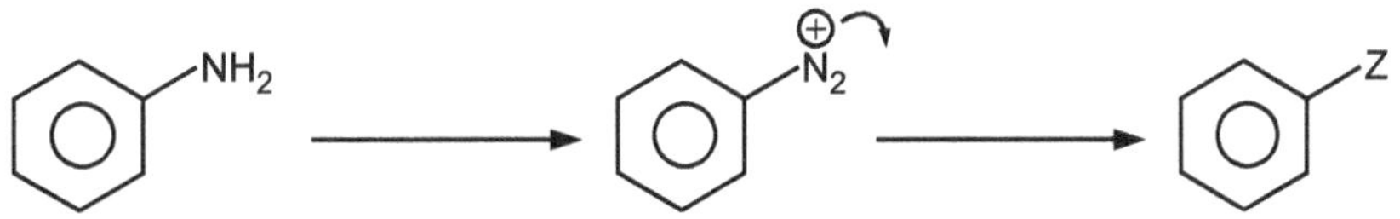

Z	Reagent
OH	H_2O
OR	ROH
CN	CuCN
Cl	CuCl
Br	CuBr
I	KI
Ar	Ar – H
H	H_3PO_4 or $EtOH/H^+$

3.6 SYNTHON APPROACH

Important Steps:

(A) Analysis:

- Recognize the functional groups in the TGM.
- Disconnect by a method corresponding to most reliable and known synthetic reaction or do FGI.
- Repeat this cycle till you reach the simplest S.M.

(B) Synthesis:

- Write out the reverse plan as per the analysis, adding the appropriate reagents and reaction conditions.
- Modify the plan as per actual laboratory experiments.

e.g. **Analysis:**

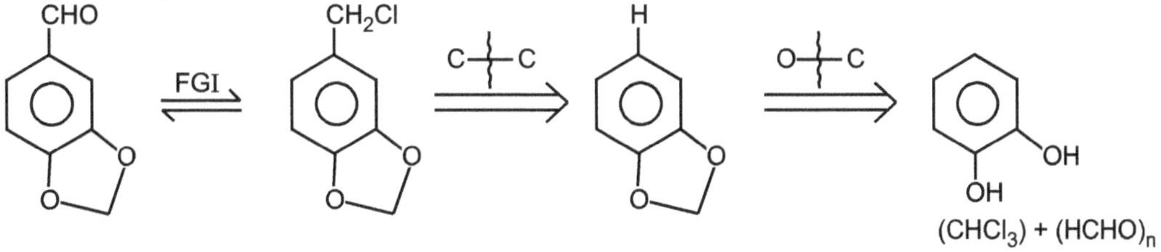

Synthesis:

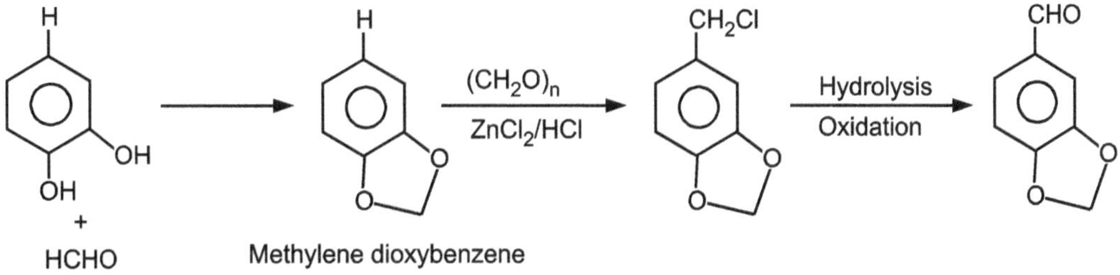

e.g. **Benzocaine:**

Analysis:

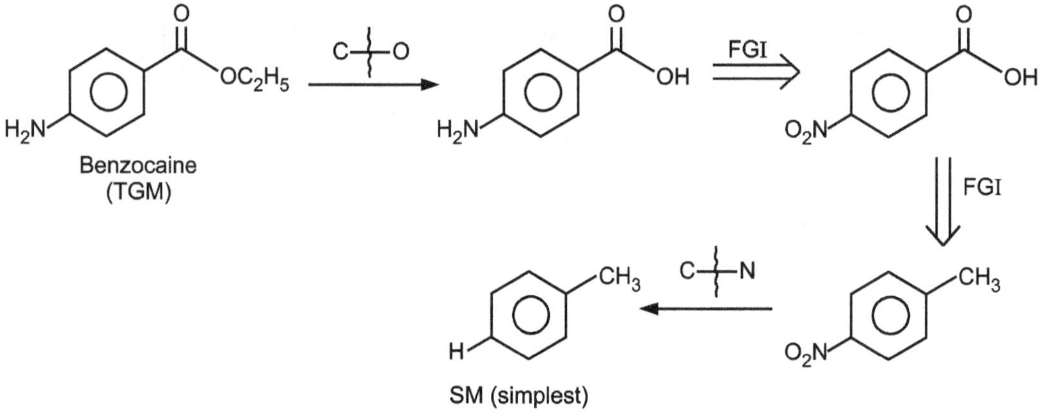

Benzocaine
(TGM)

SM (simplest)

Synthesis:

(Benzocaine)

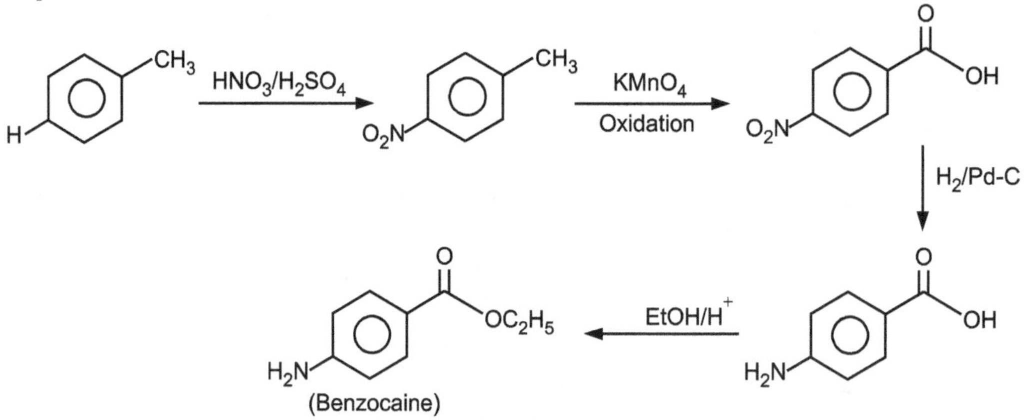

3.7 HETEROCYCLIC RING SYSTEMS

Heterocyclic ring systems are part of many drug molecules as basic skeleton.

∴ It is imperative, we should deal with a few.

Generally one performs retrosynthesis of heterocycles using the criteria of "Readily recognizable fragments".

e.g. NH_3, NH_2NH_2, NH_2OH, guanidine, urea, thiourea, $H_2N - CH_2 - CH_2 - NH_2$, $H-OC_2H_4-NH_2$ are such readily recognizable fragments.

Selected Examples:

2 – NH$_2$ Pyrimidine:

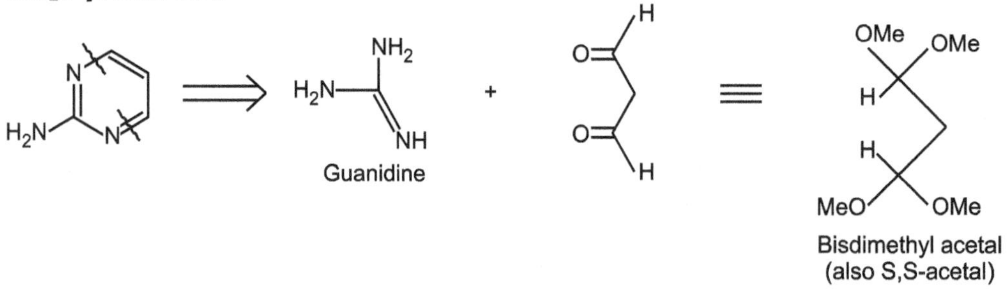

Guanidine

Bisdimethyl acetal
(also S,S-acetal)

2-NH$_2$ – 4, 6-Dimethyl pyrimidine:

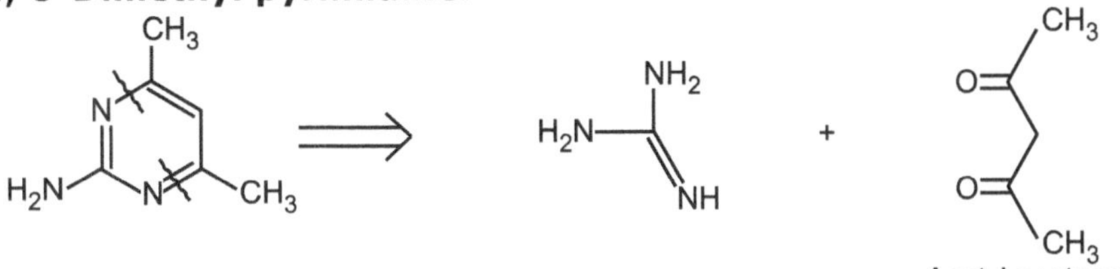

Acetyl acetone

3, 6-Dichloropyridazine:

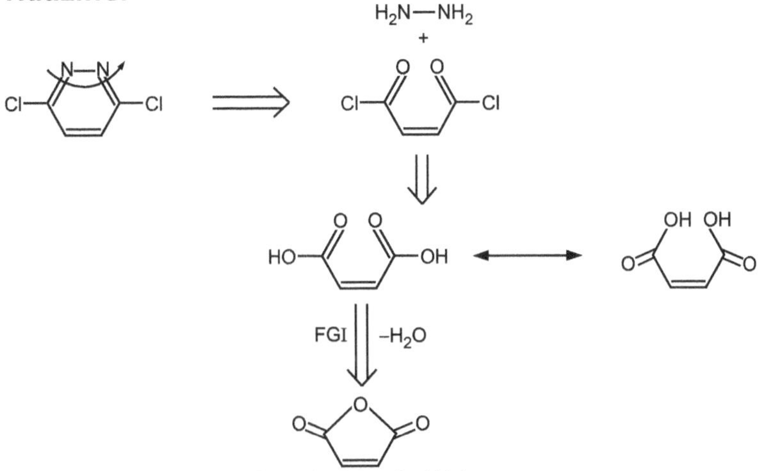

Pyran (maleic anhydride)

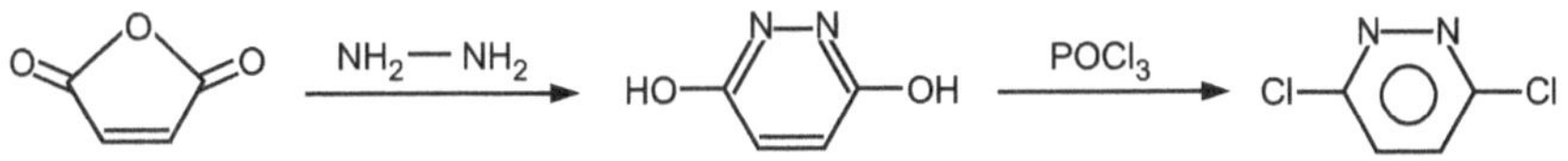

3, 4-Dimethyl-5-amino Isoxazole:

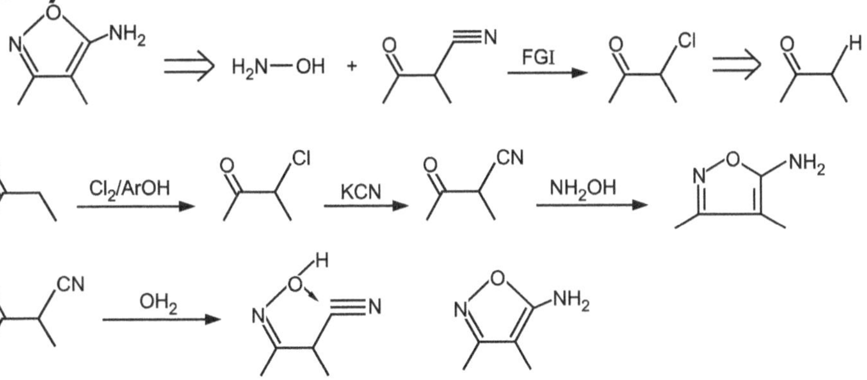

3.8 RETROSYNTHESIS OF SELECTED DRUGS

3.8.1 Retro-syntheis of Ibuprofen

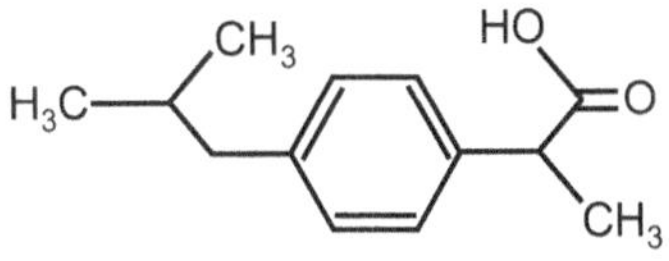

Ibuprofen

Analysis:

$$\xrightarrow{FGI} \qquad \xrightarrow{FGI}$$

$$\xrightarrow{FGI} \qquad \xrightarrow{C \nmid C}$$

$$\rangle\!=\!CH_2 \quad \text{or} \quad \text{X} \quad + \quad \text{(benzene)} \qquad a=b=S.M.$$

Synthesis:

Isobutyl benzene $\xrightarrow{Ac_2O/Acetylation}$ p-isobutyl acetophenone $\xrightarrow{HCN}$

p-isobutyl acetophenone cyanohydrin $\xrightarrow[\text{(ii) Hydrolysis}]{\text{(i) HI/P}}$ Ibuprofen

3.8.2 Retrosynthesis of Propranolol

Propranolol

Analysis:

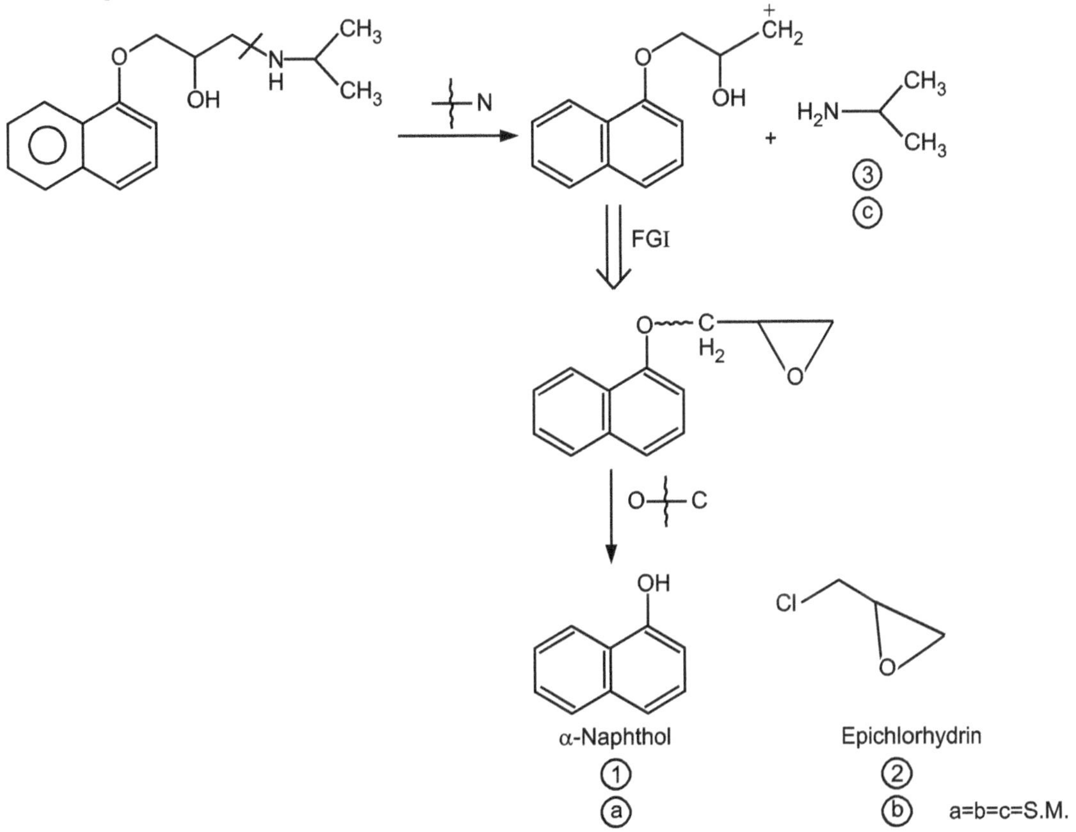

α-Naphthol   Epichlorhydrin

①   ②

ⓐ   ⓑ   a=b=c=S.M.

Synthesis of Propranolol:

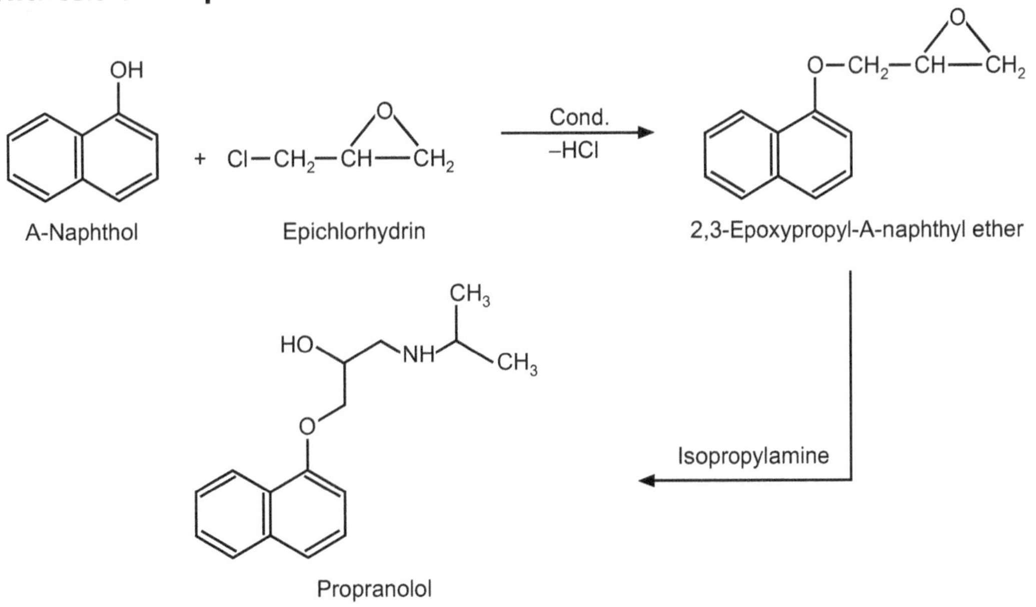

A-Naphthol   Epichlorhydrin   2,3-Epoxypropyl-A-naphthyl ether

Isopropylamine

Propranolol

3.8.3 Retro-synthesis of Ciprofloxacin

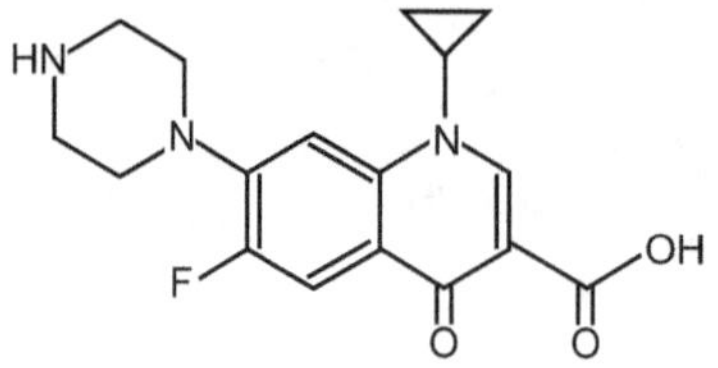
HN
N
N
F
OH
O
O

Ciprofloxacin

Analysis:

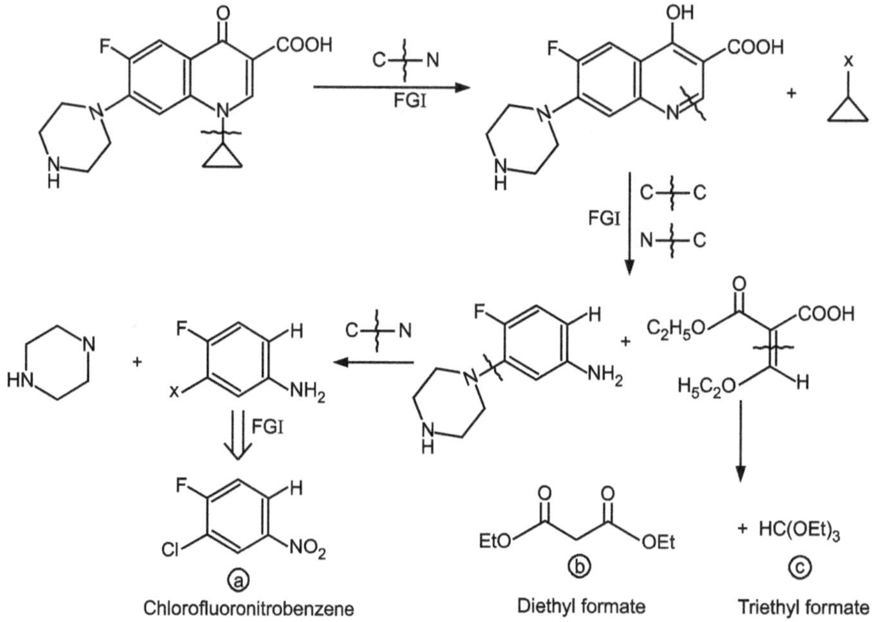
COOH
C—N
FGI
OH
x
C—C
N—C
C_2H_5O
H_5C_2O
NH_2
X
NO_2
Cl
EtO
OEt
+ $HC(OEt)_3$
ⓐ
Chlorofluoronitrobenzene
ⓑ
Diethyl formate
ⓒ
Triethyl formate

a=b=c=d=S.M.

Synthesis:

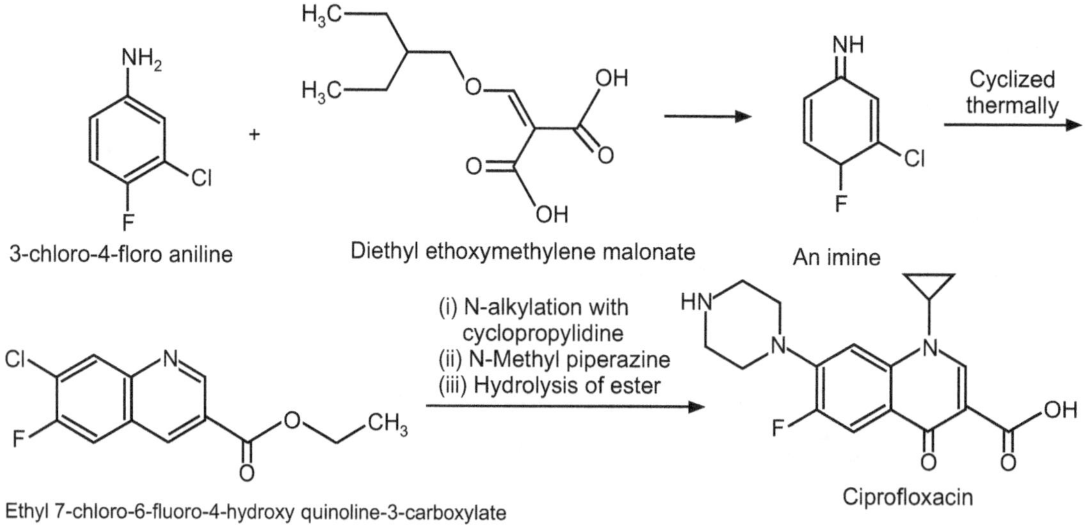
NH_2
Cl
F
H_3C
H_3C
O
OH
NH
Cyclized thermally
3-chloro-4-floro aniline
Diethyl ethoxymethylene malonate
An imine
(i) N-alkylation with cyclopropylidine
(ii) N-Methyl piperazine
(iii) Hydrolysis of ester
CH_3
HN
Ethyl 7-chloro-6-fluoro-4-hydroxy quinoline-3-carboxylate
Ciprofloxacin

3.8.4 Retro-synthesis of Sulphamethoxazole

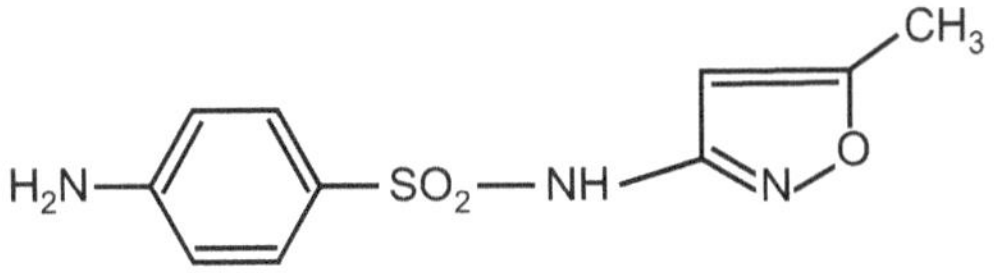

H_2N-⬡$-SO_2-NH-$[isoxazole ring with CH_3]

Sulphamethoxazole

Analysis:

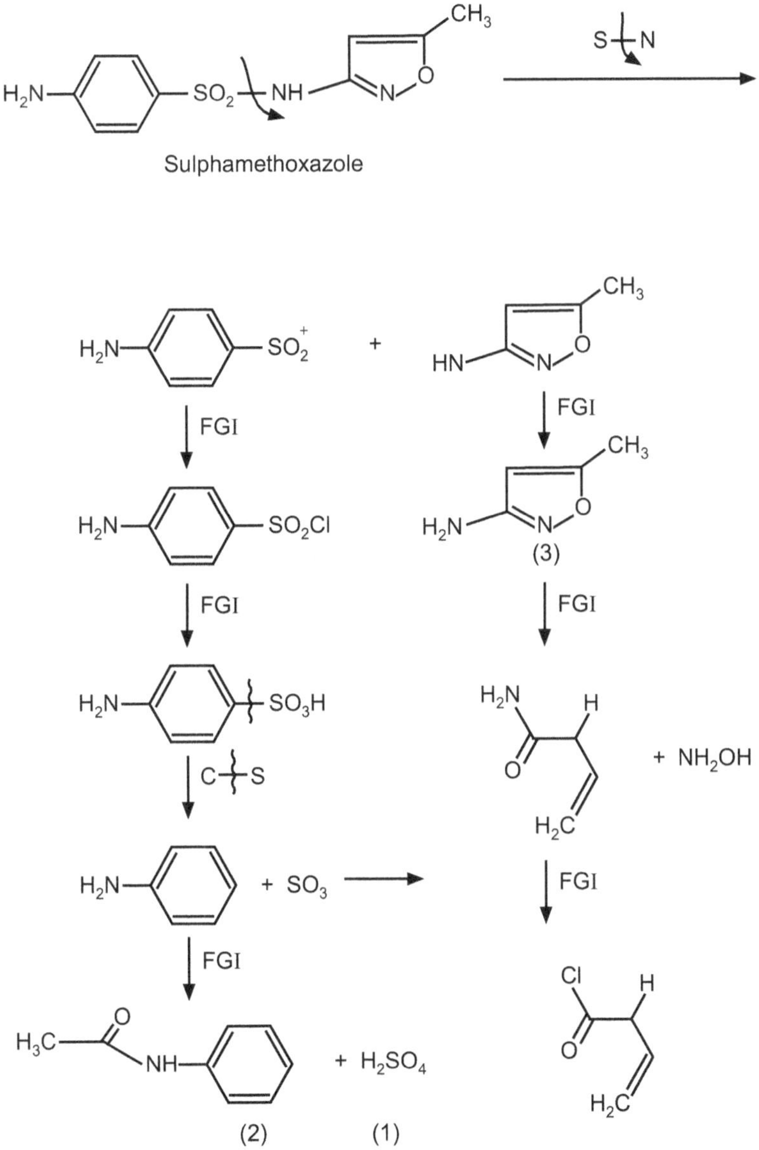

H_2N-⬡$-SO_2 \not| NH-$[isoxazole ring with CH_3] $S \not| N$ ⟶

Sulphamethoxazole

H_2N-⬡$-SO_2^+$ + $HN-$[isoxazole ring with CH_3]

↓ FGI   ↓ FGI

H_2N-⬡$-SO_2Cl$ H_2N-[isoxazole ring with CH_3]
                                          (3)

↓ FGI   ↓ FGI

H_2N-⬡$\not| SO_3H$ H_2N-[amide with H_2C] $+ NH_2OH$

↓ $C \not| S$ ↓ FGI

H_2N-⬡ $+ SO_3$ ⟶

↓ FGI   ↓ FGI

H_3C-[acetanilide structure]$-NH-$⬡ $+ H_2SO_4$ [acid chloride with Cl, H, H_2C]

       (2)   (1)

Synthesis:

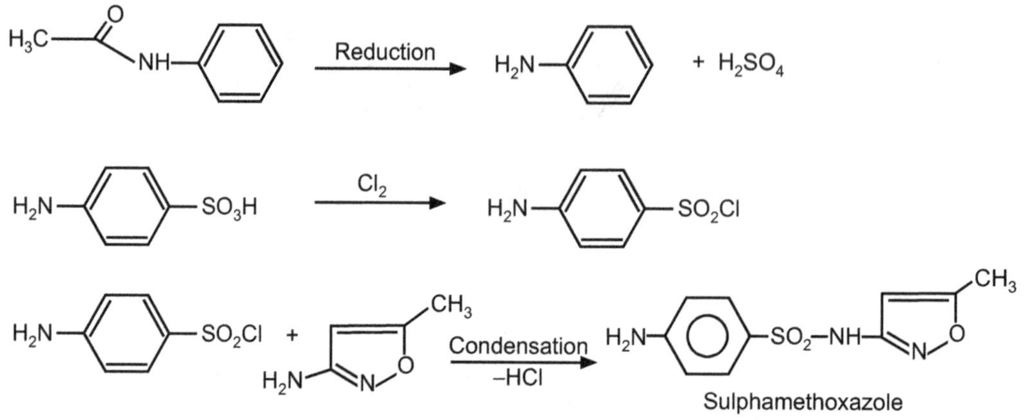

Sulphamethoxazole

QUESTIONS

1. Define the term Retro-synthesis.
2. Explain the following terms used in retro-synthesis:
   (a) Disconnection
   (b) Synthon
   (c) Reagent
   (d) Functional group equivalents
3. Explain with suitable example the basic rules applied for retro-synthesis.
4. Write a note on strategies and order of events in retro-synthesis.
5. Explain with suitable example, the heterocyclic ring system retro-synthesis.
6. Give the retro-synthesis of:
   (a) Ibuprofen
   (b) Propranolol
   (c) Sulphamethoxazole
   (d) Ciprofloxacin

■■■

Chapter 4

CHEMISTRY OF CARBOHYDRATES

Syllabus ......

Introduction, Significance and medicinal importance of carbohydrates. Classification, Method of synthesis(Killiani fischer and ruff degradation) and reactions of C5 (Arabinose) and C6 (Glucose and fructose) sugars., Mutarotation., Establishment of structures of Glucose and Fructose.

4.1 INTRODUCTION

Carbohydrates constitute one of the most important groups of natural products. Earlier carbohydrates were defined as compounds containing C, H and [O], the latter two elements being present in the same ratio as in water i.e. they were regarded as the 'hydrates of carbon' and thus correspond to the formula, $C_x(H_2O)_y$. e.g. glucose $C_6H_{12}O_6$ {$C_6(H_2O)_6$}, cane sugar $C_{12}H_{22}O_{11}$ {$C_{12}(H_2O)_{11}$}.

But later on it was found that certain carbohydrates do not correspond to this formula.

For example, Rhamnose – $C_6H_{12}O_5$; Rhamnohexose – $C_7H_{14}O_6$; Digitoxose – $C_6H_{12}O_4$. While several compounds although not carbohydrates correspond to this formula. e.g. H-CHO, CH_3COOH, lactic acid ($C_3H_6O_3$) etc.

4.2 DEFINITION

Hence, the modern definition of carbohydrate is as follows **"Carbohydrates are optically active polyhydroxy aldehydes or ketones or substances which yield such products on hydrolysis".**

Carbohydrates are widely distributed in plants and animals, the ultimate source of all carbohydrates is plants which build up them from CO_2 and H_2O by the process of photosynthesis.

$$xCO_2 + xH_2O \xrightarrow[\text{Chlorophyll}]{\text{Light (solar energy)}} (CH_2O)_x + xO_2 \uparrow$$

The chief function of carbohydrates in animals and organisms is as a source and store of energy. Certain products of carbohydrate metabolism act as catalysts or promoters in oxidation of many foods stuffs. Carbohydrates can also be used as starting material for the biological synthesis of other types of compounds in the body such as fatty acids and certain amino acids. Carbohydrates are also found in the structure of certain biologically important compounds such as glycolipids, glycoprotein, heparin, nucleic acids and other substances.

4.3 SIGNIFICANCE AND MEDICINAL IMPORTANCE OF CARBOHYDRATES

The Importance of Carbohydrates: Functions and Impact of Deficiency

The main function of carbohydrates is to provide the body and brain with energy. An adequate intake of carbohydrates also spares proteins and helps with fat metabolism.

Just like a car needs fuel to make it run, our body needs fuel to make it go. Of course, our body doesn't run on gasoline - it runs on carbohydrates. Carbohydrates, found in foods like grains, fruits, beans, milk products and vegetables, are by far your body's favorite source of energy, yet providing your body with pep is not the only role carbohydrates play. We will take a look at the functions of carbohydrates as well as what happens when you do not get enough carbohydrates in our diet.

4.3.1 Functions of Carbohydrates

After we enjoy a meal, the carbohydrates from the foods you consumed are broken down into smaller units of sugar. These small units get absorbed out of our digestive tract and into our blood stream. This blood sugar, or blood glucose, is transported through your blood stream to supply energy to our muscles and other tissues. This is an important process; in fact, we could say that of the different functions of carbohydrates, supplying energy to the body is the main role.

Most of our body cells use the simple carbohydrate glucose for energy, but our brain is particularly in need of glucose as an energy source. So, we can add that an important function of carbohydrates is supplying energy to the brain. If you have ever gone on a low- carbohydrates diet and felt like your brain was foggy for a few days, then you experienced just how important carbohydrates are to proper brain function.

Another function of carbohydrates is to prevent the breakdown of proteins for energy. By consuming sufficient amounts of carbohydrates in our diet, we ensure that our body can meet its energy needs, but if our intake of carbohydrates is too low, or we are using them up too quickly, such as during intense exercise, then our body is forced to break down proteins for energy. Protein is kind of like the backup generator when the primary energy source goes out. It is great that the body has this backup system in place, yet when proteins are used up for energy, they are no longer available to do their life-sustaining jobs, like helping with muscle contractions and maintaining muscle and other body tissues.

Carbohydrates also help with fat metabolism. If the body has enough energy for its immediate needs, it stores extra energy as fat. To access this stored energy, your body needs the working energy of carbohydrates. If your diet is deficient in carbohydrates, like if you are trying a crash diet or a strict low-carbohydrates diet, then fat metabolism cannot proceed normally, and the result is the formation of ketones. Ketones are acidic molecules formed by partially broken-down fats. Ketones can be used by your body for energy, and they can even spare some protein from being broken down, but if too many ketones are present in the blood they lead to a condition called ketosis. This makes the blood acidic, which can hinder normal body processes; a person in ketosis will also have some noticeable symptoms, including headaches, a dry mouth and an odd, fruity smell to their breath.

4.3.2 Deficiency or Medicinal Importance of Carbohydrates

So we see that a deficiency of carbohydrates can lead to ketosis. We also see that a deficiency could lead to excessive breakdown of protein. And, because a deficiency of carbohydrates means that you are not giving your body the fuel it prefers, it is easy to see that fatigue and a decreased energy level could result.

In addition, you will miss out on many important nutrients that are found in carbohydrate foods. For example, eating a diet deficient in carbohydrates would lead to a reduced fiber intake.

Fiber is a component of plant foods that cannot be digested but helps foods pass through the digestive tract. Because fiber is not digested, it travels through your system intact, acting like a scrub brush that moves food along and aids in the elimination of wastes and toxins from the body.

Our body looks at carbohydrates as fuel, so one of the main functions of carbohydrates is supplying energy to the body. Our brain is particularly in need of the simple carbohydrate glucose as an energy source. So supplying energy to the brain is another important function. We also see that having enough carbohydrates for energy can prevent the breakdown of proteins for energy. While it is great that proteins can be used as a backup energy source, if you burn them for energy, they are no longer available to carry out their usual life-sustaining jobs.

Carbohydrates also help with fat metabolism. If our diet is deficient in carbo-hydrates, then fat metabolism cannot proceed normally, and the result is the formation of ketones, which are acidic molecules formed by partially broken-down fats. If too many ketones are present in the blood, the result is ketosis, which makes the blood acidic. Ketosis comes with symptoms, including headaches, a dry mouth and a fruity smell to the breath.

Knowing these functions of carbohydrates shows us that a deficiency of carbohydrates can lead to ketosis, excessive breakdown of protein, fatigue and a decreased energy level as well as reduced fiber intake.

4.4 CLASSIFICATION OF CARBOHYDRATES

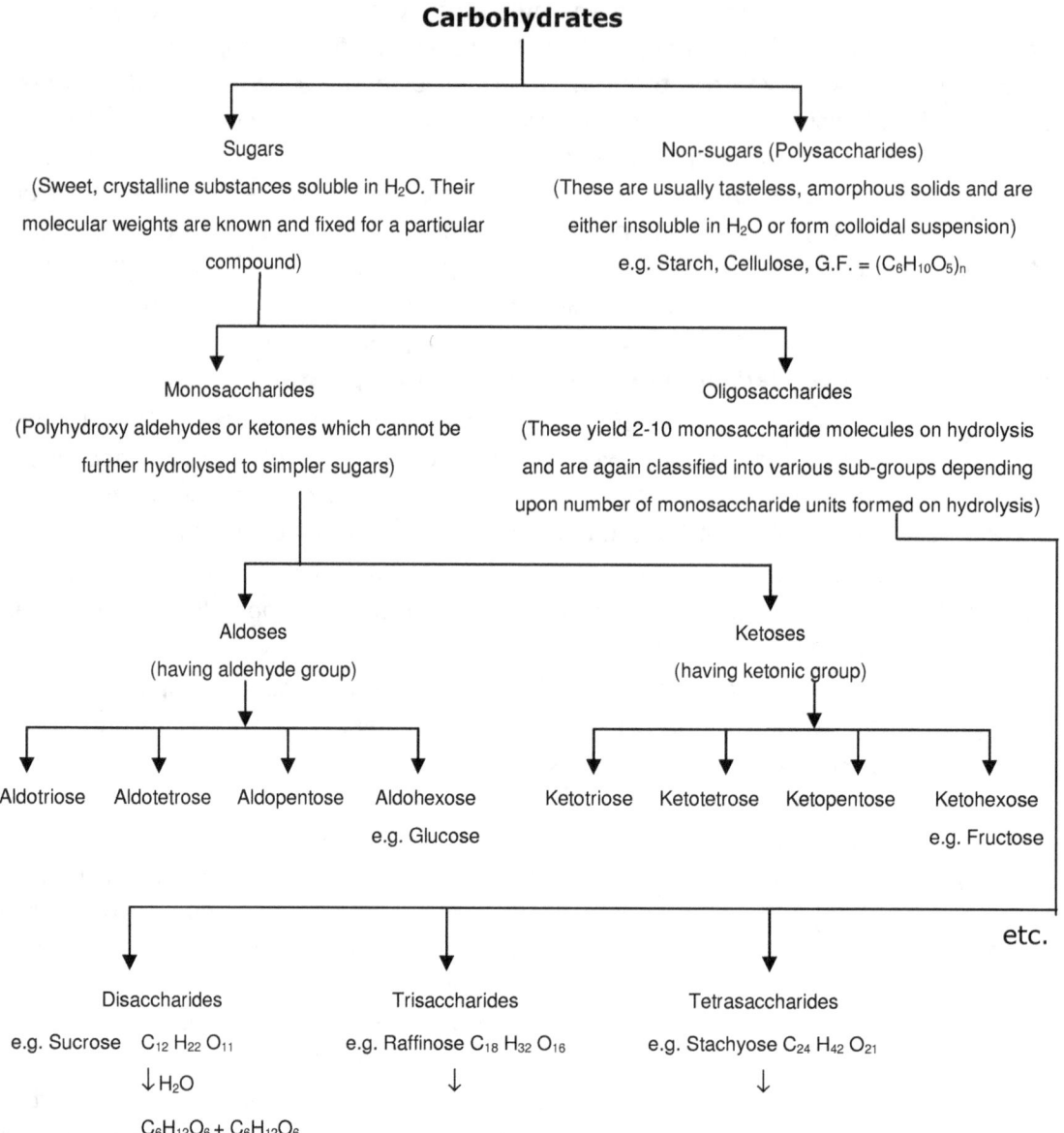

Monosaccharides	Disaccharides	Polysaccharides	Mucopoly/Hetero saccharides
1. Glucose	1. Maltose	1. Starch	1. Hyaluronic acid
2. Fructose	2. Lactose	2. Glycogen	2. Heparin
3. Galactose	3. Sucrose	3. Cellulose	

4.5 METHODS OF SYNTHESIS (KILLIANI FISCHER AND RUFF DEGRADATION)

4.5.1 Kiliani-Fischer Synthesis

This reaction is carbon chain lengthening of carbohydrates. In this method an aldose is treated with hydrogen cyanide and potassium cyanide to form corresponding cyanohydrins which on reduction with hydrogen and palladium poisoned barium sulphate to form corresponding chain lengthened imine which undergoes further hydrolysis with dilute mineral acid to give chain lengthened aldose. e.g. aldopentose is converted to aldohexose in Kiliani-Fischer synthesis.

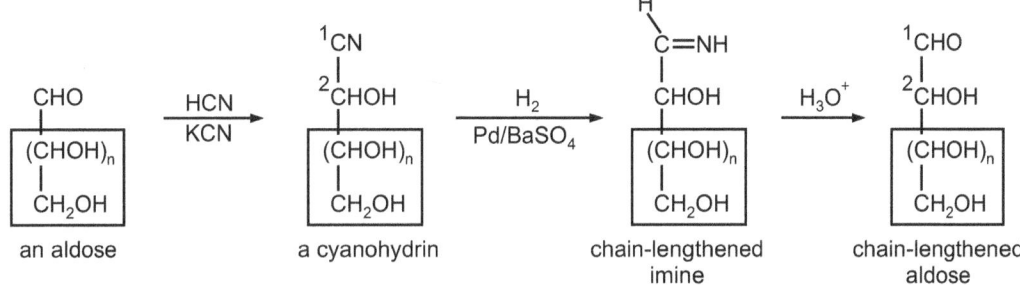

an aldose   a cyanohydrin   chain-lengthened imine   chain-lengthened aldose

4.5.2 Ruff Degradation

This is chain shortening of carbohydrate (aldoses). In this method the aldose is oxidized by bromine water to form corresponding carboxylic acid which is then decarboxylated by hydrogen peroxide and ferrous sulphate to form corresponding chain shortened aldose. e.g. D-glucose is converted to D-arabinose.

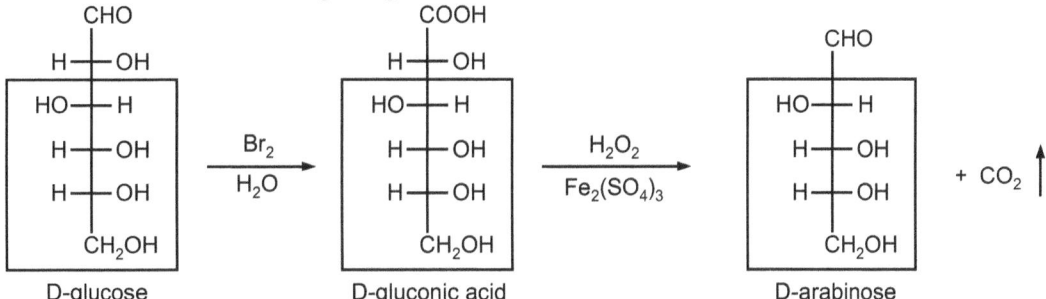

D-glucose   D-gluconic acid   D-arabinose

4.6 REACTIONS OF C_5 (ARABINOSE) AND
C_6 (GLUCOSE AND FRUCTOSE) SUGARS

4.6.1 Chemical Reactions (C_5 and C_6 Sugars)

1. Reaction of the hydroxyl group:

(i) **Formation of esters (Esterification):** Alcohol groups can be esterified. In biochemistry, the esters of phosphoric acid have special significance; the organism metabolizes almost exclusively phosphorylated sugars. In case of glucose-2-phosphates are commonly encountered in biochemistry viz. glucose-1-phosphate and glucose-6-phosphate.

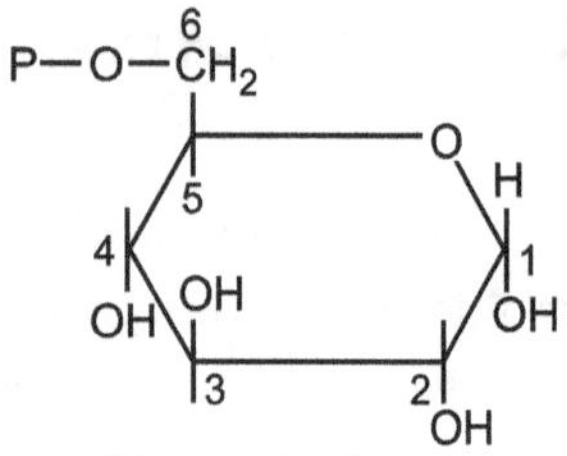

Glucose-6-phosphate 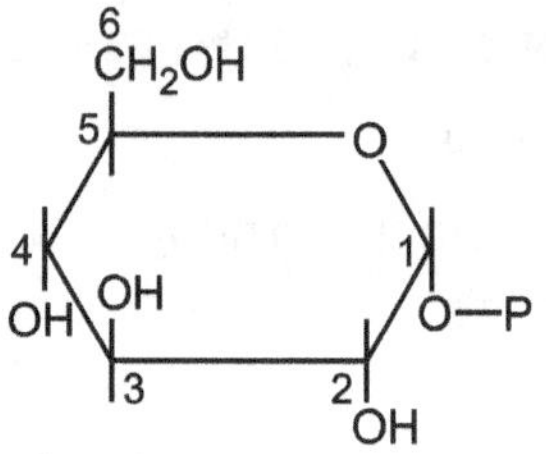   Glucose-1-phosphate   (where P=a phosphate group)

(ii) Formation of glycosides:

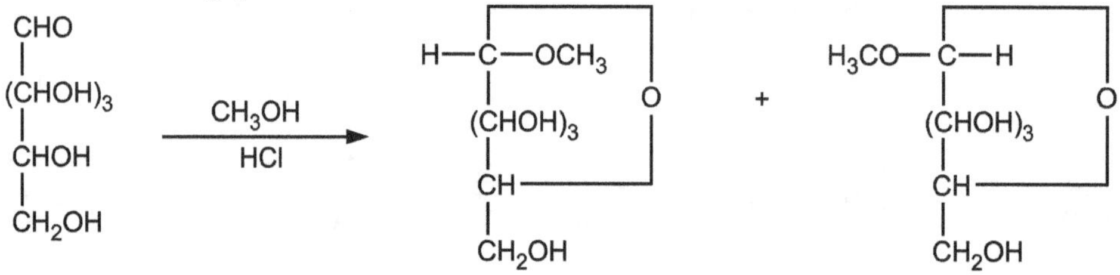

Glucose   α-methyl glucoside   β-methyl glucoside

(iii) Dehydration:

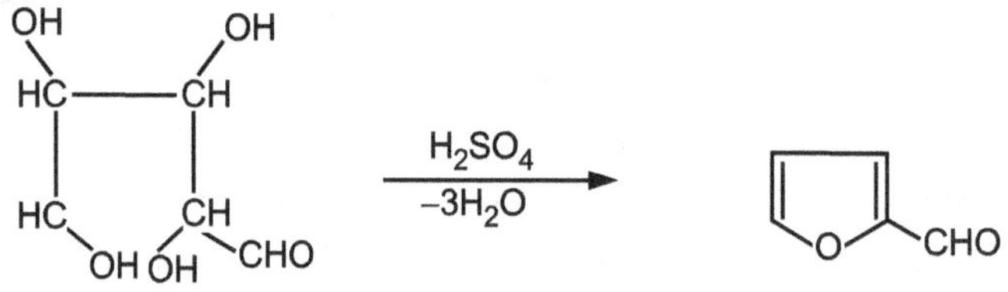

Aldopentose   Furfural

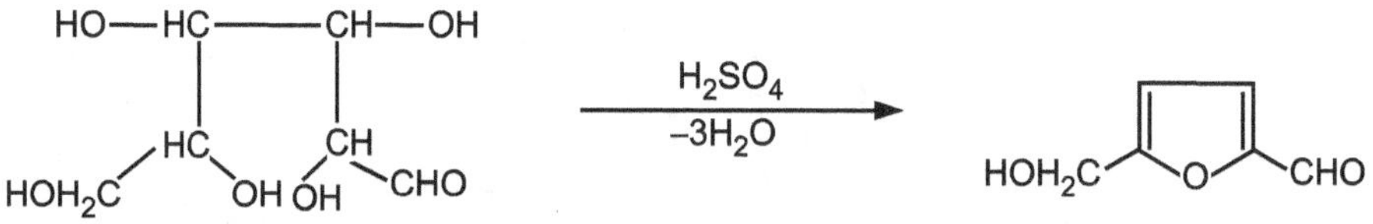

Aldohexose (glucose)   Hydroxymethyl furfural

These two compounds are very reactive and react with a number of phenolic and other compounds to form coloured products. Thus, the complete set of reaction can be used for identifying carbohydrates. Further the amount of colour can be used to determine the concentration of carbohydrates.

2. Reactions of Carbonyl Group:

(i) Reaction with HCN:

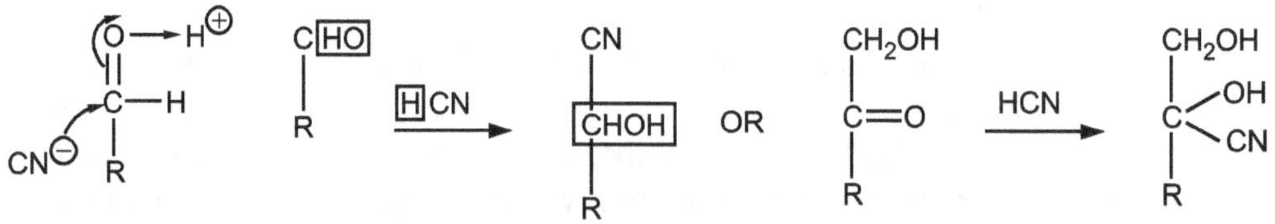

Cyanohydrin and
chain lengthened

(ii) Reaction with phenylhydrazine:

$$
\begin{array}{c}
\text{CHO} \\
| \\
\text{CHOH} \\
| \\
\text{R}
\end{array}
\quad \text{OR} \quad
\begin{array}{c}
\text{CH}_2\text{OH} \\
| \\
\text{CO} \\
| \\
\text{R}
\end{array}
\quad + 3\ \text{ph—NH.NH}_2 \longrightarrow
\begin{array}{c}
\text{CH}=\text{N.NH—ph} \\
| \\
\text{C}=\text{N.NH.ph} + \text{NH}_3 + \text{ph—NH}_2 \\
| \\
\text{R} \\
\text{Osazone}
\end{array}
$$

(iii) Alkaline interconversion:

Since glucose, fructose and mannose are identical in structure except at carbon 1 and 2, when either of these is treated with dil. alkali, mixture of all the three compounds is obtained. It is believed that in this reaction sugars first undergo tautomerism to form enol which then breaks down to yield a mixture of carbohydrates.

$$
\begin{array}{c}
\text{CHO} \\
| \\
\text{H—C—OH} \\
| \\
\text{HO—C—H} \\
| \\
\text{H—C—OH} \\
| \\
\text{H—C—OH} \\
| \\
\text{CH}_2\text{OH} \\
\text{Glucose}
\end{array}
\rightleftharpoons
\begin{array}{c}
\text{CHOH} \\
\| \\
\text{C—OH} \\
| \\
\text{HO—C—H} \\
| \\
\text{H—C—OH} \\
| \\
\text{H—C—OH} \\
| \\
\text{CH}_2\text{OH} \\
\text{Enolic form}
\end{array}
\rightleftharpoons
\begin{array}{c}
\text{CHO} \\
| \\
\text{HO—C—H} \\
| \\
\text{HO—C—H} \\
| \\
\text{H—C—OH} \\
| \\
\text{H—C—OH} \\
| \\
\text{CH}_2\text{OH} \\
\text{Mannose}
\end{array}
\rightleftharpoons
\begin{array}{c}
\text{CH}_2\text{OH} \\
| \\
\text{C}=\text{O} \\
| \\
\text{HO—C—H} \\
| \\
\text{H—C—OH} \\
| \\
\text{H—C—OH} \\
| \\
\text{CH}_2\text{OH} \\
\text{Fructose} \\
\text{(Ketonic form)}
\end{array}
$$

(iv) Reduction:

$$
\begin{array}{c}
\text{CHO} \\
| \\
(\text{CHOH})_4 \\
| \\
\text{CH}_2\text{OH} \\
\text{Glucose}
\end{array}
\xrightarrow{\text{H}_2\text{ - Pt}}
\begin{array}{c}
\text{CH}_2\text{OH} \\
| \\
(\text{CHOH})_4 \\
| \\
\text{CH}_2\text{OH} \\
\text{Sorbitol}
\end{array}
$$

(v) Oxidation:

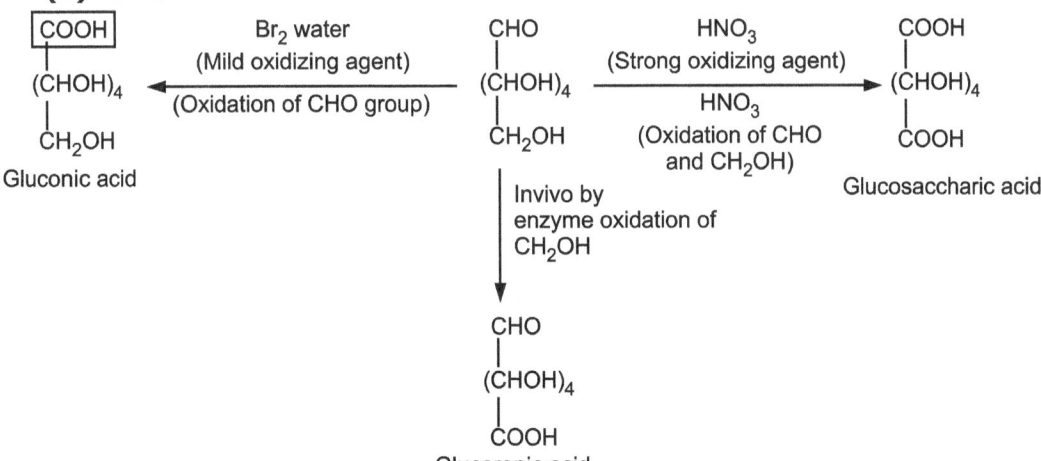

$$
\boxed{\text{COOH}}
$$
$$
\begin{array}{c}
| \\
(\text{CHOH})_4 \\
| \\
\text{CH}_2\text{OH} \\
\text{Gluconic acid}
\end{array}
$$

Br₂ water (Mild oxidizing agent) (Oxidation of CHO group)

$$
\begin{array}{c}
\text{CHO} \\
| \\
(\text{CHOH})_4 \\
| \\
\text{CH}_2\text{OH}
\end{array}
$$

HNO₃ (Strong oxidizing agent) HNO₃ (Oxidation of CHO and CH₂OH)

$$
\begin{array}{c}
\text{COOH} \\
| \\
(\text{CHOH})_4 \\
| \\
\text{COOH} \\
\text{Glucosaccharic acid}
\end{array}
$$

Invivo by enzyme oxidation of CH₂OH

$$
\begin{array}{c}
\text{CHO} \\
| \\
(\text{CHOH})_4 \\
| \\
\text{COOH} \\
\text{Glucoronic acid}
\end{array}
$$

4.7 MUTAROTATION

When ordinary glucose is crystallized from cold water or ethanol below 50°C its aqueous solution has specific rotation of + 111°. When this solution is allowed to stand the rotation comes down to a constant value of 52.5°.

On the other hand, if crystals of glucose are obtained from hot pyridine or hot water above 98°C, the specific rotation of the aqueous solution of these crystals has a specific rotation of +19°.2' but on standing this value becomes 52.5° and remain constant at this value.

This change of specific rotation in aqueous solution of each of these to the equilibrium value is known as "Mutarotation'.

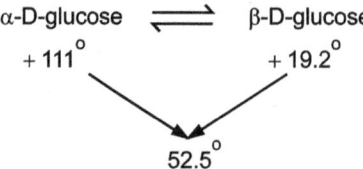

The existence of the two isomeric forms of glucose and change of specific rotation i.e. mutarotation cannot be explained by an open-chain formula.

4.8 ESTABLISHMENT OF STRUCTURES OF GLUCOSE

1. **Molecular Formula:** From elemental analysis and molecular weight determination, the molecular formula for glucose has been found to be $C_6H_{12}O_6$.

2. **Open chain structure for glucose:** Baeyer given the open chain structure for glucose and according to this glucose is pentahydroxy hexanol with four asymmetric carbon atoms but it does not give the configuration of these asymmetric carbons.

    Baeyer's open chain structure for glucose:

    H
    1C=O
    |
    2* CHOH
    |
    3* CHOH
    |
    4* CHOH ⟶ Pentahydroxy hexanol
    | where *C = asymmetric carbon atom
    5* CHOH
    |
    6 CH₂OH

3. **Configuration of glucose:** Configuration of glucose is given by Emil Fischer (1891) and was awarded Nobel Prize (1902) for this work.

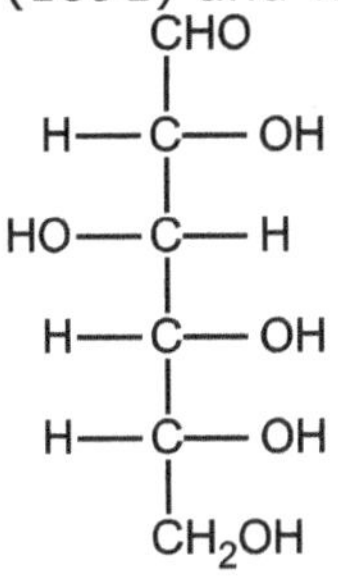

```
        CHO
         |
  H——C——OH
         |
 HO——C——H
         |
  H——C——OH
         |
  H——C——OH
         |
       CH₂OH
```

(+) –Glucose

4. Evidences for the ring structure of sugar OR Objections to the open chain structure of Glucose

1. We know that all normal aldehydes restore the pink colour of Schiff's reagent but glucose does not restore Schiff's reagent.
   ⇒ Glucose does not contain a true – CHO group.
2. Glucose does not react with $NaHSO_3$ and NH_3.
   ⇒ Glucose does not contain a true aldehydic group.
3. X-ray analysis definitely proves the existence of the ring structure and at the same time indicates the size of ring.
   ⇒ Glucose exists in furanose {1: 4 oxide} and pyranose {1: 5 oxide} form.

From the above evidences it has been found that glucose exist in alpha and beta Furanose and Pyranose ring structures as below.

5. **Cyclic Structure of Glucose:**

(i) Furanose ring structure (1 : 4 oxide) for glucose

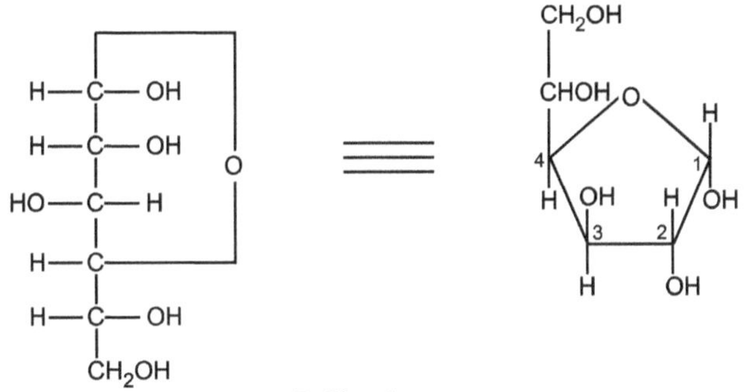

α-D-Glucofuranose

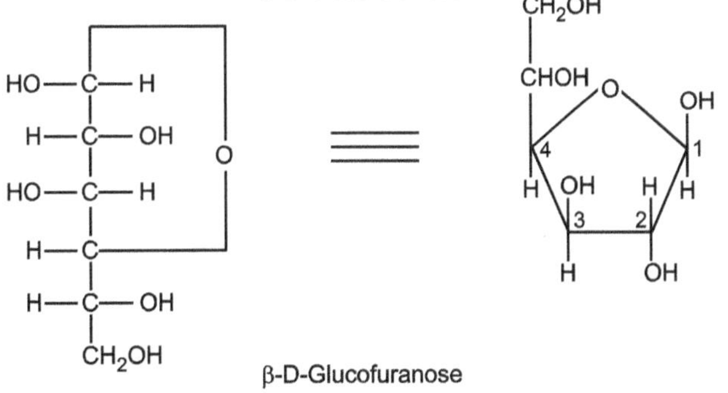

β-D-Glucofuranose

(ii) Pyranose ring structure (1 : 5 oxide) for Glucose

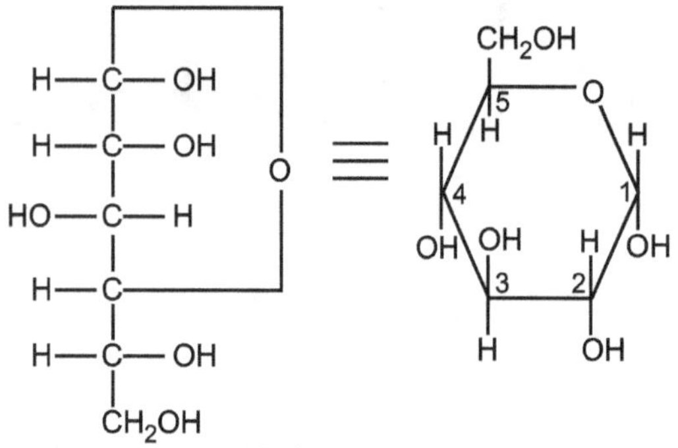

α-D-Glucopyranose

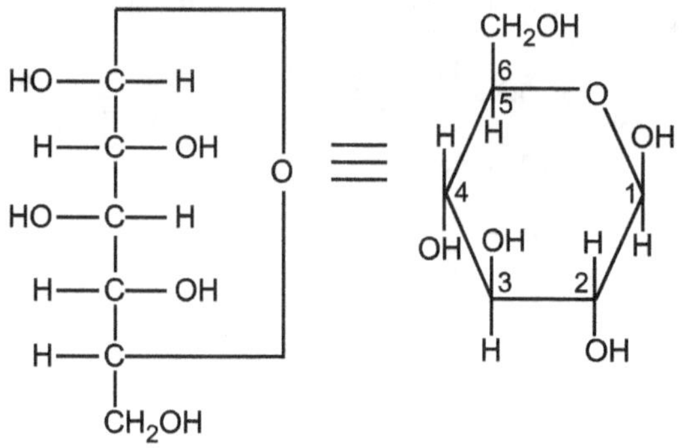

β-D-Glucopyranose

4.9 ESTABLISHMENT OF STRUCTURES OF FRUCTOSE

1. **Molecular Formula:** From elemental analysis and molecular weight determination, the molecular formula for fructose has been found to be $C_6H_{12}O_6$.

2. **Open chain structure for fructose:** Baeyer given the open chain structure for glucose and according to this fructose is pentahydroxy hexanone with four asymmetric carbon atoms but it does not give the configuration of these asymmetric carbons.

Baeyer's open chain structure for fructose:

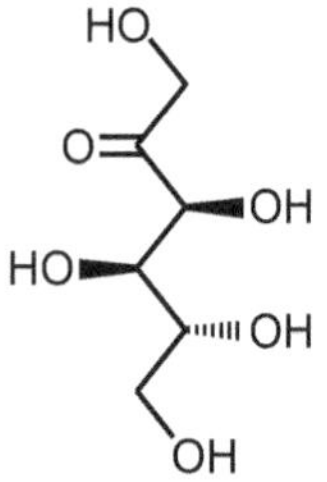

3. **Configuration of fructose:** Configuration of fructose is as given below:

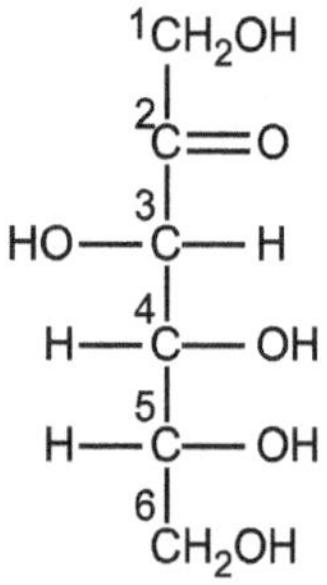

4. Evidences for the ring structure of sugar OR

Objections to the open chain structure of Fructose

1. We know that all normal ketone restore the pink colour of Schiff's reagent but fructose does not restore Schiff's reagent.

   $\Rightarrow$ fructose does not contain a true $-$ C=O group.

2. Fructose does not react with $NaHSO_3$ and NH_3.

   $\Rightarrow$ fructose does not contain a true ketonic group.

3. X-ray analysis definitely proves the existence of the ring structure and at the same time indicates the size of ring.

   $\Rightarrow$ Fructose exists in furanose {1: 4 oxide} and pyranose {1: 5 oxide} form.

From the above evidences it has been found that fructose exists in alpha and beta Furanose and Pyranose ring structures as below.

5. Cyclic Structure for Fructose

(i) Furanose ring structure (1 : 4 oxide)

(ii) Pyranose ring structure (1 : 5 oxide)

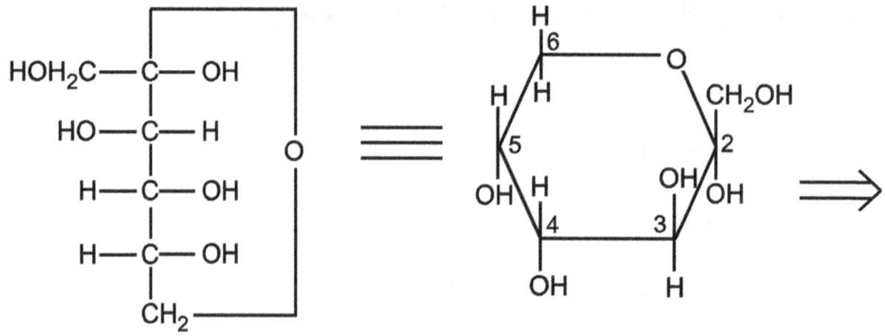

α-D-Fructopyranose

⟹ α-D-Fructopyranose

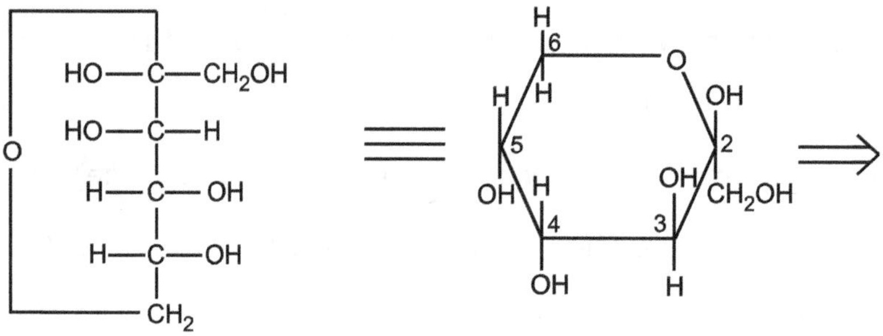

⟹ β-D-Fructopyranose

QUESTIONS

1. Provide the IUPAC names, with (R) and (S) configurational designations for D-glucose and L-glucose.

2. Show why the aldaric acids derived from ribose and xylose would not be optically active.

3. Give the modern definition of carbohydrates.

4. Give the classification of carbohydrates with suitable examples.

5. Give the various reactions of glucose.

6. Write the Emil Fischer configuration of glucose.

7. Give the evidences for the ring structure of glucose.

8. Write a short note on mutarotation.

9. Draw the furanose and pyranose ring structure of glucose.

10. Draw the furanose and pyranose ring structure of fructose.

11. Draw the furanose and pyranose ring structure of galactose.

12. Give the significance and medical importance of carbohydrates.

13. What is inversion of sugar and draw they structure of sucrose?

14. Establish the structure of glucose

15. Establish the structure of fructose.

16. A monosaccharide is treated with HCN, the product hydrolysed and reduced to carboxylic acid by heating with HI and P. What carboxylic acid is formed if the monosaccharide is:

    (a) D-glucose

    (b) D-mannose

    (c) D-fructose

    (d) D-erythrose

17. What is the enantiomer of α-D-(+)-glucose?

18. What sugars are obtained by epimerizing respectively C-2, C-3, C-4 of D-glucose?

19. Explain which of the following compounds are not carbohydrates and why:

    (a) Erythrose, $C_4H_6O_4$

    (b) 2-Hydroxy ethanal, $C_2H_4O_2$

    (c) Cyclohexanehexol (inositol, $C_6H_{12}O_6$)

    (d) Ethanoic acid, $C_2H_4O_2$

20. Distinguish between racemisation and mutarotation.

21. What were the objections raised against open chain formula of glucose?

22. What happens when D-glucose react with:

    (a) Reducing agent

    (b) Bromine water

    (c) Dil. HNO_3

    (d) Phenyl hydrazine

    (e) Hydrocyanic acid

    (f) CH_3OH in the presence of HCl

23. What is the significance of the letters 'D' and 'd' in the name of D(d)-glucose?

24. Give experimental evidences of ring structure of glucose.

25. Explain why sucrose is not a reducing sugar.

26. Mention various enzymes used in carbohydrate chemistry.

Fill in the blanks:

1. The general formula for carbohydrates is _____.

2. Carbohydrates are optically active _____ or _____.

3. Sucrose is a _____ sugar.

4. Sucrose is a _____.

5. Raffinose is _____.

6. The change of specific rotation in aqueous solution of each in equilibrium value is known as _____.

7. Milk sugar is called _____.

8. Lactose consists of the monosaccharide _____ and _____.

9. Amylose is _____ soluble.

10. Polysaccharides are also called as _____.

(Answers: (1) $C_x(H_2O)_y$, (2) Polyhydroxy aldehydes, ketones, (3) Non-reducing, (4) Disaccharide, (5) Trisaccharide, (6) Mutarotation, (7) Lactose, (8) Galactose, Glucose (9) Water, (10) Glycans**)**.

■■■

Chapter 5...

NANOCHEMISTRY AND MICROWAVE ASSISTED SYNTHESIS

Syllabus ......

Basics and Application of Nanochemistry and Microwave Assisted Synthesis in Pharmaceutical Organic Chemistry.

5.1 INTRODUCTION

Nanochemistry is concerned with generating and altering chemical systems, which develop special and often new effects as a result of the laws of the nanoworld. The bases for these are chemically active nanometric units such as supramolecules or nanocrystals. Nanochemistry looks set to make a great deal of progress for a large number of industry sectors.

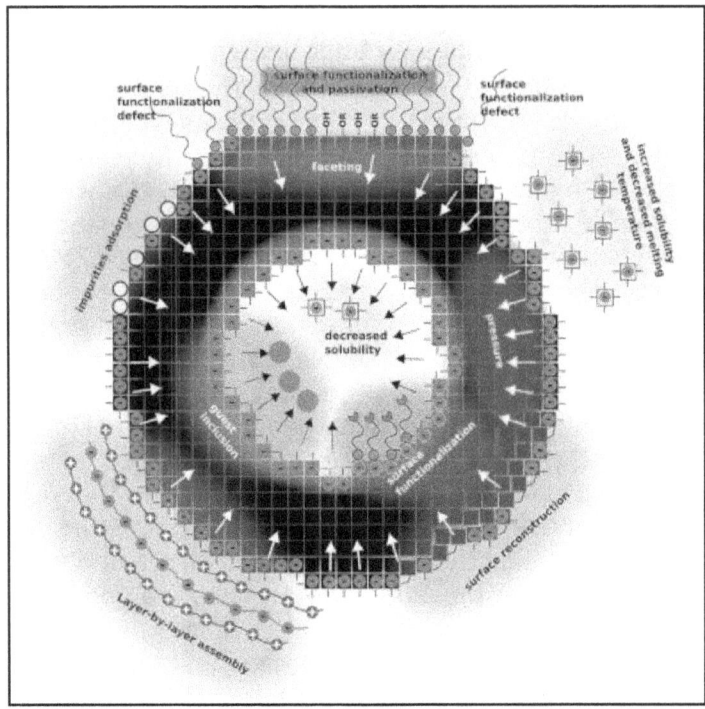

Nanochemistry focuses on the unique properties of materials in the 1–100 nm scale. The physical, chemical, electrical, optical and magnetic properties of these materials are all significantly different from both the properties of the individual building blocks (individual atoms or molecules), and also from the bulk materials. Nanochemistry is a truly multidisciplinary field, forming a bridge between nanotechnology and biotechnology, spanning the physical and life sciences.

5.2 APPLICATION OF NANOCHEMISTRY IN PHARMACEUTICAL SCIENCES

Nanochemistry applications in the materials, resources and energy sectors range from the design of crystalline catalysts and the control of crystal size, morphology, phase and purity, to the design and use of additives to control crystallization and inhibit scale formation. In the biological field, control of chemistry at the supramolecular level can lead to the development of a wide variety of new and improved biomaterials, such as artificial bones and tissues, as well as new pharmaceuticals and improved methods of drug delivery.

Nanoscale chemistry is used to synthesize a multilevel, hierarchically built nanoparticle, which we define as a nanoclinic, for targeted diagnostics and therapy. This nanoclinic, produced by multistep chemistry in a nanosize micelle, consists of a thin silica shell encapsulating magnetic (Fe_2O_3) nanoparticles and fluorescent dyes for enhanced contrast magnetic resonance and optical imaging and magnetic-induced cancer therapy.

5.3 MICROWAVE ASSISTED ORGANIC SYNTHESIS

5.3.1 Introduction

Synthesis of new chemical entities is major bottleneck in drug discovery.

Conventional methods for various chemical synthesis are very well documented and practiced. The methods of synthesis (heating process) of organic compounds has continuously modified from the decade. In 1855, Robert Bunsen invented the burner which acts as energy source for heating a reaction vessel, this was latter superseded by isomental, oil bath or hot plate, but the drawback of heating, though method remain the same. Microwave Assisted Organic Synthesis (MAOS), which has developed in recent years, has been considered superior to traditional heating. Microwave assisted organic synthesis (MAOS) has emerged as a new "lead" in organic synthesis. The technique offers simple, clean, fast, efficient, and economic for the synthesis of a large number of organic molecules. In the recent year microwave assisted organic reaction has emerged as a new tool in organic synthesis. Important advantage of this technology include highly accelerated rate of the reaction, reduction in reaction time with an improvement in the yield and quality of the product. Now-a-days technique is considered as an important approach towards green chemistry, because this technique is more environmentally friendly. This technology is still under-used in the laboratory and has the potential to have a large impact on the fields of screening, combinatorial chemistry, medicinal chemistry and drug development. Conventional method of organic synthesis usually need longer heating time, tedious apparatus setup, which result in higher cost of process and the excessive use of solvents/ reagents lead to environmental pollution. This growth of green chemistry holds significant potential for a reduction of the byproduct, a reduction in waste production and a lowering of the energy costs. Due to its ability to couple directly with the reaction molecule and by passing thermal conductivity leading to a rapid rise in the temperature, microwave irradiation has been used to improve many organic syntheses.

5.3.2 Microwave Frequency

Microwave heating refers the use of electromagnetic waves ranging from 0.01 m to 1 m wavelength of certain frequency to generate heat in the material. These microwaves lie in the region of electromagnetic spectrum between millimeter wave and radio wave i.e. between I.R. and radio wave. They are defined as those waves with wavelengths between 0.01 m to 1 m, corresponding to frequency of 30 GHz to 0.3 GHz.

5.3.3 Principle

The basic principle behind the heating in microwave oven is due to the interaction of charged particle of the reaction material with electromagnetic wavelength of particular frequency. The phenomena of producing heat by electromagnetic irradiation are either by collision or by conduction, some time by both. All the wave energy changes its polarity from positive to negative with each cycle of the wave. This causes rapid orientation and reorientation of the molecule, which cause heating by collision. If the charged particles of material are free to travel through the material (e.g. electron in a sample of carbon), a current will induce which will travel in phase with the field. If charged particles are bound within regions of the material, the electric field component will cause them to move until opposing force balancing the electric force.

5.3.4 Heating Mechanism

In microwave oven, material may be heated with the use of high frequency electromagnetic waves. The heating arises from the interaction of electric field component of the wave with charged particle in the material. Two basic principle mechanisms involve in the heating of material.

5.3.4.1 Dipolar Polarisation

Dipolar polarisation is a process by which heat is generated in polar molecules. On exposure to an oscillating electromagnetic field of appropriate frequency, polar molecules try to follow the field and align themselves in phase with the field. However, owing to intermolecular forces, polar molecules experience inertia and are unable to follow the field. This results in the random motion of particles, and this random interaction generates heat. Dipolar polarisation can generate heat by either one or both the following mechanisms:

1. Interaction between polar solvent molecules such as water, methanol and ethanol.

2. Interaction between polar solute molecules such as ammonia and formic acid. The key requirement for dipolar polarisation is that the frequency range of the oscillating field should be appropriate to enable adequate inter-particle interaction. If the frequency range is very high, intermolecular forces will stop the motion of a polar molecule before it tries to follow the field, resulting in inadequate inter-particle interaction. On the other hand, if the frequency range is low, the polar molecule gets sufficient time to align itself in phase with the field. Hence, no random interaction takes place between the adjoining particles. Microwave radiation has the appropriate frequency (0.3-30 GHz) to oscillate polar particles and enable enough inter-particle interaction. This makes it an ideal choice for heating polar solutions. In addition, the energy in a microwave photon (0.037 kcal/mol) is very low, relative to the typical energy required to break a molecular bond (80-120 kcal/mol). Therefore, microwave excitation of molecules does not affect the structure of an organic molecule, and the interaction is purely kinetic.

5.3.4.1 (a) Interfacial Polarisation

Interfacial polarisation is an effect, which is very difficult to treat in a simple manner, and easily viewed as combination of the conduction and dipolar polarisation effects. This mechanism is important for system where a dielectric material is not homogeneous, but consists of conducting inclusion of one dielectric in other.

5.3.4.2 Conduction Mechanism

The conduction mechanism generates heat through resistance to an electric current. The oscillating electromagnetic field generates an oscillation of electrons or ions in a conductor, resulting in an electric current. This current faces internal resistance, which heats the conductor. The main limitation of this method is that it is not applicable for materials that have high conductivity, since such materials reflect most of the energy that falls on them.

5.3.5 Effects of Solvents

Every solvent and reagent will absorb microwave energy differently. They each have a different degree of polarity within the molecule, and therefore, will be affected either more or less by the changing microwave field. A solvent that is more polar, for example, will have a stronger dipole to cause more rotational movement in an effort to align with the changing field. A compound that is less polar, however, will not be as disturbed by the changes of the field and, therefore, will not absorb as much microwave energy. Unfortunately, the polarity of the solvent is not the only factor in determining the true absorbance of microwave energy, but it does provide a good frame of reference. Most organic solvents can be broken into three different categories: low, medium, or high absorber. The low absorbers are generally hydro-carbons while the high absorbers are more polar compounds, such as most alcohols.

5.3.6 Conventional Versus Microwave Heating

Microwave heating is different from conventional heating in many respects. The mechanism behind microwave synthesis is quite different from conventional synthesis. Points enlisted in Table 5.1, differ the microwave heating from conventional heating.

Table 5.1

Sr. No.	Conventional	Microwave
1.	Reaction mixture heating proceeds from a surface usually inside surface of reaction vessels.	Reaction mixture heating proceeds directly inside mixture.
2.	The vessel should be in physical contact with surface source that is at a higher temperature source (e.g. mental, oil bath, steam bath etc.)	No need of physical contact of reaction with the higher tempera-ture source. While vessel is kept in microwave cavities.
3.	By thermal or electric source heating take place.	By electromagnetic wave heating take place.
4.	Heating mechanism involves conduction.	Heating mechanism involves dielectric.
5.	Transfer of energy occurs from the wall.	Surface of vessel, to the mixture.
6.	Eventually to reacting species.	The core mixture is heated directly.
7.	Heating rate is less. Heating rate is several fold high.	Heating rate is less. Heating rate is several fold high.

5.3.7 Applications of Microwave in Organic Synthesis

Following reactions have been performed through microwave heating.

1.

$$Ar-I + HS-R \xrightarrow[\substack{1.5 \text{ eq. KO}t\text{Bu, H}_2\text{O} \\ \text{MW, } 120°\text{C, } 30 \text{ min}}]{\substack{5 \text{ mol-\% CuO} \\ 5 \text{ mol-\%,1,10-phenanthroline}}} Ar^{I}R$$

1.2 eq.

R; Ar, alkyl, Bn

A combination of copper(II) oxide and 1,10-phenanthroline catalyzes a microwave-promoted C-S bond formation of thiols and aryl iodides. Various aryl iodides react smoothly with thiols to provide the corresponding aryl sulfides in very good yields in water with a short reaction time. Amino, chloro, bromo, acetyl, and nitro groups are tolerated.

2.

R—≡— + H₂O   →   (see scheme)

2 eq.

1 - 4 mol-% Au-TiO₂
(Au nanoparticles supported by TiO₂)

5 - 20 mol-% morpholine
dioxane, MW. 110 or 120°C, 1- 2 h

R: 1° alkyl,
Ar, vinyl

TiO_2-supported nanosized gold particles catalyze the hydration of alkynes using morpholine as a basic cocatalyst. As TiO_2-Au/morpholine system is weakly basic, the reaction tolerates acid-sensitive functional groups (e.g., silyl ethers, ketals) and strongly coordinating group such as pyridine. In addition, the gold catalyst can be recycled by simple filtration and works well in flow reactors.

3.

1) DCE
MW, 160°C,10 min

2) 5.2 eq. TFA
MW, 100°C,10 min

Benzimidazoles and quinoxalin-2(1*H*)-ones were synthesized by treatment of 2-(*N*-Boc-amino)phenylisocyanide with carboxylic acids and glyoxylic acids, respectively via two-component coupling, deprotection, and intermolecular cyclization.

4.

Ar—≡— + (scheme)   →

2.5 mol-% Cu-(OTf)₂

AcOH
MW (200 W, 110°C, 17 atm)
5-6.5 min

Ar: Ph, 4-Tol

An efficient hydrosulfonylation of alkynes using sodium arene sulfinates is catalyzed by Cu(OTf)₂ under microwave irradiation. Various vinyl sulfones were obtained in very good yields and with high regio- and stereoselectivity. Short reaction times, simple reaction conditions and low catalyst loading are the remarkable features of this protocol.

5.

3 eq. ClCF₂CO₂Na

THF
MW (300 W, 170°C), 5 min

R: H, alkyl, Ph,
Br, B(pin)
R: H, alkyl

A MW-based protocol enables a rapid preparation of 1,1-difluoro-cyclo-propanes, using fluorinated acetate salts. The new procedure is not only considerably faster than conventional methods, but it also employs easily removed, low boiling-point solvents and avoids the use of highly toxic or ozone-depleting substances.

6.

Microwave irradiation enables an expeditious one-pot, ligand-free, Pd(OAc)$_2$-catalyzed, three-component reaction for the synthesis of 2,3-diarylimidazo[1,2-a]pyridines. This methodology offers high availability of commercial reagents and great efficiency in expanding molecule diversity.

Use of the heterogeneous catalyst amberlist-15 A enables an efficient synthesis of N-(tert-butylsulfinyl)imines under microwave irradiation. Amberlist-15 is convenient to handle, inexpensive, safe to use and quickly separable from the reaction mixture. This method offers a number of advantages including operational simplicity, high yield of products, and broad substrate scope.

7.

Microwave-assisted conditions enabled a simple, rapid, one-pot synthesis of arylaminomethyl acetylenes in very good yields using arylboronic acids, aqueous ammonia, propargyl halides, copper(I) oxide and water as the solvent within ten minutes.

8.

Solvent-free, base-free microwave-mediated (Cp*IrCl$_2$)$_2$-catalyzed conditions for the N-alkylation of amides with a series of primary and secondary alcohols produce high yields of N-alkyl arylamides and N-alkyl arylamides.

9.

R—MgX
or
R—Li

1 eq.

SO₂·N(⌒)N·SO₂

THF
−40°C, 1 h

[R—S(=O)—OM]
(removal of THF)

3 eq. R'—X'
DMF, MW
120°C, 3 h

R—S(=O)(=O)—R'

R: alkyl, Ar, vinyl, benzyl, allyl
R'X': benzyl-Br, allyl-Br, Br-CH₂COPh, Pr-I

The addition of Grignard reagents or organolithium reagents to the SO₂⁻ surrogate DABSO generates a diverse set of metal sulfinates, which can be trapped in situ with a wide range of C-electrophiles, including alkyl, allyl, and benzyl halides, epoxides, and (hetero) aryliodoniums to give sulfone products.

10.

R—CHO + NH₂OH · HCl

1.2 eq.

15 mol-% catalyst

neat, 100°C, 10 h or
neat, MW, 140°C, 10 min

R—CN

R: Ar, benyl, Et

preparation of catalyst

15 mol-% choline chloride,
30 mol-% urea, 100°C, 30 min

A deep eutectic mixture of choline chloride and urea (1:2) is an efficient and ecofriendly catalyst for the one-pot synthesis of nitriles from aldehydes under solvent-free conditions under both conventional and microwave irradiation. Nitriles were obtained in good to excellent yields.

11.

1.2 eq.

Ar—S(=O)(=O)—NHNH₂ + X—R

0.1 eq. CuI
[DBU] [HOAc]
MW, 130°C, 10 min

Ar—S—R

XR: ArI, ArBr, BnBr, BnCl

An efficient cross-coupling reaction of aryl/het-aryl/benzyl halides with stable and easily workable sulfonyl hydrazides as thiol substitutes deliver unsymmetrical sulfides in the presence [DBU][HOAc] and CuI under microwave irradiation.

12.

2 eq.

Ar—NH₂ + H₂N—R

8 mol-% Pd/C (10 wt-%)
THF
MW (170°C, < 21 atm), 90 min

Ar—N(H)—R

R: 1° alkyl, 2° alkyl

An easy Pd-mediated oxidation of primary amines to imines followed by aniline addition enables an alkylation of anilines. The process is characterized by a high atom economy as ammonia is the only byproduct. The catalyst could be successfully recycled upto three times.

13.

A reductive cyclization of o-nitrobenzylidene amines under microwave conditions in the presence of $MoO_2Cl_2(dmf)_2$ as catalyst and Ph_3P as reducing agent delivers 2-aryl-2H-indazoles in good yields.

14.

An efficient, microwave-assisted ligand-free and catalyst-free coupling of various nitroarenes and phenols produces nonsymmetrical diaryl ethers. The newly developed method is an ecofriendly and cost-effective approach to synthesize nonsymmetrical aryl ethers.

15.

The Krapcho decarboxylation of alkyl malonate derivatives has been adapted to aqueous microwave conditions. For salt additives, a strong correlation was found between the pK_a of the anion and the reaction rate, suggesting a straightforward base-catalyzed hydrolysis. Lithium sulfate gave the best results, obviating the need for DMSO as a co-solvent.

16.

R,R': benzyl, alkyl

The key step in a new route for the construction of 2-aminoimidazolidines is an intramolecular microwave-assisted Staudinger/aza-Wittig cyclization of an in situ generated urea intermediate upon treatment with Bu_3P or polymer-supported phosphine reagent. Furthermore, a useful one-pot Staudinger/aza-Wittig/Buchwald-Hartwig protocol leading to bicyclic guanidines has been elaborated.

QUESTIONS

1. Define nanochemistry. Discuss various terms used in nanochemistry.

2. What is microwave assisted organic synthesis. Give example.

3. Give different applications of nanochemistry.

4. Comment on different applications of microwave assisted organic synthesis.

5. Give distinction between conventional and microwave assisted organic synthesis.

6. What are the advantages of microwave assisted organic synthesis.

∎∎∎